INISHOWEN

Joseph O'Connor was born and lives in Dublin. His books
include *True Believers*, the Whitbread-shortlisted *Cowboys and
Indians* and *The Salesman*. He has won a number of awards
for his work, including the Macaulay fellowship of the Irish
Arts Council, the Miramax Ireland Screenwriting Prize and the
Hennessy New Irish Writer of the Year Award.

Joseph O'Connor

INISHOWEN

Secker & Warburg
LONDON

Published by Secker & Warburg 2000

2 4 6 8 10 9 7 5 3 1

First published in Great Britain in 2000 by
Secker & Warburg
Random House, 20 Vauxhall Bridge Road,
London SW1V 2SA

Random House Australia (Pty) Limited
20 Alfred Street, Milsons Point, Sydney,
New South Wales 2061, Australia

Random House New Zealand Limited
18 Poland Road, Glenfield,
Auckland 10, New Zealand

Random House South Africa (Pty) Limited
Endulini, 5A Jubilee Road, Parktown 2193, South Africa

The Random House Group Limited Reg. No. 954009
www.randomhouse.co.uk

A CIP catalogue record for this book
is available from the British Library

ISBN 0 436 25554 5

Papers used by The Random House Group Limited are natural,
recyclable products made from wood grown in sustainable forests;
the manufacturing processes conform to the environmental
regulations of the country of origin

Typeset by Palimpsest Book Production Limited,
Polmont, Stirlingshire
Printed and bound in Great Britain by
Mackays of Chatham PLC.

For Anne-Marie

The Donegal Democrat
December 27, 1948

BABY ABANDONED NEAR BUNCRANA

THE CIVIC GUARDS at Buncrana are investigating an incident in which a newborn baby girl was abandoned last week. The child was discovered in the early afternoon of Christmas Eve, on a disused track near the spot known to local people as Father Hegarty's Rock (after a priest of the penal times who was martyred there).

An English couple who are at present guests of Lady Montgomery at New Park House, Moville, were making their way along the road towards the Bronze Age burial cairn at Croachaisil when they were alerted by faint cries. "At first we thought it was an animal of some kind," said Major Philip Penderton (rtd) of Lyme Regis, Dorset, "or possibly even Father Hegarty." On investigation they discovered the child, who had been wrapped in a tweed shawl and placed in a wicker shopping basket. Mrs Elizabeth Penderton, having nursed in London during the blitz, was able to administer first aid.

A SHOCKING OCCURRENCE

The infant was cold and distressed but is said to be in remarkably good health given the circumstances. She was taken to Saint Colmcille's hospital where she was immediately baptised. *(more on page 2.)*

Father Eamon Toland MA, parish priest of Buncrana, said this was a most shocking occurrence which would bring great shame to the town. For it to happen in the holy season was almost literally incredible. The availability of strong drink to young people and the recent opening of various local premises used for jazz dancing could only result in further such incidents. Buncrana was fast becoming the Sodom of North Donegal. "The youth of the Inishowen peninsula would be better off attuning themselves to the quiet rhythms of nature than the epileptic lurchings of the Negroid races," he added.

BRITISH PUPS

Sergeant Frank "Pack" McDaid appealed for information from anyone walking the road last week, which is two miles north of Buncrana town. Though disused, he noted, it is well known to ramblers, huntsmen, farmers and courting couples. He believed the mother was a person with local knowledge. If she came forward, even at this stage, criminal proceedings and a custodial sentence might be avoided. He was of the view that the father was probably a British soldier stationed across the border in Derry. Many of them were only pups, he averred.

FRIDAY, 23 DECEMBER 1994

Chapter One

At ten minutes to noon, on the day before Christmas Eve, 1994, an off-duty electrical repair man named Dermot Shouldice was approached outside the Busaras coach terminal in north central Dublin by an ash-haired, elegant, raw-boned woman he took to be some kind of lunatic. She might have been forty-five, maybe fifty. As she bore down towards him waving her arms, advancing purposefully through the delirium of illumination, he found himself wishing he was somewhere else.

'Help me, sir,' she managed to croak, in what he thought might be an American accent. 'Please help me, sir, I . . .' before suddenly going completely limp, as though some kind of power surge had blown her main fuse. Knees buckling, backwards she tottered, causing him to drop his turkey sandwich and grab her around the waist. An odd thought came into his mind. Nobody had ever called him 'sir' before.

The heel had broken off her right shoe. It sat there glumly on a manhole cover. As he tried to stop the fainting woman from hitting the ground, hugging her tightly in a grim slow-dance of embarrassment, Dermot Shouldice stared at the heel hard, as though it might give him inspiration. He could feel sweat between his shoulder blades now. Holy God, was she heavy. How in the name of Jesus could she be so heavy? He bent his knees to take her weight. A shower of coins fell from his pocket and hit the pavement.

It was then that he noticed two blue-blazered schoolgirls eyeing him dolefully from inside a nearby bus shelter. One of the pair was short and chubby, the other alarmingly tall and gaunt, like death warmed up but not very thoroughly. Their differing heights made him think of a comedy double act. The unknown woman slumped forward into his arms, now slithering to her knees, head lolling sideways, limbs flailing like those of a puppet with broken strings. Mr Shouldice decided the time had come when something would have to be said.

'I tend to have this effect on women,' he quipped to the girls.

At least, he found himself adding in this claim when describing the bizarre incident some twenty minutes later, to Inspector Martin Aitken of Pearse Street Station, who managed a dutiful bark of laughter as he scribbled it in his notebook.

By now an ambulance had arrived, its siren whoop-whooping as it inched through the curious crowd. Office workers in party hats stared down from their windows, shop-girls from their doorways, passers-by from cars. The oddly heavy woman was unconscious on the pavement, being tended by a pompous little countryman who insisted he had won first-aid badges in the Boy Scouts; his brother was trying to dissuade him from attempting a Heimlich manoeuvre. Another man, in a Santa Claus outfit, was uselessly fanning her face with a U2 bath towel. Taxis and trucks had stopped on the street. Several buses were clogging up the traffic, stony-faced passengers on the upper floors gawping down at the scene as though it had been put on for their entertainment. In the middle of the throng, a madwoman with a crucifix wrapped in green, white and orange ribbons had stepped up on to the rim of a granite horse-trough. She was declaiming the Hail Mary in a nervous whinny, one hand brandishing the cross like a scimitar, the other leaning to steady herself on a bus stop, a leer of orgasmic happiness in her blasted eyes.

Inspector Aitken felt uneasy as he pushed through the crowd. He squatted on his hunkers and examined the comatose woman. This was something he could do without. A week of Christmas leave was starting tomorrow and things at work had been difficult lately. He didn't need this. He needed a break.

She looked to Aitken like a woman who'd had troubles. Her long, thin face was pale as paper. Mascara stains had trickled down her cheeks. The knuckles of her right hand were grazed and bleeding. There was a small smudge of lipstick on her lower front teeth. She was wearing golden earrings in the shape of theatrical masks, one smiling, one frowning, each with elongated eyes. He took her wrist lightly and felt for a pulse, trying to look as though he knew what he was doing. ('Good man,' called the electrician, 'good man yerself.') It occurred to him now that the people milling around had expectations he probably couldn't fulfil; perhaps, he mused, this was how Jesus felt when he came across a leper. He parted her eyelids, loosened her coat buttons, checked inside her mouth to see if she had swallowed her tongue. It flashed into his memory that he had often stopped Robbie from doing that, how once, during a particularly bad fit, the poor kid had bitten into the base of his father's thumb so hard that Aitken had needed two stitches afterwards.

When was that anyway? Some time back in the eighties. In the Garden of Remembrance on Parnell Square. They'd been looking up at the statue of the Children of Lir. Himself and Robbie. Was Valerie there too?

The three unfortunate children had been conjured into swans by their evil stepmother, condemned to roam the sea and sky for nine hundred years. He'd been sitting on a damp green bench and telling Robbie the story. Such a nice-natured kid, he thought. Always ready to listen to a story. Then wham. It had happened. Down he'd flopped, his only son, trembling and wriggling like a fish on a dockside.

'Slap her in the chops,' someone said. 'Slap her face, for Jayzus' sake.'

He glanced up to find a heavy-set young man in a hooded, tasselled leather jacket glaring down at him from a few rows back.

'I'll slap your bleedin face in a minute.'

'Sure yeh will, pig. I'm rattlin here.'

There were tongue-clicks and gasps from people in the crowd. Slowly Aitken looked up at him again. 'You talkin to me, pal, or chewin a brick?'

The man was smirking. He pulled down his hood. He had a peroxide white crewcut with a shamrock shaved into the crown. He raised a cigarette to his scornful mouth and took a long, contemptuous drag. 'Arsehole Aitken. Big hat and

7

no cattle. Lost the auld bottle when they took away yer gun, didnyeh?'

Pouting, he lifted his hands to the front of his jacket, his fingers squeezing invisible breasts.

People in the crowd gaped at him in astonishment. 'Go home, you dirty bowsie,' someone said. Aitken called to one of his officers. 'Noel, get over here for a sec, willya.'

'Boss?'

'Charge Scary Mary here with loitering and breach of the peace.'

The white-haired man laughed. Scratched at a spider-web tattoo on the side of his neck. Finished his cigarette, dropped it on the pavement, never once taking his eyes off Aitken. 'Nobody's gonna charge me with nothin, pal. Cos they'll know all about it if they bleedin do.'

The garda took hold of the man's forearm. 'Will you come with me now, sir?'

The man stared hard at the garda's black-gloved hand, then absently, almost dreamily up at the sky. 'D'yeh know who yer dealin with here, kiddo?'

'Matter of fact, I was just about to ask you, sir.'

'Ask yer so-called bossman there. He knows right well. Int that right, Aitken auld son?'

'Don't be causin hassle,' said the garda, 'you can see we're busy surely. Walk over here with me till we work this out.'

The man grinned. Thrust out his sleeve. 'See that jacket? Do yeh?'

'Yes, sir, I see it.'

'Cost me more than youse piggies earn in a month.' He laughed, pulled a face, spat on the pavement. 'How's that make yeh feel, hoh?'

'There's no need to be abusive, sir.' The garda took hold of him again. 'If you don't come quietly, I'll have to use force on you.'

The man snapped his arm away. He stepped back, still smiling, although his small eyes were suddenly bright with hatred. 'You so much as put one livin finger on that jacket again, yeh culchie little dirtbird, and yeh'll know all about

8

it, I'm tellin yeh. I've wiped better than you off me boots before this.'

The ambulance men looked anxious. The garda glanced at Aitken. There was fear in his face as he asked what to do.

'You can stick a drunk and disorderly on to that, Noel. Now get him outta here before I burst his hole for him.'

'Come along now, sir, and don't be makin more trouble for yourself.'

The man clutched at the garda's lapel. 'Bleedin do's much as touch me again, pig, yeh'll be wakin up with a crowd around yeh. I'll dance yeh into that road there so I will.'

In an instant Aitken was on his feet, grabbing the man around the throat, jaw slack with rage. The man squirmed, his shocked face pale, as Aitken shoved him backwards, hard against a phone box, so hard that the perspex cracked. Jammed his knee between the man's thighs. Small eyes narrowing. Breath smelling of meat.

'You filthy godforsaken pup,' Aitken bawled in his face. 'Don't you dare speak to an officer of mine like that. You hear me? *You hear me?*'

All around him people were gasping and tutting. An elderly woman in the crowd said there was no need for that kind of talk on Christmas Eve.

'Say sorry to him. Now.'

'Go and ride yer aulwan, pig.'

His fingers moved through the man's clothes, quickly, efficiently.

'Get yer paws off me, Aitken, I'm bleedin warnin yeh.'

Aitken pulled a switchblade from the breast pocket, flicked it open, jabbed it towards the man's crotch.

'Apologise right now or so help me, pal, I'll slice off your bollocks and play bleedin marbles with them.'

The garda stepped forward, looking wild with anxiety. 'Boss, Jesus.'

'What?'

'Well, y'know . . . There's really no need like . . . I'm grand.'

'Come on, Martin, cool it,' said one of the ambulance men, trying to put his arm around Aitken's shoulder.

'Shut the fuck up, Larry.' He held the blade to the man's throat, the point pressing gently into his flesh. 'Apologise. This minute. Or I'll make a jigsaw out of you.'

The man was struggling. His sleeve rode up, revealing a bulging venous forearm.

'Yer a deadman for this, pig. A fuckin stiff.'

Aitken lowered the switchblade and cut one of the tassels off the jacket.

'Here! Christ! What the fuckarya doin?'

Another flick of the knife. A second tassel flew through the air.

'Stop it! Jayzus!'

'I said say sorry, prick.'

'*I'm sorry then, all right?* Jayzus, yeh bleedin psychoyeh.'

Aitken wheeled him around, grabbed his hands, jerked a set of cuffs on to him.

'That's right, scumbag. And don't ever forget it. Now get him out of here, Noel, before I do somethin I'll regret.'

'Let me go, for Jayzus' sake. It's Christmas, yeh miserable bastardyeh.'

The garda grasped his collar, marched him to a squad car. A large policewoman forced him into it, hand down hard on his head. The car rocked from side to side as he clambered in, struggling and kicking. Down slid the window and out came a roar:

'You'll be sorry yeh done that on me, Aitken. Yeh'll be beggin for a bullet by the time I'm finished with yeh. Yeh hear me?'

'Blow it out your arse, loser. Now stand back. All of yez! And let these men do their work.'

The ambulance men pushed in through the crowd. One sank to his knees beside the woman, quickly placing a stethoscope to her chest, while the other felt her forehead and held smelling salts under her nose.

'So,' said the first. 'How's Martin this weather?'

'If I was any better, Larry, I couldn't stick it.'

He watched as the men tried to revive her. 'Well?' he said, after a moment. 'Is she after kickin the bucket or what?'

The ambulance man shook his head. 'Course not, Martin. Some class of a faint, that's all.'

'Should we move her?'

'Yeah, we're gonna have to take her in for observation. Give us a dig out there, will you, Martin?'

She gave a soft, delirious moan as they lifted her limp body and eased her slowly on to the stretcher. 'Hold on, hold on. Take it easy.' When Aitken glanced up, he saw that the garda was standing above them again.

'Sorry, boss, we've a problem here.'

'What is it, Noel?'

'Just the guy in the squad car. You know who he is?'

'Martin! You'll have to clear the street. Right now. Her heart rate's after slippin on us.'

'Boss, that's Mousey Doogan. Mickey's brother.'

'I don't give two shites if it's the Sacred shaggin Heart in Doc Martens. Have him charged! Get on with it. And get these rubbernecks moved. Now!'

The woman had no purse or handbag, no identifying papers of any kind. Her clothes looked expensive: a velvet blouse, smartly tailored woollen skirt, designer-label snakeskin shoes, the whole effect somewhat undermined by a pair of garish emerald green socks. In the pocket of her gaberdine raincoat was a wad of hundred-dollar bills and a tube of lipstick, fireapple red.

'Who is she anyway?' asked the ambulance man.

'Haven't a monkey's,' said Martin Aitken.

Even for Christmastime in Dublin, it was more than a little perplexing.

* * *

Convent of Our Lady, Star of the Sea
Ballybeg, near Malin, Inishowen
County Donegal
Republic of Ireland

8 September 1985

Dear Madam,

Please allow me to introduce myself.

My name is Sister Mary Rose Kennedy and I am in charge of archives and records here at Our Lady's. Your letter to the Department of Justice in Dublin (dated 7 July 1984) requesting information about the identity of your birth mother was forwarded to me some months ago, along with copies of correspondence between yourself and various United States government departments and adoption agencies.

You will be wondering why you are hearing from myself. The reason is that a search of the existing records has revealed that your birth mother was a person from what became in subsequent years this electoral district.

At the outset I must apologise for the delay in responding to your request. As you can imagine, it took some time to locate the person in question. I should add that since rumours began to circulate of a scheme operated by the Irish Church in the 1940s, whereby children born out of wedlock were sent to the United States for adoption in Catholic homes, we have been, frankly, inundated with requests similar to your own.

As for your own enquiry, the position is as follows:

I can tell you that your birth mother is still living, and indeed continues to reside in the Inishowen area of North County Donegal. She is married with a family and grandchildren. For some years now she has not enjoyed the best of health.

The position is that we have contacted the lady in

question – in strictest confidence, naturally – to tell her of your interest in possibly making contact or even meeting. However, I am sorry to have to tell you that she does not wish to make any contact whatsoever with yourself. As so often happens in these unfortunate situations, she was in fact greatly shocked and distressed even to hear of your request.

As I am sure you can imagine, much has changed in her life since she felt compelled to come to the heart-rending decision she made as a young teenager to allow you to be placed for adoption. She has never discussed that course of action with anyone since – even her husband and children remain unaware of the entire matter – and she does not wish to have painful wounds opened up again after all this time.

In charity, I must ask you therefore to desist from any further enquiry and let matters rest at this point.

I am sorry not to be able to help you more than this. Do, please, let me at least assure you of my prayers at all times.

Yours sincerely in Christ
Sister Mary Rose Kennedy

PS: I return herewith all copies of your correspondence.

SATURDAY, 24 DECEMBER 1994

Chapter Two

Round about lunchtime on Christmas Eve, Doctor Milton Amery III left his surgery on Park Avenue and walked east along 65th, turning southwards on to Lexington. He prided himself on his precision, even under stress. He had done the same walk every working day for almost twenty years. He'd be damned if he didn't do it today.

Wreaths of ivy and holly hung on many doors, old-fashioned coach lanterns in windows and storm porches, tinfoil stars and angels in fanlights. Festive music was coming from the department store entrances, hosannas, noëls and soaring violins. By the main door of Bloomingdale's a choir of uniformed firefighters was belting out the Hallelujah Chorus. A goggle-eyed black man dressed as a comedy reindeer was clanging a handbell and calling 'Help the homeless'.

Amery dropped a ten-dollar bill in the reindeer's bucket. He wondered if his wife would come back this time.

Snow had fallen the night before and the city looked almost ridiculously magical, even to a native New Yorker such as Milton Amery. It was proper New York snow that was satisfyingly crunchy underfoot, almost arrogantly white, radiating a kind of chemical coldness, not like the watery grey slush that half-heartedly plopped down on less fortunate parts of the country. He walked another block, turned north again, trudged up Park as far as 65th. The thing about life was it had to go on. When you were in trouble you found consolation in the smallest of things.

Two blocks westward brought him to Fifth Avenue. The skyscrapers glistened, orchid cream, watery silver, sapphire blue. Off to the south he could see the Twin Towers, their upper storeys disappearing into the mist.

Angels we have heard on high,
Sweetly singing o'er the plain;
And the mountains in reply
Echo back their glorious strain.

He crossed Fifth, to walk by the park. Over the wall to his right, he could see joggers and jugglers, strolling couples, shuffling old men, rollerbladers slaloming through lines of traffic cones. Kids on mountain bikes, riding the mounds of earth, whooping and screeching with fearful joy. Dappled splashes of tiny white lights in the ash boughs, serpentine tubes of golden neon spiralling the trunks as though trying to strangle them.

The air was charged with the smells of roasting coffee and frying onions, the heaving streets full of crazed shoppers and mittened children. The city seemed electrified with purposefulness today. But then again, it always did. The fact that it was Christmas only meant the trains were scarcer. The sheer doggedness of the pedestrians was something you had to admire. Yellow cabs inched along the avenue blaring their horns in lugubrious chorus. Fat globes of steam came ballooning from a subway grid. On the corner of Fifth and East 61st, a princely Rastafarian with a Spanish guitar was wiggling his hips and yowling out a reggae song, while two laughing girls in anoraks took his photo.

Jah, him speak to all the nation,
Babylon burn in desolation.

He had done his best to console his son and daughter, but by ten this morning he had begun to get the feeling his wife would not be back this time. He allowed the thought to flower in his mind now; the unravelling sense of cold panic was so startlingly intense it was almost pleasurable. All these people around him dazed with celebration, drunk with shopping, virtually sexualised with glee, and his wife wasn't coming back. Last time he had seen her was three days ago, 21 December, her forty-sixth birthday. She had given no sign that she was thinking

18

of leaving. At 7.30 that Wednesday morning she had dropped him at the station, kissed him goodbye, and he had run for the New York train.

On the 7.31 into town from Scarsdale he had caught up on his paperwork, scribbled a few notes for a lecture on a new surgical technique. Then into Manhattan, and a determinedly calm saunter – through the cathedral of the Grand Central lobby, up and out on to the street, a quick espresso doppio at his favourite diner, a call at the news-stand to buy the *New York Times*, which he bought every day and never had time to read. The day had been madly busy, morning consultations every half-hour. At lunchtime he had played squash at his club, then had a wheat grass juice and a vegetable grill sandwich with a classmate who had gone into paediatrics, Mike Brockleton. They had exchanged ideas for the forthcoming lecture, Amery shamefully enjoying the hint of gentle envy he thought he saw in his friend's eyes. 'Good old Milton,' Brockleton had said, shaking hands and stepping back into his chauffeur-driven Daimler. 'Still setting the world on fire.'

'We can but try, Mike. We can but try.'

'Give my love to that gorgeous wife of yours. Sarah says you guys must come to dinner again soon.'

The afternoon was taken up with a long and complicated operation, a tricky procedure you didn't want to rush. It was a day more or less like any other, just busier. It hadn't felt like the kind of day your life would be changed for ever.

After surgery had finished he had gone for cocktails with his girlfriend, to a little jazzy place called the Red Blazer, halfway along Restaurant Row. It was a touch touristy but then they didn't want to bump into anyone. They had eaten and drunk a bit too much; they had even hit the floor and danced. Cathy had told him he was a good mover for his age. He had laughed and blushed and pulled her close for the mambo.

> *Lo siento, mi vida*
> *Yo sei que es terminado!*

He had noticed the tall, excessively cheekboned baritone winking at her in between the lines, swivelling his snake-hips in a frankly lewd manner, his fingers gently clawing at the collar of his poncho.

From the room at the Holiday Inn Crowne Plaza he had called home. Left a message on the answering machine advising his wife not to wait up. A nasty case had arisen. He would have to sort it out. Well, you couldn't allow a patient to suffer over Christmas. As he'd hung up the phone he'd felt a dull wave of guilt. He went to the window and looked down into Times Square, the converging streets dazzlingly illuminated by the phosphorescent glow of the theatre fronts and strip joints. Lines of traffic crawled along the avenue like miniature boats on a magical river. Beyond the square the wider city spread itself out, a shimmering mirage of glitzy possibility. Down to his right a matrix of moving white lights flashed the news headlines across the front of a building. The Middle East. Northern Ireland. Bosnia-Herzegovina. Maybe it wasn't too late to change his mind. Surely even now there was a way to extricate himself. He'd just say what he felt, explain the situation – he simply couldn't continue cheating on his wife. But when he'd turned around, dry-mouthed, shaking, the bathroom door was open wide. There was Cathy, in the skimpy lace outfit he'd bought her at Victoria's Secret, statuesque in a radiance of pale yellow light.

'So how do you like your Christmas gift?' he'd asked.

'Uh uh, buster. This is *your* Christmas gift. Now how about you get over here and unwrap it.'

When he'd returned that night, on the last train from Grand Central, his head swimming with gratified desire, his body so raw with sex that it felt like a layer of his skin was missing, it was one in the morning and his wife was not in the house.

His daughter had been curled up on the sofa, watching a chat show with the volume turned down low and the telephone receiver clamped to her ear.

'Where's Mom, Elizabeth?'

She put her hand over the phone. 'She's not with you?'

'I'd hardly be asking her whereabouts if that were the case, would I?'

'OK. I guess not.'

He plucked the cigarette from his daughter's mouth and mashed it out on a saucer.

'Dad? For God's sake . . .'

'Not in the house. I've told you before.'

On the screen, an obese black man in a low-cut sequined cocktail dress was attempting to punch his grandmother. Jerry Springer was pacing up and down, gnawing his lip, looking like a confused owl.

Amery went to the window and opened it wide, making a great show of fanning in fresh air.

'Dad! It's minus three out there.'

'Well, in here I need oxygen. I'm suffocating.'

His eyes came to rest on the screen again. Two muscle-bound security men were holding back Granny, while the weeping transvestite tried to head-butt her. The audience members were on their feet, punching the air and chanting wildly.

Jer-RY, Jer-RY.

His daughter continued mumbling into the phone. 'I'm like going to the mall the other day? And he shows up and he's like, are you into it or not? And I'm like, get out of my face, Carlo, you know we've been through all this crap before.'

It amazed him that a girl who was attending Yale insisted on using the word 'like' as punctuation. Fees of thirty thousand a year and she talked as though she'd been born in New Jersey.

Into the kitchen went Doctor Milton Amery. The worktops were piled high with bags of Christmas food – a turkey, a ham, tins of *foie gras*, a whole side of wild smoked salmon. Agreeable aromas permeated the air. He looked around but found no note from his wife. Went to the refrigerator and fixed himself an Emmental sandwich.

The exertions of the evening had left a tremble in his hands. His whole body felt shaky and weak. Good God, she was passionate. So needy and crazy. Some of the things she had done to him were astounding, others quite disturbing – one or two, in several of the southern states, at least in the technical sense illegal. When he closed his eyes, dull red light seemed to glow. He pictured her naked muscular body tautening in a

21

rush of pleasure, that tattoo of the roaring tiger in the small of her tanned back. Deep in his loins came a palpitation of exhausted desire.

He opened his eyes. With disgust, he now saw an extinguished cigarette butt on the rim of a plate of congealed baked beans. He took the plate and dropped it in the sink.

Elizabeth shuffled in, looking tired and mopey. She was wearing those slippers that Ellen had bought her in Paris, the ones that looked like cuddly gendarmes' heads.

'Hey, Popsicle,' she said.

'Hey yourself.'

'So how was your evening?'

'It was busy, thank you.'

'Nice restaurant?'

His heart pulsed. 'How do you mean?'

'Oh, that was Vicky Myerson on the phone. She saw you in a restaurant in the city earlier.'

He shrugged. 'Not me. I was working late.'

'The Red Blazer? On West 46th? She's waiting tables there over the holiday. She was sure it was you.'

He allowed himself a hollow laugh. 'I wish.'

She nodded vaguely. 'I wish too.'

Fetching plates and cups from the table, she brought them to the dishwasher and stacked them inside. She lifted a glass vase from the draining board to the light and examined it briefly before putting it in a cupboard. Then, sighing, she took a pot from the cooker to the sink and started half-heartedly to rinse it out. For no good reason he remembered her as a child now, a chirpy little tomboy with a tumble of almond-brown ringlets, her pockets perpetually full of crayons. One day when she was seven or eight he had come home to find she had scribbled suns and flowers all over her bedroom wallpaper. He could still see the gape of incomprehension on her face when he had scolded her for it.

'So hey,' he said. 'I guess you're smoking again.'

She gave him a half-look over her shoulder. 'Oscar Wilde said a young lady should have an occupation.'

'Oscar Wilde said a lot of remarkably dumb things.'

She laughed, wiped her mouth with the back of her hand.
'Come on, Pops. I'm eighteen years old.'

'It's for your sake, Elizabeth. You'll ruin your skin, I'm
telling you.'

'Yeah, yeah.'

'You know what smoking does to your skin? It dries it out.
Like shoe leather.'

'Whatever.'

'I had a woman in the surgery today whose face looked like
a bandolero's boot. She'd pay a million dollars to have skin like
yours. But it's too late for that.'

His daughter wasn't moving now. Her long, straight back was
as still as stone. She seemed to be staring out the window, as
though something unusual was happening in the garden.

'Dad. You don't think she's like . . . done it again, do you?'

He found himself staring hard at the tabletop while his
thumbnail worked at a lump of dried grease. 'Don't be silly,
honey. She wouldn't do it again.'

She nodded, pushed her hair behind her ears, still with her
back to him. 'You promise, Pops? It's gonna be OK, right?'

'Everything will be fine. Believe me, it will.'

She finished the dishes, dried her hands, sat down to the table
and regarded him as he ate. It seemed to Amery that there was
an edginess in the air, a jangling sense of difficult things not
being said. She fiddled for a while with the strap of her watch.
Gnawed on a fingernail. Began desultorily plaiting a handful of
her hair.

'God, I'd really like a cigarette now.'

'Well, I believe you're aware of the location of the garden.'

'Come on, Popsicle. Please? Just one?'

'No.'

'Pretty please? With a cherry on top? Hmm?'

'I said no, Elizabeth. Don't be infantile.'

She shot him a huffy, frozen look and picked up a magazine.
He looked at the backs of her graceful hands, her braceleted,
fragile wrists and aquamarine painted nails. How in the hell had
she grown up so fast?

'Oh, go on then,' he sighed. 'Kill yourself if you want.'

She beamed. 'Thanks, Milton. You're a pal and a half.'

She took a pack from the pocket of her jeans and lit one up, sighing with pleasure as she took the first drag.

'That's it,' he said. 'Suck it down good and deep there.'

'Sure thing.'

'Make sure you really pop those lungs, why don't you.'

'Yup.'

'Maybe get another one going for when you're finished that one. Because the Marlboro man really needs your money.'

She raised her eyebrows and gave him a smile of ironic tolerance that was designed to quiet him. 'It could be worse, you know, Milt. Most of my friends are on cocaine.'

'Most of mine are on their second heart attack. That doesn't necessarily mean it's a good idea.'

The dishwasher gave a churning, plosive sound. She laughed, as though conceding something, and shrugged her shoulders. 'I know I shouldn't, Dad, OK? I'm gonna try quitting for good real soon. But it's hard.'

'I know, I know. Just don't do it in front of Lee, OK?'

'OK.'

'And don't tell your mother I let you do it in the house.'

She nodded, took another quick and guilty drag, waving the smoke away towards the window.

'So. You look tired, Dad.'

'The natural result of an honest day's labour.'

'Hard afternoon down the old mineshaft, huh?'

He scrutinised her now, wondering at her choice of words. But she was flicking through her magazine again.

'Yes,' he said. 'You could put it that way.'

'Mmm.'

He would have liked her to invite him to elaborate on his day, but she showed no sign of doing so. He missed that about her lately. When she'd been younger, she had seemed quite interested in medicine. She would sometimes ask about his patients, what problems they had, why they came to him and not some other doctor. Occasionally he would even find her in his study, leafing through a textbook or a medical journal. Her term project in ninth grade had been on Alexander Fleming

24

and the discovery of penicillin; back then she'd had a picture of Professor Christiaan Barnard on her bedroom wall. There were times he had allowed himself to believe she might follow him into the practice one day. She had the brains for it, there was no doubt about that, and unlike Lee she had application too. But then, gradually, inexorably, around thirteen or fourteen, she had seemed to change and become more like Ellen, more dreamy and easily distracted – not exactly distant but somehow more difficult to reach. She had dropped chemistry and biology shortly afterwards, opting instead for art history and comparative literature. Simone de Beauvoir was on her wall now.

'Well,' she said, 'if you want to know, I started reading *Crime and Punishment* this morning. It's a very cool story indeed.'

'I'm sure Comrade Dostoevsky would be gratified to have it put that way.'

She nodded blankly, got up from the table. Took a bottle of Evian from the refrigerator and poured a glass.

'I'm gonna turn in now, Dad. Sleep tight, OK?'

'You know, that's curious, what Vicky told you. About my being in that restaurant earlier.'

'Isn't it, though?'

'Perhaps I have a *doppelgänger*. How Dostoevskian.'

'Oh, I knew it wasn't you, Popsicle.' She smiled. 'Vicky said this guy was doing the macarena.'

It was only after his daughter had gone to bed that he felt the first unfurling of real panic about Ellen.

At first he had thought he might have misunderstood some arrangement. Perhaps she'd had plans that he had forgotten. Wasn't there a play she'd been mentioning lately? Some concert of Christmas carols in the town? Another of her damn poetry readings?

Lord, how he loathed her poetry readings. At the last one, a frighteningly intense man from Nigeria who had been in solitary confinement for seven years had recited his haikus about civil liberties, then played something called 'a tone poem' on two metal bars, clanging them together and simultaneously ululating. Amery and Lee had found it almost impossible not to laugh. He remembered his son's body writhing in agonised silent mirth beside him in the back row of the town hall, the side of his hand stuffed in his mouth, tears of shameful gaiety rolling down his face.

In the shower, he still seemed to smell of his girlfriend's perfume, no matter how hard he scrubbed the hot soapy water into his skin. Dripping on the tiling, he looked at himself in the mirror. He wasn't in bad shape if he sucked in his little paunch. Fifty years old and still at least presentable. Heck, still handsome enough, in a certain light. There was a single, small bite-mark on his right shoulder. Damn. He would have to ask her to stop doing that to him. She got so carried away sometimes. Once, during a frantic post-prandial coupling at the Holiday Inn Chinatown, she had bit into his lower lip so hard that it had bled all over her complimentary paper kimono. He'd had to tell Ellen he had cut himself shaving.

At a quarter to two he climbed into bed and tried to read the notes for his lecture. Leaning back, closing his eyes, he envisioned himself on the dais – a modest bow, a small self-deprecatory wave, an embarrassed half-smile as he acknowledged the cheers. Credit belongs to others, really. Only continuing down the trail blazed by true pioneers. Yes, if adding at all to scientific knowledge, then gratified, of course, but please, enough. He imagined Ellen in the front row, applauding him wildly and looking proud. Then he managed to sleep for a while, a fitful dream-filled doze full of flickering lights and mysterious discordant sounds, the treacly slumber of the guilty and the drunk. Early next morning he got up and telephoned a couple of her colleagues from school.

'Didn't she come home last night, Milton?'

Not for the first time in his twenty-one-year marriage, he was glad to be a natural at the doctor's skill of affecting the casually unconcerned voice. 'Oh yes, Prudence, of course she did. But she went out this morning before I woke up and I need to catch up with her about something.'

'Is it something I could help you with?'

'It's kind of a personal matter, Prudence.'

His wife's friend gave an archly flirtatious chuckle. 'Lord, you two. Still love's young dream after all these years.'

'Oh,' he had laughed back. 'You know us.'

Chapter Three

Onward he walked through the festive, tinselled city. A light dust of snow began to fall, swirling softly in the gusting breeze. Workmen with shovels were clearing a pathway outside a hotel. A stately horse-drawn carriage with a top-hatted, whip-wielding driver clopped past, turning solemnly in the direction of the park. A trio of well-wrapped Japanese tourists in the back had video cameras trained on the street with the grim concentration of snipers pointing rifles. How could she do this to them, especially at Christmas? How was he going to get through the day, just himself and Lee and Elizabeth and his own parents, all sat around the table and politely avoiding mention of her?

The police had taken her description and asked for a picture. He had given them a copy of the photograph taken at the Rotary Club dinner held to honour him. They were waltzing in the picture. Her mouth was slightly open and the flash had turned her eyes into coins of scarlet. But he loved that picture, the liquid grace of her body, the way her hand rested on his chest. The way she was throwing back her head and so freely laughing. It reminded him of when they were young.

The police had told him yesterday there was not a lot they could do. Disappearing was not actually a criminal offence; Mrs Amery was hardly a juvenile runaway. These days a person could be gone for a whole week before the department would take too much of an interest.

'Perhaps *I* should take an interest in calling your superior and see if I can get you transferred to a dog pound.'

'Doctor Amery, calm down. Let's not get overexcited here.'

'Overexcited? Do you have any idea how much tax I pay?'

'She's mixed up in politics, right? Radical stuff?'

'For God's sakes, officer, she's a registered Democrat.'

The policeman grimaced painfully and wrote that in his notebook.

'And she helps out at some radical bookstore in town, right, Doctor Amery?'

'You think someone abducted my wife for selling Woody Guthrie's autobiography?'

'I don't suppose that's very likely, no.'

'I don't suppose so either, officer. Unless it was a literary critic.'

'Huh?' said the cop, his left hand working between his buttocks. He seemed to be adjusting his underwear in some fashion.

'Forget it,' said Amery.

'You get any kind of a ransom note? Strange phone calls lately? Stalker? Anything like that?'

'No, for God's sakes. Nothing like that.'

'This kind of thing ever happen before?'

'How do you mean?'

The officer took off his cap and pursed his lips. 'Well, now' – he attempted an expression of man-to-man frankness – 'you have some kinda little domestic situation there, Doctor Amery?'

'How do you mean, officer?'

'You ever fight with the missus?'

'We disagree sometimes, yes. We're married, after all.'

'What about?'

'I told you, we're married. We disagree about the usual things.'

The policeman sighed, exchanged a knowing look with his colleague. Snapped his notebook closed. Put his cap back on. 'She'll come back in a couple days, Doctor Amery. God knows mine always does.'

'Worse luck,' the colleague had smirked.

The truth was that it had happened many times before. At least twice a year she would disappear from the house. Usually it was part of an argument's aftermath, but not always; sometimes it was spontaneous. However it happened there was no planning

29

for it. Once she had walked out of a sports day at Lee's school and not come back for a whole week, having flown to California to visit an old college friend. Another time, she had failed to turn up for work and called two days later from Mexico City. Something about wanting to see a volcano. Worst of all was the occasion she had vanished around the time of her own father's funeral, leaving her mother astonished and hysterical.

'Why do you do this, Ellen?' he'd shouted, right there in the car from Newark airport. He remembered his hands actually trembling with rage.

'I can't help it, Milton,' she'd quietly replied. 'I just don't know why. So there's no point in asking me.'

And that had seemed so simple and strange to him, because it appeared to be completely true. His wife was a senior teacher with twenty years' experience and a place on the management board, a serious woman of responsibility and scrupulousness. Here was a woman who understood filing, who could operate a computer and pre-set a VCR, who had once flown home early from a vacation in Bermuda just to get her eighth grades' examination papers corrected on time. She would lecture their friends on why they should vote, go out half the night putting up posters for her candidates, shinning up ladders with people half her age. Yet she was the same woman who would simply flit like this, vanish from her family without so much as a goodbye note.

Once, after she had returned from a two-week jaunt to Baltimore – of all places! – they had agreed to attend a marriage counsellor together. But Amery had found it difficult to talk openly. The woman they'd seen – Rose, was it? Perhaps Iris – had somehow been too searching and too vague, but simultaneously. Her accent hadn't helped either; she was from Louisiana and spoke with such a ludicrous drawl that sometimes he was sure she was putting it on. She wore shapeless smocks of the type favoured by 1950s beat poets, or agricultural persons in Stalinist propaganda paintings. She was the kind of big-boned gal who ended all her sentences with a kooky smile, or, worse, a vaguely inquisitive raising of one eyebrow that made her look disconcertingly like Vegas-era Elvis in drag. And then she'd go silent. For whole minutes. The silence was something designed for falling into. And often he did. Well, he would feel that someone had better come out with some damn thing, if only to fill in the time or make the experience seem at least halfway useful. All the while he talked and talked, his wife would gaze into the empty fireplace and Lily or Daisy or Magnolia the counsellor would smile and raise her eyebrow, and sometimes do both.

'Uh-huh-huh,' she'd say. In Amery's mind.

'Baby, lemme be your lovin teddy bayuh.'

Towards the end of what turned out to be the last session Ellen had accused him of having an affair. Not that it came out as an accusation, more a simple statement of fact. 'My husband,' she said, 'has been sleeping with a younger woman.' He had denied it, put on a shocked expression, even managed a pitiful stammer. Not that that was difficult; he was astounded that she knew. He and his then girlfriend had been so careful. Well, the only course of action now was a little emotional sleight of hand.

Overwhelmed by his own vehemence rather than his guilt, he had even managed to cry at the suggestion. Besmocked Holly (or was it Petunia?) had handed him a wad of tissues – smiling, raising – and he had gladly taken them, relieved to have a way of momentarily hiding his face. He felt sure it was the only time Ellen had ever seen him cry, apart from once, briefly, just after Lee had been born. Afterwards she had looked appalled by the sight, and had never repeated the charge. He was glad about that. Admitting to an affair was merely cruelty dressed up as consideration. If you thought about it honestly, it was only looking for forgiveness.

They had decided that therapy wasn't such a good idea after all. He was glad about that too. A week in Paris was better than therapy. Off they'd gone, they'd flown first class, had a week of night-strolling and café au lait. By the time they'd come home things seemed to have settled. It wasn't fair anyway, it wasn't morally right to have to pay a stranger in order to be able to talk to your wife. There was something fundamentally wrong with a society where that could be seen as a good idea.

It struck him now to look for her passport. Maybe call the

travel agent in the town; see if she'd expressed an interest in
going anywhere recently. Outside a sporting goods store on the
corner of the park, he stopped, reached into his camelhair coat,
took out his mobile and called the surgery.

'Violet?'

'Yes, Doctor Amery?'

'Before you leave for the holiday, Violet, could you call
Westchester Tours in Scarsdale for me. Ask if my wife picked
up those tickets she booked last week.'

'Yes, Doctor Amery. Those tickets for where?'

'They'll know for where. They'll know all about it.'

His secretary sounded alarmed. 'You haven't planned a trip,
have you, Doctor Amery? Because the appointment book is
absolutely full right from 9.15 on the morning of the second,
I mean if you've planned . . .'

'Violet. Please. Just . . . do as I ask.'

But in his heart he didn't think she had left the country this
time. For some reason he suspected she was at their farmhouse
up at Saranac Lake. He must have tried the number a hundred
times in the last couple of days but it had remained unanswered.
Perhaps she had unplugged it – he wouldn't put that past her.
Maybe he would drive up there himself when the weather
cleared a little. Whatever he thought about anything else, he
hated to think of her alone in the big old creaky timber house
like that, being frightened by the extraordinary darkness outside
and the nimble scuttle of the mice in the walls.

For the first time it occurred to him that perhaps she was not
alone. He stopped on the corner of East 58th, his gut pulsing
at the possibility. Had she run off with someone this time? If
so, who might the candidates be? There was Howard Ackley,
that smarmy vegetarian anarchist who helped out at the charity
bookstore where she volunteered on Wednesday afternoons after
school. Or was it Thursday afternoons? He thought he had
noticed a certain disturbing familiarity between them once,
at a buffet they had organised together in aid of saving one
allegedly imperilled portion of the Brazilian rainforest. While
the imported tribal elder with the saucer through his lower lip
had been lording it over the devout if half-drunk audience,

Amery had seen his wife standing by the Nicaraguan coffee bar, reaching out her fingers and removing a hair from Ackley's shoulder. A gesture of startling intimacy, there was no doubt about it. He, Amery, a surgeon and a healer, a man who made a damn good living with his fingers, would never have dared do such a thing to a non-family member.

'Consumerism is death,' the tribal elder had said, through the adoring, doe-eyed interpreter seated at his naked feet. Which had seemed richly ironic to Amery. Because the big-lipped, hairy-assed old phoney hadn't seemed to mind flying first class, all the way from Rio de Janeiro, on his, Amery's, goddamn credit card. Sting good, consumerism bad. That seemed to be the gist, more or less. We should all stop buying shoes made of animal skin. All of which would be absolutely fine, Amery had reckoned, the day we could buy shoes made of Sting's skin instead.

But then again, Ackley was gay, wasn't he? Wasn't that what Ellen had said? He had married his percussionist boyfriend, Geraldo – or was it Ronaldo – in Hawaii. Or maybe he was bisexual. Good God, had his wife run off with a bisexual anarchist? Was she shacked up somewhere with a white trash epicene? A sudden mental picture formed before him, of his wife having a gymnastic threesome with Ackley and the large-lipped chieftain in a Days Inn somewhere. While Ronaldo – or Geraldo – squatted cross-legged on the carpet, playing the bongos with his dick and hooting. The image made him wince with panic.

The mobile rang. His receptionist again.

'I'm sorry, Doctor Amery, there seems to be a misunderstanding. The travel agent says Mrs Amery didn't order any tickets, they haven't seen her for several months.'

'Fine. I thought so. Excellent. Thank you.'

'Oh. It's a pleasure.' She sounded uneasy. 'Everything is all right, is it, Doctor Amery?'

'Yes, Violet, of course. Any messages?'

'Well, yes. Miss Kenneally called twice.'

'Miss Kenneally? Which one?' He affected ignorance of his lover's name.

'The one who calls us a lot, Doctor Amery. She seemed quite keen that you call her back directly.'

'All right. Thank you. And Merry Christmas, Violet.'

'Same to you and Mrs Amery, Doctor.'

Perhaps she had gone to Florida to visit Dick Spiggot. Lord in heaven, was that a possibility? Spiggot had been her teenage sweetheart; they had all hung around together at Columbia, played tennis, gone dancing and bowling together. And Spiggot and she had acted together in the more amusingly Marxist of the two student drama companies. The man was a raving imbecile and an unspeakable vulgarian who had inherited his family's rum-running millions. He had a house in South Beach, Miami, quite near Madonna's and just down the street from Gianni Versace's, a pile of such transcendentally baroque tastelessness that even a minor British royal wouldn't live in it. The wedding reception he had thrown for his eldest daughter, Chastity, had been like something Ceaucescu would have put on for a niece. For God's sake, there had been dyed pink swans. Cakes shaped like dollar signs. Topless fire-eaters! He had several airplanes and a colossal sharking boat; there was a rumour that he actually owned one of the smaller Bahamas and was conducting an ongoing legal battle with the authorities in Nassau to have it renamed for his favourite racehorse.

Perhaps every marriage needs one useful scapegoat, a figure who appears in the relationship's iconography like a leering demon in the margin of a medieval manuscript. In Amery's marriage, that was Dick Spiggot. As part of making up their milder arguments, he and Ellen had sometimes joked that she should have married Dick. It was one of their small rituals of reconciliation. It was how they knew a disagreement had truly ended.

'I guess you're going to leave me now for Dick Spiggot.'

'Maybe I will. Then you'd be happy.'

'Elizabeth, honey? Your mother's leaving for me for Dick Spiggot. She's going to let Mister Taste take care of her from now on.'

'Oh, OK. Good idea.'

'If I'd married Dick instead of you, Milton, he would have treated me like a princess.'

'What kinda weird name is Spiggot though?' their son had scoffed once, scrunching his nose in ugly displeasure. 'I woulda been called Lee Spiggot. Jesus.'

'It's a fine name and he's a fine man,' Ellen had said. 'Anyway, you shouldn't judge people by their names.'

'Dick Spiggot,' said Lee. 'It sounds like a sex aid.'

When he thought of his son, tears of shame formed in his eyes. He was a sensitive teenager, restlessly clumsy and full of a passion for which he had no vocabulary, at a raw, fearfully sullen age when he needed his mother's calm in his life. Ellen was so good with him, there was no doubt about it. She seemed to see something bright and affirmative in him, some potential for responsiveness, whereas all Amery could get most of the time was a series of grunts, barks or half-suppressed gurgles.

'Where are you going, Lee?'

'Out.'

'When will you be back?'

'Later.'

'With whom are you going out?'

'Nobody you'd know.'

'Who the hell do you think you are, Lee?'

'What the hell's this, Dad? Philosophy class?'

He would pronounce the word 'Dad' as though it was in inverted commas. Irony, in fact, was now his default position.

The older Lee got, the more distant he seemed. Soon he would be communicating with vowel sounds alone. Thirteen-year-olds could be troublesome and solipsistic, of course that was obvious; but surely to God there was something unhealthy about his obsession with aliens, machine guns and death. This was a boy who had once been fond of picking wildflowers for his mother, painting watercolours, collecting baseball cards. Now he trudged around the house like a Nike-wearing zombie, muttering darkly about Roswell and petrol bomb recipes, his face plastered with nodules of bloodied toilet paper since starting to shave three months previously. Amery remembered his own adolescence, how his mother and not his father had been the anchor of his life. He caught his guilty reflection in a storefront window. He looked like a scumbag. He looked like a criminal.

He looked like a man who had driven his wife away from her children.

Yes, she had her complications; there was no denying it. But all women were complicated, as any doctor could tell you, full of endless layers and dizzying depths of emotion. Thank God they were. He had learned to make a good living from that happy and unchangeable fact. But he wouldn't pretend to understand them. How in the hell could you hope to do that? Think of a man, then subtract reason and accountability. That's what his father used to advise. But Amery didn't think that was right. There was a lot more to women than that; in his line of work, you got to know it. Know a man for a week and you knew him for life. Like a small, confused, semi-extinct woodland creature, a man was entirely predictable in his pitiful little habits. But you could never accuse a woman of predictability. You could know a woman your whole life and she would still turn around one morning and do something that would shock you to the core of your being. Then again, women had pressures that men could only dream about. Let's face it, they were lunar. Some more than others. Ellen was so lunar she was practically tidal.

But then, in other ways, she was such a simple person. A woman of tact, of the most extraordinary gentleness, who seemed to feel not exactly pain, but great surges of unadulterated empathy, in a way that Amery simply didn't. She would cry at an old movie, a lame dog on the sidewalk, a sad song on the radio, a separation scene in a soap opera, a collection of fat and ugly persons being 'made over' on a chat show. Hell, she had cried the night Clinton was elected. He remembered the tears streaming down her face, as Slick Willie and Handsome Al had boogied around the stage, shaking their posteriors and playing air guitar – the President Elect doing his lachrymose 'aw shucks' grin and brandishing his saxophone the way Lady Liberty brandished the torch. Don't. Stop. Thinking About Tomorrow. If he could have cried with her, God knows he would have.

It was not even that they didn't love each other any more; it was just that the energy required to go on being seen to do so had become too much. And anyway, fidelity was such baloney.

36

Faithfulness to a person was highly overrated; keeping faith with an idea was much more important. To be honest, he imagined she saw things the same way. In recent years he had come to feel that all she truly wanted from him now was companionship. Someone to share the simple business of inhabiting the space in which they had mysteriously woken up. The thought that he had failed her even in that was like a poisonous worm corkscrewing through his gut.

On the corner of Fifth and 57th a Mexican policeman on a large brown horse seemed to regard him accusingly. Even the horse didn't look too happy to see him. It stared in his direction, disapprovingly munching; its huge yellow molars like those of an ageing rock star.

Happy now? it seemed to be saying. You royal son of a bitch.

He peered at the horse as it sneeringly masticated. Then reached out a hand to stroke its bridle. As if obeying some divine ordinance, it raised its tail and shat on the sidewalk.

There ya go, Milton Amery. That's what I think of you, ya big phoney.

Two black boys in windcheaters cackled and pointed. A woman in a mink coat glared at him as she passed. A blind man he tried to help cross the street shied away from him, flailing with his stick and snapping like a spaniel.

'Get your dirty hands off me, Mac. What am I, *crippled*?'

Crossing Fifth Avenue he went into Tiffany's. The heat was on so high that his spectacles fogged up and he had to try to clean them with his tie. He wandered the aisles on the ground floor for a while, feeling large and stupid and somehow out of place, the way a lapsed Roman Catholic would feel in one of those malodorous European cathedrals Ellen was so fond of traipsing around. The polished glass cases glinted. The marble and onyx pillars gleamed; the lacquered wooden panels seemed to ooze authority. Often in stores like this he would have the feeling of being watched by the security guards; he knew it was irrational, even downright ridiculous, but nevertheless there it was. It was nothing obvious, just a certain way they had of half nodding at him as he

37

passed, or grinning in his direction with their lips and not their eyes.

'I have money,' he wanted to tell them. 'I'm not going to stick the damn place up.'

'How may I help you today, sir?'

The assistant was a portly, *simpatico*, platter-faced piece of work who looked like she had a flock of adoring grandchildren. What a question. For a moment he wanted to tell her he was beyond help, that he had wrecked his life, for reasons he could not even begin to understand. That he had taken the dreams of his boyhood and thrashed them senseless, that lately he was starting to feel there was something psychologically amiss with him, some essential part of his emotional constitution that was simply absent or the wrong way around. She grinned demurely. He wondered what she would do if he were to vault one-handed over the counter, bury his face in her extraordinary bosom and bawl 'mama'.

'I wanted to get a Christmas present for my wife,' he said.

'Oh,' she beamed delightedly, as though that was the most remarkable thing she had ever heard. 'And did you see anything you liked today, sir?'

He pointed half-heartedly at a choker of pearls and diamonds.

'Might I see that one please?'

The assistant took it out of the case, rubbed it on her sleeve, then on a small yellow cloth. She placed it on a black velvet tray, which she tilted theatrically back and forth. As if on cue, the diamonds began to sparkle. Sweat was forming in the small of his back. His tongue felt dry, large as a bar of soap. The assistant was explaining where the stones were from, a hundred-year-old mine in the Transvaal region of South Africa, but Doctor Milton Amery wasn't really listening. He found himself picturing the tribal elder from the rainforest gleefully fingering the necklace, wrapping it speculatively around his foot-long penis sheath, while his wife did something unspeakable to Howard Ackley's nipples – the whole gruesome tableau being shot on home video by leering, florid-faced, drooling Dick Spiggot.

'That's very attractive. How much is that one?'

'That one is fifteen thousand five hundred, sir.'

Lord, the smooth insouciance with which she said those words.

Fifteen thousand five hundred dollars. His mind performed a quick calculation. That was ten nose jobs, a couple of tummy tucks, one pretty comprehensive bout of liposuction, on an opera singer, say, or a semi-professional wrestler.

A sudden wash of hail peppered the windows. People in the store turned to look in the direction of the sound, as though it was something miraculous. When he looked back, the assistant was peering at him eagerly. It was a little off-putting, actually. From a professional point of view, she definitely needed some work around the neck. She wasn't an oil painting and never would be, but there was a lot you could do with a woman like that. Most of it wouldn't even have to hurt too much. For one terrible moment it came into his mind to offer some kind of barter, a full neck scrape or a couple of alpha hydroxy acid peels in return for a ten per cent discount.

'Hmm,' he said instead.

She shot him a look of almost crazed expectation. If her eyebrows went any higher they would disappear into her hairline.

'If you'll allow me to show you something reasonably similar but in the five-thousand-dollar range?'

Now he felt he was disappointing the assistant. It was nothing she said, but he sensed she thought he was cheap. This was a sensation he often experienced in stores, it was ridiculous and he knew it, but it would never change now. She was probably on some pitiful commission, after all, he told himself. He imagined her apartment on Christmas night. An electric fire, one bar switched on, a mangy Jack Russell, a cracked plate of cold cuts. A framed picture of Mom and Dad back in Cleveland. A half-pint bottle of methylated spirits. Why not give her a break, for God's sakes.

Stores were difficult for Milton Amery, crucibles designed for his trial and mortification. Occasionally he would find himself in a men's department, trying on a pair of trousers he didn't really like, some obsequious assistant flirting and simpering, or, worse still, saying nothing at all. He would look at himself in these ludicrous trousers, knowing absolutely that he would never wear them. But then, if he didn't take them, he'd feel as though he were disappointing the assistant. Once or twice, he had even felt he was disappointing the trousers. He'd peer at them, lying on the chair in the changing room. *Oh please, Doctor Amery, please, please buy us. We promise we'll be good trousers, please don't leave us here.* At home he had an entire wardrobe for the clothes he never wore, sartorial testimony to his weakness and malleability. Ellen was always on at him about it.

'No, no. I believe I'll take this one.'

The assistant smiled her approbation. 'I don't think you'll regret your choice, sir. It's such a beautiful piece.'

'Well. Yes, it is. And it's Christmas after all.'

'She's one lucky lady,' the assistant said.

'No, I'm the lucky one,' said Doctor Milton Amery, wondering silently, as he reached for his Mastercard, if he would ever see his wife's face again.

*　　*　　*

STRICTLY PRIVATE AND CONFIDENTIAL

16 January 1986

Dear Mrs Amery,

May I begin by wishing you belated compliments of the season. I pray that this New Year of 1986 may be a happy one for yourself, your family and your students.

I am in receipt of your reply to my letter of 8 September.

While of course I understand the depth of your natural feelings about this matter, I really must advise that your birth mother has absolutely insisted once again that she does not wish to meet you, under any circumstances. She is most adamant and will not be persuaded otherwise.

I beg you to accept that I do fully understand the profound human need to 'make a connection', as you put it. But there are factors that you yourself must try to understand also. There are other important rights at issue here – not just those of your birth mother, but those of her family. I have done what I can. In fact, I have gone a little further than usual, given the force with which your letter to me was written, and the very obvious distress out of which it clearly came. I have gone back a second and, indeed, a third time to put your case to the person concerned, but to no avail. Her mind will not be changed on the subject. Against that background I must ask you not to put forward your request to meet with her again.

You mention in passing that you are a teacher, Mrs Amery, with an appreciation of Irish literature. I imagine, therefore, given your interest in our country, that you must have some knowledge of what Ireland was like in the 1940s. Some would say we were a terribly secretive and hypocritical society in those days, others that we formed a far more cohesive community. I do not know. Perhaps both statements are true. Perhaps each is true because of the other. In any case, young women who 'got themselves into trouble', to use the biologically inaccurate phrase of the time, were often seen as outcasts and scapegoats. Terrible things happened. Maybe our own weakness was all we saw in them, when we should have tried to see their Christ-like strength and resilience. God help them and God forgive us. For I am sorry to say that many of us in the Church would have much to examine our consciences about here, as regards charity, respect for human dignity and simple compassion. When these young women needed love and support, we all too often offered only harsh judgement. When they cried out for mercy we filled them instead with shame.

Such feelings of shame and guilt, if they have not actually ruined the lives of those who were made to experience them, have certainly made those lives much more troubled than they needed to be. Many of the young women I speak of have carried these corrosive feelings into adulthood, into their own marriages and homes, and in the case of your birth mother, well into her middle age. This may account for her reluctance to see you now. Personally, I feel it probably does.

You will know all too well that Ireland is a country at war with its past – or, at least, with conflicting versions of its several pasts. But we are each of us in struggle with those, Mrs Amery, on a much more deeply personal level than we sometimes know.

That said, by way of explanation, I do have one small piece of possibly good news for you. I implore you not to raise your hopes at what I am about to write. I may say candidly that I have agonised about whether to tell you at all, but it is my duty to do so, and so I do.

Your birth mother has asked me to say that she would be willing to receive a letter from you, if and when you want to send one. Furthermore she adds that she may – and I do stress, it is only a possibility, and, I myself feel, a remote one – that she may exchange some sort of correspondence with you in time. The conditions would be that you respect her privacy, give an absolute guarantee that matters will not go any further than written communication and undertake only to write to her care of myself, at the above address.

I repeat that a meeting is absolutely out of the question. But having accepted that fact and reflected upon it – and if you are a praying person, you may wish to pray about it too – if you still feel inclined to write something to her, I would of course be willing to pass it on.

Please, please, do not raise your hopes of getting a reply.

With sincere prayers for you and your family.

Yours in Christ

Sister Mary Rose Kennedy

PS: I hope you will not think it presumptuous or intrusive of me to enclose a little reading which has brought a sense of healing to my own life at times. It is from the writings of Julian of Norwich, a great woman mystic from the fourteenth century.

As surely as God is our father, so is he our mother. For in God our fractured being is made whole. It is I, the strength of fatherhood. It is I, the wisdom of motherhood. It is I, the trinity. It is I, the unity. It is I who teach you to love, my child. It is I who am the reward of all true desiring.

MRK

SUNDAY, 25 DECEMBER 1994

Chapter Four

Around half-past eleven on Christmas morning Inspector Martin Aitken awoke, mumbling and groaning from a dream of his marriage. He and Valerie had been lying half naked on a twilit rocky hillside, gazing straight up at the stars. He could hear her smoochy, languorous, twenty-a-day voice, identifying them one by one – *Antares, Fomalhaut, Arcturus, Mimosa* – and as she had said each name, the star in question would give a sulphurous self-important twinkle. A picnic basket sat nearby on a Black Watch tartan rug, with an uncorked bottle of red wine inside it.

His mouth salted up at the thought of the wine. He reached out and fumbled at the cardboard packing case doing duty as bedside table. He took the greasy glass, swigged down half a pint of cloudy metallic-tasting water and waited for his heart to stop whomping. A shaft of silvery dust-filled light shone in through the gap in the curtains. Along the yellowed ceiling scuttled a solitary spider.

His heart puttered like a dirty engine. He couldn't remember if anything remotely like the dream had ever happened for real. But it felt so electrically vivid that he wondered if it had, and if the conscious part of his mind had somehow forgotten. Not that it was like him to forget too much.

Inspector Martin Aitken had trained his memory. Car registrations, telephone numbers, dates of birth, national insurance codes. In the old days, before things had gone so badly wrong and his life had begun to unravel like a worn-out sweater, the younger officers would come to him for advice, for information, numbers, leads and directions. He would pretend to complain but in fact he would find it flattering. In they'd trot to his office, like sinners to confession. He could reel off details on

47

every important criminal in the city, where they lived, who they knew, what they would and wouldn't do, who they owned, where they drank, what weapons they favoured and on what kind of job. Conmen, robbers, fraudsters and cheats, burglars, muggers, pickpockets, car thieves. 'Give him a name and he'll give you the numbers.' That's what they used to say about Martin Aitken. He was famous throughout the police stations of Dublin for having once caught a leading IRA bomber by somehow remembering that he wore a size sixteen shirt collar.

But where was the place he had seen in the dream? Indignant-looking swans on choppy water, outcrops of granite and rough green marble, twisted black bushes that seemed to shake their fists at the sky. He had been there. He knew that: it had seemed so familiar, so utterly known right down to its details. People like Valerie and her daft new-age buddies sometimes said that dreams were echoes of past lives, residual rehearsals of roads already walked. And Aitken himself had often had dreams where he would know every stunted tree on a winding hillside path, each turn and twist of stony roadway ahead. He could predict the very undulations of fields and wet meadows even as they appeared before him – yet when he woke he could put no name on the landscape.

Where was this place?

Where the hell was it?

His head hurt and his vision was cloudy. Behind his itching eyes throbbed an insistent, pumping ache. He'd smoked way too many cigarettes the night before and his synapses felt fried up and desiccated. He would really have to give it up.

He listened to the stressed wheeze that was coming from his trachea. Like a distant flock of unhappy seagulls. His sad heart seemed to flutter and jounce. He imagined his lungs now as polythene bags filled with molten tar, the back of his throat scorched scarlet and raw. He would have to stop smoking; there was no doubt about it. Otherwise, one of these days he'd collapse in the street, pain shooting across the tops of his arms. Be carted into some intensive care ward, where they would break his chest open like a Dublin Bay prawn and lift out his heart in their rubber-gloved hands.

He had a vision of two grinning junior doctors chucking it to each other in rugby pass style. Lazily tossing the gloopy mess around the operating theatre. Maybe even attempting a few cheerful drop kicks, before screwing in a couple of artificial valves and shoving it back into his sternal cavity – like some foolish souvenir bought on a holiday, too big to go in a bulging suitcase. They'd probably have to sit on his chest to sew the bloody thing up again.

On the cardboard bedside table was a carton of soggy McDonald's French fries, left there the previous night, congealing as he'd fallen asleep. He picked one out and ate it slowly, trying to focus on something real. He watched the spider as it zigzagged towards the light fitting. Somehow, deep down, he envied the hell out of it.

The corners of his aching eyes were crusty with sleep, the edges of his mouth tender where the recent sharp cold had split the skin of his lips. He took the half-smoked joint from the floor by his bed and lit it up, sucking lightly at first, almost cautiously, as he began to slot together the pieces of the night before.

He and Valerie had had a bad argument. He'd been supposed to call at eight to her place in Donnybrook, see their two daughters and exchange Christmas gifts; but at the last minute he hadn't been able to make it. There'd been a fatal shooting in the north inner city. In the seasonal absence of the regular Special Branch unit he'd had to take charge of the crime scene himself. 'Just like the old days, boss,' the desk sergeant, Hughie Tynan, had grinned. 'Martin Aitken rides again, hoh?'

From the taped-off alleyway that led to Sean MacDermott Street, he'd phoned her at a quarter to nine to try to explain. But it hadn't gone well. Dangerous things had got said, old angry things that had no place between them now. The exchange had ended with her slamming the phone down.

'You'd do anything not to be here, wouldn't you Martin? You were always the same, you were never any other way. You'd shoot someone yourself if you thought it would hurt me.'

What had got to him the most was that he'd known she was right. Not quite about shooting someone; he would have drawn the line there – though admittedly, once or twice over the last five years he had considered letting her boyfriend have a blast of a sawn-off, probably around the buttock region. It was good to have an unmissable target. But apart from that, Valerie had his number. He wasn't proud of it, but he knew it was true. In the final days of their self-destructing marriage, causing trouble, undermining, needlessly sniping, had practically become an entertainment to him. It was a thing he had no control over, a fact of life from which he felt disconnected. Like standing on the shore and watching a ship sink out in the bay, knowing you had a loved one or a lot of money on board. Not that she'd been an angel herself. In some ways, he often thought now, it was what had held them together so long, the fact that they knew how to hurt each other so terribly. She had said that once, and she'd been right about that much. But then Valerie Houghton was nearly always right. It was one of the most infuriating things about her.

Sneezing in the rain, coughing and spluttering like a broken-down machine, he had helped the uniforms seal off the street, arranged for the photographer, the forensics and fingerprint teams and the uneager state pathologist who turned up with gravy on his tie. ('Jesus, Martin,' the pathologist had said. 'I thought you were stuck behind a desk these days, no?') He had cleared away the press guys, the TV and radio reporters, all hungry for a piquant story of the rainy city with which to tease the jaded palates of their Yuletide audiences. 'The public have a right to know, Inspector,' a shaven-headed girl of about twenty-five had informed him, jamming a microphone into his face.

'You can take that yoke and stick it up the public's hole, pet. And by the way, the name's Aitken, if you want to report me to someone.'

Around half-ten the pubs had shut. A gang of silent, morose-looking drunks had congregated at the barrier to watch pro-ceedings, like inbred medieval hayseeds awaiting the annual unveiling of some gory relic. One of them emitted a hollow cheer as the shattered corpse was scooped into the plastic bag and trundled away. No ambulance had been available, so one of Aitken's men had had to commandeer a taxi; it was either do that or leave the body on the street until morning. The driver had placed a lining of black plastic rubbish sacks across his back seat before accepting his grim cargo. Then off he'd sped into the night, Charon the ferryman in a Dunnes Stores shellsuit, and the crowd had drifted away as if to gather elsewhere. By 11.15 the street was empty. Aitken had helped a frightened young rookie to clean the bloodstains off the pavement.

And for some reason he didn't understand, Martin Aitken had drifted in to midnight mass on the way home. Blackrock church had been packed to the doors, the air sweetly oppressive with the smell of incense and candles, of wet dirty hair and sodden woollen clothes. A folk group was huddled around the concrete altar, denim-clad amiable youngsters strumming mandolins and banjos, while the plump priest bobbed his boulder of a head in uneasy rhythm. A shabby, flame-eyed, sour-smelling drunk in the porch had fixed on Martin Aitken, tottering over and declaiming bits of 'Boolavogue' to him, or at him, all the way through the homily.

> *Arm, arm, he cried, for I've come to lead yez*
> *For Ireland's freedom . . . we'll fight . . . and dhie!*

God never looked away, the priest was saying. There were people here tonight who looked away from God every other week of the year. But God never looked away from us. He was constant. He was beyond time. He was, in a sense, like the income tax authorities. You could run from God but in the end you couldn't hide.

The congregation chuckled a bit at this point, as if obliging the priest was something they'd get points for.

It was about time we all got straight with God. Because God would forgive the fact that we'd turned our backs on him. It was never too late, there was always time. Even God had fallen, after all. Jesus our blessed Lord himself had fallen three times on the road to Calvary.

For the cause that called youse
May call tomorra,
In one last fight, for the ghreen aghain.

Aitken had found himself thinking about the woman who had fainted outside the bus station. What was her story? What part did God play in that? All he had was the fact of her falling. But behind the raw facts of the everyday whose explication he was paid to bring about, there were almost always fiercely complicated stories; narratives of pain and bad choices, of mistakes made and wrong turnings taken, cul-de-sacs entered once and never truly left. Nothing in police work was as simple as it seemed. The craziest bank robber could be motivated by love, the most scrupulous lawman by utter malevolence. He thought about the dead man in the alleyway, a long-time addict and minor pusher called Bronco Ferris, one of seven kids who were all HIV positive before they were sixteen, only out of the Joy a wet weekend and back in the artificial happiness business already. Poor old Bronco, always acting the hardchaw, shaping around town in his dead father's leather jacket, with PHIL LYNOTT RULES done out in Tipp-Ex on the back. Was God looking down on Bronco too, as the world exploded in a stinking back alley, spike improvised from the tube of a biro still jammed deep into his bony thigh? What kind of Christmas would his four youngsters have?

At the sign of peace, the drunk had thrown his arms around Aitken and begun to cry softly about his father.

'Get the fuck off me,' Aitken said.

'Dada,' the wino wept.

'Get off me, bollix, or I'll be dug out of you.'

'Dada. Dada. I love my dada.'

After mass, the spotlight on the steeple beamed down on the car park like the beam of some hovering UFO, flooding the scene with an eerie sodium blaze. One in the morning and the place was swarming, alive with the thuds of BMW and Mercedes doors, the yelping and squealing of overexcited children. 'Hurry, Daddy,' one of them shouted, a feisty little bruiser with a mop of glossy curls, 'Santa's gonna come soon! We've to get home before Santee comes.' He'd sat in his car and watched from the shadows, John Lee Hooker moaning softly on the cassette player. He had waited and watched until everyone was gone, not really sure exactly what he was waiting for, but certain all the same that home was not yet an option.

> Rattle snake crawlin', Mama
> Gonna crawl all over you.
> Tell me why you do your lovin' man
> The way you do.

Now it was Christmas morning and he was alone.

A full week of leave stretched ahead of him, seven days and nights of nerve-shredding inactivity. He lay very still, pulling harder on the joint, sucking the sickly fumes deep into his lungs. The damp sheets were wrapped around his limbs like manacles, something like a semi-erection dying beneath the duvet. He pulled back the covers and peered downwards. As if trying its best to be seasonably joyous, it gave a piteously hopeful little twitch. Like a fat kid trying to get picked for the football team. Once upon a time that would have been major currency. Now it was small and useless change.

Slowly the marijuana started to bite. It was as though his nerve endings were being dipped one by one into ointment. The room smelt musty, of stale shirts and old socks, of cheap aftershave and ripe masculinity. The day advanced before him like a desert road in a nightmare.

People often seemed to believe that police work was action packed, one long car chase, a kind of living cop show. But one thing you learned as a Special Branch man was how to do nothing. Turning your head off was essential, finding some location where feelings weren't important, at least not for the moment. Some defined moral space where emotions weren't just a luxury but an actual impediment to clear and rapid judgement. That was true on the rare enough occasions when things got insane. When you came in through the fire escape of a city-centre flat and found a young woman bound and gagged, stabbed to death and wrapped in a sleeping bag. When you kicked in the door of a bungalow in the sticks to find blood splattered on the walls and a gang member face down in a bathtub, hands wired behind his back and his mangled kneecaps in different rooms. But it was true the rest of the time also. In this line of work – he'd told his officers often – the ability to be still was a *sine qua non*.

Sometimes back in the old days he'd get a raw and hungry newbie, dripping testosterone, with a hard-on for action. The kind of guy who would turn up for the first day's training in a *Miami Vice* sports jacket, chewing on gum; the type who would look at his new gun and quiver with excitement. He'd seen *The Untouchables* once too often. That was a man Aitken had never liked to get, back in the days when he got men to train. He'd be tricky to handle, too unpredictable. You could always tell the kind who would never understand that real police work wasn't edited. It was one of the reasons women made better Special Branch officers. They seemed to be able to do nothing without getting paranoid.

Thinking about it now, it occurred to him that most of the last twenty years had been spent in doing nothing, in waiting for some grand thing to start happening. Yes, there were moments that stood out in relief. But looking back over the landscape from his current vantage point, it was a long blurred vista of nights passed in cars, watching suburban houses, killing time, eating lukewarm hamburgers, drinking foul coffee, listening to the radio, sometimes playing cards, but mostly doing nothing. Just watching and waiting for the big thing to finally appear, or at least to start peeping over the horizon. He simply couldn't say it had all been exciting. You'd have months and months on one bank job, say, a whole season of sifting through files and account records and at the end of it all not even an arrest. Once, back in the terrible months just after Robbie died, Valerie had taken him to see *Waiting for Godot*, with some of her worry-beaded chums from the spiritualist group. He remembered them being in the bar of the Gate Theatre afterwards, throwing down gin and freaking out the tourists. They'd all thought the play was very strange. 'I mean, Holy God, Valerie, nothing really *happened* in it.' But Aitken had reckoned it was like a documentary on police work. Just that a hell of a lot more happened in the play.

I can do nothing, thought Martin Aitken. *I am trained to do nothing. That shouldn't bother me.*

The incident with Doogan came into his mind now, fresh and sharp as something imagined. Evil, vicious, head-wrecking little bollocks. He was sure there would be a complaint about it. Always trust a criminal to know his civil rights.

What the hell had possessed him to do it? Cut the guy's jacket up like that. Throwing the head with a gouger like Doogan was dangerous; he knew that well from the mad old days. Back then he was famous for never showing his emotions, and back then, in the seventies, that was saying something. Car bombs were going off in the streets of Dublin; he'd had a man gunned down by the INLA. But even with the very worst of the Provos he'd always been able to keep his calm. 'Cool as a poker player in some late-night movie.' That's what Hughie Tynan had said about him once. That wasn't the way Aitken saw it himself. Interrogating a suspect was more like being a scientist; waiting patiently for some measurable substance on a specimen plate to change colour, knowing it would, if you just kept at it and mixed what you added in the right proportions.

They'd sit silent twelve straight hours, some of the better-trained ones, arms folded, eyes fixed on the interrogation room wall. Never open their beaks except to whistle 'Christy Moore'. All around him colleagues would be having shit-fits and wanting to get into cracking heads. And Martin Aitken would be the one they'd send for then. His technique was simple, the only one that made sense. He'd just ask the questions, over and over, wear them down by attrition and calm. Often, in the quieter moments of those endless nights, he would have a mental image of the law as a mighty wave that kept breaking against a shore. Nothing could stop a wave like that. Until slowly they'd start to crack and fidget. One or two would even lose the plot, jump up and start whining about constitutional rights. With another officer, with one of the Heavy Gang, that would be the precise point when the beating would begin. But not with Martin Aitken. He'd just keep the questions coming, short and sharp, in words of one syllable, over and over till they'd start climbing the walls and throwing shapes. Even that was fine, it rarely bothered him.

They could spit in his face and he'd scarcely wince. But that was when he'd been married and had a family. Nothing at all could touch him then.

He'd explained this once, to a diehard from Belfast who was up for armed robbery on a post office van. At the end of an all-night interrogation session, he'd pulled up a chair, sat down, lit a smoke. 'I'm going home now, son, to my wife and my kids. You're going to jail. If not this time, then the next time. Or else you'll end up drinking your brains out of your cap. Bullet in the head, from my side or yours. Now, you want to die for Ireland, that's game-ball by me. But you try and kill anyone for Ireland, I'll fucking nail your balls to Patrick Pearse's gravestone first, son. Because my kids won't live in a country run by you. Not while I've a single breath left in me.'

It almost amused him now to think that once he had been able to talk like that. Because after his family had imploded, his sang-froid had simply disappeared. And lately he'd noticed his fuse getting shorter again. That was bad, it could only lead to trouble. He would really have to watch his temper. One more mistake, he'd be out of a job. End up helping yuppies park their beamers on Stephen's Green. Maybe there was a New Year resolution here.

On the floor by the bed he found an unopened envelope with a final-demand electricity bill inside. He took out a pen and began to write.

Don't lose temper.
Learn how to iron.

Right now he couldn't think of anything else.

The sheet was scratchy with old crumbs. He got up painfully and looked at the bed. For a moment he considered turning the sheet over. But it had been turned over so many times by now that the dirt must be starting to meet in the middle.

In the mirror he peered at the crow's feet around his baggy eyes, his wrinkled neck, the tufts of hair in his ears. These days the ear-hair seemed to grow in inverse proportion to that on his head. Nobody ever told you that this was going

56

to happen. That one day your life would be opening before you like a beautiful tulip, and the next you'd be checking over your shoulder before guiltily whispering to some diplomatically nodding barber, 'Take a little off the sides, then do the ears.'

He rooted around on the floor of his wardrobe and found a shirt that was almost clean, an expensive black and silver tie his daughter had given him for his forty-third birthday.

In the mirror his hair was like a madwoman's fanny. People said that by forty you had the face you deserved. But that wasn't right. He didn't deserve this face. As a matter of fact, nobody did.

Look at the bleeding state of yourself.

Inspector Martin Joseph Philip Aitken, the pride of Ireland, the thin blue line. Twelve stone of shite in a ten-stone bag.

From under the bed he got out the shoebox and looked through his bootlegs. Hendrix live at Cobo Hall. Rory Gallagher at the National Boxing Stadium, Muddy Waters at the Kit Kat Klub. He put on the Stones, Hyde Park '69, Mick drawling out lines from Shelley's 'Adonais'. *'Peace. 'E is not dead. 'E does not sleep.'* Laughing softly, he forwarded the tape, to 'Jumpin' Jack Flash', loud and raucous, Mick Taylor's chopping brash guitar, the vicious four-four backbeat of Charlie's crashing drums. *Eyes, bone. In a crossed line her cane.* That was how his brother Johnny used to insist the opening lines went. Whenever anyone said that was totally meaningless he'd just smile and say 'not when you think about it'. Aitken rolled and lit a second joint now, his stained fingers shaking badly as he took a drag. Cupped his hands to trap the smoke. Opened his mouth and swallowed it down, gulping and spluttering like a goldfish yanked from its bowl. The shake in his hands wouldn't stop. It was just like the old days.

A gas, gas, gas.

Fingers fumbling, wrists like jelly, he tried to knot his necktie now. The Stones were into 'Sympathy for the Devil', Mick screeching like a banshee on angel dust over the voodoo drumbeat and tortured guitars. The first time the knot came out the

size of a tennis ball, the second the size of a walnut. Forty-three
years old and he couldn't tie a tie. He ripped it off and threw
it on the carpet. Who the hell was going to see it anyway?

Down in the kitchen of the south-side redbrick he had once
shared with his wife and children, the sink looked as though it
had vomited. Lately he was beginning to have the feeling there
was something actually living in the plumbing. The radio was
playing a steel drum reggae version of 'Adeste Fideles', the gas
had been cut off for serial non-payment and there was nothing
in the fridge except a bottle of aspirins.

The room sang with the aroma of refrigerator freon and
advanced organic decay. The smell that says, perhaps more
than any other, 'You, loser, have lost the plot.'

Across the avenue, the eldest Bradley boy was riding a new
bicycle, pulling off wheelies and tinging the bell, while his fat
younger brother huffed along beside him, menacing him with a
stiff dead crow. Christ, that kid was fat. Like a beach ball on legs.
Through the front window of their house he could see a plump
vermilion Christmas tree, practically shrieking with lights and
gaudy tinsel stars.

If Robbie were here now, he'd be their age.

He'd be out there now, acting the maggot.

If he fell over on his backside I'd go and pick him up.

Maybe we'd kick a ball around the road.

Suddenly, like a migraine lifting, everything about the place
in the dream became clear to him.

It was Inishowen.

Inishowen.

The mordant call of screaming seagulls.

Let it go.

Leave it be.

It's a gas, gas, gas.

He knocked on the window three times hard. The Bradley
boys stared at him with uneasy curiosity, as though he was
something they had just found under a rock.

'Merry Christmas, guys,' he gaily called, throwing down a
couple of Tuinal. 'Santee bring you a new bike, did he?'

The Bradley boys said nothing. Not one word.

'Isn't Christmas only great crack, huh?'

One of them pushed his hair behind his ears.

'C'mere and tell us what you got off Santee, why don't you? How's your parents?'

They looked at each other and tittered like cartoon devils. Bowed their heads and whispered in a conspiracy. Then the eldest turned to face Aitken. Slowly, almost delicately, he raised his middle finger, jabbing it forcefully up and down, pouting his grossly purple lips. The other doubled up with maniacal laughter, twisting his face into a hideous leer.

There was no need for that attitude, Aitken thought. Though he had to admit that things had not been the same in the neighbourhood since the morning he had crashed his secondhand Mini into their father's vintage Jaguar. The man had actually wept when he'd seen the damage. A grown man, a senior architect, an adviser to the central committee of the Progressive Democrats, bawling into his hands like a big fat Bradley baby.

K-chunk! The sound came from behind him.

A plump, brown mouse had been caught in one of the traps. It twitched and tried to pull its tail free.

Poor little bastard. I know how you feel.

Down on his knees, he eased back the wire teeth and let it go. It wriggled and sped off behind the bookcase, like something on castors rather than legs.

'Happy Christmas, Mickey, me auld son.'

K-chunk!

'Ah! . . . *Jayzus!*'

The wire chomped down hard on his little finger.

'*Fuck it,*' he winced. 'Fuck, fuck, fuck.'

On the television, the Pope was in Saint Peter's Square blessing people. He moved slowly along a line of kneeling pilgrims, allowing various parts of himself to be touched or grasped. He looked very old and a little frightened, as though he was expecting to be shot again soon. A black nun in a sky-blue veil kissed his hand. Aitken found himself thinking about the Pope going to the toilet. Valerie had once confided that this was how she dealt with her 'authority issues'. Her psychotherapist had advised her to think of the powerful, dominant, controlling

people in her life as always sitting on a toilet. 'Like who?' Aitken
had asked her in gulping astonishment. 'Well, like you,' she'd
responded. 'Whenever you get thick with me, that's what I do, I
picture you sitting on the toilet, looking miserable.' And Aitken
often thought he could date the effective end of their marriage
from that precise moment; certainly, the fundamental respect
on which the spousal relationship ought to be predicated had
taken a fatal, below-the-waterline hit. It was sad, he supposed,
but in its way it was also comic. One minute you were on a
pedestal, the next you were on a toilet. That was marriage, Irish
style, in the last years of the twentieth century.

He was sorry she had told him this, because ever since she
had, the image had stuck with him, lodged somewhere in
his brain like the annoying melody of an Abba song. Try
as he might, it wouldn't go away. Now he could seldom see
any authority figure without envisioning him sitting on a toilet.
Sometimes it made meetings with his superiors quite difficult.
Often, during a case conference, or an important investigation
review, he had been asked what the blazes did he think he was
grinning at? Conversely, he could rarely sit on a toilet himself
without thinking immediately of an authority figure. And that,
understandably, had its difficulties too, for a man who worked
in the civil service.

He picked up the note by the dead geraniums. 'Dear Martin.
We are thirsty. If you do not water us, we die. Love, the plants.'
His eldest daughter Claire had written it, maybe six months
previously. It made him laugh every time he saw it. She was
a smart one, no doubt about it. She was like her mother, cool,
assured. A soul survivor from head to toe.

The air in the living room seemed thick and tainted, almost
buzzing with the redolence of damp. Two strips of the flower-
patterned wallpaper had begun to peel down from the lintels,
their frayed edges stiffened and corrugated. He caught his bleary
reflection in the mirror over the mantelpiece.

That was a mirror that had seen a thing or two.

He put his joint in an ashtray, got down on all fours, grunted
hard as he began to do push-ups.

Jesus!

What was that?

Under the sofa?

His eyes narrowed. Squinted to look.

With a dull moan of existential horror, he saw that a crop of copper-coloured mushrooms was sprouting in the carpet around the sofa leg.

Things are growing inside my house.

For one mad moment he wondered if he could eat them. Mushrooms on toast would be a nice Christmas morning breakfast. Very wholesome and inexpensive. But when he pondered it further, he had no bread to make the toast with.

Back on his feet he lit a cigarette. Looked around the malodorous room.

'Tis the season to be jolly,' said the announcer on the TV.

'Stuff the turkey's arse with holly,' said Inspector Martin Aitken. Out loud.

K-chunk!

Squeak.

Ave Maria.

He went outside, got into his Mini, started up the engine. Pushed a cassette into the tape deck. The Stones again. 'Brown Sugar'.

Yeah, yeah, yeah, WOOO.

As the wipers began to slice through the frost, he found himself wondering just where he could go.

★　　★　　★

Inishowen, County Donegal

St Patrick's Day
17 March 1986

Dear Mrs Amery,

I have been sitting here at my table for over two hours and a half, and I can tell you that I still hardly know how to begin.

I waited until it was late at night, until the house here was quiet and all were in bed, thinking that the darkness and solitude might in some way help me. But my heart is beating so hard I can hear it. Several times I have begun to write and only ended up throwing it away. My hand is trembling even now.

You cannot imagine the dread when I received the news from Sister Mary Rose that you had begun to look for me. I suppose I had felt for some time – probably for some years – that the news might come one day. I confess that some part of me prayed it never would, and another part of me yearned for the opposite. To know there is a person belonging to you out there in the world is a terrible thing. And not to know where they are.

I must begin by saying that your letter moved me to tears. I thank you for your beautiful compassion and forgiveness. You are a gentle merciful person, full of kindness. May God bless you for the things you said – it is so strange, I almost feel as though you are the mother and I the child.

What happened took place so long ago now. They say that time heals all the wounds, but I do not know. It is a thing I have carried around inside me for so long. Like a child that was never given birth to.

But I must compose myself and do what you ask me. Heaven knows it is little enough, after all this time.

You ask for a little information about my own life. I was born here in Donegal in 1930. When I was a girl of maybe four we moved to Dublin. Times were hard enough here and my father, having poor luck on the farm, had to come off the land. He felt that Dublin would be the place to go, and he had family there already, so we did go, in 1934, I think. He had great plans of making a fortune there in Dublin. And we lived in Francis Street, which is in the oldest part of the city, the Liberties. And although my father never did make his fortune – he was a carpenter and a cabinet maker then – we had some very happy times there but also some painful ones.

I can see our home so clearly still. When you went through the door the first thing you saw was an enormous staircase, which was far too large for the size of the flat. This was because the building had at one time been a single house before being broken up into what would now be called apartments, I suppose. Though boxes would have been a better word.

There was terrible poverty in many parts of the city. My mother belonged to the St Vincent de Paul society, and even though we never had much to spare ourselves she would always try and help others if she could. Often she went without herself so as to give to others. She was a very Christian and exemplary person. I can still see her face when, one night, she came home upset because she had been to visit a poor family in Parnell Square and there had been rats in the rooms where the children were sleeping.

My father became involved with trade union politics. He was an intelligent, sensitive sort of man but he had never been given the chance of an education. He read widely though, in his spare time, the works of Shaw and James Connolly, and Sidney and Beatrice Webb. He was a sympathiser with the Irish Communist Party but he, like my mother, was a deeply religious person and those principles would not allow him to join. Instead he was in a group called the Republican Congress. I remember once, when I was only six or seven, being at some kind of demonstration with him outside the Mansion House on Dawson Street in Dublin. A man was saying that one day the red flag would fly over Ireland. People in the crowd were booing him. Another man got up and said the reason the sun never set on the British Empire was that God wouldn't trust the English in the dark. The police were in our home many times and often my father was arrested.

Things came to a head in 1937 when he was beaten by a gang of Blueshirts – they were Irish Fascists – and almost died from his injuries. It was at a demonstration or meeting to do with the Spanish Civil War. For some years subsequent he had no work. In fact, he was never the same man afterwards. He became a violent, bitter person. As we children grew up, my mother had many hard years with him. We came back to Inishowen when I was maybe fifteen.

And now we come to the most difficult part.

You ask about your own father. As you can imagine, it is a painful thing for me to think about those times at all.

He was a local boy. I knew him best when we were both seventeen. I do not feel that I can tell you his name. For the moment, all I can say was that we were great with each other, but we were not free to be together owing to an ancient disagreement between our families. If it is any source of peace to you to know that there was love between us, I can tell you in complete honesty that there was. I have been blessed with a happy family life and a most understanding husband, but in the quiet moments of the day and the night, I think, to be honest, that that other boy was the love of my life. If it is true that there is a person out there who is the other half of our soul, as the poets tell us, then I truly think he was that. And although we were not fated to be together, there has rarely been a day or a week of my life when I have not thought about him and missed him so.

As for what I can tell you about him: he was a nice, gentle, uncomplicated sort of person, very handsome and tall. He was 'wide as a gate', I heard someone say about him once. He was fond of poetry and music and played the violin. I suppose he would not have been a mathematical person at all, or a scientific one. He enjoyed fishing and

64

dancing and walking in the countryside. He had a pleasant singing voice.

I had hardly any notion of real life. The education and openness that young people take for granted now would have been unthinkable at the time. My own mother, Lord rest her, had scarcely told me a thing. Even the words 'Virgin Mary' had no real meaning for me – a virgin, we were told, was simply a lady who was not yet married. 'The Immaculate Conception' just meant being born without sin. There were more people in Hell because of sins committed against the sixth commandment than all the other commandments put together, is what we were told in religion class. We were only teenagers at this time so, as you can imagine, adultery was not something we knew very much about! It will give you some idea of how things were that when I began to menstruate I thought I was dying. Occasionally in school there would be a film, and if there was a harmless scene of the 'chap' as we used to call the hero and his girl kissing or embracing, the nuns would put the lid of a shoebox over the screen to block the view. There was a harmless old man in the town called Needle Fullerton who had been in a gas attack at Passchendaele. He was seen as a terrible danger to faith and morals because once, when drunk on market day, he shouted 'my hand on your knee' at a lady teacher going past on her bicycle. All of us young girls were warned to avoid Needle like the Devil himself from then on, although it was never said exactly why. Those were the times. It would almost be funny were it not for the fear and the terrible ignorance. My mother told me not long before she passed away that she and my father had never once seen each other's naked bodies in all the years of their marriage. As for what are called the facts of life, nothing was ever explained to us. Any knowledge I gleaned about my own body or about what happens in intimacy between men and women would have been from watching the animals in the fields or from overhearing whispered conversations. Once or twice a year a man from Sligo came to a nearby farm to inseminate cattle. I learned

65

something from watching him at his work.

So that would be the background of the time.

What happened between the boy and myself was only the natural thing, but we hardly even knew what we were about. We were so much in love, we saw only the immediate pleasure and comfort of being together and were irresponsible. There is an old Irish song that goes, 'She bid me take love easy, as the blossoms on the tree. But I, being young and foolish, with her could not agree.' I remember hearing that song all those long years ago and knowing in my heart exactly what it meant. We could not take love easy.

Nature took its course. I remember that I had a little spell of sickness but it was put down to growing up. And then, after a time, it dawned on me what must have happened.

I cannot tell you the fear I felt then. To think there was something living inside me. It was like a fist clenched inside my stomach all the time. I would lie awake the whole night sometimes, praying for help. Often I thought about running away, but the world is so small when you are that age, with no money of your own and nowhere to go. Your whole world is the townland you live in.

After a few months I had to tell my mother. She was broken-hearted by what I had done but stood by me as best she could. I was sent away from home without my father being told the reason why. If he had known what was the matter, he would have put me out of the house. He was a good man in many ways, but that would have been too much for him.

Though I was sent to a kindly relative, I felt frightened, so awfully alone. For six months I was not allowed to leave her house, only go into the yard at night, or to use the toilet, which was outside, in case a neighbour might happen to see me and word might somehow travel home to my father. I cannot go into the circumstances or what happened then, after I gave birth. It was 21 December 1948, three days before Christmas Eve. Maybe I will be able to, in time.

If it had ever been found out by my father that I had

been in trouble I probably would have ended up in an institution. They were places we girls dreaded. They were so-called homes in the cities, run by the Church. The Magdalene Laundries was what they were called. The very Christian idea was that girls who had fallen pregnant were like Mary Magdalene, I suppose.

There was one in Galway, I know that much.

There has been a lot of coverage in the papers here in recent times about what went on in those places. Very cruel and inhuman things happened, with girls being beaten and starved, and some of them molested. They would have been seen as complete outcasts. 'The Maggies', they were known as, to mock them. I once saw a group of them when I was on an outing to see my aunt in Galway. I will never forget it. Their poor hungry faces and dressed in rags, with that terrible look of being crushed in their hearts. Just young women who should have had everything ahead of them, but with all the life already gone out of them, so gaunt and cold. Never a kind word or a mother's loving embrace for them. It would break your heart to see them.

It is many years now since I heard from the boy who was your father. I know that he went away to England around the time of your birth. I believe he may have joined the British army. But I do not know for certain.

I read in our local newspaper about two years ago that he had died, from heart disease, in England. But it did not give much information about him, only his name.

Often I thought about you, and wondered what kind of life you had. (I was aware that you had been adopted in America.) I hoped and prayed that the people who had taken you would give you the loving home that you deserved and that I would not have been able to. I hope they were kind people.

Sometimes when there was a television programme from America, I would allow myself to think a certain face in the crowd might be you. Never one day of my life has gone by when I did not think about you and pray for you, that God would keep you in his mercy wherever you were in the world and look down on you with a great love. I always remembered your birthday and lit a candle for you that day.

You do not say if you are married or have children yourself, nor what kind of life you have in America. I do sincerely hope it is a happy one. My husband and I were in Queens, New York, once. Our children kindly sent us for our thirtieth wedding anniversary, and we have relatives in Woodside, Queens, which is a particularly Irish area, as you will doubtless know. Imagine that I may have walked down the same streets as yourself and maybe even passed you by. When we think about it. Perhaps you might like to send me a photograph of yourself and your family if and when you write to me again.

I would like that very much, if you did. Please write to me care of the convent, if you like, and Sister will pass it on.

May God bless you for your kindness.

Yours sincerely

Margaret D. (Mrs)

PS: I send you enclosed an old photograph that I found in the bottom of a drawer recently. It is of Lough Fada, a local beauty spot.

Chapter Five

Early Christmas morning, Amery realised he was awake.
It was still dark outside, that navy blue liquidy darkness
that seems somehow more than just the absence of light.
He could see the crescent moon through a gap in the curtains;
thin black clouds were drifting past it like wisps of smoke. The
house was still. Rain was falling on the garden. Somewhere a dog
was giving a repeated two-note bark that sounded both lonesome and expectant.

He lay on his back and looked out the window, aware, or
so he fancied, of his body beginning to switch itself on. The
wardrobe door was wide open and yawning; it seemed to leer
at him like a freshly dug grave. Through the walls he could hear
Lee's soft mumbling.

Christmas morning and Ellen was gone.

He glanced across the pillow, half expecting that she might
have come back in the night, but already knowing that he would
be alone. She had done that once before, crept silently back
into bed after one of her returns, maybe the second or third
time she had run away from him. When was that anyway? Back
in the eighties maybe. Around the time she'd started going to
Ireland.

He allowed himself to recall that first flight now. The front
door wide open when he arrived home from work, the children
crying and searching the house, the slow dawning terror of
the fact of her absence, the lurching fears of what might have
happened. Then that first long night without her, lying awake
and dazed with shock, wondering what he could possibly do.
After a morning of frantic telephone calling, an afternoon of
driving the streets of Scarsdale in the pouring rain, a night
spent systematically working through every single number in

their telephone book, he had woken around three to find her in bed beside him, her face pale with remorse. They had cried and made love for the rest of the night. It was the last time they had ever made love.

He got up, padded to the bathroom, showered, gargled, flossed his teeth and shaved. His flesh felt too tight for his body. The blazing light over the mirror gave him a greenish tinge. He had a peculiar sense of being somehow inside himself, of being trapped in a form he hadn't ever chosen. He slapped on aftershave, lacquered his greying hair. He saw his father's face in his own.

Was there some actual reason she had gone this time? Some small promise he had forgotten to keep, maybe something he'd said that had gotten on her nerves? So far as he could remember, they hadn't had an argument in weeks. As a matter of fact, things had been improving.

When the news had first come, of course she'd been frightened. But that was to be expected, there was no planning for a thing like that. He thought about the words the doctor had said. Pancreatic cancer. How simple they had sounded, and yet how strange. He had sat in the office holding his wife's hand as the doctor had told her there was no hope whatsoever. There wasn't even any point in undergoing chemotherapy. There rarely was, with pancreatic cancer, since it couldn't be diagnosed until it was already too late. Ellen had less than a year to live.

They still hadn't told the children, and that had been a source of tension between them. Amery felt they should be told immediately, give them some chance to start getting used to it. But Ellen had insisted she wanted to wait. She would tell them, she said, when the time was right.

All kinds of excuses had been made. Elizabeth was about to start college. Lee was so unsettled right now; his grades were low, he was in trouble at school. Amery had gone along with her pleas to say nothing. But now he wondered if that had been the right thing to do. Was it really concern for the children that was preventing her from speaking out? Or was she denying what was going to happen?

The bad news had come six months previously. But lately

he thought he had seen a change in his wife. Some kind of calm had enveloped her, that anxious, haunted look was gone. The anniversary of their engagement fell in October, a date they had always marked and celebrated. They had gone to the Met and held hands all through *Tosca*; he had noticed her crying during 'E lucevan le stelle'. Afterwards they had dined in the simple downtown trattoria they'd frequented in their student days, then taken a stroll through the streets of the village. The night was warm; it smelt of musk and diesel, and rang with the chugging of air-conditioning machines. He had thought she looked tired, but she had absolutely insisted – it was something they did every year on this anniversary. They strolled down Perry Street, up through Christopher, stopped outside the brownstone on Bedford which they'd rented as a newly married couple, next door to the narrowest house in New York, where Edna St Vincent Millay had once lived.

He remembered the way she had looked up at the house for a long time, as though she'd expected it might reveal something important to her. A middle-aged gay couple had walked past, arm in arm carrying bags from Balducci's and Strawberry Fayre. How at ease they seemed, those plump, contented men. After a while some tourists had appeared, tall French people, elegant and beautiful. One of them had asked him to take their photograph with the narrow house in the background. Ellen smiled at his officiousness as he'd lined them all up in a neat row.

'Thanks for twenty-one wonderful years,' he'd told her when they'd left, taking her in his arms and kissing her hair. He remembered her hands reaching up to touch his neck. And then he had regretted putting it that way, had silently cursed himself for his stupidity and clumsiness. There wouldn't be twenty-one more, after all; nor would there even be that number of months. She would probably be dead before their next anniversary. The knowledge had seemed to haunt the drive back to Scarsdale, she'd been silent all the way, resting her hand on his thigh. It was almost as though Death had been sitting in the back seat.

The morning after, she'd called him back as he was about to leave for work. They had breakfasted together in bed, watching

71

the news. These early mornings were when he felt most at ease with her now, the companionship between them as comfortable as an old sofa, the quiet rhythms of quotidian marital compromise pulsing, the courtesies that remain when ardour has burned away. He loved the images that remained with him of those moments, almost as much as he loved the moments themselves: her hair spread out on the clean white pillow, the smell of hot toast and English Breakfast tea, golden light spilling into the room.

'Hey, Doctor?' she'd said, as he'd taken his jacket and made for the door.

'What's that?'

'I love you, Milton.'

Touched by her directness, he'd come back to the bed and taken her hand.

'Me too,' he said.

And then he had noticed that there were tears in her eyes.

'Come on, baby. Don't be upset now.'

'Could you hold me?' she whispered. 'I feel a little scared this morning.'

'Everything's going to be all right, honey. I don't want you to worry about a thing. We're going to get through this thing together.'

The banality of his words made him loathe himself. A woman as unspeakably brave as Ellen deserved better, but it frightened him so much to think of what was happening that, try as he might, cliché was all he could manage.

She touched his cheek, drew him down to her, held his face tenderly in both hands. Then she had softly kissed his mouth. He had kissed her back, though in truth he hadn't been sure he wanted to. When they'd broken away she sighed and smoothed down his hair.

'You're still a beautiful kisser. You know that, Doctor Amery?'

'Thank you, Miss Donnelly. I practise a lot on my own.'

Instead of the smile he was looking for, a soft look of yearning had lit up her eyes. 'So would you like to come back to bed for a while, Milton?'

'I'm not really in the mood, Ellen.'

She slid her hand gently inside his jacket and touched his ribs through his shirt. 'Well, I don't know. Maybe we can do something about that?'

'The kids are downstairs, honey. And I'm late for work.'

She looked at him for a time with an expression he couldn't read. And then silently nodded and lay back down.

'But everything's going to be fine. I promise.'

'I know it is, Milton. Have a good day, OK?'

He'd gone to the window and pulled open the curtains, silently praying for some words that could possibly make a difference; that could cut through the ectoplasm of fear in which they had lived for four months. Down in the street the postman waved. When he turned back she had the TV on again.

'So I'll go then, OK? You've got everything you need?'

She changed the channel without looking up at him. 'It's not because of my news, is it, Milton? That you don't want to come back to bed?'

'I'm late, Ellen, really. And it isn't that, I promise.'

She smiled, then, warmly and hopefully. It was as though he was the one who needed reassurance. What hurt the most, looking back on it now, was how deeply he knew that had always been true. Christmas morning. He needed her today.

He pulled on a bathrobe and crossed the landing, knocked gently on his son's graffiti'd door. ABANDON HOPE ALL YE WHO ENTER HERE one slogan said, scarlet blood-dripping letters on thick black gloss, skulls and crossbones all around. When there was no answer, he opened it and crept in.

The ruined room stank of rancid food and pinecone deodorant. On the tubular steel desk, the computer's screensaver showed a pattern of flashing stars and moons. His son was face down on the bed in Freddy Kruger boxer shorts, his arms splayed out at right angles as though he were embracing the mattress, his girlish mouth drooling on the pillow, muttering 'Definitely . . . I said so . . . What do you want from me?' The walls were plastered with photographs of diseased-looking young women in black leather bikinis or shroud-like robes, tour posters for leering rock bands, cartoon aliens with suckers and

73

tentacles, assorted members of a televisual entity that Amery believed to be the Simpson family.

In his own day, American children had admired astronauts or baseball players, FBI detectives, sometimes heroes of the West. Now such figures were discredited or ridiculed. You couldn't even say the word 'Indian' without getting told you were a racist oppressor. Now balding, corpulent underachievers like Homer Simpson were the guys you saw on posters in boys' rooms. And people wondered why the country was in ten types of trouble.

He pulled the barbed-wire-patterned duvet up to his son's shoulders. Then bent and gently kissed his dirty yellow hair.

'If it isn't,' murmured Lee. 'It sometimes is.'

Turning to leave, his eye was drawn to a poster of that blond leggy tennis player hitching up her skirt and showing her lack of underwear. But the girl wasn't what caught his attention. It was the improvised speech bubble containing Lee's scrawled handwriting and coming, arrestingly, from the peach-like cleft of her backside.

I HATE MYSELF AND I WANT TO DIE

Sometimes, he felt, that boy needed a therapist.

Down in the kitchen he made coffee and a slice of cinnamon toast. Slit a blood orange and squeezed the juice. Opened a half-bottle of chilled Dom Perignon, glumly mixed himself a Bucks Fizz in one of the Waterford flutes they'd been given as a wedding present. If Ellen were here, they would do that together, as they had done every year of their marriage on Christmas morning. The dawn was rising fast over the golf course, the sky outside the kitchen window turning pink and pale yellow. It was a time of day that Ellen loved, although Amery himself had always found it vaguely disturbing. He listened to the sound of the birds for a while, a vile susurration of screeches, squawks and croaks. Lord above, it was truly horrible.

What the hell did poets see in the dawn? It was a time of day that made him anxious and kvetchy, and always had, even as a child. Dawn, to poets, was daffodils and lambs. But to Amery it was things crawling out of ponds, rubbing the slime out of their big bad eyes. It served as ample reminder that if mankind was cruel, so was nature; the appearance of the day, like every birth, an intimation of mortality, but in the case of the dawn on a planetary scale.

As a young medical student he had seen the simple business of waking up as an extraordinary miracle. What an awesome machine was the human body, to shut itself down like that and switch itself on again eight hours later. Think of the millions of biological processes involved in just one wakening – that was what his Professor of Ethics used to say – each functioning at exactly the same time, an incomparably glorious piece of engineering, a living work of art. How exactly did the body know how to do that? Even to a sceptic – even to a scientist – it was the kind of question you could get religious about.

Whenever he thought about it, which was not terribly often, Amery saw the planet in a similar way. It was a thing that slept and a thing that woke, and, really, nobody could understand why. And just as death was kind enough to come to most people in their sleep, that was how the earth would die too, when the time came for it to happen. One of these mornings the sun just wouldn't come up. There would be no dawn. That would be that. Goodnight Saigon, it was nice while it lasted. The tree-huggers and tofu-munchers had it completely wrong, the greens and vegans and cranks and rootsuckers who Ellen had made her so-called friends; when the end came it would make no difference whether people had used unleaded gas or chlorofluorocarbon-free hairspray. For God's sake, the sheer laughable arrogance of it all. There would be no big bang, no catastrophic collision. The world would simply forget to wake up. Darkness would remain, deep and all-enveloping, along with freezing, looting, bad manners and cannibalism. It would make *Lord of the Flies* look like a pyjama party.

He pictured his receptionist, Violet, being eaten by her neighbours in Weehawken, New Jersey. A thick slice of her bottom between two hunks of rye. He found it an oddly pleasing thought. Mind you, the world wouldn't have to end for that to happen. Not in New Jersey.

He took a small sip of his drink. Heard the soft, comforting cough of the pipes as the central heating clicked on. Looked at his watch. The boiler was running two minutes late. He made a mental note to call the plumber, just as soon as the holiday was over.

The radio news said there had been more snow overnight, two whole inches followed by a freezing frost. From the outskirts of Manhattan all the way up to New England, conditions were severe, in some places dangerous. The National Weather Service was tracking several major storms and had issued a stockman and traveller warning. Drivers should look out for snowdrifts, black ice, freezing fog. Power lines were down in Maine and rural Massachusetts. Closed by the baggage handlers' dispute anyway, JFK and O'Hare were under six inches of snow. A teenage girl from Minneapolis had fallen through the ice on Lake Michigan. Police divers had still not recovered her body.

He drained his glass and changed the channel. A heartbreakingly beautiful soprano voice drifted from the speaker.

> *Oh, holy night, the stars are brightly shining.*
> *It is the night of the dear Saviour's birth.*

Brightening a little, he pictured his pretty girlfriend, at home now and opening his gift to her. Wrapping the choker around her swanlike neck. He thought of her pale pink lips, her bob-cut hair, the long straight back he had once spent a whole hour kissing. She liked diamonds, he knew that much, though she had never, of course, actually owned any. Fifteen thousand five hundred was a lot to spend on her, but what the hell, he could afford it. These days he needed all the Brownie points he could rack up. And anyway, he'd get it back off someone else come January. If he couldn't scrape fifteen grand's worth of cellulite off some menopausal socialite's gluteus maximus his name was not Milton Longfellow Amery.

> *Fall on your knees,*
> *Oh, hear the angels' voices.*
> *Oh, night divine. Oh, night when Christ was born.*

How did he know she liked diamonds? One wet afternoon back in April he had skipped surgery and accompanied her out to Astoria, to the Museum of the Moving Image. Together, arms linked, they had wandered the three vast floors, safe in the relative certainty of not bumping into anyone. Down aisles of framed posters and masks of movie stars they strolled, pausing for a kiss by a full-size model of a hirsute creature apparently named Chewbacca who reminded Amery, oddly, of the singer Kenny Rogers.

At one point Cathy had gone to make a phone call. Amery had ambled away on his own, into an anteroom where a gargantuan video machine had been set up. On the screen was bespangled, voluptuous Marilyn Monroe, her hips swaying like a church bell in a breeze, her extraordinary mouth in a wounded pout as she cooed and trilled to the almost empty room that diamonds were a girl's best friend.

'Quite the lady, wasn't she?' Amery had remarked to the glum security guard, a stocky liver-lipped Bostonian pugnose with dandruff speckling his shoulders.

The guard shrugged and pinched his nostrils. 'Get a little tired of it when you're watchin it all day.'

'Yes. I suppose so.'

'Better believe it.'

'I wonder if Arthur Miller encountered the same difficulty.'

'Kept quiet about it if he did. Mean to say, she could give you a blowjob would leave you cross-eyed for a week.'

'I happen to think she was a comic genius.'

'Oh yeah, sure. But this guy came in here once who knew her when she was startin out. Italian guy, had a restaurant in Hollywood. She'd ride you like a Harley on a rough road. S'what he said. No word of a lie.'

'How noble of him to share that piece of vital information.' By now, Cathy was standing beside Amery again, grinning naughtily up at the screen.

'Sexy little thing, wasn't she, Milton?'

'She was certainly attractive, yes.'

'And so talented too.'

'Better believe it,' the security guard said, archly crossing his eyes at Amery with such violence that his pupils almost appeared to merge.

'Hey, I guess you guys remember her the first time around?'

The security guard had laughed out loud, then. 'Your daddy and me ain't quite antiques just yet, sweetheart.'

'*Man*,' she sighed, 'would you look at those diamonds.'

Coming up to Christmas, she had begged him not to buy her anything too expensive, she would have problems explaining to her parents where it had come from. But what the heck. Let her invent something. Oddly, it excited him to think of her lying.

Down in the living room, he struck a match and lit the candles on the windowsill. It was an old Celtic tradition Ellen had picked up on one of her trips to Ireland. Light a candle to show the magi the way to Bethlehem. He had scoffed when she explained it, but he'd found the idea quite moving. It was one of the things he loved about her most, that she provided secret ways for him to find things moving.

Sometimes on the weekends, when he had a little time to read, Amery would wearily scan those articles that filled the Sunday supplements, about how men found it difficult to express their feelings. He'd wonder if he was one of those men: silent, sullen, full of suppressed rage. In the old days, women had liked quiet men. To be quiet was manly, dependable, calm. The shorthand for this was the Strong Silent Type, and the Strong Silent Type was what women had wanted. But now that didn't seem a good thing to be. Now you had to get in touch with yourself, discover something called the Inner Child. You weren't actually a person any more. You were a set of those Russian dolls that fit into each other. Once he had asked Ellen to tell him straight out, was he one of those men who concealed his emotions. He'd been disconcerted by the time it had taken her to answer.

'I always know how you feel,' she'd said, appearing to Amery as though choosing her words with scrupulous care, like an expert witness in a difficult trial. 'It's always more or less clear to me, even if you don't actually say it.'

He would laugh long and loud at these courses men did nowadays, where they'd all pile into the woods for a weekend, to paint rings around their nipples and thump their bongos

78

and weep in each other's arms about being emasculated. He would ridicule them, with wryness and irony, and Ellen would allow him to, she would even laugh back, though he knew she must be aware that privately he envied them – these crestfallen boobies squatting around fires in the forest, wishing they were ninjas instead of Rotarians. She knew him so well. That was the thing. She loved him so much that she allowed him to believe his deceptions about himself; and that, he often thought, when you looked at it in broad terms, was really the only true measure of love. But then again, he went along with her too. He indulged her penchant for standing up for the oppressed, that oddly un-American streak she possessed of what could only be called – though he despised the phrase – Catholic guilt. Guilt for what you had done yourself was one thing. Personal shame for the fact that Guatemalans were poor, well, that was something else again; that was relatively easy when you had two homes, three cars, and a dependable after-tax income of four hundred thousand a year. Often he felt she would rather be poor, living in a project and existing on food stamps, with a son in prison named after a Sandinista. But she wouldn't stick that life for a week. Not that he would ever dream of saying that aloud to her. Not saying things aloud was the only firm foundation for matrimony. Nobody ever told you this, but in fact it was true. He and Ellen had become skilled at silence – the dynamic of their marriage the quietly shared intuition that every such relationship is a game of masks. If marriage had a secret geometry, Amery thought, it would be a pattern of initially parallel trajectories that sometimes intersect and sometimes flow away, the better to flow together again, or at least to have that possibility some other time. Love, honour and shut the hell up. That was how the wedding vows should read.

He placed his gifts under the tree, the sweet smell of the pine needles almost desperately evocative. The house was quiet, as though some violent thing had happened there recently. He plugged in the fairy lights and watched them flash for a while. Big deal, big deal, they seemed to say.

On his knees by the grate, he began to build the fire. First the firelighters, then the twigs, now the kindling and the lumps of coal. Another of his Christmas morning tasks.

These small rituals were the parts he liked best about the day. The insignificant, primal ceremonies of domesticity and calm. If there was anything truly sacred, it was surely the home. The Romans were right about the household gods. Or was that the Japanese? Well, whoever it was, it didn't matter. Probably the damned Irish. Ellen seemed to feel they'd invented everything else.

Yeats, Joyce, Oscar Wilde. From the way Ellen talked about Leprechaun Land, you would imagine that no other country on the face of God's earth had ever produced a trickster capable of attaching polysyllabic adjectives to his neuroses and calling the result literature. He had to laugh at the way she did this, how every major artist in history could be press-ganged into the cause. Scott Fitzgerald? Irish. Eugene O'Neill? Irish. Henry James? A down-home shillelagh-waver. Honest to God, it was like being married to Ted Kennedy. One of these days she would say Mahler was Irish. As a matter of fact, he couldn't swear she hadn't already.

Lighting the fire now, he remembered one of their first trips there, to Galway and the west. All that bleakness and Becketty nothingness; the dreadful service in the lard-smelling restaurants, the astounding dental problems of the indigenous peoples, the loaded way they had of talking, their frankly morbid fascination with death and the ancient, the tendentious sadness of their unending songs. Those ruined castles everywhere, falling down like drunks in the fields. Was there ever a country so fortified for defence and so utterly, irredeemably bellicose. While their fellow tourists had oohed and aahed at the scenery, Amery had been secretly struck by how appropriately savage it all was. How the trees in Connemara, battered and lashed by the Atlantic gales, grew at every possible angle to the ground except the strictly vertical. How every town in West Cork had a Celtic cross in the square to commemorate some local act of squalid historical slaughter, by one side or the other, it didn't matter much to Amery, and nor, he suspected, had it ultimately done to the commemorated. The streets, the parks, the railway stations

80

were all named for dead people. It was one of the problems with Ireland, he felt. Everything you saw was named after someone dead. There was something unhealthy about a place like that.

One bright, rainy Sunday morning, while their party had been sipping Irish coffees in a theatre in Sligo and listening to some honey-toned nonentity recite derivative odes about birth, an enormous bomb had exploded in a town across the border, killing war veterans at their Armistice Day parade. The town was less than fifty miles away, but at lunch the tour guide had barely even mentioned it, so obsessed had she been with putting across her shtick. 'Ireland,' she said, 'is the land of saints and scholars.' And the tourists had nodded and smiled, and the poet had started talking about how much he loved his wife, how his wife was the other half of his soul, how, really, he couldn't go on without his wife. A sure sign, if ever there was one, of a man who would pork the crack of dawn if given half a chance.

Later, when he mentioned this to Ellen, she'd gotten defensive. Well, perhaps it was the way he had put it that had hurt her. 'I bet you're glad your mother gave you up for adoption. Imagine growing up in this God-awful place.' They'd had a bad quarrel and she'd stormed out of the hotel room, returning four hours later, as if to spite him, in a tweed beret she'd bought duty free, with a record of rebel songs under her arm.

The next year, against his repeatedly expressed wishes, she had applied for summer work with the cultural group that had organised their trip. She had accompanied a party of university students from Boston on a two-week tour of heritage sights in the West, taken them to plays about the potato famine, lectures on emigration, recitals, readings, puppet shows, barbecues, traditional music concerts held in barns and other outbuildings. And every summer since, she had gone to Ireland, for longer periods each time. Now she was a director of the group. Every spare hour was spent on fundraising. For a while, until the bad news had come, she had seriously talked about giving up teaching and devoting herself to the group full time. She talked about The Group the way communists used to talk about The Party. And after a while, he had stopped arguing, because one thing he had come to learn about Ellen was that the more you approached her with anything like reason the more she would do what she wanted anyway. She was certainly Irish in that way.

'Encounter the Real Ireland', the group was called. (Rather appropriately, in Amery's view, Elizabeth had acronymised it to 'EERIE'.)

Real Ireland, my ass, as Lee would say. And real Irish monkeys might fly out of my butt. The programme didn't include any exhibitions on knee-capping teenagers or blowing up pensioners. That was as real as the Aran Islands. There was a good deal more to the Irish than illuminating ancient manuscripts and tediously singing through their noses about fishermen. As a matter of fact, if it came right down to it, the main talent the Irish had now, and the main one they had always had, was for beating the living bejesus out of each other. Not that you could say that around Ellen. Not if you wanted something like a quiet life.

He went into the downstairs guestroom and made up the bed. His parents were coming down from Keene tonight. They'd been sympathetic as ever when he called with the news about her skedaddling off again, but he hated himself for having to trouble them. He had agreed with Lee and Elizabeth to postpone Christmas lunch until tomorrow. Maybe Mom would be back by then.

He opened the window, let in a blast of cold air. A plump vicious robin was hopping along the lawn; the tree trunks were silver, glittering with frost. The bunkers on the golf course were full of snow. Across the hills and pine forests in the distance, whiteness lay like icing on a Christmas cake.

Back in the lounge he saw now that a bottle of Coke had overturned and spilled its contents on the carpet. Only four days since Ellen had gone, and already the place was turning into a speakeasy. Cursing and fuming he fetched a dishcloth from the kitchen. Down on his knees he rubbed hard at the mark. It spread out on the carpet, a dark-pink, accusatory stain, shaped just like the map of Africa. The more he rubbed, the worse it got.

From upstairs he heard the shower come on. Elizabeth must be up; he could hear her singing.

A stab of abject terror pierced him. Christmas Day was beginning in earnest. He had an image of himself about to jump from a high-dive board, taking deep breaths, preparing for the plunge.

Desperation rolled out of some unseen depth and broke against his heart like a cold, black wave. It was the first time he had felt this since he'd realised she was gone again. Other feelings had paid him a visit – concern, anger, grief, even jealousy. But here was blank suppurating despair, coming at last, as he had known it would.

He loved her so much that once, as a young man, about to be anaesthetised for a minor operation, he had found himself shamefully praying for her to die before he did. He had hated himself straight away, even as he was saying the words. It was probably the worst thing he had ever done. But the thought of being old and without her was unbearable.

In one long, still moment, he imagined that reality now. It made him feel physically sick. She's gone, he thought. Ellen is gone. Lines from a poem he had read decades before in high school came into his mind. *Time present and time past are both perhaps present in time future.* For the first time in his life, he knew what those words might truly mean.

Still kneeling, he put down the ruined dishcloth and joined his hands.

'Dear God,' he said, 'this is Doctor Milton Amery speaking.'

The clock ticked, the pipes gurgled.

'Please,' he whispered. 'Please, I'm begging you. If there's anyone out there, just let her come home.'

He heard his daughter singing in the shower.

The pipes, the pipes, the pipes are calling.

He felt like the world was about to end.

Inishowen
County Donegal
Republic of Ireland
14 April 1986
Dear Mrs Amery,

I cannot do what you ask. Please, please do not ask me again.

I simply cannot meet you, I am sorry. It would cause too much turmoil.

If you come to Ireland again, as you say you plan to do in the summer, please do not try to contact me directly. Please, I beg you, never do that.

It is *impossible* for me to give you my home address. If you want to write, you must continue to do so care of Sister Mary Rose at the convent.

I am sorry. Please forgive me.

Yours sincerely

Margaret D. (Mrs)

             ★   ★   ★

Chapter Six

Saint Michael's in Dun Laoghaire was the hospital to which Robbie had been taken after the accident. Often when he found himself there, in the course of his work, Martin Aitken had a mental image that was hard to explain. He would see himself moving through the gleaming corridors with the broken body of his son in his arms. It had not happened the way he remembered it; in fact, his son's remains had been brought to the hospital in an ambulance. There was little doubt about it: he had died immediately the car hit him. *Cranial contusions and massive fracturing.* That's what the forms had said. *Pronounced dead on arrival at Saint Michael's Hospital.* But in Aitken's imagination, and whenever he dreamed about it, the scene was always the same: Robbie would be fearfully crying, trembling in trauma, and he himself would be climbing endless staircases, calling out for help, with his son in his arms.

'I won't leave you, Scout. Don't worry. Daddy's here.'

It was not as if he had never said those words. But by the time he had got to say them, it was already too late. He remembered now, as he stood waiting for the lift to the public wards, how the call had come to the station on that sweltering afternoon, 8 August 1988. He'd been in the middle of an interrogation when Hughie Tynan had burst in and said there was a caller on the phone who needed him urgently.

At first Aitken had been unable to believe it. He had thought the man on the line was some evil practical joker, some thug he had once put away trying to wreak his sick revenge. He had hung up immediately, searched out the hospital's number in the phone book and rung it. But the same man had answered. He was the priest whose job it was to do these things. 'I'm sorry,

Detective,' he'd said, in his studied, gentle voice. 'But it isn't a joke, I'm afraid Robbie's dead.'

He had no memory whatsoever of the next twenty minutes. And his recollection of the whole day was patchy. It seemed to come in flashes of disconnected pictures, as though an album of photographs had been thrown in the air by a child and shuffled back together in too much of a hurry. Valerie in the kitchen holding on to the edge of the sink. The race out to Dun Laoghaire in the back of a squad car. The stark whiteness of the morgue. The noxious reek of formalin. A nun calling Julie in from a hockey pitch to tell her that her brother was dead. A bloodstained folded towel beneath his son's head, the sight of the weary-looking chaplain putting on the purple stole and the two mortuary attendants taking off their paper hats to pray.

Valerie seemed to derive some kind of peace from the knowledge that Robbie's death had been instant. But for Aitken that was the worst of all the terrible things about it. Simply put, it didn't make sense. It mocked the laws of nature, it seemed grotesque and obscene that a spirit so loud and obstreperous could be stilled in such a way, so suddenly, so utterly, without even a chance to prepare yourself for missing it. They didn't make shrouds to fit a nine-year-old boy, the undertaker had whispered, with an expression on his face that looked strangely like fear. Perhaps you'd like to buy him something yourselves? Or maybe he had a favourite garment?

Aitken remembered being in the funeral parlour two days later, his son's waxen face in the coffin, small pale hands folded across his Manchester United shirt, a photograph of the Ireland football team removed from his bedroom wall and tucked into the pocket of his shorts. Julie and Claire had been weeping in their Uncle Johnny's arms. As Valerie bent to kiss her son goodbye she too had broken down in gulping tears. Aitken had gone to her then and tried to hold her, but for almost half an hour she had refused to let go of Robbie's hands. The sight of her doing that was like having a spear driven through him. It was the worst thing he had ever seen.

Even the undertaker looked close to tears that day. But Aitken had not been able to cry. It was too soon to do that, the whole morning had felt artificial, like something watched on a screen or through a lens, a set of unreal events that had nothing to do with him. He remembered the requiem mass, the gifts being brought up at the offertory, a soccer ball, a skateboard, the bread and the wine. He recalled the Police Commissioner and the Deputy Minister for Justice filing by to shake his hand, their faces ashen and taut. Even as they were doing that, some part of him was wondering why they were there. The line of silent, frightened-looking boys outside the church, all in Scouts' uniforms and saluting as the small coffin was led past and put into the hearse, one of them gnawing his lip and visibly trembling with the effort of trying not to cry. Until the two Scout leaders had moved forward to place the wreaths done out to read OUR FRIEND in the back of the hearse. And then that boy too had raised his hands to his face and begun to shake with silent tears. They looked so fragile and young to Aitken, so milky-faced and skinny. Who would have dreamed that the one among them who would die too early would be Robbie?

It was in the weeks after the funeral that the true grief had come. He would wake up in its grip, try to shake it off, but it would follow him around all day like a black, ragged dog. He had been secretly amazed at how Valerie managed to go on, seeing a strength in her he'd never suspected, moved to the core of his heart by her quietly heroic resolution simply to continue. Meals were cooked, clothes were cleaned; Julie was driven to dance class on Wednesdays. Valerie seemed to want to act as though nothing had changed. Though the attempt to do that had made him love her more, it had also begun to separate them; before Robbie's death he had felt he knew everything about her; now she was drawing on some part of herself that he simply could not touch. In truth, at least sometimes, he even resented it.

There were things about her now that he could not explain. He noticed that since Robbie died she laughed more often, with a wild gaiety that often unnerved him. One afternoon about two months after the funeral they had all gone for a drive to the Glendalough lakes. Claire had started in Trinity by then, had borrowed a camera from a college friend. Every photograph taken of Valerie that day showed her laughing. He couldn't understand it. How could she laugh?

It was only after the girls had gone to bed that she would allow herself to stop pretending. She and Aitken would sit in the living room together, watching the television, smoking, sometimes drinking wine, but saying hardly anything. If an advert came on which featured a child she would silently look away to reach for a cigarette or pour another glass. One night a feature film opened with a scene of a young boy being pursued by a car. She turned away as sharply as if something had stung her.

The feeling between them came to seem to Aiken like that between two hostages on the eve of their execution. Often he would wonder what she was thinking about, but whenever he tried to ask she would simply change the subject. Before long she had become almost unreachably silent; it was as though a carapace had formed around her. Only one evening, during an item on the TV news about a boy from a troubled part of Belfast who had won an award for singing, he had looked over and noticed that she was bitterly crying. When he'd tried to comfort her she had jumped up and run from the room.

Loss seeped into the house like a faint smell of winter. The smallest of things brought the pain into sharp focus. Having to cancel his appointment with the orthodontist. Writing a note to the milkman to say they needed one less pint every day. Explaining to the dapper little traveller man who called once a year to sweep the chimneys what had happened – why 'the nipper', as he'd always called Robbie, wasn't there any more. Two months after the funeral Aitken would still find the dog sitting hopefully by the door, waiting for its owner to get home from school.

In time his absence became so sharp that it began to feel to Aitken like a presence. He would find himself in Robbie's room late at night, looking through his copybooks, holding his clothes. Taking out his books one by one and searching the shelves behind, as though some clue might be hidden there that could somehow explain what had happened. He would feel the shame of the invader as the room gave up its childish secrets. Four cigarettes in the toe of a soccer boot. A page torn out of a *Cosmopolitan* showing a winsome Japanese model in a skimpy lace bra. A pyjama shirt stuffed under the wardrobe with a melted chocolate biscuit still in the breast pocket. Sometimes he would sit in the room until dawn, until he would hear Valerie or one of the girls stir in bed or get up to use the bathroom. And then he would slip quickly out of the house and drive into work. Mornings in particular were difficult to bear. He couldn't be around his family in the mornings any more.

He would wonder as he drove the streets of the city, stalking terrorists and shadowing informants, if it were possible for a scar to form around a memory. Could you encase what had happened in such a way that Robbie could be recollected still, without the act of remembrance involving such merciless pain? His men, his superiors seemed to change. Even the criminals would fall silent when he walked into the room. People stopped looking at him directly.

For months they left his bedroom exactly as it was. And then Valerie started to give his things away: his bicycle, his books, his CDs and computer games. A friendly, smiling man from the Salvation Army arrived one afternoon to take all his toys away in a van. Shortly afterwards Valerie said they should redecorate the room and give the furniture to a charity. They had a violent quarrel about it. He told her he couldn't understand why she would want to forget their son like that.

It was the only time she had ever struck him.

And it was around that time that something like madness had stalked into Martin Aitken's life, slipping in silently, gently as a burglar. He began to have dreams of startling vividness, where he heard Robbie's voice or laugh; once he woke up to see him standing by the bedroom window, the bright lace curtains blowing about him, his bloodied face tilted in that playfully challenging grin of his. 'You didn't help me, Daddy. I called and you never came.' He sat up drenched with sweat and whispered his son's name, only to have the image melt away and reveal itself as nothing more than an arrangement of clothes hung over a chair in the half-light.

He found he was drinking more. Before long he was drinking every night. And often after the bar had closed, he would take a bottle and drive to the stretch of dual carriageway where his son had been killed. There he would park and sit for a while, as though the uncomplicated act of simply being at the place could connect him in some secret way to what had happened. Those were the ash trees that were the last thing he saw. That was the house where the old lady had called the ambulance. For months the scene had remained unchanged: cellophane-wrapped bunches of chrysanthemums taped to the twisted lamppost against which his son's body had been hammered. And then, in time, the flowers had been taken away; men from the council had put in a new lamppost. The scene had been restored to what it must have been on the August afternoon when his son had decided to take the short cut home from football practice, the walk to the crossroads towards which death was already roaring.

Sometimes, drunk, he would see a boy of Robbie's age in the street and tell himself that was his son. Once, in the clutch of a violent hangover, he had even followed a boy halfway home through Dun Laoghaire, letting himself fantasise that there had been some awful mistake, that the lad was Robbie and that everything would be all right now. Other times a smell – old training shoes, the eucalyptus-scented lotion his son had used for his eczema, the bleachy reek of a hospital corridor – would bring Robbie back from the grave. His mocking mournful ghost would hover around Martin Aitken, like a fragment of a melody from a childhood summer, only played out of tune, in a minor key.

The hospital ward was hung with balloons and tinsel. In a curtained-off corner the woman from the bus station was still unconscious. A blue rubber nametag around her wrist had a paper slip inserted, reading 'name + d.o.b. unknown'. An impatient Kerry nurse with pimpled skin told him the woman had been given ten milligrams of intravenous Valium and probably wouldn't wake for at least a day. 'And I bloody well envy her that much,' she added, venomously. 'I hate Christmas. With a passion.'

The woman had on a light green tissue-paper gown. Her nose

90

and right cheek were slightly red, her left eyelid a little puffed up; one slender forearm was bound in a gauze bandage stained russet brown with blood. He sat by her bed and looked around the ward, waiting for something unusual to happen. An orderly in a paper hat was draping a string of tinsel across the window. A wilted poinsettia sat on top of a radiator, its tear-like petals drooping in the heat. By the bedside of an emaciated man in lurid pink pyjamas, two little girls were kicking each other's shins while their harassed mother peered at the ceiling and looked like she was about to scream.

A Sikh doctor came in and did a double-take.

'Season's greetings,' Aitken said. The doctor laughed and shook his hand. He was a stocky, muscular man who carried himself well, with clear, bright eyes and a neat moustache, a golden leaf-shaped pin in the knot of his burgundy tie.

'Hopalong Aitken, the king of the West. What the hell has you among us today?'

'Christmas Day shift.' He shrugged. 'Luck of the draw.'

'Want to book in for a service now you're here?'

'Yeah, right. Just what I need.'

Doctor Ranjiv Singh ruefully pursed his lips, poked him in the belly with the edge of his clipboard. 'What you need is to lose some of that upholstery, Inspector. You could wear that beergut as a kilt these days.'

'I'm not fat, Ranj. There were never any fat people in my family.'

'There were never any psychos in the Bates family either, before little Norman came along. Look at yourself, man. You're a heart attack waiting to happen.'

'We're all gonna die, Ranj. I think you better start gettin' your head round that. Make your job a good bit easier.'

The doctor put his fingers on the woman's wrist. 'If you're planning on doing any dying today, my friend, do it on someone else's watch, OK?'

Aitken nodded at the woman in the bed. 'Any gen on Sleeping Beauty here?'

Singh shook his head. 'Barely woke up. Didn't say a word.'

He took an electric thermometer from a breast pocket full of pens, held it to the woman's ear. 'Well, actually, she did say one word. In kind of a whisper.' He clicked the thermometer and peered at the dial, scribbling something in his notebook.

'So?'

Singh looked at him quizzically.

'So are you going to tell me the word, Professor, or do I have to be clairvoyant now?'

'Oh, sorry, Martin . . . Inishowen.'

'Inishowen?'

'That's what she said. And for God's sake put out that cigarette, Hopalong. You're in a bloody hospital.'

'Inishowen? As in County Donegal?'

'I dunno.' Singh shrugged. 'You're the mick.'

Aitken said nothing. A dirty yellow tennis ball came rolling along the floor. He picked it up and squeezed it with his fingertips, chucked it back to one of the little girls. She caught it and smiled before running away, her shoes sliding on the smooth, red floor. Singh put on a weary face and held out a paper cup. Aitken dropped his cigarette into it.

'So Martin. You know this Inishowen?'

His son's grave was at the foot of a rolling heathery hillside that looked down over Trawbreaga Bay. From the summit you could see Five Fingers beach; further to the south, the peak of Sliabh Sneachta. He was buried close to his maternal grandparents, not far from his grandmother's own mother and father. Near the grave of a local man named Logue, a blacksmith, who died in Market Harborough, England. Across the way from one Peggy Duffy, who had been a servant all her life at Malin Hall. The field beyond the drystone wall had rabbits and sheep in it. In the summer the gorse on Soldiers Hill smelt sweet as coconut milk; in winter the aroma of turf drifted over from the cottages on the shore of Doagh Isle.

'Martin? I was asking about Inishowen?'

'It's where Valerie's folks are from. In Donegal.'

'Where's Donegal?'

'Jesus Christ, you bloody foreigner. It's way up in the north.'

'Oh yeah? Nice place?'

'Kind of hick, to be honest. You plug in a kettle and the streetlights dim.'

The doctor nodded as he felt the woman's neck. He moved his probing fingertips to behind her ears, massaging her.

'It's mentioned in the stuff we found in her coat.'

'What stuff's that, Ranj?'

'She had these . . . I don't know . . . letters or something. In her pocket.'

'Jayzus. Did she? I didn't find anything on her.'

'In a pocket inside her coat. Like down at the hem.'

'Can I have a goo?'

'Yeah, sure. Get them yourself. They're in the locker over there.'

Aitken went to the bedside locker and opened a drawer. Inside was a sheaf of folded papers, tied in a length of thin red ribbon. They did seem to be letters – some typed on an old-fashioned typewriter, others in a minuscule, untidy scrawl that was almost illegible without his glasses. There was also a cutting from an old Donegal newspaper, with a headline about a baby abandoned on a boreen.

'I'll need to take these with me, Ranj.'

Singh was finishing taking her blood pressure. 'I can't allow that, Martin. They're hers.'

'She's officially a missing person. They might give me a lead.'

He shook his head firmly. 'No can do, Kimo Sabe. I can't give you a patient's private property.'

'I can get a court order if you want.'

'Listen, spare me the Starsky and Hutch routine, Mr Bigshot.' He did a mocking chuckle. 'Come back in a few days. If she's still out cold you can have 'em then.'

Aitken nodded and sat on the edge of the bed. He watched Singh part the woman's eyelids and shine a pencil-torch into them, bending low to examine her closely.

'So how's that peg-leg treating you these days, Martin?'

'It only bothers me when the weather's cold.'

'If you'd done your physiotherapy that wouldn't have happened. But you know best. And always did.'

93

'Yeah. Anyway. What's wrong with my friend here?'

Singh stood up straight and looked at the woman, shaking his head in gentle exasperation. He put his large smooth hand on her forehead, tenderly moving a strand of moist hair. 'Most probably just exhaustion, Martin. She's a little underweight. Her pulse is on the button. Blood pressure normal enough in the circumstances.'

'What circumstances would those be?'

'Well . . . pressure. Stress of some kind. You see it a lot at this time of year.'

'So it's not the season to be jolly, after all?'

'It's called Einstein's theory of relativity, my friend. Time goes a lot slower when you're with your relatives.'

'Nothing more than that, Ranj?'

He shrugged. 'Pathology lab's closed until Friday. I can't give you the whole story till then. If there is a story.'

'We've a witness says he thought she was American.'

'It's hard to tell that from a medical examination, Martin. Unfortunately they don't have a third nipple.'

'She had a rake of dollars in her pocket.'

'Lucky her.'

'Maybe she was planning to go.'

'Or maybe she'd just arrived, Hopalong.'

'Makes you say that?'

'Well, it's obvious even to an Irish fool she was out of the country recently.'

'Oh yeah? How's that so obvious?'

Singh winked, went to the locker and pulled out a plastic bag.

'So, look, Kojak.' He reached inside. 'Know what these are?'

'Yeah. Green socks.'

'Not just socks, Hopalong. They're the cheap socks they give you on a long-distance flight. Throwaway things.' He put his hand inside one, his fingers forming a puppet-like mouth. 'I mean, you don't think anyone'd *buy* those, do you?' He raised the hand-filled sock to his nose and pinched his nostrils with it – 'Hello, Ranji, hello, you handsome thing' – and gave a

94

soft, stertorous moan of pleasure. 'Feminine feet, Martin,' he grinned. 'The sexiest smell in the world.'

'Jayzus, fair play, Ranj. Sherlock Holmes lives.'

He took the socks and tucked them into his pocket.

'Give us a buzz on the mobile when she wakes up, OK?'

'You want me to take a look at the leg now you're here, Martin?'

'No, it's grand. I'm practically line dancing.'

'Hard to do the mashed potato with a bullet in your femur. Unless you're a stubborn Irish mick, of course.'

'You're charming, Ranj. You know that, don't you?'

'Sorry, Martin. I just need to get laid.'

'Well, climb up a chicken's arse and wait. OK?'

'Ah, *Daddy*,' came a laughing call from down the ward. 'Daddy, don't! It's too embarrassing.'

A man in a wheelchair was holding a hairbrush to his mouth, curling his lip and pouting like Elvis, while his wife laughed in joyful mortification. The little girl with the tennis ball was tugging on the hem of his pyjama leg and pleading with him to stop.

'Hey. Seriously. Are you OK, Martin?'

'I'm delirious, Ranj. Why wouldn't I be?'

The doctor laughed fondly and shook his head. 'Get off the bloody stage, man. You look like a dog's breakfast. If you want to talk, you know where I am.'

He picked up his stethoscope and put it around his neck.

'Any time. I mean it, Martin. Come out to the house or something.'

'I'd want to be bleedin desperate though, wouldn't I? Before I'd talk to you.'

The doctor put his hands in his pockets and gave him a look. 'Same old tough-guy Martin, right? A cowboy to the end.'

'I'll take that as a compliment, Ranj. Coming from an Indian.'

The lift got stuck on the way down. He took out the letter he had stolen and began to try to read it. When the lift started to move again, he imagined it continuing down through the ground, all the way to Hell.

95

Chapter Seven

It was one of the few fixed points of Inspector Martin Aitken's life that holidays of all kinds were to be avoided if at all possible, and if not, got over quickly and with minimum fuss.

In the six years since his marriage had ended, Easter had been spent walking alone in the Kerry mountains, bank holiday weekends in London with his brother and sister-in-law, Saint Patrick's Day in any place other than Ireland. As for Christmas, that had usually been four Seconal and a couple of amitriptyline, washed down with a mouthful of Night Nurse cough mixture, a heady seasonal cocktail that would wake you up smiling on December twenty-seventh with fewer brain cells than you had before but a measurable amount more tranquillity.

Why did you need your brain cells at Christmas anyway? Was there any time of year that was more fundamentally stupid? Ranjiv Singh was right about that much. Take your closest relations, their children, their pets, their smiling jealousies and antediluvian resentments, lock them all in a room with enough drink to satisfy a rugby team and then act surprised when disorder breaks out. As a policeman, he knew that Christmas meant problems. The murder rate went through the roof, assaults and batteries multiplied, spousal abuse flowered like love in the spring. Shoplifters, burglars, fraudsters, pimps and pickpockets all saw it as an opportunity for market dominance. It was a time of year that meant nothing but hassle: trouble with a Coke and fries to go.

Some of his colleagues liked the overtime. But Aitken saw Christmas as torture with tinsel, a cold turkey sandwich of misery and cant. This was a season when rules were forgotten, when sensible people did things that were extraordinary. Drink and sentiment were only part of it. The holiday fostered a regression to infantilism that Aitken saw as fundamentally unhealthy. Grown men going carolling, mature adults wassailing. People old enough to vote dressing up as elves. After a departmental booze-up one year, he had seen one of his own officers – a quiet, solid Limerick man who went purple when anyone spoke to him – drop his trousers and photocopy his penis while serenading his howling, inebriated colleagues with 'Long Live the Rifles of the IRA'.

He drove around St Stephen's Green, throwing a glance down a deserted Grafton Street. Bits of paper drifted on the air like scraggy birds. In the window of Laura Ashley the SALE signs were already displayed. A wino in a topcoat was shuffling along, lurching from one side of the street to the other like a sailor on the deck of a ship in a storm. The lights had been up since the day after Hallowe'en. They'd be still there at the end of January. One of these years they'd forget to take them down. That was the future for the prosperous new Dublin. Bloody Christmas all year round.

Christmas was when he and Valerie had married. And Christmas was the time their marriage had ended. Turning down Dawson Street he did a calculation. The day before yesterday would have been their twenty-fifth anniversary. In front of the Mansion House, a man was showing the outdoor crib to two laughing children. A hundred yards further along, outside St Anne's church, choirboys in red soutanes were singing 'Good King Wenceslas'. A memory floated up. He allowed it to come.

It was almost five months after Robbie's death. Aitken and Valerie had been driving home from the station Christmas party. Neither of them had truly wanted to go, but each had lied about it, he understood later, thinking a lie was what the other had wanted.

As soon as they arrived, Aitken knew it had been a mistake to come. It was fancy dress, which he had forgotten; everyone in the room except himself and Valerie was dressed as a vicar or a tart. There was a loud disco and a wall of flashing lights, people were badly drunk; in that late and dangerous stage of drunkenness that suffuses a room with unease. His men were lurching in a ring on the dance floor, looking florid with lust, shirts open to the navel, arms around each other. The women officers were sitting in small groups at tables, smoking a lot and looking exhausted. The party had been strained; hardly anyone had talked to Aitken and Valerie. Those who did seemed either anxious or falsely casual; it was as though they didn't know what to say. He had felt like a man walking around in a spotlight, people stared so hard as he moved through the room.

They had left as soon as they thought it polite. On the way home it had started to rain, suddenly the streets were sleek and wet. A Bob Dylan song was playing on the radio. The signal had been weak and the sound was crackling.

'Martin,' she said. 'I want a separation.'

His first response was to laugh.

'I mean it, Martin, love. I've thought it over.'

He had driven on in silence for a while, vaguely aware that he was concentrating too hard on the controls. His mind began slowly admitting the knowledge that however it turned out – and right now there was no way of knowing that – he would remember the conversation that was about to happen for the rest of his life.

'Don't you have anything to say, Martin?'

Even now, after all this time, he recalled that a small orange light on the panel behind the wheel had flickered on, and he hadn't known what it meant. He had hit a few switches to see what would happen, but it had stayed on. Cursing, he had begun to talk about the light then, asked if Valerie had noticed the car acting up lately, talked about bringing it in for a service as soon as Christmas was over.

'Listen to me, Martin. I'm leaving you.'

'You're upset, pet,' he finally said. 'You're still a bit down about August, that's all.'

The word 'August' was shorthand for the death of their son. Neither of them could mention it in any other way.

He had driven on through the damp streets. The midnight news came on, something about a weapons find in the North. In Westland Row two drunken girls in sodden ball gowns had waved and made thumbs-up signs as they passed. Distracted, he had swerved a little, before righting the car again.

'Jesus,' Valerie gasped, gripping his arm.

He clipped a dustbin, knocking it into the gutter.

'Christ Almighty, would you mind your driving!'

'I'm fine.'

'You're over the limit.'

'I'm not over the limit, Valerie. I only had two beers.'

'You're over the bloody limit, Martin. You know it well.'

He remembered stopping at traffic lights on Merrion Square, a grid of white headlights moving across her face.

'You had at least five beers, Martin. That's not counting before we went out.'

'You want to drive yourself, then?'

'I'm over the limit too.'

'Because you can fucking drive any time you want, Valerie. That's fine with me. You want to do that? You're such a fucking expert, why don't you drive?'

She had turned to him then, her eyes bright with anger. 'Don't fucking talk to me like that, Martin. I'm not one of your men, all right?'

When the light went green he hadn't moved. A taxi behind them had begun to honk.

'Martin, for God's sake, drive the car.'

Finally the taxi had pulled out and squealed past him, the driver leaning over to wave two fingers and bawl.

His heart was thudding as he eased the car forward. She was peering at the floor with her arms folded tightly.

'It's strange,' he said, nodding at the dash, 'I really don't know why that light is on.'

'I don't want to talk about the light.'

'Look . . . It's August, Valerie. That's all it is. You're after being through a terrible time.'

'Don't make this harder than it needs to be.'

'For God's sake, pet. It's Christmas Eve.'

'I'm sorry to tell you now. But my mind's made up.'

'Let's go somewhere and have a quiet drink, all right?'

'I don't want a bloody drink! OK? Does it ever cross your

bloody mind that people might want to do more with their lives than drink?'

'All right. Calm down. Let's have a talk, then.'

'It's too late for talking.'

'It's only midnight, Valerie.'

'I know the time, Martin. That isn't what I meant.'

By now they were driving through Ringsend village. He pulled into the car park on Sandymount Strand. When he switched off the ignition the orange light stayed on. For a minute or two, the only sound was the soft, repeated, metallic click of the engine cooling down. He remembered strangely incongruous thoughts forming in his mind. How ugly the red and black tower of the Pigeon House suddenly seemed. How had they ever got permission to build something like that? All around them were cars in which couples were making out. Here in his own car, his marriage was ending.

'Do you believe in Heaven, Martin?'

'I don't know if I do.'

'Do you think that's where he is now?'

'I suppose I haven't thought about that.'

She opened the glove box and closed it again. 'I don't know what kind of world it is any more. Where someone could hit a little boy with their car and just drive on like that. Without even stopping. Not even for a minute.'

'Valerie, please.'

'I mean, if I hit a dog I think I'd at least stop. Wouldn't you?'

'I don't know,' he said. 'I hope I would.'

She nodded. 'Are you seeing another woman, Martin?'

He laughed with shock. 'What are you on about? Of course I'm not.'

He remembered suddenly feeling very drunk, his jaw heavy, tongue too large.

'You're lying to me, Martin. I'm not a fool.'

'I'm not lying, Valerie, I swear to Christ.'

'One night last month you told me you were working. And you weren't. I rang the station to ask for you and they hadn't seen you all day.'

'Well, so what? I was probably out on a case.'

'I got Hughie to check the roster. Your shift ended at five.'

The truth was that lately he had taken to staying out all night. It was nothing he understood – or cared to try and understand – beyond a desire to be alone that was so deep it sometimes frightened him. He would remain in the pub until closing time, then drive out of town by the quiet, winding back roads he knew to be rarely patrolled, and head up into the Dublin mountains. He'd park the car and listen to the radio, looking down at the lights of the distant city and, beyond those, the twinkling lighthouses out in the bay.

'I must have gone for a spin on my own, that's all.'

'And you lied to me about it?'

'Well, I didn't fucking realise you'd be checking up on me, did I?'

She flinched as though he had slapped her across the face. Her eyes filled with tears as she turned away. She bowed her head and started to weep, her chest softly heaving, her fingers covering her mouth and nose.

'Don't be crying, for Jesus' sake.'

'I wanted to hear your voice, that's all.' She took a tissue from her sleeve and wiped her eyes. 'I was lonely. I missed you, Martin.'

'I'm sorry, then,' he said. 'Come on, let's be friends.'

'It's all right for you.' She pushed him away. 'You're out all day. Moping around in his room half the night. Talking in your sleep. Looking through his things. We haven't made love in five months, Martin. What do you think that does to me? To have all the closeness taken away.'

'Jesus, Valerie, he was my son too. Don't you think I'm hurt as well?'

'I know you're hurt. And I've tried to make it better. But I can't be married for the two of us any more.'

'Come on, stop it.'

'Telling me I want to forget him. In front of the girls like that.' Fresh tears spilled over her eyelids, her face twisted with anguish. 'How in Christ could you ever say that to me, Martin? When I brought the child into the world.'

'It upset me when you threw his stuff out that time.'

A bitter sob convulsed her now. 'God Almighty, Martin. Do you understand nothing?'

'What do you mean?'

'It broke my heart to give away his things. I did it to stop you being hurt any more.'

He went to touch her, but she pulled away again.

'I never know what you're thinking now. You snap the head off the girls for nothing.'

'I just don't want them walking the roads at night.'

'That's a little brother they've lost. Is that really so hard for you to understand? Can you not go easy and give them a tender word sometimes?'

'I do understand.'

'You used to be such a gentle person, Martin. It's what made me love you. And now it's over.'

That was Christmas Eve, 1988. By New Year's Day, Valerie and the girls were gone.

The separation hearing had been listed for March. Aitken had not recognised the marriage that had been described in the court. He had been cold, unfeeling, distant and controlling. His work had taken him away from the family. His drinking had made things very much worse. The death of their son had seemed to make things worse again. He was incapable, drifting, indecisive, lost. He was a man, said the barrister, who couldn't tie a tie.

'Irreconcilable differences', it had said in Valerie's affidavit. The moment Aitken saw those words written down, he had finally accepted that they must be true.

She didn't turn up to hear the judgment. It came the morning after Saint Patrick's Day. He'd been up all night on a stakeout in the city, watching a flat where it was suspected two IRA men were hiding. The courtroom was modern, with central heating and venetian blinds, empty except for a couple of lawyers. When the judge came in, he asked Valerie's solicitor to stand.

'There's no hope of a reconciliation?'

'No, my Lord.'

'But surely with two teenagers to think about? Perhaps with counselling this could still be resolved happily.'

'My client indicates not, my Lord.'

'These are good caring people who had a cruel loss. Maybe all they need is a chance? Won't you ask your client to give her husband another chance?'

'With respect, my Lord, the position is that this marriage has become a work of fiction.'

And Aitken had found that an oddly appropriate way to put it. Because it had sometimes seemed to him that every marriage could be read in that way. Particularly a marriage in which a child had been lost. A certain streak of imagination was required to go on pulling off the trick, and that kind of artistry was something he knew by now he didn't have. Valerie was right to perceive that about him. It simply wasn't the way he was made.

The court had awarded custody of Julie to Valerie; Claire had turned eighteen that year and was too old for the court to say where she must live. She herself had made it clear in a meeting with the barristers that she wanted to stay with her mother. Aitken was given weekend visiting rights. The judge ordered regular psychiatric assessments, not only for Julie but for both parents also.

Once a month throughout 1989 Aitken had trooped along to the psychiatrist's office. The doctor had a collection of coffee mugs on his bookshelf, one with the slogan stamped in black letters, 'Do those voices you hear say anything about my fees?' Another, his favourite, the only one Aitken ever saw him actually use, featured a Gary Larson cartoon of a crestfallen cow lying on a couch, while the frizzy-haired shrink in the foreground scribbled in his notebook, 'Just Plain Crazy'.

Aitken hadn't enjoyed his visits much. He had talked about his childhood, his relationships with his parents; once or twice he had touched on his drinking, but the psychiatrist never seemed too interested in that. He had put questions so startlingly personal that a criminal in an interrogation would punch you out for asking them. Aitken had done Rorschach tests, free-association word games, spontaneous role-plays based on scenarios from his adolescence. After a while he realised he was making things

103

up, partly to keep the psychiatrist happy but also to feel he was getting value for money. Eighty-five pounds an hour for a guy who stirred his coffee with a screwdriver and looked like he secretly stirred it with his cock when all the patients had disappeared home.

★

At Pearse Street station, a stack of stolen bicycles lay in the lobby. WANTED posters of thugs and robbers covered the walls, photographs of people who had disappeared, warnings about pickpockets and the dangers of speeding.

In the office behind the counter, Hughie Tynan, the desk sergeant, was playing computer chess and munching on a sandwich. He peered up in mid-gulp and wiped his lips with the back of his hand.

'Holy moly. Good morrow, my liege.'

'What?'

'Didn't expect you in today, boss. I've you down in the book for a week's leave.'

'Couldn't keep away from your beauty, Huge. Any action?'

'Methinks thou pullest me wire, goodly captain. We'd action right enough. Your man Doogan. Broke the gaff up a bit last night. Like Hiroshima in here it was.'

'Bad little bastard. Where's he now?'

'Verily, we had to lurry him up to the Joy. Breaking the gaff up he was. Tried to start a fire in the cells.'

'Fuck him anyway. Anything else?'

Tynan shrugged and looked at his ledger. 'Few breaking and enterings. Ruction down in some kebab kip on Usher's Quay after closing time, ten rounds, but not of Lord Queensberry's rules. Shower of drunken Trinity lads sleeping it off inside. Theology students, if you don't mind. One of them says he's a prince from Nigeria.'

The chess machine bleeped. An acrid stench of disinfectant washed through the office. The sergeant scratched his balding head and slid a piece across the board.

'Any enquiries come in on a missing person, Huge?'

The sergeant glanced in the ledger again. 'Couple of out-standings. Nothing new. Why?'

104

'I got a woman.'

'You and Elvis,' the sergeant said, reaching for his notebook and pen. 'Would she have a sister for a lonely man?'

'Her mother'd be more your style, Huge.'

'Gimme the story, boss, and don't be slaggin.'

'What the fuck's this? Bad humour are you?'

'Noreen made a curry last night. Woke up with me arse like the Japanese flag.'

'Merciful Christ but you're only lovely.'

'Do you want to gimme the details or not, boss? For we have not here a lasting city.'

'From the day before yesterday when you were off. No name on her yet. Five seven or so. Hundred and ten, hundred and fifteen. Dark hair, shoulder length, streaks of grey. Forty-five to fifty. Might be an American tourist. Dropped out of her standing outside Busaras. She's in a scratcher out in Michael's if anyone asks.'

The sergeant nodded as he noted down the details. 'Tell you what, boss. I could give a bell around the hotels, see if someone's AWOL from a room.'

'Do you know what it is, Huge? You've brains to burn.'

Chapter Eight

He went into his office and opened the blinds. The sky looked stormy, the colour of cold porridge. A home-made Christmas card sat on the windowsill; Claire's daughter Elsie had made it in kindergarten. On the front was a drawing of a rotund cop waving a gun, with ransom-note lettering snipped out of newspaper headlines: **To GrAnD-dad MaRTin, T*H*e bEst policeman iN tHe wOrlD. FiGhT ThE PoWeR**. He wondered what the psychiatrist would make of that.

He crossed the room and sat at the desk. An envelope with his name on it was leaning against his telephone. It had arrived several days ago but he'd left it in his pigeon-hole, already knowing what was inside. Hughie must have brought it in this morning. He picked it up now and ripped it open.

AN GARDA SIOCHÁNA: DISCIPLINARY BOARD
17 December 1994
Dear Inspector Aitken,

I am directed to inform you that the disciplinary board has considered your case once again and has decided, as previously, that reinstatement to Special Branch duties would not be appropriate.

I am further advised that the matter has been examined comprehensively at this stage. The board does not envisage any change in the near future, if ever.

May we take this opportunity to wish you and your family a Merry Christmas.

He crumpled up the paper and lobbed it into the bin. Fucking suits. Amoebas in pinstripes, sitting on little amoeba toilets. They wouldn't rest easy until they'd driven him out.

He lit up a joint and stared at the pile of paperwork overflowing from the in-tray. How in Christ had it got that big? He pulled the bin over from the corner and began working through the stack, dropping in papers and announcements from head office.

He took out the letter he had stolen from the hospital, put on his glasses and tried to make out the writing. It was so spidery and small that he had to squint. An old woman seemed to be telling some kind of story. Place names he recognised were mentioned here and there. Carrowmenagh, Ballyliffin, Bulbinmore, Graignahulla. The blotted pages were yellowed and creased, as though they had been folded many times.

He went to his bookshelves and looked for an atlas. Where the hell was the bloody thing? He knew he'd got one free a few months back for buying a tank of petrol in some garage down the sticks. He shuffled stacks of papers, mounds of files and folders. There it was, wedged between the Golden Pages and a copy of the constitution.

He opened the atlas and looked up Inishowen, the tiny diamond-shaped peninsula that formed the north-eastern tip of Donegal. The map of Ireland was a little punk rocker and Inishowen was his Mohican haircut. Julie had said that once, the first or second time they'd brought her up there. When was that anyway? Around the time she started school. He remembered her sitting on his knee by Malin Head, asking him how he had met and married Mammy.

There was a question to slice open your heart. Tell us, how did you meet Mammy?

The summer he had left school, 1969, his elder brother Johnny had been injured in an accident at work and given two hundred pounds as compensation. Things at home were tough at the time; Aitken's father had died the September before. The union people had tried to do their best, but the owners of the factory were fighting his pension claim. Johnny had wanted to give all the money to his mother. She insisted she would only take half.

It was their mother who had suggested they go away for a while. Get out of the city and knock around together. It was Martin's last summer of freedom, she said. His life as an adult was about to begin.

He and his brother had taken their guitars and rucksacks and headed off to Clare on a skite. There was a music festival in Doolin; they had some kind of notion to support themselves by busking. When the fleadh was over they'd headed north to Galway, then Spiddal, Clifden, Westport, Inishbofin. They had drifted up to Sligo in a haphazard way, hitching lifts from salesmen and tourists, sleeping in a tent or sometimes under the stars. There was vague talk of looking for jobs, but mostly they had just kicked around, drinking the few pounds their busking earned them, sometimes trying in a half-hearted way to pick up American girls. It was a summer over which hung a sense of things ending, like the smell of something starting to rot.

In October, Aitken hoped, he would start in Templemore, the college in Tipperary where the police recruits were trained. The day the interview results were announced, he rang his mother from a coin box on the desolate shore of Lough Erne, while his hungover brother chain-smoked and paced the gravel road. He had been accepted, she told him, subject to his exam results, her voice breathless with excitement and pride.

Things in Ireland were beginning to change. From across the border, news of trouble was coming. By late June there were riots in the streets of Derry; in Belfast, Catholics were being burnt out of their homes, RUC patrols had been attacked with pistols and grenades.

By the middle of July the brothers had drifted up the coast to Buncrana, a seaside resort at the southern end of Inishowen. The pubs and cafés were full of people who had come across the border. July was the marching season in the North, a time when things boiled over and you wanted to get out.

That summer, in a town called Dungiven, an Orange Lodge was burned in a riot; the cops tried to break it up, a man called McCloskey was killed. Soon afterwards a man named Devenney died, having been beaten senseless by the police in Derry. An RUC station on the Falls Road was raided by a gang of local kids who battered down the door with a telegraph pole. Catholics were attacked in Unity Flats; a man named Corry was fatally injured by the police. In a lounge bar in Buncrana, Aitken watched a report on the news about how a civil rights march had been attacked by the RUC, broken up with batons and dogs. There was talk of British soldiers being sent in to keep the Protestants and Catholics apart, but the barman said it would never happen.

Aitken's brother rushed into the pub at that point.

'Did you hear?' Johnny gasped.

'About the North?'

'Fuck the North. I'm talkin about Taste.'

'Taste?'

'They're playin in town tonight. Come on, quick.'

The pastel-coloured dance hall on the seafront had been built in the 1940s and looked as though it was about to fall down at any minute. Weeds and moss were growing on the roof; rusting jagged holes punctured the corrugated iron walls. Faded ancient signs in the upper windows announced THE NORTHERN STAR CEILIDH BAND THIS THURSDAY and TRADITIONAL MUSIC EVERY NIGHT. On either side of the main doors were cracked glass noticeboards containing crumpled showband posters: Con Dunphy and the Deportees, Red Hurley, Big Tom, Cahir O'Doherty 'Ireland's Elvis'. Outside, as well as young local people, there were tourists wandering around in small groups, taking photographs of each other in front of the building. Most of them wore tweeds and Aran sweaters. One or two were carrying souvenir shillelaghs. Aitken and his brother pushed through the crowd and into the dank, tumbledown hall.

A small statue of the Sacred Heart smiled down from a plinth in the balcony wall. Up in the rafters a seagull was flapping. The wooden floor was so badly warped that it dipped several inches in the middle. On the rickety stage a drum kit and amplifiers had been set up. Three electric guitars were resting on stands; a skinny, pony-tailed roadie was on his knees, tuning an acoustic. A banner saying TASTE had been draped over an upright piano, near an old hand-painted notice that said NO JIVING: BY ORDER OF THE MANAGEMENT. A revolving mirror ball sent spangles of light across the shabby walls. An announcement was made over the loudspeaker: the concert would begin in five minutes.

Johnny was so excited he could hardly speak. He pulled a bottle of vodka from his pocket, took a long swig, handed it to his brother. 'You're about to have the night of your life, kiddo,' he said, embracing Aitken, hugging him hard. The hall began to fill up quickly; before long there was hardly room to move. The front doors were opened wide, outside there were still people trying to crush in. At nine o'clock the house lights suddenly darkened. A rig of red and yellow spots flickered on over the stage. A roar of applause filled the hall. A cherub-faced, slightly awkward-looking youngfella with long shaggy hair and a tartan lumberjack shirt ambled out from the wings and waved to the cheering crowd.

The frenzied applause seemed to embarrass him. He blushed deeply and bowed several times. 'Anyone here from Donegal?' he chuckled into the microphone. The crazed howl that came back made him smile. He donned the acoustic guitar, thrashed out a few chords, fine-tuned it, strummed again, started hammering into a steady, urgent, country blues rhythm. A scream of longing and happiness came from the audience; they began to stamp and clap along in time. His name was Rory Gallagher, and he was from Ballyshannon, a neat and sleepy little town through which Aitken and his brother had passed a few weeks before. The blond Aran-sweatered tourists gaped in disbelief as he stepped up to the microphone and began to sing:

> *Gonna tell you 'bout the wildest showdown*
> *Ever shook the Texas plains,*
> *That made the prairies rumble*
> *And the bullets fall like rain,*
> *When a bunch of foolish lawmen messed*
> *With Frank and Jesse James*

He stood slightly hunched in the single white spotlight, the long fingers of his claw-like left hand racing up and down the fretboard, his head bobbing from side to side as he closed his eyes, cried out and growled, wrenching the notes from the guitar.

Aitken had never heard anything like it in his life. It sent a wild fizz racing through his blood. The song finished to a storm of applause, maniacal cheers, anguished whoops. The stamp of feet on the floorboards was as loud as rolling thunder.

'*Rory!*' howled his brother. 'Gallagher is God.'

'Ah, now,' laughed Rory Gallagher, his voice hoarse and breathy. 'Say hello to Johnny Wilson on drums, and Mister bassman, Ritchie McCracken. Yeah!' Two long-haired lads came on in bellbottoms and flowery waistcoats, waving and grinning, blowing kisses to the audience. 'Here's a Muddy Waters song you might like,' said Gallagher, tossing his hair. 'All about the Gypsy Woman Blues.' He picked up a battered Fender Stratocaster, strapped it on, plugged it in. A wail of screeching feedback echoed around the hall. Three denim-clad boys in front of Aitken began jumping up and down with their arms around each other. Johnny Wilson bashed at his cymbals, flailed at his snare drums. Ritchie McCracken turned up his volume so the thunk of the bass throbbed through the floor. The tourists looked at one another with disapproving frowns. TRADITIONAL MUSIC EVERY NIGHT. That's what the sign in the window said. This was certainly not traditional. In Mississippi maybe. But not in Donegal.

'Sing "Danny Boy",' one of them shouted.

'Danny Boy's dead, man,' Aitken's brother yelled back.

'But Ledbelly lives,' said Rory Gallagher into his microphone.

A bawl of laughter and applause filled the hall. Rory Gallagher counted off an intro. The band lashed into a savage twelve-bar blues, blistering guitar riffs piercing the air, loud, distorted power chords, clattering drums. A lad in a leather jacket ran forward and wrapped his arms around the bass amplifier, trying to stick his head inside the speaker well. And then in through the door that led from the ladies' toilets strolled this lissom girl in a tight blue cotton dress. Her hair was dark, full of curls. She had a way of walking that made you want to look at her. All around, people were shouting and dancing, jumping up on each other's shoulders, madly head-banging. But she moved through the throng smoothly, assuredly, almost as though nobody else was there. She glanced across and seemed to wave at Aitken. When he waved back cautiously, he thought she smiled, a dazzling radiant smile that lit up her suntanned face. But then a scrawny bearded guy in denim flares and platform shoes stepped out of the crowd and embraced her, and she hugged him back hard, clapping him on the shoulders.

'You fuckin great eejit,' his brother laughed.

'What are you talkin about? I wasn't even lookin at her.'

'Me arse and parsley,' Johnny said. 'Get back in your league there, Georgie Best.'

The song segued into another. Rory Gallagher grabbed the microphone and sang loud and sweet, as the seagull flapped down madly from the rafters and came to rest on the floor of the stage.

> *Same old story, it's gettin' me down.*
> *Same old story, in this one horse town.*

Johnny waved his hands in the air and squealed. *'Fuckin kill me, Rory, man.'*

Around midnight, when the Taste gig was over, Aitken and Johnny had gone to a hotel up the town where Dickie Rock and the Miami Showband played a late set on Friday nights. Showband wasn't exactly Johnny's kind of music, but the hotel was the last place in town to get a drink. They had sat at the bar for an hour or so, watching the people waltz and do the hucklebuck, laughing together at some of the dancers. They were drunk by now and Johnny seemed in strangely bitter mood. He told Aitken he was leaving for England in the autumn. He was fed up with Dublin, the rest of Ireland was worse. A glorified kip, the arse-end of nowhere. The sad little land that time forgot.

'Ireland's not so bad,' Martin said. 'What about Rory Gallagher?'

'Look,' sighed his brother, pointing towards the floor. A middle-aged man with a wide flowery tie was trying to persuade a tipsy woman to dance with him. 'Look at Mr Brylcreem thinkin he's groovy. Fuckin desperado. Doing the twist with cowshite on his wellies. You want to know what Ireland is, take a gander at that.'

Aitken had turned away from his brother for a moment and seen the beautiful girl from the Taste concert coming in with her friends.

The band was playing 'The Green Glens of Antrim' as he crossed the floor and asked her to dance. She looked him in the eye and seemed to think about it. He could see the friends quietly laughing.

'Dublin?' she said. The first word she ever spoke to him.

At the end of the night, the band played the National Anthem. Everyone in the room stopped talking and stood up. Some of them clenched their fists in the air. A young man clambered on to the stage and took the microphone. 'God save Ireland,' he roared. 'And fuck the Brits,' came a cry from the back.

'Bloody gobshite,' Valerie said. 'As if the Brits would even want him.'

Afterwards they went for a walk on the beach. She was from Carndonagh, a small town further up the peninsula. She had five sisters, her mother was dead. She was studying French and folklore down in Dublin, at UCD, but home for the summer, working as a receptionist in a small hotel near the seafront.

When they had kissed, he asked if he could see her again. She agreed to meet him the next day for coffee. By the end of that week, they were meeting every day, and every night when she had finished her work.

That was the end of the brothers' journey. The rest of the summer had been spent in Inishowen. What could he remember of those carefree times now? Swimming in the sea at Five Fingers beach, where the water was always bitterly cold, even on the hottest days. The taste of salt on clean, wet skin. A walk one afternoon through a field of wild fuchsia and bog cotton. A long night in a tiny bar in Culdaff, he and his brother, with Valerie and her cousin Karen who flirted with Johnny the whole night long, all of them merry on cider, trying to waltz to the jukebox of showband tunes.

113

He was his father's only son,
His mother's pride and joy.
And dearly did his parents love
The wild colonial boy.

Later that night, he and Valerie had gone up to Inishowen Head. This was the place she loved best in the world, she told him. It was where Saint Colmcille had blessed Ireland for the last time before going into exile. It became the place they would go to be alone. One night, in mid-August, they lay together in the long grass and watched strange lights flickering across the bay in Derry. She had never seen them before, she said, there definitely wasn't a town over there. They had wondered if the lights were ghostly apparitions. It was said by some of the old people of the area that the ghosts of those who had died in the famine woke and walked at this time of the year, on the nights around the feast of the Assumption. But the next day someone in Malin explained. The lights were from the wartime British army camp at Magilligan point. Soldiers had come to open it up again.

That night in Belfast, eight people were killed. The RUC riddled the Divis flats with a machine gun mounted on an armoured car. A nine-year-old boy was among the dead. A Protestant named Herbert Roy was shot to pieces. Bombay Street was set alight, two-thirds of the houses burned to the ground. As he looked at the newspapers the following morning Martin Aitken could scarcely believe what had happened while he'd been lying on the hillside in his girlfriend's arms. Bombay Street looked as though it had been blitz-bombed. War had come to Ireland again.

On the afternoon he was due to return to Dublin, he agreed to go to her house for tea. She met him outside the church in the town and told him tearfully that she had missed her period. He remembered the smell of bacon frying in the small council house, the framed photograph of her mother over the fireplace, the way her sisters had playfully laughed at him as they set the table and poured glasses of milk from a pewter pitcher.

After a time her father came in, a strikingly handsome, barrel-chested Derryman who captained a trawler out of Greencastle

114

port. When Valerie introduced them he looked at Aitken closely, waiting several moments before shaking his hand.

'So you're the big city flyboy keeps my daughter out half the night.'

'Yes, Mr Houghton.'

'It's as well you're away back to Dublin so. Isn't it?'

'I suppose it is. Though I like it well enough here.'

'Oh,' said her father, turning to his daughters. 'He likes it well enough here, ladies. Aren't we wild lucky now to have buck's approval?'

The girls laughed loud and Valerie blushed.

'And is it true you're to join the Garda?'

'Yes, I am. At least I hope so. If I get the results in the leaving cert.'

'That's a dangerous job these times. Specially for a man in the Free State uniform.'

'What do you mean, the Free State?'

In his memory, the room grew suddenly silent, as though a phantom had appeared through the floorboards. Houghton's daughters looked shocked that anyone would question him. A long moment passed before he peered at Aitken again, this time with a mirthless smile.

'I mean the so-called Republic of Ireland. That turns its back on those in the North.'

'Daddy, now,' said one of the girls.

He sat down at the table and unbuttoned his cuffs. 'There'll be no peace in this country till it's our country again. That's my opinion if anyone wants it. Maybe they think different down in Dublin. Shower of west British, the whole shoot of them.'

'Daddy,' said Valerie, 'don't be starting all that.'

'I'll start what I like in my own house, madam. And I'll finish it too, if that's all right.'

Scarcely a word had been said during the meal. Afterwards Valerie walked him through the town to the bus station. With hardly any discussion, they had agreed to get married. She kissed him gently and touched his face.

'You'll never forget Inishowen now, Martin Aitken.'

Inishowen. He closed his eyes and said the name aloud. It made him think of waves breaking on a shore.

It was where his only son was buried. He saw the lights glinting across the lough. Wild irises and rhododendrons fluttering on Soldiers Hill. A couple at the altar in the Star of the Sea Church, Malin, the girl largely pregnant, the boy in his brother's suit, the two of them crying with happiness and love. The inscription over the door of the little meeting room where the families had arranged for beer and sandwiches. St Mary's Hall. Erected By Priests And People United, 1912. The wild sea beating the rocks at Altnadarrow. A group of mourners carrying a small coffin around a Bronze Age burial mound before taking it to the graveyard. A local tradition, somebody had insisted. A thing that had always been done in Inishowen.

'Shame about poor auld Bronco last night, wasn't it?'

The sergeant had come in with a cup of beige tea and a mince pie in an aluminium wrapper. He plonked them on the desk, hung around, softly whistling as his thumbnail scratched at a stain on the window.

'Yeah,' said Aitken. 'He wasn't the worst.'

'Any ideas on a suspect, boss?'

'Maybe them fuckin Doogans. Maybe renegade Provos. He wasn't exactly the force's sweetheart.'

The sergeant didn't seem to want to leave.

'You waitin on me to give you a kiss there, Huge?'

'No, boss. But thanks for the offer.'

'So what are you gawkin at?'

'Well, just . . . ' He tugged on his earlobe. 'You're not seein the kids today, boss, no?'

'You see that door over there, Huge?'

'Aye, goodly nuncle.'

'Close it on your way out like a good man, would you?'

He read back over the notes of his interview with Shouldice, the electrician. He'd got shorter statements from serial bank robbers about to go into retirement. But its six pages said almost nothing of any importance. Imagine someone as stupid as that doing your wiring. Plug in your toaster and you'd be

116

blown yelping through the roof slates. Had the woman been with anyone before she fainted? What exactly had she said before hitting the pavement? Was she distressed, delirious, ecstatic, what? It irritated him how little people noticed, how they tottered around the city half asleep and helpless. What the hell was wrong with people now? In his former life, as an armed Special Branch officer, what you noticed was not just the difference between your children eating and going hungry, it was sometimes the way you stayed alive. Maybe it was something in the water these days that wrapped people's brains up in cotton wool.

The phone on his desk rang.

'Call for you, my Lord.'

'Take a message, Huge, I'm up to me gicker.'

'Well, I would, boss. Only it's the Assistant Commissioner.'

'Jayzus, Bollocky Bill? Today?'

'Sounds like he's having a head-throw too.'

'Mother of Christ. Put him on.'

He picked up the letter and looked at it again. A verse of some song or poem had been written out in a careful deliberate print, shakily underlined. It was in medieval Irish, Aitken reckoned, with an English translation underneath.

Do-ell Erinn, indell cor
cechaing noib newed mbled.

He turned away from Ireland, entered a pact,
He crossed the sea in ships, the sanctuary of the whales.

'Aitken, this is the Assistant Commissioner speaking. Did you harass Mickey Doogan's brother?'

'Merry Christmas to you too, sir.'

'Answer me, Aitken, when I'm talking to you.'

'I had him arrested, if that's what you mean.'

The AC's voice was breathless and angry. 'I don't know, I just don't. Lawyers ringing me up on a Christmas morning. Threatening to drag me into court. What the blazes did you think you were at, man?'

117

'What I was at, sir, was doing my job.'

'A chap gives you a bit of harmless lip, you choke the living shite halfway out of him, bang him up in a cell for the night. Then into the Joy. On a *Christmas Eve*!'

'Tell him apply to the courts if he wants out. He's plenty of dough for a barrister's fee. Smack's fetching good prices these days.'

'What are you gabbing about, man? He's out already.'

'He's *what*?'

The AC gave a sigh of frustration. 'He's working for us undercover, Aitken. All right, Aitken? Do you understand now, Aitken? It's called police work. Didn't you read the memo I sent you about it? I must have sent it three whole months ago!'

'That dirtbird on the payroll? He'd rob a poorbox and come back for more.'

'It's up to me to implement policy.'

'You call that policy? Holy Christ. It's no wonder the papers are all over us these days.'

'It is up to me,' the AC continued, raising his voice with practised ease, riding over him, 'to implement policy and it's up to those who don't like it to think about alternative employment and to do so toot fucking sweet.'

'I know you'd like that, Mellowes, don't worry. You think I haven't copped you're stymieing me with the board?'

'Aitken, do you want a battle of wits? Because by Christ you can have one if that's what you're after.'

'I wouldn't have a battle with an unarmed man, sir.'

A strangled splutter sounded down the line. 'You little . . . Are you drinking again, Aitken?'

'No.'

'No bloody what, man?'

'No, I'm not drinking again.'

'You are hanging on by your bootlaces, Aitken. I'll tell you that much. Did you get me those files?'

'What files?'

'Holy Christ . . . the ones I asked you for back in February. On the seventies and eighties. The Nicky Kelly case and all of that?'

'No.'

'I told you I need them.'

'I'm not actually a secretary, sir.'

'Holy God, Aitken, you're some monkey. Aren't you? Some monkey. And that's a fact.'

'Look . . . Excuse me, sir, are you wearing trousers?'

'What?'

'Are you wearing trousers at the moment?'

'Amusing, aren't you, Aitken. Yes, I'm wearing trousers.'

'Well, next time you ring me could you pull them down first, sir. So I can hear what you're saying more fuckin clearly.'

He slammed down the phone. Lit a cigarette. Picked the phone up and slammed it down again, leaving the receiver off the hook this time.

Back in the main office, Tynan was at his desk, noting down numbers from the telephone directory. Shouts and wolf-whistles were coming from the cells. The flytrap made a zizzing sound. A caterwauling song began, in a chanted, football terrace style:

> Low lie the fields of Athenry,
> Where once we watched the small seabirds fly.
> Our love was on the wing.
> We had dreams and songs to sing,
> Now it's lonely
> Round the fields of Athenry.

The sergeant grinned. 'The AC rang back.'

'Oh, did he?'

'I told him thou had withdrawn thy presence. Faded away like the mountain dew.'

'Good. The slimy poxbottle.'

'Aye, my liege.'

'Listen . . . Would you ever have a dekko around for some files for me, Huge. Anything on the seventies and eighties, he wants.'

The sergeant scowled. 'That's all comin up again, is it? Our friends in the press tellin tales out of school.'

'I don't know. Arse-face says he wants them anyway.'

The sergeant nodded. 'What'll I do with the Pavarottis in beyond? One of them says his auldfella's a Supreme Court judge. Talks like the seam of his bollocks is hand-stitched.'

'Well, shag that one into solitary and let the rest go home.'

'*Ceart go leor,*' said the sergeant, reaching for the keys. 'Live long and prosper, oh thane of Glasthule.'

Aitken paused, door in hand.

'Here, Huge?'

'Boss?'

'You don't want to go and have a bite somewhere later, do you? When you knock off, like. Bit of Christmas cheer?' He tried to say the last two words with a heavy layering of irony.

The sergeant shot him a wide-eyed grimace of pantomime fear. 'I'm due home for the turkey and trimmings at three, boss. She'll mangle me if I'm late. We've her mother up from the country, you know?'

'Oh yeah. Course. I forgot.'

'But you'd be welcome to join us, boss. We'll shove up in the bed and make room.'

Aitken said nothing. A sudden composite mental picture of last year's Christmas Day in the Tynan household floated into his mind. Twenty-something Hughie junior, a devoted Ecstasy fiend if ever there was one, eighteen-year-old Niamh and her oafish boyfriend Teddy, drunken rural Mammy singing 'Wrap the Green Flag Round Me, Boys' in a voice that would peel a carrot, drunken rural Daddy piddling in his slippers and popping down Prozac like it was going out of fashion (which, according to Niamh, it was), and, worst of all, Joxer, the yapping, flea-bitten, alleged Pomeranian, vigorously humping Aitken's leg all the way through *The Sound of Music*.

'I think I'll pass on it this year, Huge. I've made plans.'

Tynan winked suggestively and snuffled with laughter. 'Oh yeah? Would I know her?'

Since Aitken's separation, the sergeant seemed to enjoy thinking of him as some kind of character. Most of the time it was easier to play along with it.

'You know how it is, Huge. A man has his needs.'

'Give her a goose for Christmas, eh? As Robert Emmet said from the dock.'

'You've a wonderful way with words, Sergeant Tynan. Should've gone in for poetry instead of police work.'

'Bring the lucky lady as well if you want. If she's good-lookin at all she can sit on me lap.' He beamed excitedly as he picked up the phone. 'I'll ring Noreen now and tell her chuck two more names in the pot, all right?'

'Well, she's a bit shy, Huge. We've only just met.'

A curious look came over the sergeant's face. 'Is this one . . . somethin special then?'

'I dunno. Maybe.'

Tynan nodded understandingly. 'I'd be made up if you did come over, boss. So would Noreen, honest. She's always askin after you. I think she has designs on your body.'

He saw an opportunity to change the subject. 'How's your better half these days?'

'Never better, Martin. Honest to God, since she had the last operation you wouldn't know her. Lovely and bright in herself she is. Just like the old Noreen.'

'That's a miracle, right enough, livin with you.'

'Come home with me later, Martin, it'd make her day. And bring the ladyfriend too, all right? Sure there's plenty of room at the inn, eh?'

'I'd love to, Hugh. But I really can't.'

'At least say you'll wander over for a jar tonight. The kids'd love to see you too.'

'Some other time, Huge. We agreed we'd just . . . keep to ourselves this year.'

The sergeant sighed and shook his head.

'We owe you so much, boss. Noreen and me. We could never repay you for what you done for us.'

'You owe me shag all, man. Don't be annoyin me.'

Chapter Nine

Crossing Pearse Street to his car, he thought about what Tynan had been through. Two years back, on his way home from visiting his wife in hospital, he had walked in on a jump-over robbery in a newsagent's on the quays, been laid-into by a junkie who stabbed him twice in the neck with a syringe. He'd been dragged into a box-room and beaten with a crowbar, so badly that they'd had to rebuild his leg. All that, and then the sleeveen Judases in head office had tried to pension him off. They'd have done it too, if it weren't for Aitken. He had threatened to go to the papers if it was ever so much as suggested again.

He stopped in his tracks. Gave a soft yelp of shock. The right front tyre of the Mini had been slashed. The word PIG was scratched into the driver's door.

Cursing under his breath, he opened the boot. He knew for a fact the spare wouldn't be in there, but he went to the trouble of looking anyway; rummaging among the bits of old newspapers, shoeboxes of battered cassettes, mud-spattered wellingtons. Anger tightened his throat muscles now. He took a few breaths and let it subside.

Though the air was bitterly cold, he was sweating hard. A thirst like a dredger formed deep in his throat. He was lusting for a drink now; things were getting urgent. He felt the familiar desire seep through his veins. Just one pint of cold lager. One glass of smoky vodka. The bar in Heuston Station would be the only place open; he knew that from the old days, knew it too well. He could be there in five minutes, drunk in thirty. Or maybe he'd be lucky today. That was always possible. Maybe one might be enough to put out the fire.

Back in the station, he asked Tynan to get his tyre changed

and somehow cover up the graffiti on the door. Then he signed out a set of keys and found an unmarked squad car out front.

Heuston was closed, despite what he had thought. He swung north up through Dorset Street, towards Drumcondra and the airport road.

The streets were wide and empty, so deserted it felt like a bomb must have gone off. Mounds of grey snow were piled up on the pavements, and on the roofs of the shuttered shops slush lay like melted plastic. When he flicked on the radio, Cliff Richard was singing 'Mistletoe and Wine'. He switched it off as fast as possible and jammed in a tape. Rory Gallagher doing a cocky Muddy Waters number.

> *The blues had a baby*
> *And they named it rock and roll.*

His battered mobile rang in his pocket.

'Martin, it's me.'

'Oh. Hi.'

The line crackled and bleeped. In the background he could hear classical music, violins and blasting trumpets and a male voice choir.

'Don't you have anything to say about last night, Martin?'

'You're the bloody psychic, Valerie. You tell me.'

'I'm not a psychic, smart-arse. As you know, I'm a medium.'

'Oh yeah, I forgot. The happy medium. How's all the girls down at the circus?'

She said nothing.

'Talked to Napoleon again lately, have you? Or was it Buddy Holly this time around?'

She gave a soft, placatory sigh. 'Jesus, Aitken . . . you're impossible sometimes.'

'But you love me to death really, right?'

'That's for me to know, isn't it? And you to find out.'

Throughout their marriage this was the mood he had loved best. The playful way she had of making up. He imagined her sitting on the floor of her living room, her knees making a sack of her nightdress. She'd be painting her toenails or plaiting

123

her hair, while she clutched the phone between her shoulder and chin. She never could talk on the phone without doing something else. For some reason he'd always found that almost painfully endearing.

'So what are you doing for Christmas, Martin?'

'Dying me balls green, white and orange.'

Off in the distance he saw a 737 banking to the left, its tail-lights flashing as it moved in from the east towards the airport.

'Are you away to Hughie's again this year?'

'Yeah, I am. Want to come with me?'

She chuckled flirtatiously, deep in her throat.

'Maybe I'll turn up and surprise you. See if you have a little Christmas present for me.'

She was teasing him now. But that was OK. That was another mood he liked.

'Yeah, why don't you come over. I'll see what I can rustle up.'

She laughed again. 'You'd run a mile.'

'I suppose old misery-guts wouldn't like it if you did.'

He heard her drag on a cigarette. 'He's a good man, Martin. You shouldn't talk about him like that.'

'Yeah, yeah. He's a dote, I know. The patron saint of the single-flush jacks.'

'I miss you, Martin. Specially at this time of year. I hope you know that.'

Disarmed by her candour, he didn't know what to say for a moment. He looked out at the messy stretch of road. A chipper here, a pub there. A revolving metal sign stood on a corner, advertising papers, bread, milk, Lotto tickets.

'I miss you too, Valerie,' he finally said.

'I still miss talking to you. Just being in your company. We used to have great old talks, didn't we?'

'Yeah, we did.'

'I often think I never really knew what happiness was until I got married.'

Now it was his turn to laugh. 'And then it was too late, right?'

124

'Come on now, don't be like that. It's Christmas.'

He stopped at the lights by Drumcondra church. A red and gold banner hung down the façade, showing the three wise men on their knees by the manger. People were going into mass in small groups. He watched an old couple shuffling up the path, the man linking the woman's arm.

'Christmas is rough, Martin, isn't it?'

'Yeah, it is.'

'Are you thinking of him today?'

'You know I am, Valerie.'

'I know you'll probably laugh. But I'm certain he's in a really special place, Martin. I feel him so close to me when I let myself.'

Ordinarily he couldn't stand it when she talked like this. But today, he thought, he could afford to let it go. What the hell, if it made her happy.

'I wouldn't laugh at that,' he said.

'I read something the other night, Martin. It said the dead are our closest companions.' The old man slithered on the ice. 'We think they're gone but really they're not. It's only when we forget them that that happens.' The old woman caught the man's arm and helped to straighten him.

'I know you'd never forget him, love. And I wouldn't either.'

'Do you ever think you'd like to get married again, Martin?'

'Why? You proposing?'

She clicked her tongue. 'Come on, Aitken, you know what I mean.'

The old couple had almost reached the church door now. He wished the lights would turn green. When they didn't, he found himself playing a mental game. If they went green before the old folks got to the door, he would drink today. And if they stayed red, he'd remain on the dry.

'I don't really think about things like that any more, Valerie. Being with someone the way it was with us.'

'You can't even say the word marriage, no?'

'Marriage isn't a word, pet. It's a whole fuckin sentence.'

She laughed. 'The girls'd love to see you, Martin. It's Christmas Day, after all.'

'I might swing by tomorrow night,' he said. 'If you promise not to set the dog on me.' But by the time he'd finished what he was saying the line had bleeped and gone dead. The old folks were still shuffling churchwards as the lights changed and he shot away.

★   ★   ★

DUBLIN AIRPORT SAYS WELCOME HOME FOR CHRISTMAS

The neon sign on the façade of the terminal had been switched off; blackbirds and gulls were perched in the curves of the letters. A low-lying mist was drifting in from the fields, wrapping the buildings in a gauzy gloom. A twenty-foot Christmas tree stood by the entrance, decorated with grinning cartoon aeroplanes.

He parked on the slip road outside the departure lounge. The longing for a drink had begun to fade but still he was feeling decidedly uneasy. It was something to do with that army of plastic snowmen that had been placed around the grounds and on either side of the approach road. They'd been arranged in various cheerful poses, some standing to attention or gamely saluting, others leaning chipperly on each other's shoulders, a couple of them climbing the side of the arrivals terminal like cat-burglars. One poor individual had had the plastic carrot that formed his nose unscrewed and somehow attached to his crotch. Others had been stabbed, maimed, hacked in two or decapitated.

Dublin airport at Christmas, Aitken thought, would be a terrible place to get the DTs.

The departures floor was surprisingly full, though most of the stores and concession stands were shuttered up. Here and there, people milled around in untidy groups, forming ragged lines at the check-in counters. Two priests were sitting in the smoking area, sharing sandwiches and laughing together. A fat breathless woman in a fur coat was trying to run for the gates, lugging her suitcase behind her. A couple of backpackers were asleep on the benches, newspapers spread over their faces.

He took the airline socks from his pocket and wondered exactly how to do this. Where did you start? What exactly did

126

you ask? Should he just forget the whole bloody thing and go home to bed?

A chubby, imperious man marched quickly past. If he wasn't in a pilot's uniform, he might have been a Roman emperor.

'Excuse me?' Aitken said. The pilot stopped, looking harassed.

'Are these yours?' Aitken said.

He looked at the socks. Then he looked at Aitken.

'Would you ever rev up and fuck off,' he snapped.

'I didn't mean yours personally,' said Aitken. 'I meant . . .'

But it was too late. The pilot was gone.

He felt his headache begin to threaten again. To make things worse, his bad leg was starting to throb. The announcement board showed flights for London, Paris, Gran Canaria, Rome. For one mad moment it occurred to him that maybe he should go somewhere. Just get on a plane and to fuck with everything. There was a flight leaving for London in just over an hour, he could get on that without any passport. What was to stop him, after all?

A small sprig of hope sprouted inside him. He could be in London in a couple of hours! What a laugh. Why not? For a gas, gas, gas. He could get the tube from Heathrow into town, maybe have a dander around for a while, turn up at his brother's house in Greenwich, just stroll right up and knock on the door. It had been over a year now since he had seen Johnny and Rachel. What a surprise they'd get.

He crossed to the Aer Lingus counter and took out his wallet. A middle-aged ground attendant was perched on a stool, talking into a wraparound phone mouthpiece, a clump of limp holly pinned to her lapel. She seemed to be flirting down the phone as she sorted through a box of cards. He gave the gentlest cough he could. She glanced forbiddingly up at him.

'Yes?'

'Merry Christmas.'

'Yes?'

'I'd like to go to London please. On the next flight.'

'It's full, sorry.'

She went back to her phone call, whispering softly, while she

127

began separating credit card slips from receipts. Her fingernails were so long that she was having trouble getting the embossing machine to work. 'I never said that,' she smilingly murmured. 'You really think you can get on my soft side, don't you?' After a moment she looked up at him again. She squinted, as though shocked to see him still there.

'What about the flight after that?' he asked.

'Everything is absolutely full today. I've nothing at all for you.'

A sudden and terrible vision of her sitting on a toilet began to form in his mind. He blinked hard and made it go away.

'I could sit in the thing. You know. Where the pilot is.'

'Do you mean the cockpit?'

'Exactly. The cockpit. I could sit in there.'

She scoffed. 'Nobody's allowed to sit in there, sir. It's against the regulations.'

'Well, yes. But you could make an exception, couldn't you? It's Christmas Day, after all.'

'It'd be against the regulations to do that, sir.'

'Well, I know. I accept that. I'm just asking you to bend them.'

She gaped at him as though he had suggested a bout of no-questions-asked sex. 'The regulations can't be "bent", sir. Now if you don't mind, I have work to do.'

'Look, I'll level with you here, love. I'm desperate. I just have to get to London, I can't take no for an answer.'

'I'm sorry. No is the only answer I have.'

'But you don't understand,' he said. 'My mother's died.'

Well, that much was true. His mother was dead. And just because it had happened eleven years previously didn't mean he wasn't still upset about it.

'I'll call you back,' she sighed, into the phone.

'Yes. My mother died. Over in London. Just like that. One minute fine and then, you know . . . Arrivederci Roma.'

'I'm sorry,' she said. 'I'll see what I can do for you.'

A few minutes passed while she tapped at her keyboard, muttering to herself, sometimes softly humming. But then she pursed her lips and shook her head.

'There's really nothing at all I can do for you. I'm sorry. You could try British Midland but I know they're packed out too.'

He pulled back inside himself like a snail. Walked away from the counter, feeling weepy with frustration.

He noticed three Virgin Cityjet flight attendants, gathered around a fountain like a trio of gazelles. What the hell. He was here now. Might as well go over and ask.

He approached the women and flashed his badge. 'Excuse me, ladies, can I have a quick word?'

One of them had a sticker on her holdall that said FRAGILE: VIRGIN. He wondered, if he asked her nicely, whether she'd let him borrow it.

'I'm on the case of a missing person. A woman of about fifty, pale colouring. Greying hair. Possibly American.'

'You're looking for her?'

'No, no, we have her.'

The attendant peered at him. 'So why are you looking for her then? If you have her?'

'No, no, you don't understand. See, I need to find out about her.'

'What do you need to find out?'

'Well, you know . . . where she's from. That kind of thing.'

'I thought you said she was from America.'

'We think she is. I'm not sure.'

'Is she in trouble or something?'

'Not trouble exactly. I just need to find out as much as I can about her. We think she might have come into the country in the last few days.'

'Well, she couldn't have come from America.'

'Why not?'

'There's a baggage handlers' strike over there. Since the day before yesterday.' She turned to one of her colleagues. 'Isn't that right, Siobhan?'

The other girl said yes, that was right. No flights had come in from America for three days now.

'So you didn't notice a woman like that? Here in the airport maybe? Acting a bit strange? Or a bit fainty?'

The attendants shrugged and said no, they hadn't. But then

it would have been difficult to notice anyone. Tens of thousands of people had come through in the last few days; it was by far the busiest time of the year. Then they said they had to go.

And now he thought he'd go himself. What the hell was he doing anyway? Why should he care about this bloody woman and her horrible green socks? In truth, he knew, he really didn't. He didn't give a fiddler's mickey whether she lived or died. Suddenly he saw himself as utterly pathetic, a man who would rather invent reasons to work on Christmas Day than just sit at home and be quietly depressed like everyone else.

His phone rang. He took it out.

'Boss, it's Hughie. Listen I'm after tryin twenty hotels at this stage and nobody's got any skulls missin. What'll I do?'

'Just leave it, Huge.'

'You sure, boss?'

'Yeah. Go on home. I'll call around a few of them myself later.'

On his way out of the terminal his limp worsened. A hot seam of pain rippled in his right thigh. He sat down on a bollard, wincing and groaning. He wondered if anyone would notice if he lit up a joint now. He looked left. He looked right.

It was then he noticed that the squad car was gone.

He stood up. That's where he'd left it. Right there. By the car-park payment machines. Right where it wasn't.

He rushed back inside and up to the Aer Lingus desk. A phone was ringing on the wall behind the counter. The attendant was sorting through a filing cabinet.

'Call security for me. Quick.'

'What's the matter?'

'Quick, love. I'm a cop. Do it, please . . .'

She grabbed a walkie-talkie from her desk and pressed some buttons.

'Con, are you there?'

'Hurry, please.'

'What's the matter?'

'Someone's after nickin my car. My police car.'

The attendant punched the buttons again. 'Con, come in, I

need you urgently.' The phone on the wall kept ringing. Cursing softly, she snatched it up with her free hand.

'Yes? Yes?' A curious look came over her face. She turned towards him.

'Is your name Martin Aitken?'

'Yeah. Why?'

She held out the phone. 'It's for you.'

'It couldn't be. Nobody knows I'm here.'

She shrugged. 'Inspector Martin Aitken? From Pearse Street station?'

He took the phone and held it to his ear. He heard an almost gentle laugh.

'Howya, Martin. Me auld segocia.'

'Who's this?'

'Nice set of wheels, man. Real classy.'

'Tell me who this is. Right now.'

'Happy fuckin Christmas, piggie. Vroom fuckin vrooom!'

The line went dead. He leaned on the counter. There was no mistaking the voice of Mousey Doogan.

MONDAY, 26 DECEMBER 1994

Chapter Ten

It was almost lunchtime on the day after Christmas and Amery's father was already quite drunk. He was sitting at the dinner table, chewing on a stick of celery and staring at his reflection in the back of a dessert spoon, in between holding forth on the subject of plastic surgery, a thing he enjoyed doing to taunt his son.

'See, Milton, the thing about liposuction is: I wouldn't mind having it all sucked out.'

'That's gratifying to know, Dad.'

'But I'd want to know who was doing the sucking.'

'Really, Dad. How utterly fascinating.'

'Yeah, really. And depending on that, I'd want to be the one suggesting where they put the incision.'

'Yes, Dad. Thank you, Dad. Your comments are really most helpful, Dad.'

Amery was helping his daughter set the table. Her new boyfriend, Everard, a militant socialist who wanted to be a rock star, was polishing the wine glasses on the hem of his grimy Alice Cooper T-shirt. Most of Everard's visible parts contained metal piercings. All morning he had clanked around the house like a medieval knight, glaring at the furniture as though he didn't like it.

A pine log fire was banked in the grate, softly spitting and crackling, throwing washes of pale red light around the room. Lengths of mistletoe and ivy were draped around the candelabra. The kitchen door opened. Amery's mother and Lee came in, pushing a hostess trolley on which sat serving plates, dishes of vegetables, a large, old-fashioned silver salver. At a signal from his grandmother, Lee whipped off the lid. A fat, juicy turkey sat underneath with strips of sizzling bacon across its back.

135

'Lord Almighty,' Amery's father sighed. 'There's an animal lived a happy life. And I'm not talking about your grandmother.'

'I sure hope everyone's hungry,' said his wife, ignoring him. 'There's enough food here to satisfy an army.'

'Man, I hate those skinny turkeys you get these days,' her husband cackled. 'They import 'em from some damn place like Uganda. They have to swim the whole way across. Surrender to the coastguard off Plymouth Rock.'

Lee and his grandmother set out the dishes, the warm, heavy smell of the meats filling the room. While Amery carved, Elizabeth circled the table, serving everyone except Everard with slices of turkey and baked ham, big dollops of thick, steaming gravy. Everard was a committed vegetarian, she explained. He piled his plate with potatoes and sweetcorn, flushing with embarrassment as she continued to talk about him.

'Matter of fact, Everard's a vegan. That's like a special kind of vegetarian.'

'Of course,' sneered Lee. 'He'd have to be special.'

'Vegans don't just not eat meat, they don't eat any animal products at all. Isn't that right, Everard?'

'Uh . . . yes, that's right, honey.'

'Not even fish?' said Amery's father.

'No, sir. Not even fish.'

'Why the hell's that, though? A fish doesn't feel pain, does it?'

'The jury's out on that one, I guess, sir. And it's more of a general principle anyway.'

'He doesn't eat anything that once had a mother,' Elizabeth explained.

'Well, that's the most insane thing I ever heard,' said her grandfather. 'When half the world is starving to death. When there's Africans who'd bludgeon us all in our beds for a hot dog.'

'Everard thinks the reason for famine is the international conspiracy of the capitalist system. Don't you, Everard?'

'Well, yes, I do. I mean, broadly speaking.'

'Oh, Christ,' said Amery's father. 'Christmas lunch with Che Guevara.'

Amery sat down at the head of the table. He replaced the

136

cover on the serving dish and looked around. 'May we all join hands for grace now, please?'

'Come on, Pops,' Elizabeth said. 'Do we have to do that?'

'Yes, we do.'

'But Everard's a Buddhist.'

'Grace is said in this house every Christmas. No matter what exotic persuasion our guests happen to be.'

'But we're a whole day late now. It's not Christmas any more, Dad.'

'Yes it is. It's still Christmas. And grace has been said in this house every Christmas that I can remember and will be as long as I have any say. So we're going to say grace and that's final. Those of us who are uninteresting enough to be part of Western civilisation, feel free to say amen at the end.'

Amery's father smirked at Everard. 'The rest of us can just rattle our chains.'

'Lord,' said Amery, 'we thank you for this food and this good fellowship. We pray for those who produced it and prepared it. We thank you that we all survived another year.' A sudden vision of Ellen's face swam before him. He wondered where she was right at that moment. Lost for words and glancing up dumbly, he noticed Everard grimly scowling. 'We pray for those in the world who are hungry today,' Amery continued. 'For all those who have nothing, when we ourselves have so much. That we might remember the blessings we have in our own lives and try to be a little more grateful sometimes. Amen!'

'Aren't you forgetting something, Milton?'

'What's that, Mother?'

'Well . . . Isn't there someone else we should be remembering today?'

'We pray,' he said quietly, 'for absent friends.'

He picked up a bottle of vintage Mouton Cadet and poured himself a glass. A long, painful silence descended over the table.

'What?' Lee said. 'We can't even say her name any more?'

'Lee,' said his grandmother gently.

Amery took his son's hand and squeezed it. 'God bless Mom, wherever she is. We send her our prayers and all our love. We hope she'll come home to us just as soon as possible.'

'Yeah, right,' said Lee sulkily.

'Amen,' said Elizabeth.

'Om,' said Everard, nervously turning his nose ring.

They pulled the crackers Amery's parents had brought and donned the paper hats they found inside. Lee had on a cardboard crown, Elizabeth a stetson, Everard a bowler. Amery's cracker turned out to contain a pirate's skull-and-crossbones cap, which he didn't want to wear at first because the skull was anatomically inaccurate.

'Milton, please. Don't be a stuffed shirt.'

'I don't find sloppiness amusing, Mother, that's all. The number of ventricular molars is completely wrong.'

His mother stared hard at the ceiling. Amery sighed and put on the hat.

'Yo ho ho,' his father said. 'Sixteen men on a dead man's chest.'

The turkey was dry. The mashed potato was lumpy. An individual with a Mao Tse Tung tattoo was having sex with his only daughter.

Still, at least it was Christmas dinner. Despite Ellen's latest disappearance, life was going on. The dishes were passed around the table again and all present helped themselves to seconds. For two or three minutes no words were exchanged, just occasional sounds of general approval, or at least of non-specific reaction. The chink of glasses, the scrape of a fork against a plate, interrupted finally by Lee giving a soft belch.

'Jesus,' said Elizabeth. 'What trailer park are *you* from?'

'The one up your ass.'

'Lee, please,' Amery sighed.

His son did not even look at him. Instead he scowled at Elizabeth and snuffled dramatically, before going back to his meal, pushing the peas into his mouth with the end of his knife, breaking up a bread roll and mopping disconsolately at the gravy.

Elizabeth shot him another look. 'Would you like that in a dog bowl, Lee? That way you could just stick your head into it.'

'Better than some of the places you stick yours, butt rash.'

She put down her cutlery. 'You think you're all that? Huh?'
He ignored her.

'Yeah?' She poked him. 'Because you're not all that, Lee, let me tell you.'

'Whatever,' he said.

'You're not.' She prodded again.

'Touch me again, you're gonna die.'

'Come on then,' she said. 'Bring it on, wuss.'

'Oh, scare me, bitch. I'm shaking here.'

'Please,' said Amery, more sharply. 'Could we all try to behave in a reasonably civilised manner for just this one day at least?'

'Is he allowed to speak to me like that, Dad?'

Lee pulled a sneering face, repeating her words in a pleading mock falsetto.

Amery looked across at his son. Lee was pushing his food around with his cutlery. He looked so angry and knotted up. With his eyes Amery made a gesture of appeal to his daughter. She glanced away towards the window and folded her arms. Amery's mother suddenly beamed

'So tell me, Everard, what's this band of yours called?'

'The Multiple Orgasms, Mrs Amery.'

Amery's father gave a choking splutter.

'Oh my,' said his mother, 'that's a striking name.'

Everard dabbed at his lips with his napkin. 'Yes, ma'am. Thank you. We were gonna call ourselves Barking Pope and the Cajun Cardinals but we thought it might be a little too bourgeois.'

'I see,' she said, smiling uncertainly, her fingers forcing apart the wishbone. 'And you play the guitar, do you?'

'Electric guitar and chainsaw, yes, ma'am.'

'Oh. How nice.'

'Everard's the frontman, Grandma,' Elizabeth said. 'He plays guitar, writes the lyrics. He even drives the van.'

'My gosh,' said Amery's mother. 'Good for you, dear. You're the regular Renaissance man, right?'

'I guess so, ma'am,' said Everard, his pierced face turning claret with mortification.

Silence fell on the room again. Lee began slowly sucking through his straw, making a gurgling sound in the bottom of his glass. When nobody reacted, he threw back his head, making louder gargling noises as he drained his drink.

'Jesus Christ,' Elizabeth sighed.

'What? What I do now?'

'You're such a child sometimes. You know that?'

'Oh right. And you're such an adult.'

A malicious grin came over her face. She turned to Everard but kept her eyes on her brother. 'Lee was abducted by aliens. Weren't you, Lee?'

'Shut up, ho-ass.'

'Yes. Two years ago a spaceship landed on the ball field at school and aliens took him away for a few hours. Didn't they, Lee?'

'I never said it happened at the ball field.'

'That's what he wrote in his sad little diary, which he very intelligently left lying around for me to read. They took him up to the mother ship, isn't that right, kiddo? Because you're so incredibly special and wonderful?'

'Eat my shorts,' said Lee.

'And they did all these big experiments on him. Didn't they, Superboy? And then they beamed him all the way back down here to Scarsdale to save the world.'

'I wish they hadn't bothered,' Lee said. 'Not back to this excuse for a family.'

Nobody said anything. It was almost as though he had stood up and overturned the table. Everard was staring hard at his plate. Amery's parents' heads were bowed low. He saw that his daughter was looking at him with something like sympathy. Lee took a bottle of Pepsi and silently poured himself another glass.

'Well, honey,' Everard said, gently, 'a lot of people do believe in aliens.'

She laughed in disbelief. 'Are you taking his side? Against me?'

'I'm not taking anybody's side exactly . . . I'm just saying, a lot of people do claim to have seen aliens.'

140

'Now that's very true,' said Amery's mother, brightly. 'Jimmy Carter saw one.' She turned to her husband. 'Do you remember that, dear?'

'Jimmy Carter had several in his administration,' said Amery's father.

His wife shot him a cold look. He lifted the lid off the salver and took another forkful of meat. Placed it on his plate and cleared his throat.

'And I believe you have your peter pierced, Everard? Is that right?'

Lee tittered so hard into his Pepsi that it foamed up his nostrils and made him sneeze. Everard glanced at Elizabeth. To Amery's horror, they exchanged warm, knowing grins, as though some eccentric but essentially lovable relative had just been mentioned.

'As a matter of fact, yes I do, Mr Amery, sir.'

'My God. Didn't that hurt some?'

'Well . . . For a while, it did, sir. Till the scar tissue healed up.'

'And the pustules,' Elizabeth said.

'Yeah, those too,' Everard agreed. 'But they give you like an ointment to put on those.'

'You have to rub it in like real carefully,' Elizabeth said, 'in case you tear the suturing. Don't you, babe?'

'Absolutely. Real carefully. That stitching is kinda delicate down there.'

He and Elizabeth giggled at each other.

'Somebody pass me a sick-bag,' muttered Lee.

'Just take a look at yourself in the mirror, pimple boy,' said Elizabeth.

Amery's mother pulled a face. 'But why would you do something like that to yourself, dear? Go about mutilating yourself in that fashion.'

'I don't really see it that way, ma'am. I guess I wanted to make a statement.'

'A statement?'

'Yes, ma'am. A political statement.'

'Jesus Christ Almighty,' said Amery's father. 'You have to

have your weenie skewered to make a statement? You ever hear of a press release, son?'

'What's it look like?' Lee said suddenly.

'Well,' said Everard, 'I could show you later if you like.'

'Cool,' said Lee. 'Is it, like, right through the glans or what?'

Everard laughed. 'No, it isn't.'

'Aw, man. Not through the *eye*?'

'God Almighty,' said Amery now. 'Do we have to be having this particular conversation at the dinner table?'

His mother turned and regarded him admonishingly. 'There is nothing wrong with the human body, Milton. You'd think as a doctor you'd know that.'

'I'm not saying there is, Mother. But surely there's a time and a place.'

'Milton hath spoken,' Lee said. 'Thus spake the Lord on high.'

The fire spat and cracked in the grate. A rush of charged air filled the room. Amery saw that his parents were staring at him. Elizabeth asked if anyone wanted more wine.

'Lee,' said Amery. 'I know you're upset right now. But I'd rather you didn't speak to me in that offensive manner.'

His son said nothing.

'Do you hear me, Lee?'

'Whatever,' he shrugged.

'Now, I think we're all a little tired today,' said Amery's mother. 'And when we're tired we can all be antsy.'

'I don't consider the word "whatever" an answer, Lee.'

'Whatever.'

'If you speak to me in that fashion again I'll have to ask you to leave the company.'

Lee laughed snidely. 'Is that right?'

'Yes, it is.'

He looked up at his father. 'Fuck you, Milton,' he said.

Before Amery knew what he was doing, he had lunged across the table and slapped his son across the face, so hard that he almost knocked him off the chair.

'Milton!' his mother shouted.

Lee touched his cheek, as though he was surprised he had one. He smiled through the tears of shock that were already moistening his eyes. 'Good one, Dad,' he said.

'Lee . . .'

He stood up and walked quietly from the room.

For a moment they sat at the table without moving. They heard his heavy metal music come on upstairs. Amery picked up his cutlery and went back to his food. His hands were trembling as he poured a glass of Evian.

'Hey, maybe I should leave,' Everard muttered to Elizabeth.

'Nobody's going to leave until dinner is finished,' Amery snapped.

'I just think it might be better, sir.'

'Nobody's going to leave this table and ever be welcome in this house again. You understand me?'

Everard sighed and peered into his glass. They ate on in silence for a while longer. From upstairs, the raucous music got louder, and then stopped. Amery saw his father push his plate away and light a cigar. His mother picked up a lettuce leaf and began to gently tear it.

'Well,' Amery said. 'I believe this was the nicest Christmas lunch I've ever had.'

Nobody said anything. He said again:

'Very tasty, Mother. Thank you for preparing it.'

Still nobody spoke. He glanced at his father, who was chewing on the cigar as he stared hard into the fire. He looked around at the others then, whose faces were bent towards their plates.

'Would anyone like a little more?' he asked.

Elizabeth threw down her knife and fork. Everard put his arm around her shoulder. Amery's mother nodded in silence and began to clear away the dishes.

After lunch, Amery and his father took the dog for a walk. They strolled out past the edge of the town, past the furniture stores and car showrooms, the pizza restaurants and supermarkets, until the pavement gave way to a muddy track with high hedges on each side, and their feet were crunching through frozen puddles.

There were hardly any houses now. Just pale green and dark green meadows, laid out in neat squares, receding up towards the hills. Away in the distance they could see Long Island Sound, a line of sport-fishing boats leaving Mamaroneck harbour. They trudged on further, past a scarecrow in a long black coat and a George Bush facemask. The dog tore into a field, howling at something.

'You've really no idea why she went this time?'

'I don't know, Dad. I really don't.'

His father stopped. His pink-veined eyes seemed to be scanning the landscape. 'You fool around on her a little bit, son?'

'No, Dad. Of course not.'

'You sure?'

'Course I'm sure. My God, I'd never do that.'

'Son, it's none of my business. But your mother hears things. You know she and Ellen are close.'

'What kind of things would those be?'

'Look . . . Every marriage has good years and bad years, son. But that doesn't matter, not in the end. If there's love there, there can be forgiveness too.'

'I'm sure there can. But I'm really not following this.'

His father closed his eyes for what seemed like a long time. When he opened them again he was looking in a different direction.

'I once knew this girl when we lived in Ohio. Big happy girl, she was, cocktail waitress in a Holiday Inn up there in Columbus.' He turned to Amery. 'Well, we used to go out sometimes, have a few laughs, a few drinks. And I'd be lying if I said nothing ever happened there. But I didn't feel too big about it later, son. Even though I had my deeper feelings for this person. But I had a mortgage and kids and a dog too. With your mother, I had a whole life.'

'Exactly why are you telling me this, Dad?'

His father regarded him closely. 'I don't really know. I guess I figured you needed to hear it.'

'Why?'

'What I'm saying is your mother never knew. I saw to that. Even after I ended it. And when you've got a mortgage and

144

kids and a dog, well, that's the way it has to be. Otherwise you're breaking somebody's heart. And honestly, son, it's just not worth it.'

'Dad, I'm sorry. I simply don't understand you when you're being gnomic.'

His father pulled a face. 'What's that mean? Is that like a gnome?'

The dog appeared through a gap in the hedge with a dead rat in its mouth. It ran to Amery's father and cheerfully dropped the bloodied pulp at his feet.

'Hey, Milton,' his father chuckled, toeing the rat into the ditch. 'Say hello to our second cousin.'

He walked off down the track, calling out to the dog, picking up a stick to throw for it. Amery followed, feeling heavy and full, wishing he hadn't eaten so much. He would have to take a nap later; something he hated to do, even at Christmas. Waking up twice on the same day made him feel depressed, as though he was losing control of his life.

He found himself remembering the first day he had met Cathy. Late one afternoon, some two years ago now, he had been about to leave the office when Violet had said there was a last-minute patient, a young woman who claimed to be a friend of his family. Impatient to leave, he had asked who she was. Her name was Catherine Kenneally; she was from White Plains, a former student of Mrs Amery. She had sometimes babysat Lee, apparently. Amery had no recollection of ever having met her, but he agreed reluctantly to see her anyway.

An alert-looking girl in a lumberjack shirt and black denim jeans strolled into his office as though she owned it. She shook his hand, and sat down.

'What can we do for you today?' he had asked.

'Guess,' she laughed.

'Guess?'

'Yeah. See if you can guess.'

'Well, OK.' He had blushed. 'Would you mind standing up for me?'

She stood, put her arms out; began to turn in a slow graceful circle.

'You look just perfect to me, Catherine.'

'You need to look just a little harder, Doctor Amery.'

He smiled. 'Oh, do call me Milton, for heaven's sakes. Why, after all, we're practically old friends.'

'Milton Amery. Cool name.'

'Yes, I'm named for the famous Milton.'

'Milton who?'

'Well . . . John Milton, the renowned English poet. It's a family tradition. I have brothers called Browning, Wyatt, Wordsworth and Chaucer.'

'Wild,' she said.

'Indeed. Had my parents thought of the king of the dandies, no doubt he would also have been included.'

She laughed a little uncertainly at this point.

'I always tell my sister she got off remarkably lightly.'

'Why's that, Milton?'

'She's called Shelley. Now, tell me . . . is it something in the upper body area?'

'Yes, Milton,' she said. 'It's my breasts.'

'OK.' He nodded. 'What about them?'

'It's a little embarrassing. But my boyfriend thinks they're too big.'

'Well . . . let's take a little look-see, shall we?'

Milton Amery often thought that when he was dying, and the major events of his life were being played back before him, prominent among them would be the moment when seventeen-year-old Cathy Kenneally had pulled her red and black lumberjack shirt out of her jeans, opened the buttons, unclipped her bra, and peered up at him with a smile of orthodontic perfection.

'Oh,' she'd said. 'Such warm hands.'

And that was the day it had all begun.

'Guess,' she had said. That was what started it. A single monosyllabic invitation. And now he made it a point to tell all his patients he could guess what was wrong with them. They seemed to go crazy for that. He would look them over, put on an expression of scrupulous intensity; write something surreptitious on his notepad, wait for several long dramatic moments before announcing his conclusion. Breasts, chin, thighs, nose, buttocks, eyelids, whatever. And how were they to know he cheated? Well, naturally he would check their request forms in Violet's office before they came in. But what the hell. Give 'em the old razzle-dazzle; let them see you in a mysterious light. So what if you threw in a little smoke and mirrors? It wasn't as if you hadn't passed your exams, after all. It was just a little extra reassurance, compelling proof of your uncanny expertise.

He caught up with his father, who was leaning on a stile.

'Listen, Milton.' He sighed and patted his pockets, as though he were looking for something. 'I have something I need to tell you about Lee.'

'What's that?'

His father frowned and shook his head. 'Well . . . I was sworn to secrecy by your mother, but I think I should tell you anyway. Seems to me there's too many damn secrets in this family sometimes. It's like living with the CIA.'

'So go on.'

'Look, son . . . He told your mother that Ellen called him the other day.'

'He *what*?'

'Yeah. Apparently she called the house the day before yesterday.'

'Well . . . what did she say? Do you know? Did she say where she was, Dad?'

'She didn't say that, no . . .'

'So . . .'

'I'm telling you, for God's sakes . . . Look, as far as I know, she said she was fine. And something about visiting Europe next year. Going to Paris to see EuroDisney, you and Lee and Elizabeth together. I mean it didn't sound like she wasn't coming back. It was just like a thirty-second conversation.'

'Jesus Christ. Why didn't he tell me that, Dad?'

'I really don't know, son. You better ask him that yourself.'

Chapter Eleven

Back at the house, Amery's mother was cleaning the kitchen. The dishwasher had broken down but she seemed quite happy, up to her arms in suds and water, while Everard stood beside her doing the drying and intermittently sipping from a can of alcohol-free beer.

'The thing about it, Mrs Amery, is that it gives the woman more sexual pleasure.'

'Does it really?'

He nodded seriously. 'Oh yeah, it does. A Prince Albert bar, it's called. It's named after the British royal family.'

'I see, Everard. How nice that you take an interest in history.'

'Yes, ma'am. Some of the other guys in the band have it too. And all of us have our nipples pierced.'

'Do you really?'

'Sure do.' He beamed. 'We got a group discount on that. Eight nipples for the price of seven.'

'Well, how marvellous.' She handed him a dish. 'You know, I often wished Milton junior would take to rock and roll. But he was such a sober child. Kind of strait-laced. It was Beethoven this, Shostakovich that. His daddy bought him a Beatles wig in London once and when poor Milton junior saw it, he burst into tears like you never saw.' She turned and saw them. 'Oh. There you are, dear.'

Amery watched as his parents embraced.

'Wish I still had me that wig now,' his father chuckled. 'I could certainly use it these days.'

'Should I call you Ringo?' said Amery's mother, patting her husband's scalp.

'Nah.' He did a Groucho-style waggle of his cigar. 'You can just call me rich.'

She scowled mockingly. 'I sure know what I want to call you sometimes. But I wouldn't repeat it or I'd get me in trouble.'

He threw back his head and laughed out loud. 'Say, you know how I met this beautiful woman here, Everard?'

'No, sir.'

'Well, I was sitting at the bar in the Daytona Hotel in Columbus, Ohio, with my brother Coleridge and cousin Spenser and Uncle Omar Khayyám. She was waiting for a date in the lobby, but she comes in and wants to know if I got the time. So I ask her what did Big Ben say to the leaning tower of Pisa? And she doesn't know. So I say, I got the time, baby, if you got the inclination. She says to me, you're a pretty short guy, aren't you? For such a comedian. And I say I'm one hell of a lot taller when I'm sitting on my wallet.'

'And that was that,' said Amery's mother. 'I dated him out of pity.'

'Pity and sex, honey.'

'But mainly pity.'

'And there was no cock-piercing in my day, son, I can tell you that much for nothing.'

Everard laughed. 'Well, it's never too late, sir. I can give you some numbers.'

'I hate to interrupt this lively discussion,' Amery said. 'But did anyone call when we were out?'

He watched the laughter die in his mother's eyes. It made him think of a fading coal. 'I probably would have mentioned if someone had called, Milton.'

He went to the bathroom and washed his hands. Back in the lounge, Elizabeth and Everard were making goo-goo faces across the carcass of the turkey. Lee was playing the computer game his grandparents had given him for Christmas. In the bay window, they were settling down to sherry and a game of cards.

Amery went to his son. 'You OK, Lee?'

He nodded but kept his eyes on what he was doing. The screen showed a landscape of fields and lakes seen from above.

'Hey,' said Amery, 'what's your new game do?'

'It isn't a game.'

149

'Oh. OK. So what's it do?'

'It's a flight simulator programme. New York to Aspen, Colorado.'

'Oh yeah? That's interesting.'

Amery saw that his father was looking at him now. 'Lee mentioned to us that he liked stuff like that.'

'Is that right, son?'

Lee said nothing.

'He's got London to Athens,' said Amery's father. 'Cairo to Moscow. Los Angeles to Mexico City. Isn't that right, Lee?'

'Yeah,' Lee said.

'Hey, I didn't know you were interested in aviation, son.'

'I know you didn't.'

'Say, Lee,' said Amery's father. 'You know your daddy was interested in that too? When he was your age? He had model planes and all kinds of stuff. He even used to make his own.'

Lee remained silent, his eyes locked on the screen.

'Might I have a try, son? That looks like fun.'

Lee said nothing, just tapped efficiently at the controls. On the screen, the fields began to loom up close and fast. Details of trees and buildings came into view. A whining engine sound started coming from the speakers. 'Mayday, mayday,' came an electronic male voice, followed moments later by a dull boom, and a graphic of a mushroom cloud blossoming over a city's black skyline.

'Guess I just suicide-bombed,' Lee said. He turned and reached for another game.

'Lee,' said Amery. 'I need to ask you something.'

Amery caught his father's eye. His father shook his head in warning.

'Lee, did Mom call you the other day?'

His son shrugged. On the screen a skyscraper burst into flames, over a soundtrack of bloodcurdling screeches.

'Did she call you, Lee?'

'Yeah.'

Everard looked across at them. Elizabeth stood up.

'So did she say where she was, son?'

'Uh-uh.'

150

'Was she OK?'

'I guess.'

Amery looked at his mother now. She raised her hands in an imploring gesture and shook her head.

'You know your dad loves you, son? Right?'

Lee said nothing. He slotted the new game into the disc drive.

'And I'm sorry I hit you, Lee. I shouldn't have done that. I'm ashamed to say I lost control of my feelings.'

He put his hand on Lee's shoulder. His son gently shrugged it away and tugged a set of headphones over his ears.

Out in the hall, the wind was blowing under the door. He found the draught-excluder and toed it into place. The cat slunk sleekly in through the flap, curling its tail into a question mark.

'Well, Puccini,' Amery said. 'You still love your daddy, don't you?'

He lifted the receiver, checked that the line was working. Tried the farmhouse up at Saranac Lake. There was no answer, the line just kept on ringing. He pictured her sitting on the bottom step in the hall and letting it ring to spite him. She could be stubborn sometimes; there was no denying it.

Suddenly it occurred to him to try calling some of the neighbours up there. There was Eliot Morris – or was it Morris Eliot? – that divorce lawyer from Philadelphia, who came up every Christmas with his third wife and their kids; he could ask him to stop by and see if she was all right. Surely a man like that could be trusted to be discreet. He took out the spiral binder in which Ellen kept telephone numbers. The book was open already, at Dick Spiggot's address. That was odd. He wondered what it meant. Why on earth would she be calling Spiggot?

He felt a cold sensation lick down his spine. Had his crazy suspicion been true after all? She hadn't run off with that vulgar creep? Surely to God, that wasn't possible. Ellen and Spiggot locked in frenzied, thrashing bliss. The cat looked up at him and yawned.

Finger trembling slightly, he dialled the number. It rang three times, an answering machine clicked on.

'Greetings, friend, you've reached Richard Milhous Spiggot. Speak at the beep or for ever hold thy peace.'

'Dick . . . Hello. It's Milton Amery here, calling from Scarsdale. How are you? I was just wondering if . . .'

There was a merry and possibly inebriated laugh as the phone was picked up. 'Milton, old sport, how's your ass for love bites?'

'Why, Dick . . . You're there after all.'

'Naw, I'm not here, I'm in Nassau.'

'Bahamas Nassau?'

'No, New Jersey Nassau. Of course Bahamas Nassau, you dope. I get the calls punched through.'

'Oh . . . OK. So how are you, Dick?'

'Just tubular, buddy. How's yourself?'

'Fine. Yes. And how's Miriam?'

'Fuck Miriam, it's Consuela now. But yeah, she's fine. Came down here with me for the surfing.'

A frighteningly high-pitched laugh like a female impersonator's rang out in the background. Spiggot began to bark with mirth.

'Hey, Milton. Consuela says we're giving a new meaning to the phrase bed and board.'

Listening to his braying cackle now, Amery felt something close to relief. How could he have thought Spiggot was any kind of threat? The man was an imbecile, pure and simple. In the Darwinian league table, Ellen was a thoroughbred. Whereas Spiggot, at best, was some kind of donkey.

'So, Milton, old buddy. How the hell are you?'

'Oh, fine, Dick, fine. Just enjoying the holiday.'

'Christmas comes but once a year. Bit like you and me, Milton, huh? At our age. Huh? HA HA HA HA.'

His laugh was like a burst of machine-gun fire.

'Still quite the wag, eh, Dick?' Amery was looking forward to a little joust now. It wouldn't solve too many problems, but it might make him feel a bit better.

'Oh, you know me, Milt, old sport. I like to pull people's wires a little, that's all. Now. That gorgeous woman you're married to OK, is she?'

'Yes, Dick, she's very well.'

'She get home OK?'

Amery paused. 'How do you mean?'

'I'm asking if she got home, Milton. What's that, a trick question?'

'From where?'

'Jesus Christ, from here, you gimp. Where do you think?'

'From the Bahamas?'

'Yeah, from my party. Wednesday night.' He chuckled. 'Milton, are you drunk or something? You do know she flew down here for the night on Wednesday, right?'

A laugh that sounded wild and unhinged forced its way up Amery's throat. 'Of course I know.'

'Yeah. Shame you couldn't make it yourself, buddy. But Ellen explained you were all tied up. I said I wouldn't mind tying you up myself. And feeding you to the barracudas. HA HA HA HA.'

What the hell was the fool blathering about? Ellen had gone to the *Bahamas* last week? 'Yes. I was sorry not to make it, Dick.'

'It was fun, you would have loved it. You're working too hard, buddy, you really are. You want to apply the old brakes some time.'

Amery's heart was pumping now. He sank to the floor, feeling weak and jittery. A strangely intense thirst formed in his throat.

'Hey,' said Spiggot. 'Everything *is* OK, Milton, is it?'

'Of course, Dick. Why wouldn't it be?'

'I dunno. You sound a little . . . anxious or something.'

'Actually, Dick . . .' he began again, feeling like a man plunging into the sea and not knowing just where he'd come up, 'actually, Dick, the plain fact is, we're having a little domestic crisis here.'

'Oh?'

'It's nothing serious, you understand.' He closed his eyes and let the words come. 'But Ellen left her address book on the plane back home. From your party.'

'Shit.'

'Yes. Exactly, Dick. So you wouldn't know what exact time her flight back to New York left Thursday? She just can't seem to remember and we're trying to trace the flight number here.'

'Jeez, Milton, I don't know. She was gone by the time I got up. I just assumed she'd gotten a cab to the airport.'

'Yes, she did.'

'Matter of fact, we were surprised about that.'

'You were?'

'Well, yeah. Just this airport strike you guys have up there, Milton. I thought the flights to the States were affected.'

'Yes.'

'Because you know I had to have my guests flown down myself from La Guardia?'

'You did?'

'Yeah. They came down in my Lear.'

'Oh . . . Yes. Of course.'

'And she didn't wait for the flight back next day. That surprised me. But all's well that ends well, I guess.'

'Yes. Absolutely. All's well that ends well.'

'Sorry I can't help, buddy, about the flight number. But be sure and give her our love, Milton, OK? And come down here and see us yourself some time. I'd give a lot to see your wasp ass in a wetsuit.'

And with a final grunt of porcine laughter, Spiggot was gone.

The cat was staring at him from the bottom stair. It wrapped its tail around the banister and purred. A tumbling sensation swept across Amery's mind. Once, perhaps ten years ago, while watching a cartoon with Lee, he had seen a cross-section of Bugs Bunny's head, filled with revolving clockwork cogs. For some reason, he had a vivid flash of that now. But the cogs were in his own head this time, and spinning so hard they were leaking smoke. *What the hell had Ellen done?* Where had she gone? Was she still in the Bahamas? Could it be possible that Spiggot was lying, that she was still there, by his pool? Were the two of them laughing, sharing pina coladas? Was he smearing suntan lotion across her abdomen?

He got to his feet and looked in the mirror over the hall stand.

154

Was there someone – anyone – he could talk to about this? His fingers began idling through the telephone book, but he didn't know who half these people were. More of her damn friends from the Bolshevik bookstore, he supposed. Who *were* these people who filled her life?

He went down the hall and into her study. It smelt of her perfume and her damned cigarettes. On the walls were posters of Nicaragua, South Africa, Cuba. A print of the map of Ireland wrapped in chains, with the slogan BRITS OUT stamped across it. A signed photograph of Nelson Mandela wearing one of his colourful shirts.

The drawers of her desk were locked. There was a notebook on the blotter and he opened that. Her spidery scrawl filled the pages. John Keats. The Sympathetic Imagination. Notes for one of her classes, he assumed.

He looked at the bookshelves, full of hardback novels. What on earth did she see in them? All these stories of people who never lived, and who wouldn't have mattered much even if they had. It was utterly mysterious to him. How could you get yourself excited about events that had merely been imagined when the real world was waiting to be swung by the tail? To live just your own life was magical enough. What, exactly, was the point of art?

Back when he was a young medical student, their disagreements on the subject had been flirtatious and amused. He remembered a playful quarrel that had happened one night in a coffee-house on Prince Street. Ellen had been wearing hipster jeans, a short red T-shirt that showed her bare midriff; it was the early phase of their courtship when they'd hardly been able to keep their hands off each other. A novel never saved anyone's life, he'd said. 'That's where you're wrong, Doctor,' she'd replied, her eyes flashing, her hand reaching under the table and coming to rest on his thigh.

He had thought that after they married she would come to see things his way. But that had never happened. If anything, she had become ever more dreamy, while he had seen less to value in art with each year that had passed. Once they had had a quarrel because she had wanted to offer the attic of the Saranac

Lake house to some third-rate Irish poet she had met on one of her trips. Amery had resisted at first, but she had pleaded, as though installing a sonneteer in the loft would somehow bring them luck. He couldn't even remember the fellow's name now, but it was Gaelic; it had a lot of strangled vowels and spitting sounds in it. He'd turned out to be a dark-eyed, lugubrious cove with a personal hygiene problem that wasn't much helped by his wearing the same thick black polo neck all the way through July. What a fraud. What a phoney. Skulking around the farm like a manic depressive and claiming that he could tell each of the seventy sheep on the hillside apart. That was the kind of thing that would really impress Ellen.

He looked at the books again. For God's sake. Ten thousand dollars' worth of books and they weren't even alphabetised. How could you reason with someone like that?

His fingers idly scanned the shelves; he took down a thin battered volume of Yeats's love poetry he had bought for her years earlier in a SoHo bookstore. He recalled that day very clearly, a bright hot afternoon in late August, the sunlight slanting in from Spring Street through the dusty window, the old-fashioned fan perched on a ragged pile of remaindered detective novels.

The inscription on the flyleaf caught his eye. *To my darling wife, Ellen. One man loves the pilgrim soul in you.* He couldn't remember having written that, but there it was, it was definitely his handwriting. Many of the pages were dog-eared and bent; one or two had whole stanzas underlined in red ink.

It was the cheapest gift he had ever given her, but the only one that had seemed to mean anything at all. She'd taken it from him, eyes moist with tears of happiness. They had made passionate love that night. He thought it might be the night that Lee had been conceived.

In the back pages of the book he found a photograph, creased four ways and corrugated with age. It showed the sun sinking into an oxbow lake; black ragged mountains looming in the background, long streaks of cumulus cloud.

He turned it over. One word was written on the back, in a small unruly hand that was not his wife's.

Inishowen.

As if alerted by some otherworldly message, he turned towards the door. His daughter was standing in the frame, warm pink light behind her.

'Hi, Popsicle.'

It shocked him how like her mother she was. The same half-closed eyes, the same long straight back, lending her an air of haughty complacency. No doubt about it, she had grown into a beautiful woman. Though to be absolutely frank, he thought she could use a little work on her nose.

'Hi, honey. How are you doing?'

'OK, I guess. Have you seen Everard?'

'I thought I heard him clank by a few minutes ago. He was being sucked towards magnetic north.'

'Very funny. What you up to, anyway?'

He wondered how long she had been watching him. 'Nothing much, just looking around.'

She pushed her hair out of her eyes. 'Checking out Mom's books?'

'My enemies,' he said, waving towards the shelves, and immediately wondering why he had said that. Lately he had been doing this a lot, coming out with words that were close to what he meant, but not what he meant quite precisely enough: he guessed it was something to do with getting older. All this stress didn't help either.

He held out the photograph. 'You know where this is?'

She glanced at it quickly, then shook her head.

'It's the damnedest thing,' he said, groping towards acknowledgement. 'All this about your mother. It must be very upsetting for you. I can really imagine that.'

'It'll be OK,' she said. 'It's good Grandma and Grandad are here.'

'Your mother's . . . such a complicated person. When I was younger, I thought that would go away in time. But it didn't. She has her own way of looking at things, that's all. But I guess you know that much already.'

She shrugged. 'Men are from Mars, women are from Venus.'

'How do you mean?'

She laughed softly. 'It's the title of a book, Pops.'

'Ah.' He scowled. 'I guess your old dad should read that particular classic of contemporary literature, huh?'

She shrugged. 'That's a whole nother story.'

She approached the desk. Sifted half-heartedly through some papers in the out-tray, picked one up and looked at it briefly.

'Does your mother ever confide in you, Elizabeth? About her and me? . . . May I ask you that?'

She turned away from him. 'Not really.'

'OK.'

She took a drawing pin from the pen tray and pushed it into the mouse mat.

'I hope you don't mind me asking you, honey. I'm just trying to get a handle on all this, I guess.'

She nodded. 'She did tell me once you were the great love of her life. That she was lucky to marry you.'

'She said that?'

'Yeah. She said she was lucky to marry the love of her life. That hardly anyone gets to do that. That I should wait to do that too.'

'Your mother's a very romantic person,' he said.

She picked up an ivory letter opener and turned it around a few times.

'So Dad. I got a favour to ask.'

'You got?' He smiled. 'What does that mean?'

'I'm sorry. I have. I *have* a favour.'

'So ask.'

'Well, it's just . . . can Everard stay tonight?'

He looked at the backs of his hands. 'We've talked about this before, Elizabeth.'

'Come on, Dad. It's Christmas.'

'You know how your mother and I feel about this.'

'Mom's not here, Dad. Or hadn't you noticed?'

He was taken aback by the sudden sharpness.

'I had noticed, yes. But thank you for pointing it out to me.'

She sighed. 'OK, I'm sorry. I shouldn't have said that.'

'It's all right.'

'No, that was a really bitchy thing to say. I'm sorry.'

He went to her now and put his hands on her shoulders.

'Baby, I've nothing against Everard,' he said. 'But you know how we feel on that subject. When you're a little older, we can talk about it. You and me and Mom together. OK?'

'Dad, I'm eighteen. We want to be together. That can happen here or someplace else.'

'Elizabeth, I don't care to know about that.'

'Jesus, Dad, what planet are you on?'

'What do you mean?'

'You really think we don't sleep together?'

He pushed her away, his face hot with anger. 'I don't care to know the details of that. Do you hear? Don't you think I have enough on my mind just now without my daughter acting like some kind of . . . cocktail waitress?'

She shot him a glare of fury and hurt.

'Maybe you'd rather we did it in hotel rooms. Follow the old family tradition.'

'What on earth are you talking about, Elizabeth?'

She scoffed. 'I guess Little Miss Bigtits screwed your brains right out, Dad.'

'What? . . . How dare you speak to me like that?'

'It's no wonder Mom left you, Milton. I really don't blame her one little bit.'

And out she went, slamming the door behind her, leaving him alone with the wall of books.

Chapter Twelve

On all of her many trips to Dublin, Ellen Donnelly had never tried Hannigan's Quayside Hotel.

She had noticed it one sticky humid afternoon, possibly, she now thought, when she'd accompanied that freshman tour from the University of Michigan, back in the hot summer of 1991. ('The thing I like about poetry,' one of the students had happily confided that day, 'is you can read a whole poem while you're taking a shit.')

Looking at it now she was not so sure she should try it. The façade was not at all impressive at this time of evening, even with its strings of red and blue Christmas lights. She crossed quickly from the bus stop through the damp cold air that smelt of peat and hops from the brewery. The place had seen better days; it showed severe signs of wear and tear. The whole building appeared exhausted. In fact, it looked as though it was about to fall down into the street. But fair is fair, she told herself; perhaps these things could be said with some justification about herself. She had mixed feelings. But at least she had those. Mixed feelings were better than none at all.

As soon as she pushed through the revolving door she knew she had been right to come after all. Even here, in the small, crumbling lobby so redolent of decay, she felt a surge of the blissful thrill to which she had looked forward for many weeks now. It gripped her heart. It curled around her spine.

She was alone in Dublin once again. There was no place else she would rather be now.

Queuing at the counter and asking for a room made her feel illicit and furtive; especially when the receptionist informed her that there was only a king-size double left. Her face grew suddenly and terrifically hot. She turned away from the counter towards the breeze from the door, only to find a grinning young man behind her with crazy hair and twisted teeth and an ugly yellow T-shirt that said **U2 LOVE YOU TOO** in lurid pink letters. He winked at her, she was sure of it. Or was he winking at the receptionist? Well, perhaps he was winking because there was something wrong with him; he looked as though there might well be. For a moment she had the idea that he was some kind of lunatic recently released on one of those Care In The Community schemes. People nowadays had all sorts of ideas about lunatics and what to do with them. Especially in Dublin. Here in Dublin, they were fascinated by lunacy, all the way back to the time of Swift. In any case, she was sure she was blushing even more deeply as she turned back and told the girl that the king-size double would be just fine.

'Grand, so,' said the receptionist, in a chirpy voice. 'Room ten. First floor. Lift over there. Can we help you with your luggage at all?'

'Oh, no, thank you. I have no luggage. I mean it's coming later. From the airport.'

The strange grinning man followed her to the lift and got in. His mad, gelled hair looked like a mound of cold tagliatelle. The doors closed. He began humming to himself. He was clearly looking for attention, she thought.

She turned away and pretended to ignore him. In the mirror she gazed at her reflection and thought herself – yes, she had to admit it – still attractive. Maybe her husband was not just being polite and salving his conscience when he told her she was beautiful. His guilt for what he was secretly doing would be appalling, she knew that much. Milton was not a bad man at heart, not nearly so bad as he wished to be. He was simply the kind of man who finds his own innate decency an embarrassment. Something in him needed to be more of a bastard than he was, she had long since given up trying to find out why. She went closer to the mirror, licked her finger; smoothed her right eyebrow.

The lift stopped at the first floor. To her dismay, her companion stepped out. She was in two minds about whether to follow, but after a moment she did. *Be assertive, Ellen,* she could hear her self-defence teacher bark. *Head up, chest out, walk like you own the street.* The young man didn't look as though he would do her any harm. The fact that he was whistling she found reassuring. Lunatics of the dangerous variety didn't whistle, she told herself. Charles Manson, for example, it was pretty hard to imagine whistling.

Alone in her room, she felt giddy with anticipation. Thinking about what might be going on all around her was thrilling, in the rooms above and below and on either side. She wished the walls were transparent. She knew it was ridiculous, quite irrational, but she felt the excitement of being alone in a new hotel room fizzle inside her, like champagne overflowing the rim of a glass.

She went to the window and glanced out. The Liffey was muddy and very high tonight, full of oily-looking swirls and eddies. Gulls flew at the surface as though attacking it. Here and there, a branch or battered bough sped past, madly rotating in the foamy tea-coloured water; the result, she told herself, of the violent storms she'd read about in that three-day-old copy of the *Irish Times* she'd found in her seat pocket during the flight to Dublin.

Over on the north bank, something seemed to be burning. Her eyes narrowed as she tried to focus. Was it . . . ? It couldn't be. Good Lord. It was.

Across the river, a car was on fire. She wondered if she should do something about it. But when she picked up the phone, the line was dead. Perhaps that was just as well, after all. She didn't want to get involved in anything demanding.

She sat on the bed and looked around.

The room was small and far too hot. It smelt of dust, stale cigarette smoke, laundered linen not properly dried. She lay on the bed and peered up at the ceiling. Beneath the thick layers of cream-coloured gloss she thought she could make out the ghostly outlines of the original plaster ornamentation: palm, myrtle, willow and citron motifs, all seemingly struggling to escape.

She lay still, her eyes fixed hard on the shapes. Half-remembered lines from Keats came into her mind. The 'Ode

162

on a Grecian Urn'. What wild ecstasy? What struggle to escape? She had discussed the poem only a few weeks ago with her tenth-graders. It had been a Monday morning, her favourite class of the whole week, the upturned, curious faces still raw with weekend kisses and hungry for poetry. Well, as hungry for poetry as they were ever going to get. Peckish, at any rate. What good would poetry do them? She had often faced that question – what good's poetry gonna be on a résumé, Miss? – and had argued back that poetry was sustenance for the soul, that poetry was for the moments in every life that conventional language could not encompass. In her heart, however, she knew they were right. The young were almost always right these days.

What must they think of her, these absurdly confident teenagers? She envisioned herself in front of her class, a foolish, fond, frumpy schoolmarm rigorously anatomising the exquisite similes that young men and women had dredged from the depths of love. Her husband's jowly handsome face seemed to loom up at her; an image from some recent domestic argument, followed, a moment later, by the grim picture of his buttocks between the outspread thighs of Cathy Kenneally, a pleasant and bright teenage girl to whom she had once taught the definition of pathetic fallacy.

Would she stay in Dublin for the whole weekend or start out first thing tomorrow for Inishowen? Well, perhaps she would remain in the city for a while. It was Christmas, after all. The buses and trains might not be running. Dublin was beautiful at this time of year and she was still feeling washed out and woozy from whatever drugs they'd given her at the hospital.

What a start to the journey. A stay in hospital. What a relief that they had allowed her to leave before the results of the tests had all come back.

Perhaps she'd go to a play, or a recital at the concert hall. There was always research for the group to be done. Or maybe she'd just be by herself. Dawdle the length of Grafton Street, window-shopping. Stroll through Stephen's Green if the weather eased. Look at the ducks and the piles of golden leaves. She might even go to mass. Why not?

Through the window she could see a forest of lit-up cranes

163

over the city; another hotel was being built on the north bank. They were constructing new hotels in Dublin all the time now; throwing them up faster than the guidebooks could include them. Maybe she'd amble down to Temple Bar later. Have a glass of Guinness in one of the cafés. She liked Temple Bar, its small daubed shop fronts, its hysterical giddiness; the cool young people skulking about in sunglasses even on the rainiest of Dublin days.

She thought about Manhattan. Hard Atlantic rain falling on the tree-lined streets of Greenwich Village. An apartment she and Milton had lived in once, beside a narrow house on Bedford Street that tourists loved to photograph. They'd walked past the house only two months ago. She hadn't really wanted to, but Milton had insisted. He was so sentimental sometimes, she'd always found that charming. The day of their engagement was something he loved to celebrate. But the day, like the narrow house, seemed far away from her now.

In the shower, she felt a surge of intensely sensual excitement as the warm water sprayed her tired face and splashed over her breasts. Soap stung her eyes and made her moan. She thought about the pleading voice of her son on the telephone. Could the family go to EuroDisney next summer? The chatter in the departure lounge at Nassau airport had been so loud that it was hard to talk; and she had been glad about that. She could not have brought herself to tell him the bitter truth: that there would be no family holiday next summer. Or ever again. That the days of being a family were almost over. It was one of the few things she knew for sure. Soon enough, she supposed, Lee would know it too.

She dried herself in a half-hearted way but did not dress. Instead she lay on the bed again, her fingers exploring her body. She touched the soft, small rolls of fat on her abdomen, the nodes in her armpits, the wiry hair of her pubic mound. It came into her mind what the doctor had told her on that bright afternoon six months ago now. She wasn't suffering from stomach ulcers or chronic indigestion; actually she was dying of pancreatic cancer. She thought about her body, how it was failing her. Another line of poetry came. 'My soul is fastened to a dying animal.' Yeats had written those cold, magnificent words, near the end of his own life. Through the floor she fancied that she could hear a radio playing. She was sure it was that song by Oasis, 'Supersonic'; her students were absolutely crazy about it. She had allowed them to have a special class where they discussed the lyrics, even though she was not completely convinced that Oasis lyrics meant anything at all.

The wind threw dust and leaves against the window. A plastic bag flapped by like a gull. Her mind began aimlessly trying to recall the words of the song – *Something something Elsa, she's something Alka Seltzer* – but nothing after this half-forgotten line would come. Some minutes later, as though emerging, startled, from a trance, she realised she was crying.

She sat up and began to get dressed, deciding not to bother with underwear, just pulling back on her old clothes, which smelt a little ripe now. Her skirt had been ripped down one seam in her fall outside the coach station. She had no stockings or sweaters and Dublin was cold. She would have to get some clothes tomorrow, if any of the stores were open downtown.

The phone on the table beside the bed was a modern-looking cube of gleaming white plastic with a keypad that seemed far too complicated. She had a stabbing sense that she should call her son or daughter now, at least let them know she was safe and alive. She wondered how they were getting by without her. How was Milton? Would he be all right? She picked up the phone and tried it again. But the line was still completely dead.

She heard a man's voice in the corridor.

'I'm so hungry I'd ate a tinker's mickey.'

A second male voice giggled and said, 'You're bleedin lovely, you really are.'

The two men walked away down the landing. How she envied them. These laughing companionable men.

She switched on the television and flicked through the channels. A newsreader saying the cease-fire in the North was holding. Christmas shoppers in the stores of Belfast. A leather-clad black man chasing a girl through an underground car park. Young British soldiers clambering on to a military aeroplane. Julie Andrews singing 'Edelweiss'. A close-up shot of a Pacman game. Little circular munching monsters. How those greedy scavengers raced around the screen, devouring everything in their path.

They made her think of cancer cells.

*

Down in the lobby, a party of savagely tanned Americans had congregated around a noticeboard on which was a poster of the ancient triple spiral carving on the boulder outside Newgrange. Some of them were drinking Irish coffee, others sipping at glasses of wine. A smaller group had converged on a stocky handsome man who seemed from the way they jabbered and poked at him to be important. Was he a tour guide, someone from a travel company?

Outside the wind was gusting so hard that the revolving door was slowly turning, as though placed in motion by the hand of some restless god. She wondered if one of the tourists might come and talk to her. There were poorly done charcoal portraits of famous Irish writers on the lobby walls; she lingered, recognised Joyce and Brendan Behan immediately, but confused Beckett with Sean O'Casey, only correcting her mistake when she went up close to see if she could make out the artist's signature. She looked at the pictures, waiting, hoping. She glanced around, but nobody seemed to have noticed her.

The small square restaurant that looked over the river smelt of grease and lemon disinfectant. Staff were moving between the tables, setting them with plates and cups for breakfast. Two middle-aged men, one small and thin with a horsy face, the other as large as a football player, were sitting at a circular table in the middle of the room. Although they were whispering to each other, she thought she could just make out their Dublin vowels and intonation; she told herself, yes, these were the men whose conversation she had overheard upstairs. They looked so completely at ease with each other; she felt vaguely ashamed for trying to eavesdrop.

The middle-aged waitress had a flat nose with prominent purple veins.

'Dinner's over, love,' she said apologetically.

'It says on the noticeboard you're open till ten.'

'We're closed early for Stephen's Night, pet. December the 26th is a holiday here.'

'Oh, you could squeeze me in,' Ellen said, with a smile. 'Go on. See if you can.'

The woman sighed and said all right, if she was quick about it, and nodded towards one of the circular tables. Ellen asked if she could have a booth.

'You don't want one of them booths, love. A table in the middle's nicer.'

'I'd really rather a booth,' Ellen said. 'If it isn't any trouble, of course.'

The waitress gave another plangent sigh and beckoned her towards a booth, making a great show of shaking loose the conically folded serviette and spreading it across Ellen's lap. The menu was made of plastic – she noticed, with a small shudder, that it offered 'a bowel of fresh soup'. As she read it through, she tried hard not to listen to the two men, but once the horsy-faced fellow raised his voice he was almost impossible to ignore.

'It's all please this and please that and wharrever yer havin yerself like . . .'

She opened her copy of *Hello!* but still could not concentrate. The horse-faced man was growing more animated all the time, waving his hands in the air and rocking from side to side.

'And then, says he to me, "Mr Dunne, we'd be thrilled skinny if you'd join us for a bite t'ate." And I go, "Ah, shag off, no," not wantin t'impose like, although be now I'd ate a nun's arse through a convent gate.'

'Merciful hour, but you're lovely,' the larger one said. 'Lovely is the only word for you, Sean.'

Just then the stocky man she had seen in the lobby and thought to be a tour guide came strolling into the restaurant. He caught her eye, nodded quickly and formally in her direction.

The waitress approached him and led him straight to a table. She wondered why he had not been told that the restaurant was closed, when she herself had had to plead for a favour. The horse-faced man leaned in close to his friend and began to speak in a confidential whisper that Ellen could not hear. What on earth were they talking about?

When she turned to attract the waitress's attention she got the odd feeling that the tour guide was staring at her. He had a wind-burnt, wrinkled face, thick and slightly untidy grey hair, eyebrows that met above his long straight nose. Yes, there was no doubt, he was looking straight at her. She averted her eyes and went back to her magazine. He stood up and crossed to her table with a quizzical look.

'Excuse me.'

'Yes?'

'I'm sorry. I wonder could we have a quick word?'

'How are you,' she shrugged. 'I'm Ellen Donnelly.'

His handshake was warm and strong.

'It's very nice to meet you, Mrs Donnelly.'

'OK,' she said. 'Nice to meet you too.'

'Well, that's just it.' He smiled pleasantly. 'We've met already. In a manner of speaking.'

'I don't think so,' she laughed.

'Well, yes, actually. I helped put you into an ambulance the other day. Outside Busaras?'

Her hand with its glass of water seemed to freeze *en route* to her lips.

'What?'

'Outside Busaras. The coach station in town?'

'Oh, my God,' she said. 'You're kidding me.'

He shook his head and produced an identity badge in a wallet. 'My name is Martin Aitken. I'm an inspector with the police here in town.'

'You were there?' She looked at the badge. 'But that's amazing.'

'Yes, I was called there. You took a little fall and hopped your head on the pavement. The sidewalk, I suppose you'd say. You're American, are you?'

'Yes, I am. I just signed myself out of the hospital three hours ago.'

He pinched his nose and laughed. 'Well, I've been traipsing around hotels the last few days trying to track down some information on you. A right old treasure hunt it was too.'

'Oh, no.'

He nodded. 'This was my last port of call before jacking it in for the night. Between yesterday and today I must have been in every hotel in Dublin. I could nearly write a travel guide by now.'

'God,' she said. 'I am so embarrassed here. You spent your Christmas holiday doing that?'

'All part of the job, don't be worrying about it. You're OK now, are you?'

'Yes, I'm fine, really. I can't believe you did that, though. I feel just dreadful causing such a fuss.'

'Oh, I was on duty anyway, don't give it a thought. What made it tricky was you had no papers.'

'Yes, I had my handbag stolen in the alleyway beside the station. I guess I just panicked and next thing I knew I was waking up in the hospital.'

'And you're all right now?'

'Fine, fine,' she said. 'But my purse was in it and all my papers.'

'You want to report it?'

'I don't know. Is there any point?'

'There might be. If you're staying in Dublin the next few days, you might drop down to Pearse Street station. If you see the duty sergeant, Hughie Tynan, he'll take all your details.' He reached into his pocket and handed her a card. 'Tell him I asked you to make a report.'

'OK, I will. Thanks again.'

'So there we are.'

'Yes. Here we are.'

'How did old Singy take your checking out?'

'Who?'

'Doctor Singh out in Michael's. He was in a right fret about you, I don't mind saying. I think he wanted to run some tests.'

169

'I guess he was off duty today,' she said. 'I didn't meet a doctor by that name.'

'He's a good pal of mine, works in the hospital. I called in Christmas Day, he was performing his magic on you.'

'You were at the hospital Christmas Day?' She put her hands to her face and groaned.

'Well, it's only routine. For a person in your situation. We don't just drop you in the doctors' laps and scarper.'

'I can't believe I've met you here like this.'

'Well, once you're OK, that's the main thing. So I'll say Happy Christmas then. And mind how you go, all right?'

They shook hands. He went back to his table and sat down. She picked up her magazine, feeling light-headed and flabbergasted. Dublin was such a tiny city. She could never get used to how small it was. Even her group members would joke with her about it. Spend a week in Dublin, you start bumping into people on the street.

Milton had always found that annoying. It was a city you couldn't have any peace in, he'd say. It wasn't really a city at all; it was a relatively unimportant medieval village with an inefficient airport and too many pubs.

She glanced across at the policeman again. To her surprise, she saw he was still looking at her.

'She knocked around with Bryan Ferry,' he said. 'Isn't that right? Who used to be in Roxy Music.'

'Who's that?'

'Yer woman. Jerry Hall. The model.'

'Did she?'

He smiled again. 'I'm sorry, I just saw her there.' He pointed with his fork. 'I mean on the cover of your magazine. And for some reason that came into my mind.'

'The fact she used to go out with Bryan Ferry came into your mind?'

'Yeah.'

'I see.'

'Yeah.' He broke a bread roll in half. 'Just as well they never got married, isn't it?'

'Why's that?'

'Because then she would've been Jerry Ferry, wouldn't she?'

His crimson cheeks crinkled into a grin. The joke was so corny that she couldn't help laughing.

'I suppose that's right,' she said. 'I never really thought of it that way.'

'That is right,' he chuckled. 'My kid told me that once. Cracker, isn't it?'

'Yeah. That's a good one.'

Something about his timorous smile was encouraging. In a way he looked like a small boy, but also like a man who was genuinely comfortable with women, a rare enough thing in an Irishman of his age.

'Listen,' he suddenly said. 'Won't you join me this evening? If you're eating alone.'

'Oh, gosh, no . . . Thank you. I wouldn't interrupt you.'

'You wouldn't be. As you see, I'm alone too.'

She thought about his suggestion for a moment. This was certainly not what she had planned. But what harm, when you looked at it? It was a public place, after all, and he was a police officer. What could happen? It was a very long time since she had had dinner with a handsome Irishman possessed of a sense of humour. If she ever had. Before she had quite made up her mind to accept his invitation he had stood up and was pulling out the second chair at his table.

'Please, won't you?' he asked again. 'You'd be doing me a real favour. I hate eating alone.' He laughed, softly. 'Specially around Christmastime.'

How inky-black his eyes seemed, and how white his small, straight teeth.

'Sure come on,' he grinned. 'I won't bite, I promise. The devil you know, and all of that.'

Chapter Thirteen

Her mind was racing during the few minutes they spent looking at the menu. And yet she felt immediately comfortable with him. He was so unthreatening, for a policeman especially. It was something to do with the largeness of his hands, the incipience of his gestures, the slight clumsiness in the way he held himself, always seeming to abandon a movement halfway through. She told the waitress she wanted plain sole, grilled, and a side salad. The policeman ordered a large rare steak, with mashed potato, carrots and extra fried onions.

'We're lucky to get anything at all,' she said, when the waitress had taken their order and left. 'They told me they were closing.'

'Oh, they sometimes bend the rules a bit for me here. One good thing about being a copper on the inner-city beat.'

'One of the few perks, I'd imagine.'

'That's true, I suppose.' He shrugged. 'But tell me, what do you do yourself, Ellen? Are you a working lady?'

'I'm afraid so, yes. I teach part time, at home in New York.'

He nodded. 'Oh, you teach. What? You teach high school or college?'

She noticed that his accent was beginning to change now, an odd phenomenon she had observed before when Irish people were talking to Americans, a rising inflection, an implied question-mark at the end of every sentence.

'I teach thirteen- to eighteen-year-olds. English lit.'

'Oh, that's great. That's lovely. I'd say you enjoy that, do you, Ellen?'

She looked at him as he peered back at her, his bushy

eyebrows raised in speculation. It was such an obvious question to ask, but nobody had ever asked it before.

'I suppose I do, yes. I mean the kids are great. They keep you on your toes too.'

'I bet they bloody do.'

'Well, they're so aware these days. They grow up so fast now, I feel sorry for them sometimes.'

He pointed towards the ceiling. 'We have tested and tasted too much, lover,' he slowly said. 'Through a chink too wide there comes in no wonder.'

'Patrick Kavanagh,' she smiled.

He laughed brightly. 'The Christian Brothers didn't leave much of a mark on me. Apart from on my backside. But I always liked Kavanagh. "Advent", isn't it? That poem?'

'Yes, it is. I love Kavanagh myself.'

'It puts it well, that old thing.'

'Right. It does. Kids now, they get everything so soon. Whether they want it or whether they don't.'

'That's a fact,' he agreed. 'I've an eighteen- and a twenty-three-year-old daughter myself, so I know all about it. Trying to keep up with them drives me just about bananas. You have kids yourself, Ellen?'

She paused for a moment and glanced across at the window.

'Yes,' she said, then, 'We have a boy and a girl.' She stopped again, before allowing the lie to come. 'They're grown up now, both married themselves. One lives in Wyoming and raises horses.'

'Horses?'

'Ponies, yes.'

He smiled. 'I see. So you're a glamorous granny?'

'I don't exactly know about the glamorous part.'

'And you've Irish blood, have you? With a name like Donnelly.'

'Second generation. Dad from County Kerry, Mom from Poland.'

'Jaypers,' said the policeman. 'There's a mix and a half.'

'It certainly is. They've both passed away now.'

'Did they visit much themselves?'

'Once or twice. But my dad had this weird thing about

Ireland. This love-hate thing? Most of the time it was, "Oh, that awful place, I'd rain bombs down on that priest-ridden dump if I could." But when he'd had a couple beers it was different. When he was drunk it was long live the IRA and three cheers for James Connolly.'

'Oh, I know, I know.'

'He'd get these . . . I guess Republican newspapers mailed over from Belfast and read them to us. It was funny. "I'm a Democrat every place in the world, sweetie, but in the North of Ireland I'm a damn Republican and you should be too."'

'I know a lot of republicans myself,' the policeman said.

'Oh you do? Socially?'

He grinned. 'More professionally.'

The hotel manager stalked up to the table like an executioner and asked if everything was all right. They both murmured a few words of satisfaction, even though the sole was as dry as a lump of old cardboard. He peered down at their plates, nodding seriously, then clicked his heels and moved off with a bow.

His officiousness amused them; when he had left they allowed themselves a small conspiratorial laugh at his expense. But her companion seemed like a man who could laugh without being cruel or superior, and she liked that about him.

After the dinner they talked some more, but she found it difficult to concentrate. She kept asking herself why she had lied earlier about the ages of the children. And why had she said they were grown up and married? It was a thing she had been doing lately, for no reason at all, telling the most ludicrous lies. A waiter came and poured coffee. She found it oddly touching that her new acquaintance was so polite to the waiter, and said please and thank you and called him by name. When the waiter left, he took a sip of his coffee and looked at her.

'Ellen,' he said. 'I have something a bit naughty I want to ask you now.'

'What?'

'I have a guilty secret. You promise you won't tell?'

'Well . . . I guess.'

He leaned quickly forward and frowned.

174

'Would you mind if I had a cigarette, Ellen? I'll tell you the truth, I've a weakness for a coffin nail with my coffee.'

'Not at all,' she laughed. 'Smoke, please.'

He laughed back. 'I had you looking a bit worried there. I know some Americans don't like it, that's all.'

'No, no, I don't mind. Go ahead.'

Chuckling lightly, he took a pack of Marlboros from his jacket pocket and lit one up. Then a thought seemed to occur to him.

'God, I'm sorry, Ellen. Would you like one yourself?'

'You know?' she said. 'I think I will actually, Martin.'

He handed her a cigarette and lit it for her, brushing against her knuckles as he curled his long fingers around the flickering flame. She dragged hard, sucked the thick smoke deep into her throat. God, it felt good to smoke again.

'So, Ellen?' he said. 'What brings you to Ireland yourself? Just a holiday, is it?'

Why not just say it out, she thought. Don't tell him any more lies. What is there to lose?

'The truth is, Martin, I've come to find my mother.'

He looked confused. 'Your mother?'

'My real mother. My blood mother. I was adopted.'

'Oh,' he said. 'You were adopted.'

'I was exported,' she laughed. 'Like a piece of Waterford crystal. Back in the forties the Church sent babies to Irish families in America. You know. The children of girls who got in trouble.'

'Bad old times,' he said, and clicked his tongue. 'We're putting them behind us now.'

'Yes,' she agreed. 'Bad old times.'

'And she knows you're coming? Your mother, I mean.'

'No, she doesn't. Not yet.'

'Where's she live?'

'Inishowen,' she said. 'In County Donegal.'

For some reason he looked startled.

'You know it, Martin?'

He was silent for a moment. 'Yeah,' he nodded, then, 'I know it a bit.'

175

The waitress brought the bill, slapped it down with a flourish on the table and flounced off. He put his hand on it.

'Listen, I'd be honoured to get this, Ellen.'

'Oh, no, I couldn't possibly let you do that. Thanks. Let me put it on my room.'

He shrugged his assent. 'Well then, maybe you'd let me buy you a little Christmas drink. Bit of a nightcap. If you're not too busy?'

'I don't know,' she said. 'I'm a little tired.'

He nodded. 'I understand. But thanks very much for your company over dinner. I must say it was grand to meet you, Ellen.'

'Well, you too.'

'Especially now you're conscious, right?'

'Oh yeah. I'm always better company when I'm conscious.'

'I can't change your mind, so? About the drink?'

She glanced at her watch, feeling hot and flustered. It was just after six o'clock in New York. She wondered if Milton would have spent the afternoon with his girlfriend. He probably had, especially now she herself was gone. She pictured him coming into the kitchen and running water over his hands. That was something he always did when he'd been with Cathy. She knew his routine better than he did himself. He'd come in looking weary, go straight to the sink and thoroughly wash his hands and wrists, up to his elbows. For months after he had begun his present affair, she had wondered why he did this. Then one night he had forgotten to do it, and when he had murmuringly stroked her face in his sleep, a thing he still did, especially when he was feeling guilty, she had got the faint but unmistakable smell of condom rubber from his fingers. She had lain beside him that night and wept like a child. It was just before he started bringing her flowers every day.

'Well, all right then,' she laughed. 'I guess a quick nightcap wouldn't hurt.'

He beamed. 'Won't we be a long time dead? As they say.'

They left the restaurant and walked across the lobby towards the public bar. Halfway over he held out his arm with playful self-mockery, and she linked it. Behind the reception desk a radio was playing a song she thought she recognised from her youth but she couldn't think of its name. Years ago Milton had bought her the LP as a birthday gift. Was it shortly after they had gotten engaged? Or married? She wasn't certain. Was it around the time of her first pregnancy? He had brought her to an expensive restaurant in Manhattan, One If By Land, Two If By Sea, and given it to her over dessert. It struck her as strange that she could remember the restaurant and could even recall the record's appearance, all wrapped up in blue and silver paper, but couldn't summon up the name of the song.

She asked the policeman about it. He tilted his head and listened.

'Christ, yeah, that old thing. That's "You're So Vain" by Carly Simon.'

She squeezed his arm. 'So it is, so it is.'

'I have a bit of her stuff at home.' He nodded along to it. 'I love the way she gets inside a song, don't you?'

'Oh, yes,' she said. 'Absolutely.'

Ellen Donnelly, she said to herself, what an unbelievable liar you are sometimes.

They entered the small smoke-filled bar and moved slowly through the crowd. The room was almost completely full – people were very drunk and a fat woman was attempting to start a singsong – but as if by preordination there were two empty high stools by the bar and they went and sat on those. When he asked what she wanted, she said a glass of dry white wine. He called for that, and a tonic water and ice for himself.

'Penny for your thoughts,' he said.

'Oh, just Carly Simon. Brings back a few memories.'

'Christ, me too. Before all this wojus rap stuff they're into now, eh?'

'You're not into rap?' she chuckled. 'The kids in my class seem to love it.'

He gave an exaggerated scowl. 'I hear a bit of it, Ellen, you know, when my two lassies are around the house. But I just don't get it. All that MC Hammer drives me scats. I prefer the old stuff, Dylan, the Stones, you know? That's my era.'

'Yes. Mine too.'

'The Jurassic era, that's what the girls tell me. They think their auldfella was brought up in a cave.'

'Did you know she was engaged to Bob Marley once, Martin?'

'Who?'

'Carly Simon.'

He turned and peered into her eyes. 'Jayzus, really? I never knew that.'

She felt herself blush. 'No, no. It's a joke . . . Carly Marley, you see?'

'Carly Marley?'

He threw back his head and laughed out loud. They clinked their glasses and smiled.

'Bang to rights,' he said. 'You got me, Ellen. Fair play.'

He drained his glass in one long slug, checked if she wanted more wine and called for another large tonic water.

'Don't drink on duty, officer?'

'Ah no, no, it isn't that.' He put his finger into his tumbler and stirred the ice cubes around. 'Actually there was a time I liked it too much. So I can't drink any more. I'm an alcoholic.' He laughed. 'The Irish flu, you know?'

She felt stupid and embarrassed now. 'Oh, I'm sorry, Martin.'

'Don't be sorry, it's grand. What are you so sorry about?'

'I shoot my mouth off sometimes. You must think I'm dreadful.'

'That's not what I think at all.' His eyes stayed on hers for a couple of moments too long.

The flirtation unsettled her and she glanced away to collect her thoughts. The restaurant in New York, why was it called that? One If By Land, Two If By Sea. What did that mean? It wasn't even *on* the sea. Though it came back to her now that after the meal they had walked all the way down to Battery Park and looked out at the water for a while. The words 'the end' had been daubed in whitewash on a broken wall at the end of the jetty. They had joked about it together, she and Milton. Then they had slipped into a copse of evergreens in the park and made out like teenagers in the darkness between the trees.

'An uncle of mine is an alcoholic,' she said.

'Oh, really?' He nodded. 'I must look him up in the directory.'

'God,' she laughed guiltily. 'I didn't mean it like that.'

'I'm only hopping the ball,' he said.

He offered her another cigarette and she took it. She felt the smoke burn the back of her throat.

'But why did you stop drinking finally? Do you know?'

'Christ.' He grinned at her directness. 'Who's the copper here anyway?'

'You don't like to talk about it, no?'

He shrugged. 'My drinking cost me my marriage, is the truth. Valerie – my wife – she left me and took the two girls with her. I couldn't blame her. I did some bad things. She was a great girl. Big heart, you know? But marriage to a drunk is a full-time job. I suppose she hadn't signed on for that.'

The round of drinks came and he insisted on paying. Then he took out a frayed leather wallet, opened it; removed a creased Polaroid of two girls, the taller wearing an academic gown and mortarboard and holding a laughing baby in her arms. 'That's Julie on the right, and Claire, the day of her graduation. And the little one's Elsie, Claire's baby.'

'Gosh, she's young to be married.'

'She hasn't actually got around to that yet. Made a bit of an early start, you might say.'

'Oh. OK.'

'We weren't exactly overjoyed, as you can imagine. But it happens nowadays. She's a fantastic kid.'

'They're beautiful girls,' she said.

'Yeah. They take after their mother in the looks department. All the poor youngfellas beating a path to the door.'

'Do you still see her now? Your ex-wife?'

'No, not really. She's moved on now.'

'Married again?'

'Not married, no. But she's with a nice enough chap. Morris. Sells bathrooms in a shop the size of a field.'

'Does she work herself?'

179

'Nah. She studies what do you call it? Talking to dead people. Spiritualism.'

'She's a medium?'

'Yeah, that's right. The happy medium, I call her.'

'How interesting.'

He chuckled. 'That's one word for it, right enough.'

He put the photograph back in his wallet and took a sip of his drink.

'And you didn't get involved again yourself, no?'

He paused a moment, as though trying to think of a reply, or weighing the reply that he had thought of. 'There was someone for a while, yeah. A younger woman than me. I met her at AA. We knocked around for a bit but it didn't work out in the end.'

'Oh well. The path of true love doesn't run smooth.'

He laughed. 'I don't know if it was that. She wanted to have kids and I suppose I didn't.'

'I guess you felt two was enough?'

'Three,' he said.

'Three?'

'We had a son too. My wife and myself. But he died six years ago.' He dragged on his cigarette. 'Six and a half now.'

He crushed the cigarette out slowly in the ashtray on the bar. 'Yeah. He was killed in a car accident. A hit and run.'

'God . . . I'm so sorry, Martin.'

He said nothing.

She touched his arm. 'How truly awful for you.'

'That hurt, yeah,' he said. 'That did hurt.' He seemed lost for words. His eyes ranged around the room and took on a strangely mystified expression, as though he was suddenly confused about how he'd got there. 'Yes. I don't know what else I can tell you about it.'

'No. Of course.'

'I suppose life must go on,' he said. Then he stared at his fingernails and shook his head. 'Well, actually, I don't really know that it must. But it just kind of . . . seems to anyway.'

It made her uncomfortable, the sudden darkening of his mood, the downward curl of his mouth. He lit another cigarette and took a long drag. Then he held it between his middle finger and thumb and rolled it to and fro, staring hard at the glowing red tip. For a few moments she could think of nothing to say. She peered around the bar, desperate to find a subject for conversation. The fat bright-faced woman was singing now, conducting a trio of drunken admirers as she sang:

> *Will you go, lassie, go,*
> *And we'll all go together.*
> *Where the wild mountain thyme*
> *Grows around the blooming heather.*

'And are you a religious man, Martin? Would that be a consolation to you?'

He stared into his glass. 'Not really, Ellen. I couldn't say I was.'

When he glanced up again, he was trying to smile. But she was horrified to see that there were tears forming in his dark eyes. 'I hope I'm not offending you, Ellen. But to me all that God crack just creates fear, when there's nothing out there to fear' – he paused and dragged on his cigarette – 'and it gives you hope. When actually there's nothing much to hope for.'

'I guess I never thought of it like that,' she said.

'No. Well anyway.' He pinched the bridge of his nose and suddenly grinned again. 'No politics or religion in the bar, right? Isn't that what the Pope advises?'

He brushed the ash from the knees of his trousers.

'So are you married yourself at the moment, Ellen?'

'Well,' she said, 'I'm entangled.'

He nodded quickly, diplomatically, as though he had been fully expecting an answer like this. 'One of those complicated situations. I had that feeling.'

She pondered his phrase for a moment. 'Well, I guess. One of those complicated situations. Do you mind if we don't talk about it?'

'I've been through a separation,' he said. 'I understand the pain of that. The pain of being left, yes. But there's pain in leaving too, I think. It takes a real kind of courage to say goodbye.'

'I suppose it does.' She sipped some wine and glanced around the bar. A middle-aged bespectacled priest was on his feet and singing now, in a beautifully smooth tenor voice:

> *One pleasant summer's evening*
> *The birds were sweetly singing-oh;*
> *Nature was adorning,*
> *The flowers were sweetly blooming-oh.*

'Maybe entangled is the wrong word,' she said.

'OK,' he said. 'So tell me the right word. If you like.'

She gazed into his generous, innocent face. He looked quite like Milton, she thought, just more messed up and unruly. If he had a haircut and a shave, they might well be brothers.

'I'm a nun,' she said.

('Good God,' she thought.)

He giggled into his glass.

'I am,' she said. 'Really.'

(*Jesus Christ, woman, what are you saying to him?*)

'Yeah, yeah. Get out of here, Ellen, willya.'

'Martin, I'm a nun.'

'Right,' he said. 'And I'm Billy J. Kramer and the bleedin Dakotas.'

'Honestly,' she laughed. 'I am.'

He gaped at her blankly for a few moments. Then he pointed. 'Ha! Hold on a tick there. I'm after catching you out.'

'How do you mean?'

'You told me earlier you had two kids, Mother Superior. How'd you acquire them pair? Immaculate conception, was it?'

(*Don't, Ellen. Stop. That's enough.*)

'My husband died twelve years ago,' she said. 'Of pancreatic cancer.'

The smile died on the policeman's face.

'Yes.' She felt the words begin to come tumbling. 'He . . . the day he got the news he came home and told me. I was in the kitchen. At the sink. Washing my hands. And I . . . my hands smelt of rubber, you see. From my gloves. Because I'd

182

been washing the dishes and my hands smelt of rubber. And I was too shocked to say anything. So I just held him for a long time. Close. I told him I loved him. Because if it had been me, I remember thinking, that's all I would have wanted. Just someone to hold me. And to say "I love you, Ellen, I'm going to take care of you." But he didn't . . . I mean, I didn't. And in the months that came then we . . . we got on badly. We drifted apart. It was as though he thought I was blaming him for being sick. I couldn't ever understand what it must have been like for him. I'm sure I must have seemed very cold. I maybe didn't say how much, how desperately I loved him. Maybe I couldn't show him. I'm not good with my emotions. And I must have seemed so unfeeling to him, although of course in my heart I loved him so much that . . . that if I could have died in his place, then I would have. But I couldn't, of course. I couldn't. And then he died. Without me ever being able to say what I felt. Without us ever even saying goodbye properly. Because we never once actually talked about it, though we knew for a year that it was going to happen. It was never said. Nothing was verbalised. And then one day he just died. And my kids were all grown up, you see . . . And so I entered the convent then.'

His face was pale with shock. 'You're a nun,' he said.

She felt hot tears spill down her cheeks. 'That's right.'

'Ellen, I . . . I'm terribly sorry for being so flippant.'

'It's OK. You weren't to know.'

'That's just terrible for you, though. Your husband dying like that.'

'Yes,' she said, wiping her eyes. 'He was . . . he was so in love with life. He really loved being alive. The way some people don't. But he really did. In his last few months I think he loved it even more. It began to show itself in strange ways. Most people would find them strange.'

'Like what?'

'He used to disappear sometimes. Just run away. Without saying anything.'

'Disappear?'

'Go away, yes. He'd go to the airport and get a commuter flight somewhere. Or get on a train. The first train, anywhere.

183

When I confronted him about it he said he wanted to see the country one last time. Before he died. Or he'd go to a hotel somewhere. A small hotel usually. And just be by himself. It seemed to give him something he couldn't find at home.'

He offered her a handkerchief and she dried her eyes again.

'You'd be amazed at how often that happens,' he said. 'People get closed in, they need to just run. We get a call about a thing like that three times a week in work.'

'I'm so sorry, Martin,' she said. 'I'm OK now. I've had too much to drink, I think. I just haven't talked about it for a long time. I'm fine. Let's just talk about something else now. Can we?'

He looked limp with amazement as he tried to begin a new conversation. 'Well, you're a nun now. Isn't that gas.'

'Yes. It is.'

'And should I be sitting here in a bar with a nun? Isn't that some kind of a mortal sin?'

'Well, I'm OK with it,' she said. 'If you are.'

'I think I need to go to the bathroom now. Would you excuse me for a minute, Ellen, please?'

She watched him walk quickly out the door, hands in his pockets, his shoulders low.

> *When boyhood's fire was in my blood*
> *I read of ancient freemen.*
> *Of Greece and Rome where bravely stood*
> *Three hundred men and three men.*
> *And then I prayed I yet might see*
> *Our fetters rent in twain,*
> *And Ireland, long a province, be*
> *A nation once again!*

Chapter Fourteen

Why in the name of God and all the saints, she asked herself, did you have to say you were a damn nun? Of all things. What was that about? Where did it come from? All right, yes, the man was trying to flirt with you. But all he wanted to know was whether you were married or not before persisting. A nun? Jesus Christ. You don't even *like* nuns. Why are you doing this kind of thing? Why? Her mind drifted back over some of her recent lies. In the foyer of the Algonquin Hotel in Manhattan she had found herself telling the concierge that she was separated from her husband, a well-known poet whose name she could not reveal, but a close friend of Allen Ginsberg. *(A very close friend, if you know what I mean.)* On the flight from Nassau to London she had told the plump black woman beside her that she was a secret agent for the CIA, off to do some undercover work in Northern Ireland. Recently, in a diner, just near school, she had told a Lebanese waitress who had served her breakfast that she was a widow whose second husband had been blown up in a bombing in Sweden. In *Sweden* for God's sake. Everybody knew they didn't *have* bombs in Sweden. How did that happen? Now she was a nun. She amazed herself.

To her considerable surprise, her companion finally came back. He sat down, sank what was left of his drink in one go and said he thought there had been some trouble outside.

A uniformed policeman strode in quickly, followed by the manager, who raised his hands in the air and clapped them together. The lights in the bar came on one by one. The conversation quickly faded.

'This bar is closed as of now,' the policeman announced.

A low groan filled the room.

'Is the residents' lounge still open?' the fat woman shouted.

'Only to residents,' the barman replied.

'Is it too late to book a bleedin room?' a man called, and everyone around him laughed and cheered.

'I have only one thing to say,' said the young policemen, and he paused, looking uncertain about what that might be. 'It'd be as well now,' he said at last, 'if you'd all head yourselves off to bed or the residents' lounge or wherever it is you're bound for. Because otherwise I'll have to take a statement off everyone here.'

Grumbling and complaining, people began to get to their feet and shuffle out, some with glasses or pint bottles concealed beneath their coats.

Out in the lobby policemen were standing around, looking chilly and tired, their black and yellow tunics glistening with rain. One man noticed Ellen and her companion, and strode over to them.

'Excuse me,' he said. 'Are you Inspector Aitken from Pearse Street?'

'That's right.'

'The one who had the squad car went for a walk yesterday?'

'Yeah. Is it after turnin up?'

The policeman chuckled. 'You could say that all right. It was set on fire three hours ago. Just across the river out there.'

'Fuck,' said Aitken. 'You're not serious.'

'I think I saw it from my room,' Ellen said. 'A dark-coloured car?'

'Well, it isn't too dark just now, missus,' the policeman said, turning and going back to join his colleagues.

The lobby seemed suddenly cold and miserable. Her companion had a washed-out look in his eyes. He stared around for several moments as though he was trying to think of something to say.

'The licensing laws in this country,' he finally did say.

'Yes,' she agreed, 'it makes for a very sudden goodnight.'

'It does,' he said. 'It does. Oh well.'

'If we were in New York now, we could keep on drinking until we fell over.'

'We could.' He laughed. 'You're my kind of nun, Sister.'

'Yes, well,' she said. 'I guess I should let you get home.'

He glanced at his watch. 'I suppose I should. Unless you feel like a trip to the famous residents' lounge. Maybe they'd give us a cup of tea. I'd murder my granny for a cup of tea now.'

Her face felt as though it was sunburnt. Her heart seemed to speed up a little. She felt another strange feeling then, like a small propeller whirling inside her abdomen. *(Ellen, don't. Just leave now. It's late.)*

'I don't know,' she said. 'Would you like to come to my room for a while? I believe I saw a kettle up there earlier.'

He pursed his lips and stared at his watch again, refusing to meet her eyes. 'OK, sure,' he shrugged. 'Why not? Maybe we've had enough of bars for one night.'

'And we'll be a long time dead, like you said, right?'

'Yes,' he agreed. 'We certainly will.'

In the lift they said nothing at all to each other. She thought about what Milton would say if he could see her now, inviting a man she hardly knew to her bedroom. There was no doubt he'd be terribly shocked. He'd probably find it unbelievable. In a few hours he would go to bed himself. He would have the radio switched on in the bedroom, as he always did when she wasn't there. It was such a sweet and attractive thing about him that in her absence he couldn't sleep without the radio playing. Really, he was like a little boy sometimes. She could almost see him, curled up on his side, in the bed where their two beautiful children had been conceived.

Walking down the corridor, her shoes felt uncomfortable. The pumps she was wearing were only medium-heeled, but one of the heels had broken off and that made her limp and slowed her down. Oddly, her companion seemed also to be limping, but with a brisker step. How strange. Was he somehow imitating her, the way he'd taken on her accent? How eccentric the Irish were sometimes. They passed a room where a TV was on too loud. *'It's Shearer now, to take the free. The referee having a word or two there.'* She hoped that she hadn't left her underwear lying on the floor. But she needn't have worried. The room was as bare and neat as a cell. Someone had come in to turn down the bedsheets. A couple of mints had been placed on the pillows.

She filled the kettle and told him to sit down somewhere.

'You're travelling light, I see,' he said.

'Sorry?'

'You don't seem to have any luggage.'

'Oh yes,' she flustered. 'That is, no. The airline lost it. I hope it's coming in the morning.'

A headache was tightening the skin of her forehead. He ambled over to the window and stared out for a while, as though something specific and unusual had caught his attention.

'You know,' he said suddenly. 'I used to have a friend who was religious. A Catholic priest.'

'I must look him up in the directory,' she said.

He pointed at her and winked as he laughed.

'Good one.'

'Thanks.'

'But I was just thinking – it's a funny thing – but he's the one responsible for turning me into a godless pagan in the end. Indirectly.'

'How so?'

He was sitting on the windowsill when she turned around, nervously twining the curtain-cord between his fingers. 'Oh, he was up to his oxters in this born-again lark. Here in Dublin. Prayer groups and stuff, I don't know. A few years back when I was in trouble with my drinking, he put the screws on me to come along one night. Only it turned me off the God crack for good.'

'Why was that?' she said. 'Tell me about it.'

'You don't want to know.'

'I do, Martin. Tell me.'

He gave her a rueful grin. 'Some other time. It's a very boring story. Really it's just that it wasn't my thing. And they say the Devil has all the best tunes anyway.'

She handed him a cup of tea and sat on the edge of the bed. He crossed the room and sat in the armchair.

'Mud in your eye,' he said, raising the cup.

Suddenly her headache pulsed, hard and hot. A flash of bright pain shot across the front of her skull, making her wince.

'Are you OK?'

She put her fingertips to her temples. 'Yes, fine.' She tried to rub it away.

'Are you sure? You want me to call a doctor or something?'

'No, I'm fine really. Just a little migraine.'

'You want me to run you back out to Michael's? Get Ranj or one of the others to have a dekko at you?'

'Oh no, honestly. It's just the wine, that's all.'

He was sitting forward, looking at her anxiously. 'I'm living out that way myself. It wouldn't be any bother.'

'No. Really. It's going now.'

He seemed a little disappointed to hear it. She watched him sit back and carefully sip his tea. There was a restlessness about him she hadn't seen earlier, a sense that the air around him was acquiring a colour. She tried to picture him in a police uniform. He didn't look like that kind of man.

'So how do you know him? This doctor you mentioned?'

'Oh.' He laughed. 'He dug a bullet out of my thigh five or six years ago. Be in a wheelchair now if it wasn't for Ranj.'

'How did that happen?'

'In the line of work, I suppose you'd say.'

'You got yourself shot in the line of work?'

'I was a senior Special Branch detective at the time. They carry weapons.'

'You're not one any more?'

'No. I'm not one any more.'

'You left?'

'I was demoted.' He stirred the tea. 'You could say I had a little falling out with those on high.'

She had the feeling he didn't want to be asked about it. But to her surprise he started to speak again anyway.

'It was just two months after Robbie – my son – died. Was killed. This gang in town had a plan to rob a bank. Out in Dalkey. I'd been after the leader for donkey's years. Never was able to get the evidence. The dogs in the street knew he was a scumbag, but no matter what we did we just couldn't nail him.'

'I see.'

'Only this time we had a lot of intelligence on the job. An

insider was after givin us information. We had the names, the places, everything. Their conversations on tape, surveillance photos, the works. We even had the numbers of the cars they were gonna use.'

He thrust forward his jaw and uttered a dry short cough.

'Well, it was a big operation. Planned for months. We knew everything. We'd worked with the bank, all the tellers were cops, so were the customers, cameras hidden, the lot. The whole thing was set up beautiful.'

'So what happened?'

Idly he picked up the Gideon bible from the table beside him, hefting it in his right hand, as though trying to guess its weight.

'We were waitin outside for them. Me and some others. It was supposed to just be a clean arrest . . . But it didn't work out the way we thought.'

'So how did it work out?'

'They came out the wrong door. Would you believe.'

'The wrong door?'

'We thought they were comin out the back, the way they'd gone in. But they came out the front, shootin. Like somethin out of a cowboy picture. Hit a woman pushin a pram along the street and killed her. Just like that.'

'My God.'

'Yeah. Dead on the floor. They had these three other guys out in the street and we hadn't reckoned on that. Dressed up as phone guys, you know, diggin up the road. Opened up on us with pistols. Fella beside me was hit in the chest.'

His brow furrowed up like a piece of cloth.

'One of the four who'd been in the bank ran down the street with a bag of money. I knew who he was soon as I saw him. The gang leader. Fella called Doogan.'

He nodded a few times, as though the name meant something.

'I go after him anyway. Roarin for him to stop. He hares off hard, with a cash bag still under his arm. There was this' – he pointed, as though he could see it – 'this little alleyway leadin from the main street to a supermarket car park. I chase him down that anyway. Up these steps at the end of it. But I'm a heavy smoker. Out of condition. And he's a good bit younger than me. Anyways I can't gain on him. He's just about to get away from me when he trips over himself and hits the ground.'

He began to turn the bible around slowly in his hands, staring at it, as though he had never seen one before.

'Well, he lifts his gun, then. And he's pointin it right at me. Tells me if I take one more step he'll kill me stone dead. I warn him to drop it and get up his hands. He says he won't, I amn't gonna to take him. I give him the warning again. And that's when he shoots. Hits me there' – he pointed with the bible – 'in the thigh. Tries to fire again but his gun's after jamming.'

There was a strange change of rhythm in his voice now. And although he was looking in her direction, his eyes seemed focused on some other point in space.

'I can hardly stand up with the pain. Like my leg's on fire. But I manage not to fall some way. Kick the gun off him. He asks me to let him get away. Offers me the money he's after robbin. Oh, this and that money, in bank accounts all over the shop. I can still see him doing that, plain as the day. Blood runnin down my leg. Can hardly stand, like. But I tell him it's over this time, I'm takin him in.'

'But no. He says I lay one finger on him and I'll never forget it. What he'll have done to me, what he won't do. But you don't mind: they say that, these guys. It's only panic talkin; it's just actin the hardchaw. Mostly they know it won't get them anywhere, it's just they have to say some bloody thing . . . It was what he said then caused all the trouble.'

'What was that?'

He stared at the tip of his cigarette with a dreamy expression. 'I told him this was it. I was takin him in. He said, "You fuckin touch me, Aitken" – he called me by name – "you so much as touch me, Martin Aitken, and we'll do your two daughters. The way we did your fuckin son two months back."'

'Oh my God. He didn't say that?'

'Right in my face. That's what he said. In this kind of a sneer.

191

"Yeh don't think that was an accident, do yeh, Martin? That was done to teach you a good fuckin lesson."'

'So what did you do?'

He avoided her glance now. 'I took one step forward. And I shot him in the face.'

'You killed him?'

'Oh yeah, I killed him all right.' There was a nakedness about his half-lowered eyes. 'I killed him for sure.' He sat still as a rock for a long, silent moment, and then he nodded to himself, as though he had suddenly understood something difficult.

His fingers riffled the pages of the bible. Rain spattered against the windows. The tick of the clock on the wall seemed louder than before. Down in the street, people were singing.

'I'm sorry. I haven't talked about this for a while. Not for a very long time. Not since the inquiry.'

'There was an inquiry?'

'Oh yeah. That's standard. It wasn't just what happened, but money went missing too. When the take was counted up, there was a lot of money gone walking. There was big trouble over the whole thing. I ended up demoted back into uniform. Put on tranquillisers for a year afterwards.'

'That's understandable . . . What a terrible experience.'

He exhaled a mouthful of smoke. 'It was the worst thing I ever did in my life.'

'But Martin . . .'

He stood up abruptly and put his cup on the dresser, so quickly that some of the tea slopped into the saucer.

'Look, I better go. It was nice to meet you.'

'Martin . . . You don't have to go yet.'

He gazed intensely around the room, his eyes scanning it carefully as though he had left a prized possession somewhere. It was the first time all evening he had looked like a policeman. 'I do. It's late.'

'Have I upset you or something?'

'No, not at all, I'm just tired. I have to go.'

'Martin, if I've upset you in some way, I'm truly sorry.'

'It isn't that,' he said. 'You're very easy to talk to. Thank you.'

He held out his hand.

'So are you,' she said, shaking his hand.

'The things we go gabbing about late at night,' he said, trying to smile. 'When we'd all be better off at home in our beds.'

'Sometimes it's easier to talk to a stranger.'

'I'll head on now,' he said. 'Good luck.'

He stopped in the doorway and half turned around, his finger tracing the gilded moulding on the back of the door. 'I hope you find your mother,' he said.

'Thanks,' said Ellen. 'Enjoy the rest of the holiday.'

He nodded and left, closing the door behind him. She sat still, listened to his footsteps go down the corridor. She heard the clank and hum of the elevator as it rose through the building. She turned off the lights and got into bed.

TUESDAY, 27 DECEMBER 1994

Chapter Fifteen

It was shortly after midnight, early Tuesday morning, when Amery climbed the stairs to the landing. It had been a long day and he was dazed with exhaustion. He entered his bedroom, switched on the radio. Soft piano jazz was playing, a lyrical, complex improvisation on a minor chord sequence. When Ellen wasn't there the radio helped him sleep. How pathetic that was. How she'd laugh if she knew. He crossed the floor to close the curtains.

Startled, he saw there was someone in the garden. He looked again. He wasn't mistaken. There in the moonlight, on the love-seat by the sycamore, a woman was sitting with her back to him. She had on a pale yellow gaberdine, a thick woollen scarf. She was smoking a cigarette and reading a book.

He knocked on the glass and opened the window. Cold air rushed against his face. The woman stood and slowly turned.

'*Ellen*,' he whispered. 'Is that you?'

Her hair was badly crumpled and her lips had a bruised look. She seemed to be barefoot, slightly stooped. Somewhere downstairs a telephone began to ring. She smiled up at him and gently waved.

'Please let me in, Milton. I'm expecting that call.'

'You can't come in. *Go away*.'

'But I love you, Milton.' She held out her arms. 'I always did. Let me in?'

He sat bolt upright in bed, his brow and cheeks soaked with sweat. His heart was walloping against his ribcage. The radio was turned down low, playing wild percussive bebop. The alarm clock told him it was just after two.

By the time he got down to the hall, Elizabeth had answered the phone. She had on a T-shirt that came down to her thighs, her hair looked dishevelled and her face was white. Everard emerged sheepishly from her bedroom, tousled and weary, wearing a bath towel around his waist. His entire torso was covered with tattoos. A length of thin chain hung between his nipple rings.

Elizabeth's eyes were wide and fearful.

'Is it Mom?' Amery said.

She shook her head. Handed him the phone. He watched as she went across to Everard, who put his arms around her and tried to hold her close. She pulled away from him, sat down on the bottom stair. Raised her shaking fingers to her face.

'Doctor Amery?'

The man's voice was efficient, brisk. In the background Amery could hear another man shouting.

'Yes.'

'Doctor Milton Amery?'

'Yes, yes.'

'Doctor Amery, it's the police department here, in Saranac Lake, New York. I believe you own a property up here, sir?'

'What's happened?'

'I need you to prepare for some bad news, Doctor Amery.'

Lee had stolen his father's car. Somewhere outside Warrensburg he'd hit a patch of black ice; skidded off the road, ploughed into a tractor. The car had been totalled, the tractor badly damaged. Lee had been arrested for driving without a licence or insurance. He was in the hospital now, in Saratoga Springs, with a fractured left ankle and a cracked rib. Apparently, the policeman said, in a gravely accusing tone, he'd been driving to the farmhouse to try to find his mother.

Amery hung up, feeling hollow with panic.

'You'll have to drive me up there, Elizabeth. Come on.'

'Pops . . . I'm over the limit.'

'Don't tell me you've been drinking alcohol again?'

'It's Christmas, Dad. I had a few glasses of wine.'

'I don't know what's happening to this goddamn family. My son is a car thief and my daughter's a drunk. Give me your keys, I'll drive myself.'

She looked at him blankly. 'But Grandma and I left the cars in town earlier.'

'You what?'

'When we got back to the mall car park it was closed for the night. We had to take a cab home. I told you, Dad.'

'I don't believe this. I buy you a car, what do you do? Show the same carelessness you do with every damn thing else.'

'For God's sakes, it isn't my fault. OK?'

'No, no, it's mine. Like your maxed-out credit card and your poor essay marks. Like everything else in this damn house. Your mother vanishes, that's my fault. Lee's a juvenile delinquent, that's my fault. My daughter openly ignores the rules about having guests of the opposite sex stay over, and, yes, you guessed it, that's my fault too.'

'Dad, look . . .'

'World War Two was my fault also, they just haven't gotten around to arresting me yet.'

'Dad, please, wait till the morning. It's a four-hour drive. Have you seen the weather out there?'

'I'm going now and that's the end of the matter.'

'I could drive you, sir,' Everard said.

Amery looked at him. His chest said TERRORVISION.

'Oh, wonderful. You're telling me you're sober, are you?'

'As a matter of fact, sir, I don't drink.'

Amery scoffed. 'Another one of your principled Buddhist stands, I suppose.'

'Well, not exactly, sir. I'm diabetic.'

Everard's car looked like something found on a dump. Originally, Amery guessed, it might have been dark blue, but now it had a bright red cannibalised tailpiece and its bonnet and roof had been spray-painted gold. Speckled with rust holes and rough patches of sealant, it sat in the driveway looking weary and hopeless. The passenger door didn't work, so Amery had to clamber in the driver's side and manoeuvre himself across the gearstick, finally sitting down on something that turned out to be an old banana wrapped in a Texaco road map.

The evil stench almost brought tears to his eyes. The dash was covered with parking tickets, paper cups, crumpled soda cans, and the words IMMEDIATE DEATH TO THE CAPITALIST SYSTEM had been scrawled in white paint across it.

Everard hopped in and attempted to start up. He was wearing leather jeans and one of Elizabeth's sweatshirts. The engine gave a low chug and immediately died. He tried again. It coughed and cut out again.

'Try turning the key more slowly,' Amery said.

'There isn't exactly a key, sir. You just hold these two wires together and hope for the best.'

The car vibrated, burbling into weak life. Everard pumped hard at the pedals. The hacking sound reminded Amery of an asthmatic drunk trying to get out of bed. 'I think we're in business,' Everard said. 'Hang on to your hat, sir.' He reached into the driver's door pocket, took out a pair of battered glasses which had been repaired with tape and slipped them on.

As they reversed slowly down the icy drive, Amery watched Elizabeth waving in the headlights. She had put on a long white robe now, which gave her a regal, imperious look. The light came on in his parents' room. He saw his father come to the window and open it. Elizabeth looked up. They exchanged some words.

'Should I wait?' asked Everard.

'No,' said Amery. 'Just go.'

For the first few miles they said nothing. They drove north out of town towards Briarcliff Manor, turned on to Highway Nine. The moon shone bright on the snowy fields, the high barns and brooding houses. On the left, the Hudson was flat and peaceful, though warnings of imminent flooding had been posted up at intervals. From time to time rhythmic metallic bangs would come from under the bonnet, like Japanese drumming. Whenever that happened, Everard would wince and slow down for a few moments; wait for the thudding to stop before speeding up again.

Amery wished so desperately that Ellen were here. How much worse could things get now? Elizabeth was intent on flouting his authority; Lee might well be looking at a criminal record. For three solid hours last night he had tried calling Nassau airport to get a list of flights out the day she had left. Most of the time the line had been busy. Whenever anyone did answer, they put him in a loop of recorded messages which cut itself off after fifteen minutes. Six whole days since the last time he'd seen her and still he had no idea of where she might be.

They crossed the river just past Annsville, turned north again towards Highland Falls. The academy at West Point sped by on the left, the buildings neat, a line of armoured cars in the yard, sentries on duty outside the main gates, a Stars and Stripes flag the size of a minibus fluttering over the quadrangle.

'Sorry about the smell,' Everard said. 'Elizabeth spilled a carton of milk. It gets in the carpet and rots it up.'

The night was getting colder. The heating in the car wasn't working. Amery wished he'd thought to grab his overcoat before coming out. As it was, he was wearing nothing but pyjamas and a cardigan. With a dull sprouting of embarrassment, he realised he had forgotten to put on shoes. God above, how could he go into a hospital in bare feet? They'd take one look and haul him off to the mental ward. But perhaps that wouldn't be the end of the world. The way he was feeling just at this moment, even the end of the world wouldn't be the end of the world. Certainly, a month in a padded cell was far from the worst prospect available. A shiver moved slowly down his back. Cold flowed through the car like melting ice.

'You want to hear some music, sir? I got some Beethoven in the glove box.'

'I have other matters on my mind besides music, thank you.'

Everard nodded, his hands clamped on the wheel. 'I guess this is a pretty heavy situation for you.'

'You could say that.'

'I guess you must be in a lot of pain.'

'Thank you so much for your devastating insight, Everard.'

Everard sighed and gave a small chuckle. 'Man, I guess you don't like me one little bit. But that's cool.' He pushed the glasses up on his nose. They gave him a comical, fancy dress look. 'Nobody likes me much. You get used to it.'

'Spare me your paranoia, Everard, would you?'

'The way I see it, Doctor Amery, when you get past the need

for everyone to like you – even assholes? – that's when you know you've reached nirvana.'

It was the kind of remark that closed down a conversation.

Amery had an odd sense of being static now, of the silent landscape unrolling past the window. The moon cast strong black shadows all around. The water tank of a town loomed over the landscape like a Martian spaceship about to descend. Houses and stores became further apart. Before long they were moving through real countryside, long, neat fields on either side, stalked by ghostly power stanchions, the grey road ahead wet in the headlights.

They crossed a river and sped on. Everard lit a cigarette and opened his window. His calmness was beginning to get on Amery's nerves. He wondered if Everard was the jousting type. What the hell. It might pass the time.

'So I suppose you think you're going to marry my daughter. Do you?'

Everard laughed, taken aback. 'No, I don't actually.'

'Oh, you don't. Well, that's something for which to be thankful.'

'Yeah. See, we don't believe in marriage.'

'Of course. Except for lesbians, I suppose.'

Everard swerved to the right, braking hard on gravel. He stared straight ahead and pursed his lips.

'Hey, Doctor Amery, when I'm in your home, I keep my views to myself.'

'So?'

He turned. 'So you're in my home now, OK? So keep your reactionary fucking Pat Buchanan views to yourself, man. Or you can walk to Saranac Lake for all I care.'

Amery scoffed. 'Are you threatening me, son?'

'Get one thing straight, man, I'm not your son. I'm grateful for that much too. Now you want to walk or you want to ride? It's pretty much the same to me.'

For one moment he did actually consider getting out. But they were in the middle of absolutely nowhere now; he couldn't even see through his frosted window. The wind groaned and blew snow against the windscreen.

'Well, I'm sorry if I offended you,' Amery said. 'I hadn't realised you were the sensitive sort.'

'We understand each other now?'

'I believe we're on each other's wavelength, yes. In the parlance of the times.'

Everard glared at him as though about to say something else. But then he just shook his head and pulled out again, revving the car so hard that it shuddered.

They drove ten miles in complete silence, turned right at Newburgh on to Interstate 87, passing a sign for Saratoga Springs. From then on the road ahead was straight and unremittingly featureless. Amery had always found this journey a trial, so boringly flat was the surrounding land. What the hell did Ellen see in it? How could you deal with a person who actually found farms interesting? Everard's silence began to make him uneasy him again.

'You really live in your car?' he tried.

'That's what I said.'

'How do you manage?'

'I manage just fine.'

'That can't be easy for you, though.'

'Easier than living some place my folks don't want me. Or paying some scumbag landlord to rip me off.'

'Your parents don't want you?'

He gave a bitter laugh. 'Would you?'

Amery found himself thrown by the question. 'Every father should want his children,' he said, after a moment. 'My own are the best thing that ever happened to me.'

'Better than being married?'

He considered it. 'I suppose being married is a thing that has seasons. But being a parent is something else. That gives you an investment in the future.'

'I guess so. I can't imagine it.'

'I'm sure you will. When you have children of your own.'

'That's my dream. But I don't think I can ever see it happening.'

Everard wiped the windscreen with the back of his hand. Suddenly he seemed heartbreakingly young.

'Well, I sometimes thought that too, Everard, when I was your age.'

'You did?'

'Yes . . . I was frightened about it maybe.'

'You don't seem the frightened type.'

Amery laughed, but he wasn't sure why. 'I guess my context is that my own parents had their ups and downs. Back when we were growing up.'

'Why was that?'

'I don't know . . . They married too soon maybe. When my father came home safe from the war.'

'He wasn't ready?'

'Maybe not. There were other women involved from time to time. It caused a lot of unhappiness between them. We kids picked up on that.'

'She knew about it? Your mom?'

'Oh yes, she did . . . Of course it wasn't ever discussed in front of us. But I think it hurt her very deeply.'

'I bet. She's a nice lady.'

'I always promised myself I'd be a rock for my wife and children. If I was ever blessed enough for those things to come along. That's what you do when you're young. You think it's all controllable. Like setting out on some journey.'

'Actually mine are divorced. I got beef with my mom's new boyfriend.'

'Why's that?'

'Likes to express his feelings with his fists.'

'Well . . . has she involved the police in that?'

Everard sighed. 'Man, if you knew. He is the police. I'd've killed him already if he was anything else.'

Silence filled the car again. The boy didn't seem to want to talk any more. He was concentrating hard on the road ahead, his eyes fixed, almost squinting.

Amery leaned his cheek against the window. Trees and gates drifted past, a tractor parked by a stack of logs, a rusting plough on the roof of a closed-down bar. He found himself idly counting the posts of a weathered wooden fence that stretched endlessly along the roadside. Before long his eyelids felt heavy. He nodded into an uneasy doze, thick blackness engulfing him, a sea of ink. The faces of his family shimmered before him. Other pictures flickered then. A boy he had once known but whose name he could not remember. A pretty girl on a bicycle crossing a bridge.

Some time later he felt Everard shake him. When he opened his eyes he had a dirty woollen blanket over his knees. They were in a vast car park that was almost empty, with bright beams of yellow light flooding down from the roof of a five-storey concrete and glass building.

'We're at the hospital, Doctor Amery. You want to wake up.'

'We're not here already?'

'Yeah. You've been asleep nearly three hours.'

'Good God. I'm so sorry, Everard.'

'Don't worry about it. You needed to sleep.'

His legs were numb and his head was pounding as they got out of the car. His watch told him it was almost 6.30. The sky was beginning to brighten at the edges; the cold, damp air was fresh and sweet. Everard looked completely exhausted. He took off his glasses and blotted his eyes with his sleeves.

'I guess the A and E is over here. Look.'

'Everard, there's something I'd like to say at this point.'

'So shoot.'

'If I spoke injudiciously earlier, I want to apologise. Truly. And to express my sincere appreciation for your bringing me here.'

Everard slipped his hands into the back pockets of his jeans. He peered at Amery sceptically, his large eyes gleaming.

'Man,' he said, 'I love the way you talk.'

'I'm just trying to convey my appreciation.'

'I didn't do it for you, I did it for Elizabeth. But I guess you're welcome all the same.'

Inside the hospital everything was quiet. Behind the counter in the lobby, a sleepy-looking black man was watching a Spanish soap opera on a portable TV. He looked amazed and happy that someone had come in, as he lifted the phone and called one of the doctors. After a minute a thin, olive-skinned young woman in a white coat came walking briskly across the reception area. She reached out to shake Amery's hand.

'I am Doctor Lachelle.' A drawling Southern accent lengthened her vowels. 'You must be Lee's dad?'

'I'm Doctor Amery, yes.'

'Oh. Lee didn't say his daddy was in medicine.'

'I'm a cosmetic surgeon. I practise in New York.'

'He's mighty lucky he won't be needing your services.'

She turned to Everard with a warm smile. 'This here is big brother, is it?'

'Brother-in-law,' explained Everard helpfully.

They walked down a long corridor that was painted in washed-out institutional pastels, turned right and climbed a flight of stairs, went along a grim landing the colour of a cancerous lung, somehow made even more depressing by the noticeboards plastered with children's paintings. Amery's bare feet felt sticky on the scrubbed floors.

'Your boy's had quite a shock,' the doctor said, holding open a door for them. 'He's shook up some and we have a minor fracture. But he's going to be fine in a couple weeks.'

By the doorway that led to the accident room a plump, copper-haired, slightly bulgy-eyed policeman was slumped in a chair. When he saw them coming he stood up, looking bleary, and put on his cap.

'This is the father,' the doctor said, 'this here is Officer Monroe.'

Amery shook the policeman's hand.

'Your son's been charged with various offences. No licence, no insurance, resisting arrest.'

'Resisting arrest?'

'Absolutely.' He held up a bandaged thumb. 'Kid tried to bite me.'

Everard giggled. The policeman shot him a look.

'It's certainly no laughing matter, I can tell you that. Anyone's asking *me*, he should be looking at grievous assault.'

'I'm sorry he did that, officer,' said Amery. 'But with respect, you don't exactly look like you're mortally wounded.'

The cop sighed. 'OK. It's Christmas. I guess we might be able to forget about that one.'

'We couldn't just forget about the whole matter?'

He frowned. 'Can't do it. It's official now.'

'Come on, officer. It's a small enough thing.'

A look of disbelief came over the policeman's face. 'A thirteen-year-old boy riding around in a stolen car? On roads like these? At one o'clock in the morning? It's only the mercy of God that boy's in the accident room and not in the morgue. If you ask me, his parents should be ashamed of themselves.'

'Didn't you ever act unwisely when you were that age, officer?'

'I did, yeah. Until my father found out. And then I guess he did a little fathering.'

'Hey,' said the doctor, 'can we get through this please? I've a sick boy inside needs to see his dad.'

Amery signed the bail form. The policeman checked it over, eyeing Everard with ruminative contempt. 'You'll be needed when the case comes up in court. Drive carefully on your way back home,' he told Amery.

The doctor led them into a large bright room that was sectioned off into curtained cubicles. Inside one of them, Lee was asleep on a gurney. The lower half of his body was naked, his left ankle bound in a plaster cast. The skin on his leg was torn from the knee to the thigh. His T-shirt had been cut open and a thick bandage wrapped around his chest. When Amery went closer he could hear him muttering softly, 'Why he did . . . I don't know . . . If he did . . . Yes.'

'What's he saying?' Everard asked.

'Nothing,' whispered Amery. 'He talks in his sleep.'

Lee stirred and gave a grunt. He opened his eyes wide, as though he'd been surprised. His head remained still but his eyes moved left and right.

'Hey, Lee,' said Amery. 'It's Dad here.'

His son blinked. Peered around. Tears welled up.

'Lee, you're in the hospital, soldier, everything's OK.'

His son turned to look away. The side of his neck was badly bruised. He covered his face with the backs of his hands.

'Soldier, it's OK, I promise.'

A wrenching, gulping sob broke from him now.

'Lee. I'm here. Don't worry, son.'

'I'm sorry, Dad.'

'It's OK.'

'I totalled your car, Dad, I'm sorry.'

'Lee, it's all right, it's only a car.'

'I just wanted to go see Mom. I thought she might be up at the farmhouse.'

'I know you did . . . I know, son.'

He tried to lean up on his elbows. 'But there was all this snow and ice on the road.'

'I know there was, soldier. And it's OK now, I promise. Just relax and take it easy.'

Lee lay back down and closed his wet eyes. His breathing was laboured, coming in soft gasps.

'So,' said Amery, attempting brightness, 'that's a heck of a shiner you have. Isn't it, Everard?'

'Sure is. Cool plaster cast too.'

'Well, we're gonna fix you up real nice,' the doctor said. 'Handsome young man like you has to think of his appearance.'

Lee said nothing. The doctor stroked his forehead. 'Can't disappoint all those pretty girls want to look at you and dream, now can we?'

He opened his eyes and peered at his father.

'Is Mom here now?'

Amery felt a piercing in his heart. 'Well, no, son, she's not.'

'Is she coming later?'

'Lee . . . I don't think so, soldier.'

His son closed his eyes again and began to tremble. The doctor took his hand and tenderly squeezed it. 'Hey there,' she sighed. He gnawed hard at his lower lip, his face contorting with the effort not to cry.

'Tell you what,' Amery said. 'We'll get you cleaned up, then we'll get a motel room. And in the morning take a ride up to the farmhouse, you, me and Everard. All us guys together. And see if Mom's there. How about that?'

'You don't understand, Dad.'

'Lee . . . I do.'

'I've been to the house already,' he said, his voice cracking. 'And she's not there, Dad. *She's not there.*'

Amery moved forward and touched his son's bruised face.

'And it's all my fault she went away,' Lee went on.

'Son, it isn't. It's nobody's fault.'

'It is. It's because I got in trouble in school.'

'Lee. Believe me. Your mom loves you so much.'

His son's arms came up and wrapped themselves around his shoulders. 'I'm so scared, Dad,' he sobbed.

Amery kissed his hair and held him close.

'There's nothing to be scared of. We're here together now.'

'But how are we gonna get her back, Dad?'

'I don't know, soldier. But we will. I promise.'

Chapter Sixteen

It was just after nine when Aitken woke up on the couch, still wearing his clothes from yesterday. At least, he was reasonably sure they were his, though they seemed several sizes too small for him now.

He'd got back from the hotel around one in the morning, washed down two sleeping pills with a good swig of Benylin, sat back to watch an old black and white movie that was starting. That was the last thing he remembered. He had slept marvellously and now he felt good. It was the best sleep he'd had in months.

In the shower he thought about the strange American woman. How bright and amusing she had been, how much he had enjoyed her company. He imagined she must have been attractive when she was younger. As a matter of fact, she was still attractive now. One of the most attractive nuns he had ever met.

It amazed him to realise he was in such a good mood. Only five nights to go and it would be time to return to work. He would have survived another Christmas. He wondered how he would kill the day. Drive into town; perhaps call in at the station. Catch up on his overdue paperwork, maybe find those files for the AC; see if any of the lads felt like a game of pool. Already it was almost ten o'clock. Only twelve hours to go until he could reasonably get back into bed.

Downstairs in the hall his answering machine was flashing. When he pressed play, Valerie's voice came on, sounding cross.

'Martin, I thought you were coming over. We did say Stephen's Night, didn't we? The girls are here, we're all waiting for you.'

Shit, shite and fucking shinola.

How had he managed to forget?

When he tried her number it was busy. He went into the kitchen and spooned some instant coffee into a mug, which he filled with water from the hot tap. The room was beginning to smell like something quite large had died in it. Maybe he should spend the day cleaning the house. But where to start, that was the thing. Then again, wasn't that always the thing.

Out in the hall again, her number was still engaged. What the hell, the house could wait. He decided to drive over to her place and do a little grovelling.

The day was bright and very cold. As he went to get into the Mini he saw, across the road, a star-shaped hole in the Murphys' living-room window and a turkey lying upside down in the grass. He wondered if he should knock on the door and make sure everything was OK. But then again, he didn't want trouble, and the Murphys usually wanted as much as they could get. The two Bradley boys emerged from behind a hedge. When they noticed Aitken, they nudged each other and stood up straight.

'What?' said Aitken, zipping up his flies.

'Nothing,' one said.

As he opened the door of the Mini they started to sing.

> *Wanker Aitken,*
> *He looked out,*
> *On the feast of Stephen.*
> *Piggy with a piggy snout.*
> *Can't blame his bitch for leavin'.*

It wasn't the song that made him think they were eerie. It was the fact that they were singing in perfect choirboy harmony.

He drove to Donnybrook and pulled into the cul-de-sac of yellow-brick modern apartments. A white customised Hiace van was parked in her designated driveway. He got out of the Mini and read the legend on the side. MORRIS NUNN AND COMPANY. FOR THE BATHROOM EXPERIENCE YOU DESERVE. Nearby was Valerie's brand-new Datsun. It had a sticker along the rear windscreen saying MEDIUMS DO IT IN THE DARK.

As he waited in the porch, he found himself wondering exactly what kind of bathroom experience he deserved himself. Certainly, back in his drinking days, he'd had bathroom experiences aplenty, but none – or at least very few – that might be worth repeating. An astronomically fat, frizzy-haired man in a pink dressing gown opened the door. His sad, moist eyes widened with surprise.

'Jayzus Christ All-fuckin-mighty.'

'No need for formality, Morris. Martin will do.'

'Jayzus, Martin, come on in. Sorry.'

Although it wasn't yet eleven in the morning, Morris Nunn seemed already a bit drunk. His breath smelt like decaying apples. He looked as though he was about to have a heart attack. The belt of his dressing gown was doing some kind of job of holding his enormous belly in place, but his forehead was sweaty and his large lips were pale blue. As he waddled down the hallway, which smelt of pine needles and wine, Aitken had the feeling he might topple over at any moment. He hoped that wouldn't happen. He wasn't sure he'd be able to pick him up. At least, not without the aid of a block and tackle.

'Come through in here, Martin. Sorry the place is like knackeragua.'

It was clearly a room in which a child spent a lot of time. Here and there the wallpaper had been grazed, an explosion of toys lay spread across the carpet; dolls, stuffed animals and giant Lego bricks were strewn in a tea chest beside the sofa.

'We were expecting you down last evening, Martin.'

'I got held up, Morris.'

He nodded understandingly. 'Police business, was it?'

'Yeah.'

His piggy little eyes lit up as though powered by batteries. 'Wiping the scum off the streets, hoh?'

'Something like that, yes.'

'They should bring back the birch, if you ask me, Martin.'

'You think?'

'Do I what?' He pointed to an armchair. 'They should get those little bastards and thrash them senseless. Birch some fucking sense into them. I'd give it to them myself if I was asked.'

'Would you, Morris?'

'Would I what? Who wouldn't? I'd bend them over and birch the living daylights out of them. And do you know what it is, Martin?'

'What?'

'They'd thank me afterwards.'

A gleaming, complicated-looking exercise bicycle sat in the bay window, lengths of stiff cardboard still around the base, polythene tubing covering the bars, and a faded green bath towel folded over the saddle. Morris sat painfully in the deep sofa and rested his hands on his globular abdomen. Aitken perched on the arm and lit a cigarette. Something about Morris's posture made him think of a chicken sitting on a nest. A very large and sweaty chicken, the kind that would never be *à la king*.

'So,' said Morris. 'There we are.'

'Yes,' Aitken said. 'True enough.'

'Yes indeed. Yes indeed.'

'Ah well. Not to worry.'

Desperate for inspiration Aitken looked around the room. There was a Christmas tree in the corner with decorations made to look like various Simpsons. Hanging down one wall was a kindergarten crayoned Nativity scene clearly done by his granddaughter, or, possibly, by Morris. A cake with a wedge cut out of it sat on the table. A tin of sweets had spilled its contents onto the floor.

'Will you have an auld jar, Martin? The season that's in it?'

'Hmm? . . . Oh no, thanks, Morris.'

'There's lemonade and stuff there. On the trolley.'

'Lemonade?'

'Well, you know.' Morris blushed a little. 'Non-alcoholic like.'

'Oh right.' Aitken said. 'No. I'm grand.'

'No offence like. I know you don't drink, that's all.'

'None taken, Morris.'

'Personally I don't blame you, Martin.'

'Good.'

'I admire you, in fact. The same drink is a terrible thing.'

'It is.'

213

'And the kids these days.'

'Don't be talking.'

'Sure they'd suck it off a sore leg, Martin.'

'They would, Morris.'

'It's the curse of the Irish people. Patrick Pearse said that.'

'Did he?'

'Oh, he did, he did. Ireland sober is Ireland free. We had that bet into us by the Brothers. And divil the bit of harm it ever did us.'

'Yes.'

Morris regarded him seriously. 'We had one particular brother where I went to school, Martin. Brother Maloney by name. An absolute fucking sadistic cunt, Lord have mercy on him. But he talked a lot of sense when it came to the drink.'

'Did he, Morris?'

'The devil's buttermilk. That's what he called it.'

'Did he really? Well, well, well.'

Morris gave a fond sigh of reminiscence. 'I remember a lad coming into school with a bottle of beer once. And by Jayzus, Brother Maloney bet him half stupid, so he did. Took his trousers down and lashed him stupid. With a rope. Flailed the arse halfway off him. Literally. Then he kicked him from one end of the school to the other. And then he tied him to a bus stop outside. With the rope.'

'Jesus.'

'But he thanked him afterwards.'

'Brother Murphy?'

'No, you thick. The lad.'

'Oh. Sorry.'

'Yes.'

'Mm.'

'Yes . . . but you don't mind if I have a quick one myself, Martin, do you? Just to keep the auld chill out of me chest.'

'Not at all, Morris. Fire away.'

Morris reached a plump scrabbling hand down by the arm of the sofa. When it came back into view it had a wine bottle in it. He filled a nearby plastic beaker almost to the brim and took a long swig that was more like a suck, wiping his mouth on the sleeve of his dressing gown. He seemed to be grinning at Aitken now, which wasn't a sight Aitken felt too comfortable with. How in the name of the sanctified Christ could Valerie sleep with that glorified troglodyte? When she'd first met him, he'd been half chicken and half man. Now he was half chicken and half walrus. He found himself staring downwards. Morris's feet were forced into training shoes and his swollen, flabby calves had crinkled up like a row of frankfurters.

Swallowing hard, Aitken nodded across at the exercise bike. 'You're . . . taking up training, are you, Morris?'

'Hmm? Oh right. That's my Christmas present from Valerie.'

'Very nice.'

'Yeah. Two and a half grand, that set her back. Had it imported specially from Norway.'

'It looks like a good one.'

'Oh it is, it is. Shaggin thing'd give yeh a blowjob nearly.'

'Is that right?'

'Oh Jayzus, yeah. The very latest. Dunno if it's gonna do me much good though.' He clutched his belly. It wobbled. 'I always tell her, "Sweetheart, I could've bought a palace with the money I spent acquiring that."'

'You're looking fairly prosperous right enough.'

'Big belly, no brain. That's what they call me in work.'

'I'm sure they don't, Morris.'

'They do, they do.' Suddenly he looked crestfallen. 'I mean I'd love to lose some of it, Martin. But I can't seem to. No matter what.'

'Some people can't, though. It's the way they're put together.'

'Well, that's right, that's right. It's my metabolics.'

'Your?'

'Metabolics is what's at the heart of my problem. I've had it all explained to me, Martin. Doctors and specialists to beat the band. The shoes worn off me trooping along to quacks and snake-oil salesmen, needles stuck into me, hoses stuck up me.'

'Go way.'

'Stop. I mean I hardly ate a fucking thing any more. I subsist on a diet wouldn't keep a sparrow.'

'Or a swallow,' Aitken found himself saying, for some reason.

'Well, yes,' replied Morris, uncertainly. 'A bird in general.'

The TV was on, showing a concert from Vienna. An almost offensively handsome man in a tuxedo was swaying from side to side with his hands above his head. People in the audience were waving cigarette lighters. Morris picked up the remote control and glumly began to flick through the channels.

'So, Morris,' Aitken said, doing his best to sound sprightly. 'How's the bathroom business these times?'

'Oh, grand, Martin. Yes.' He peered suddenly into his glass as though it contained something disturbing. 'I mean, I say grand. But you know, it's always ups and downs with bathrooms.'

'I can imagine.'

'Yes. Well, it's a big investment for people. Specially a younger couple starting out in life.'

'I suppose it is.'

'I mean, if you're talking about a bath on its own, that's four hundred pound now.'

'It is not.' He knew Morris liked this game.

'Straight up. Four hundred pound. That's before you even look at a toilet, Martin.'

'Good God.'

'How much to look at a toilet, Martin?'

'I don't know, Morris.'

'Guess.'

'Really, Morris, I wouldn't have a clue.'

'Guess though. First number comes into your noggin.'

'Jayzus, I don't know.' He thought he'd better come up with some laughably low figure. 'Fifty quid?'

Morris scoffed. 'Fifty quid, he says. The poor innocent.' He gave Aitken an almost violent glare of triumph. 'To look at a toilet these days is two hundred pound.'

'Go way.'

'Two hundred pound. And that's just to look at one. To actually buy one is another matter altogether.'

'Good Christ. Make you think, though, Morris, wouldn't it?'

'Stop.' Morris nodded. 'No, it's not the best time in the bathroom business. Because you've all these cowboys flooding the market too. But a lot of doors would have to open and close before anything bad would happen to me.'

'Before you'd go down the plug hole, you mean.'

'Yes exactly.' He chortled. 'Very good. Very good.'

He poured himself another beaker of wine.

'Very droll. As they say. Hmmm.'

He gave a strangled squawk of laughter.

'Are you . . . OK there, Morris?'

'Sorry,' he said. 'That was just quite humorous. What you said before. About the plug hole.'

He guffawed once more and blew his nose on his dressing gown.

It seemed like a long time before either of them spoke again.

'Martin,' he said then. 'Can I ask you something?'

'What's that, Morris?'

'Do you ever feel like . . . you want to fucking die? Just actually stop existing?'

'Well . . . Not really, Morris, no.'

A melancholic look invaded his pudgy face. 'No,' he said. 'I sometimes think about that.'

'Do you, Morris?'

Gloomily he took another swig. 'But that's expensive too now, Martin.'

'What is?'

'A funeral.'

'Oh. Right.'

'Five grand now, a funeral, Martin.'

'Really?'

'Five grand plus VAT. It's enough to make you want to go on living.'

He wasn't sure if Morris was joking.

'When *I* go, Martin, I want none of that palaver. I want to be fucked in a sack and left on the side of a mountain in Connemara. For the eagles to eat.'

'Do you, Morris?'

'I've told Valerie, I want no palaver or hocus pocus or waste of good money. If I'm going into the food chain anyway, I'd like to go in pretty high up.'

'Very good, very good.'

'High up. That's me.'

He gave a rat-like squeak of mirth.

'So . . . Valerie's upstairs, is she, Morris?'

Morris looked at him blearily. 'Sorry, Martin?'

'Well . . . Where are they? Valerie and the girls.'

'Well . . . but didn't you know, Martin? They're gone to London this morning.'

'. . . *London*?'

'Well yes. It was a surprise present from me. Week's break in London. Did you not know?'

'Morris, why in the name of the step-dancing Christ would I be sittin here shootin the breeze with you if they're gone to London?'

Morris looked confused. 'Well, I *was* kind of wondering that, Martin.'

'You fuckin . . . So when'll they be back?'

'Monday or Tuesday, I suppose. Sure one word from me and they do as they like.'

Aitken got up. 'Tell them I called in, OK?'

'But . . . you're not leaving, are you, Martin?'

'Take it easy, Morris, all right?'

Suffering Jesus. What a man. As he opened the door of the Mini, he turned to look back. The pulsing, blue light of the television screen was flickering in the window. And there was Morris, perched on the saddle of the exercise bike, his short chubby legs steadily pedalling as he chomped his way through a giant-size Toblerone.

That was the entity his ex-wife had sex with. What could you do? There was no God.

He drove off feeling restless, a little panicky. He couldn't go into the station again this early, Hughie would think he was having a breakdown. An idea occurred to him. But was that ridiculous? He took out his phone, punched in a number and waited.

'Hannigan's Hotel, Merry Christmas.'

'Yeah. I want to speak to a guest of yours, Sister Ellen Donnelly.

A computerised version of 'Für Elise' came on, segueing into 'Molly Malone'.

'No reply from the room, sir.'

'She's checked out?'

'No, sir, just not in her room. Would you like me to page her for you?'

'No . . . no, that's OK.'

Chapter Seventeen

He spent the rest of the morning on a bench in Stephen's Green, reading the newspapers and smoking a lot. The papers were full of end-of-year round-ups, most of them making much of the cease-fire in the North. There were photographs of people waving tricolours in Belfast on the August day the peace had been announced. An anonymous senior policeman was widely quoted; he hoped all the terrorists wouldn't be released, at least not until weapons had been handed in. The head of the Orange Order was interviewed too. He felt it was important for his members' right to march to be upheld.

Aitken finished the papers and idled down Grafton Street, ate a turkey-burger lunch in McDonald's on O'Connell Street, swilling down a triple-thick shake that he could almost feel gluing up his arteries. A trio of toddlers at the next table kept glaring at him. When he tried to smile, one of them burst into tears and performed a Fosbury flop into the arms of its mother.

For some odd reason, right at that moment, he had a terrifying vision of a group of bowler-hatted Orangemen on a line of exercise bicycles, just like the one poor old Morris had at home. Or a line of walking machines, even better. That way they could get in some practice for their marching.

He'd get it in the neck from Valerie for not turning up. How the hell had he managed to forget? She'd tear a strip off him, no doubt about it. He could almost hear her already, accusing him of doing it deliberately. But she had a point; he couldn't deny it. He hadn't seen the girls for nearly three months now. It occurred to him to call Morris and see if he had the number of her hotel in London. But when he tried his mobile the battery was flat and none of the payphones seemed to be working.

He was halfway up D'Olier Street when he got the feeling he was being followed.

He stopped and looked in the window of the *Irish Times* office. Out of the corner of his eye he saw a young man stop too, further down and across the street by the doorway of the Harp Bar. He turned and looked straight at him, but the man glanced away, down towards the river, as though he had heard some unusual sound. He looked familiar, but Aitken couldn't think how.

He walked on slowly around the corner, pausing by a specialist bakery shop. The window was full of multi-tiered wedding cakes, with miniature brides and grooms on top. After a moment the young man appeared from around the corner and walked straight past him gazing at the ground. He had long dirty hair, unusual sunglasses with white rims, a loping, athletic stride that didn't seem to go with his bowed head. He marched along, crossed the street to the public toilets, went down the steps and disappeared from view. Aitken wondered now if he was being paranoid. Lately that had happened more than once.

He went into the station to see if there were any messages. Hughie Tynan was off duty; the desk sergeant was a young woman Aitken didn't know, on holiday cover from head office. A call had come from a Doctor Singh at the hospital, she said, and several from the Assistant Commissioner. Apparently he was looking for some urgent files.

Aitken's office was cold and smelt of stale smoke. He opened his mail and tried to sort through it, but after a while he couldn't concentrate. Really, he thought, he should lay off the amitriptyline. It had a way of zonking you out and making the world seem fuzzy at the edges.

The atlas was still open on his desk from yesterday, the page showing Inishowen stained by a coffee mug. Maybe he'd take a drive up there one of these days. In the six years since Robbie's death he had never once visited the grave. It was such a long way to go; the time just never seemed quite right. Well, if those were justifications, they were at least pretty good ones. Maybe in the New Year, he thought, or maybe in the spring, when the weather would be better. Donegal was always beautiful in the spring.

Slowly an idea bubbled up in his mind. Perhaps Valerie might like to come with him. Was that ridiculous, after all this time? Maybe it was. But you never knew. Thinking about it now, he couldn't remember one single occasion when they had actually talked about what had happened, except in euphemisms and occasional asides. For the first few months, he had been unable to do more than that. And then, by the time he could have begun to imagine it, it was too late, his marriage had imploded and she was gone. Any exchanges that took place after that were conducted through lawyers, or, worse, through the girls. They would turn up to meet him on a Saturday afternoon with sheaves of school bills, doctors' accounts, long letters from angry creditors. His salary had been cut following his demotion and it had been hard from then on to make ends meet. He had resented the way she used the girls, had got his lawyer to ask her to stop. She'd written back to say it didn't matter any more. She had met a man who would take care of their expenses. A man who had his own bathroom business. From that day onwards, Aitken had never missed a maintenance payment.

He wondered if secretly he wanted her back. Was that what was at the root of his fantasy, the two of them going to see their son's grave? Did he want her to break down and cry in his arms? Tell him she had never loved anyone else? Take him back to a hotel room and drag him into bed? Tell him he was better in the sack than Morris? Jesus Christ, was that the height of his ambition now?

Certainly there had been jealousy, particularly in the early days of their separation. To think about her talking and laughing with someone else would send a bolt of electricity through his heart. The thought of her making love to another had been almost unbearable. He would dream about it, all night long sometimes. He would wake up shaking, almost sobbing with what he told himself was need for her, although, as he had known even back then, it wasn't truly need but only its black-hearted cousin, envy. But even that had passed in time. You couldn't beat the phone company. There was no such person as Santa Claus. His wife was bonking a drunken right-wing walrus. It was amazing, really, the things you could get used to.

222

He picked up his car from outside the station; decided he'd take a spin somewhere quiet. Maybe down to Glendalough or up to the mountains. Walk around for a while and smoke a few joints. He was in an odd and restless state of mind, which he knew from bitter experience could end up being dangerous. If he didn't get a grip, his depression would. At times like this it could seem like a battle, almost a physical fight to keep control. He paused and took a few deep breaths. It was almost like trying to swallow away nausea. Hold it in, he told himself, *hold it in*. And after a moment it did seem to pass, that desire to open his mouth and scream. He looked at the winking clock on the dash. It was already almost half-past three. Another short time, he'd have broken the back of the day, he could begin to think about slinking home to bed. But first he'd have to get out of the city, see if at least that small thing could be achieved.

As he was reversing out into the street he was sure he saw the young man again, standing near a bus stop by the wall outside Trinity. He was watching carefully, still in the sunglasses, though the afternoon was so gloomy the cars already had their lights on. He looked again. It was definitely him. A light drizzle began to fall.

A chugging bus pulled out from the stop, breaking into his line of vision. He stopped the Mini and climbed quickly out. But when the bus had passed, the man was gone.

A gleam of feeble sunlight peered out from behind the clouds. The drizzle became a cold, steady rain.

Who was the man? His face seemed familiar. Even the way he stood. A feeling of danger loomed up, as powerful as a hand placed on his shoulder from behind. He felt a prickly, clammy sensation as he hunkered down to look under the car, checked to make sure nothing was attached, searched for batteries or protruding wires.

He made a mental note to change his routine, alter the routes he took into work. OK, there was a cease-fire now, but you could never be certain with some of these guys. There were still plenty of cowboys with Armalites around. A lot of them, he felt sure, would have old scores to settle before shuffling off to write their memoirs. The very day before the peace had been announced the Provos had gunned down the leading crime boss in Dublin. He was rumoured to have helped organise an attack on a republican pub. Though nothing was proved, the rumours were enough. They had long, cool, detailed memories, these guys.

Many times back in the seventies he'd led raids on the Sinn Fein headquarters. He and his men had never found much – the Shinners were way too clever for that – but the thinking of the hard-line government at the time was that it was important to hassle them, not to let them take root in the South. He'd got to know the building like he knew his own home. It was a tall, shabby tenement on Parnell Square, with a Marxist bookshop on the street level and ramshackle offices upstairs. Bizarrely enough, there was a photographer's studio in the back of the ground floor, run by a short, pudgy man from Belfast who took the pictures for the republican newspaper, but also did the usual portraits, of married couples, children making confirmation. He remembered now, as he eased along Nassau Street, how one day he'd come bursting through the door waving his Uzi, only to find the man in his messy little studio, taking a picture of a beautiful girl in a first communion dress. The girl's mother had gone almost hysterical, accused Aitken of being a fascist and a traitor to Ireland. It was the first time he had ever doubted the rightness of his work. Maybe the woman had a point. Dark things were happening inside the police force – he'd be lying if he said he didn't know anything about them. Confessions were being beaten out of prisoners; a secret unit had been set up to get results no matter what. Journalists' phones were being illegally tapped; there was widespread harassment of suspected republicans. To have attended a meeting or signed a petition, to have sung the wrong song had almost become a crime. He thought as he drove of what might be in those files the AC was so keen to get. Only half the story, if that much. Not that Aitken himself had ever done anything to stop what went on. He had defended a state that was attacking its own citizens – a state that owed its very existence to militant republicans, depending on how you chose to look at it. But that was simply what had to be done. It wasn't his job to ask too many questions, or, at least, to ask them of the wrong people.

A startling sight made him brake hard. He looked again. It was definitely her.

Halfway up Kildare Street, the American woman was standing outside the National Museum with a notebook in her hand and a paper bag shielding her head. He moved forward again and rolled down the passenger window. The rain began to surge down hard.

'Hey, Missus,' he called out. 'Did you ring for a taxi?'

'Well, hey,' she said. 'Look who it is.'

'Small town again,' he laughed. 'Step in for God's sake, you're getting drowned.'

She climbed in, smelling of the cold and the rain. Her wet hair clung in strands to her forehead, giving her a look of vulnerability he found somehow charming. As she shook his hand, shivering lightly, he had the impression that her eyes were slightly different shades of green.

'My God, you're destroyed. Here.'

He took an old jersey from the back seat and handed it to her. 'Dry yourself off with that if you like.'

'Are you sure?'

'Course.'

She dabbed her cheeks with the sleeve of the sweater.

'Oh, that's better. What a downpour.'

'What were you looking for?'

'Hmm?'

'Heading into the museum, were you?'

'Oh no, I was trying the National Library. I wanted to look up some of the records. But they're closed right now. Damn, I'm wet.'

'Well, the Christmas holiday, you see. It goes on a bloody week over here.'

'Yeah. I hadn't figured on that. They're closed for a fortnight as a matter of fact.'

'Civil service,' he said. 'They've a great life altogether.'

She smiled. 'Isn't that what you are too?'

'Dunno about that. Not very civil sometimes.'

She laughed lightly. 'You were to me. And now you're my knight in shining armour again.'

He said he was happy to hear it. She lowered the sunshield to glance at herself in the mirror.

'God, what a sight. I look like something the cat dragged in.'

'You're grand,' he said.

'Oh sure. Regular homecoming queen.' She was searching the pockets of her raincoat now. 'You wouldn't have a tissue, would you, Martin?'

He didn't, but he offered her a J-cloth he kept in the glove box for cleaning the windscreen. She folded it in two and dried her face. The rain turned suddenly to sleet, hammering down on the roof of the Mini like a drum roll.

The policeman on duty outside the Dáil came shuffling towards them, skidding a little on the icy pavement, waving impatiently for them to move on.

She smiled at Aitken. 'Tell him you'll sack him if he's rude to us.'

'Poor guy's only doing his job.'

He pulled out from the kerb and turned right into Molesworth Street. Two ragged homeless men were sitting on the bollards outside the European Parliament office, eating something out of a mushroom punnet, plastic supermarket bags wrapped around their legs.

'So there we are. Can I drop you back up to Hannigan's?'

She looked dreamy and restless now. 'I don't know. Maybe I could invite you for a coffee or something?'

'Sure, if you like.'

'Unless you're busy, Martin. Are you?'

'No, no, I'm not too busy.'

'You're not working today?'

'Well, I was, yes, earlier. Just kickin around at the minute.'

'Where could we go that's really nice? I feel like splashing out. Do you know somewhere?'

He found it pleasant to listen to her voice, its soft vowels and intonations.

'The Shelbourne Hotel's just up there and round the block. It's a bit pricey but it's a grand old place.'

'Oh, yes,' she sighed happily, as though he had mentioned an

226

old friend. 'The Shelbourne. Do you know, I haven't been in there for years?'

'Come on, so. Only it's my treat, I insist.'

He parked on Stephen's Green and they entered the hotel. A log fire was blazing in the warm lobby; in the tea room on the right were chandeliers and mirrors, plush red velvet seats, overstuffed russet leather armchairs, tables with small trays of cakes and sandwiches set out. A girl was playing 'Galway Bay' on the grand piano. They found a banquette just inside the door. Waitresses in black dresses and white aprons moved quickly between the tables. A plump white-haired man on a nearby sofa was telling two impressed-looking younger women how the building had been occupied by the British during the Easter Rising. How you could still see the bullet-marks in the stone arch down the street that led into Stephen's Green. How the first constitution of the Republic had been drafted in a room upstairs.

'Welcome to Ireland,' Aitken said sardonically. 'You can't even have a cup of tea in peace.'

She cut her eyes at him in a quick surmising way that made him laugh.

'West Briton,' she grinned.

'That's me all over.'

'Aren't you proud to be Irish at all?'

'I'm delirious, yeah. It keeps me awake at night.'

A waitress came by and they ordered coffee. The girl at the piano started into 'Love Me Tender'. A concierge in a purple jacket came into the room and called, 'Telephone for Miss Evans', and everyone glanced around.

'You sure you're all right, Ellen? You look a bit tired.'

'I didn't sleep so well after you left.'

'Probably my fault. Did my story give you the heebies?'

'No, it wasn't that. I had the strangest dream. That I was walking by myself through a forest somewhere. And this man I didn't know was following me. But every time I stopped to look around he wasn't there.'

'That's gas,' he said.

'Probably just something I ate.'

'So what plans have you for the next few days?'

'I guess I need to think about getting to Inishowen.'

'Why don't you let me take you?' he found himself saying.

Her first response was to stare and then to laugh. 'Martin, please. I couldn't let you do that.'

'I've a week off for Christmas. I'd fancy getting out of town.'

'Martin, I'm not saying it isn't kind of you.'

'It's not meant as kindness.'

'It's amazingly generous. But I couldn't allow it.'

'Look, I'll tell you the truth, Ellen. I'm driving up that neck of the woods anyway. I planned it all six weeks ago.'

'Why on earth would you be doing that?'

'I just am. No real reason.'

'When were you thinking of going?'

'Right now, actually.'

She laughed. 'Come on, be serious.'

'I was.'

'Martin, you can't go now, it's dark outside.'

A voice he knew came from the doorway behind him.

'Boss? Is that you?'

Hughie Tynan was dressed in a suit and tie, looking ten years younger out of his uniform, his face crimson, a string of silver tinsel around his neck.

'Jayzus, Hughie . . . What are you doing here?'

'We came in for our lunch. Give the baggage a break from cooking for the troops.'

He could see Tynan noticing his companion.

'This is a friend. Ellen Donnelly.'

Tynan's eyes took on a delighted look.

'Well, hello there,' he said, in a significant way, shaking her hand and sitting down. 'My name's Hughie, but you can call me darling.'

'OK,' she said uncertainly.

'I have the dubious pleasure of working for this man here. Ten years off me spell in Purgatory every morning I sign in.'

'You're a police officer too?'

'Tynan of the Yard,' he grinned, saluting. 'At your service, ma'am. Early and often.'

228

'We keep him on out of pity,' Aitken said. 'He'd be beggin on the streets if we didn't give him something to do.'

'Do you guys know each other long?'

'Don't be talking, love,' Tynan said. 'I know this gauger since Adam was a boy. But is he treating you well, pet, tell me that?'

'Very well.'

'Lovely, lovely. I'm delighted to hear it. Because he's from Glasthule where they ate their young. I'm glad to see someone putting a few manners on him. Specially a lady as beautiful as yourself.'

'Charming, isn't he?' Aitken said.

'Aha,' said Hughie, 'here's the Mahatma now.'

Tynan's wife came in with a bunch of geraniums and a handbag the size of a small sack. She was a thin pale woman with silvery hair and pale blue eyes that looked straight into you.

'Hugh, come on. Are you ready to go?'

'But see who's here, oh love of my life.'

'Martin Aitken,' she cooed, coming over and embracing him warmly. 'Look at you, you're thin as a rake.'

'Everyone else tells me I'm gettin chubby, Noreen.'

'Not at all.' She clutched his wrist. 'You'd see more meat on a butcher's bike. But you're handsome still if you go for that type.'

'See what I mean?' Tynan rolled his eyes. 'She has adulterous thoughts about you, my liege.'

'Well, I did, I admit it, but not any more. I've a crow to pick with you, Inspector, as a matter of fact.'

'Oh, God,' said Tynan. 'You're for the high jump now, boss.'

'What am I after doing on you, Noreen?'

'I thought you were coming over to us Christmas night. I was mortally wounded and I'm not speaking to you any more.'

Tynan turned to his wife. 'Now I told you, love, he was busy elsewhere.' He glanced at Ellen and gave her a wink.

His wife peered at her over the rim of her glasses.

'This is Ellen,' Tynan said. 'My dear, this is Noreen, my sexual plaything.'

The women shook hands amiably and Mrs Tynan sat down, taking a spectacle case out of her bag.

'Well now, my dear,' Hughie said to Ellen. 'What do you think of her?'

'Who?'

'The baggage here. The war department.'

Ellen laughed. 'You have a beautiful wife.'

'Well, it was our thirtieth anniversary the other week. And she says why don't you nibble on me ear like you used to, Hughie.'

'I did not, you dirty beast.'

'But I said, by the time I remembered where me false teeth were, she'd be asleep.'

'Will you stop making a show of us please?'

'Well, this is lovely altogether, what? Will you have a drink, Ellen? And yourself, boss?'

'We don't want to keep you, Huge,' Aitken said. 'You'll be wanting to get on now, I'm sure.'

'Not at all, boss, we're free as the birds. Oh, be the hokey. Here's the mammy now.'

A frail woman on a zimmer frame came shuffling into the room, aided by a slim rangy teenage girl with raggy jeans and a bob of chestnut hair.

Tynan stood up and took the old woman's arm gently.

'Well, Mammy. Are you all right now? Here's an old friend come to see you.'

She cocked her head. 'What?'

'You remember Martin, Mammy?'

'What's that? Speak up, can't you?'

He raised his voice so loudly that people at the nearby tables turned to see what was happening. '*We had Christmas with him last year. You remember, don't you? He's the man who's over me in work.*'

'He's what?'

'*Martin, his name is. He came last Christmas. You sang a little song for him, Mammy.*'

'Oh yes, oh yes.' The old woman nodded blearily. 'Is it the poor unfortunate man whose wife ran off on him?'

'Well . . .'

'The alcoholic, isn't it?'

The girl beside her sniggered and raised her hand to her lips. Tynan shot her a look of correction, before glancing back at Aitken and Ellen.

'You remember this rip of a daughter I have, Martin?'

'I do indeed. You're looking beautiful, Niamh.'

'Isn't she, Martin. She has the young lads demented. I do have to beat them away from the door with a stick.'

'Shut up, Daddy,' she laughed, embarrassed.

The old woman peered at Aitken. 'Did she come back yet so? The wife?'

'Well . . . No, Mrs Tynan, she didn't.'

'Why not? Did you beat her or something?'

'Now, Mammy. This is his new young lady, Ellen Donnelly.'

Ellen laughed and turned to Aitken. 'Is that what I am?'

Aitken felt himself blush.

'Ellen's actually a nun, Hughie,' he said.

Tynan gave a lascivious chortle. 'I'd say she is, right enough.'

'She is. Honest.'

'Would you ever go and . . .'

'Hughie, she is. I swear to God.'

'I am,' said Ellen.

Aitken enjoyed what happened to Tynan's face then. It looked like it was trying to somehow turn itself upside down, before finally settling in an expression of mortification.

'I'm terribly sorry, Sister . . . I didn't mean any disrespect.'

'None taken,' she smiled, 'please don't worry.'

'You dirty great gormless eejit,' his wife said. 'Please, Sister, don't be minding him. I can't bring him anywhere nice.'

'It's just that Martin told me he was seeing some lassie. Naturally I assumed . . .'

She turned to Aitken again, smiling broadly. 'Is that right? You're seeing some lassie?'

'I don't know if I'd put it quite like that.'

Tynan clapped him hard on the back. 'He has a girl in every port, Sister. You wouldn't think it to look at him, I know, the great long streak of Glasthule misery. But it's them quiet ones you want to watch.'

231

The young woman at the piano half stood and asked if anyone wanted to sing. An embarrassed murmur went around the room. Tynan waved and called across to her.

'I'll sing, love.'

'You will not, you dirty-looking gom,' said his wife.

'Indeed and I will, my little bag of happiness.' He called again: 'What about a blast of Gilbert and Sullivan? In C?'

The young woman nodded and somebody cheered. Tynan stood up, marched to the piano and thrust one hand inside his blazer. The pianist sounded a loud major chord. Tynan began to croon, in a self-mockingly rumbling bass voice.

> *When a felon's not engaged in his employment,*
> *Or maturing his felonious little plans . . .*

He held his hand to his ear. Some people chimed in 'Little plans'. Tynan nodded seriously before continuing:

> *His capacity for innocent enjoyment*
> *'Cent enjoyment*
> *Is just as great as any honest man's.*

'Honest man's,' yelped a toddler, which made Tynan crease with laughter. He stood up straight and solemn then, pointing one finger at the ceiling.

> *Our feelings we with difficulty smother*
> *Ah, take one consideration with another . . .*
> *All together –*

He raised his hands in the air and began to conduct.

> *When constabulary duty's to be do-hone, to be done,*
> *A policeman's lot is not a happy one.*
> *Happy one.*

Everyone laughed and clapped. The girl on the piano vamped

a tinkling fill.

'What's he bloody like?' sighed Tynan's wife.

'Ladies and gentlemen, I thank you,' said Tynan, over the music, 'but now, for the second verse I will be assisted by my superior, Inspector Martin Aitken of Pearse Street station.'

'No way, Huge,' Aitken said.

'He needs a little encouragement, friends. So give him the clap he so richly deserves.'

'Go on,' Ellen smiled.

'No *way*.'

'Go on there, Uncle Martin,' Niamh grinned. 'Please? For Daddy?'

Aitken rolled his eyes and stood slowly up, feeling weak with awkwardness as everyone cheered and applauded.

Hughie stuck two fingers in his mouth and whistled. Then he did a sombre scowl and began to sing again.

> *When the enterprising burglar's not a burgling.*

'Not a burgling,' sang Aitken, to a whoop from Niamh.

> *When the cut-throat's not preoccupied in crime,*
> *'Pied in crime.*
> *He loves to hear the little brook a gurgling,*
> *Brook a gurgling*
> *And listen to the merry village chime.*

'Join in, one and all,' cried Hughie. Aitken laughed and took the lead line.

> *When the coster's finished jumping on his mother,*
> *He loves to lie a basking in the sun.*
> *Ah, take one consideration with another,*
> *A policeman's lot is not a happy one.*
> *Happy one!*

'Let's hear you,' bawled Tynan, punching the air.

Oh, when constabulary duty's to be done, to be done,
A policeman's lot is not a happy one.
Happy one!

Applause and cheers filled the room. Tynan did a mock curtsey and kissed the piano player's hand. Noreen hugged Aitken hard. Then she and Ellen went off to the bathroom together.

'You've a grand voice, Martin,' said Tynan's mother feebly. 'You remind me of John McCormack in his heyday.'

Laughing he turned away towards the light.

What he saw made his heart kick.

The young man with the sunglasses was staring through the window. Standing still as a statue in the pouring rain, pulling slowly on a cigarette and gazing in. The rain was running in rivulets down his face. He flicked his cigarette butt and it hit the glass.

Tynan came back to the table and sat down.

'Well, boss,' he said, 'you're the star of the show. Now we'll have another drink by way of medicinal celebration. What do you say, Mammy?'

'Huge?' said Aitken, quietly.

'What, boss?'

'Don't look now. Look in a minute.'

'Where?'

'There's a youngfella over there. At the window. Who is he?'

He watched as Tynan took a long sip of tea and glanced surreptitiously towards the light.

'There's nobody at the window, boss.'

'Look again.'

'Boss, there's no one. I swear to God.'

Aitken turned to look himself. People were rushing past in the rain. The sky was already darkening down to a bruised and purple gloom. An articulated truck had stopped on the street, with a silhouetted map of Ireland painted on the side.

'There was a guy there a second ago, Huge. Some head in his twenties. Wearing shades and a leather coat.'

'Well . . . Was he bothering you some way?'

234

'He was givin me the thousand-yard stare, yeah.'

Tynan chuckled. 'Maybe he fancied you. Or liked your singing.'

'Huge, I'm dead serious. He's following me around. I saw him earlier outside the station.'

'Jesus, Martin,' Tynan sighed dismissively. 'Relax for God's sake and enjoy your tea.'

'What the fuck is that supposed to mean?'

'Just . . . nothing. Put your eyes back in your head, OK? Don't be gettin paranoid.'

'Oh, right. You think I'm paranoid?'

'Well, I don't know. I think you're . . . preoccupied or something. Just relax. It's Christmas. Pull a cracker.'

He watched as Tynan turned to his daughter and laughed, reaching out to stroke her hair. He felt a sudden rage grip at his throat, a boiling sensation deep in his chest. 'Everything's a joke, isn't it, Huge?'

Tynan looked across at him with disbelief.

'Jesus . . . what's ailing you, Martin?'

The words came out before he could stop them. 'The joke of the station, that's our Hughie. Performing flea for the real policemen. Now he's propping up a desk.'

Tynan bowed his head and peered at the backs of his hands. His daughter's mouth opened wide with shock. When he looked up again it was with a dead smile. 'Who the hell do you think you are, Martin?'

'I tell you there's some freak followin me and you crack a joke. Nice, Hughie.'

'I said who the *fuck* do you think you are to speak to me like that? In front of my family?'

'I'm sorry then,' said Aitken. 'If you're going to get sensitive about it.'

Tynan's eyes were gleaming with anger now. 'You ever in your life speak to me like that again and you fucking will be sorry, sunshine. And very sorry. Because I'll put you through a fucking window, Martin, big and bold as you think you are.'

Aitken said nothing.

235

'Come on, Daddy,' said Niamh, moving her arm around his shoulder.

'Did you ever hear tell of respect in your life, Aitken? I know you've none for your fucking self, but the man who'll talk to me like that in front of my daughter isn't born yet, I'll tell you that.'

'I said I'm sorry. Are you gone deaf now or what?'

'I'm not the joke, friend. If you want to know the truth. Only nobody's laughing so much these days.'

Ellen and Tynan's wife came back from the bathroom, chatting together, their arms linked. They sat back down and looked around. Tynan's mother looked frightened and pale. His daughter was close to tears.

'Anything wrong?' Ellen said.

Aitken managed. 'Nothing at all.'

'What's the matter, Hugh?' Tynan's wife was peering at him. 'What's the matter, pet? Did something happen?'

Tynan said nothing. When he lit a cigarette his fingers were trembling. He stared away towards the fireplace, with a lost expression.

'What's after happening?' She touched his wrist. 'Did something happen to upset you, love?'

He shook his head and silently locked his hand in hers. She turned to Aitken with an anxious questioning look. He picked up his coffee cup and drained it dry.

Ellen glanced at her watch. 'I think I better get back to the hotel.'

'I'll drive you,' Aitken said, standing up.

'I'll get a taxi. That's just as easy.'

'There's really no need. I don't mind driving you.'

She shook hands with Tynan's daughter and his mother, kissed his wife, who hugged her back.

'It was a pleasure to meet you, Sister,' she said confusedly. 'I'm sorry now if it all's gone wrong some way.'

Ellen went to Tynan and held out her hand. He stood up and shook it, looking dazed and exhausted, as though he didn't quite know who she was.

'I'm sorry we didn't have more time,' he murmured. 'You're very welcome to Ireland anyway.'

His wife laughed gently and ruffled his hair. 'Sister's as Irish as you and me, love.'

Aitken picked up his cigarettes and put them in his pocket. 'I'll see you back in work next week then, Huge?'

Tynan said nothing, just sat back down.

They went into the lobby and looked out at the rain.

'Will you let me drive you to Inishowen tomorrow?'

'I can't, Martin. Really I can't.'

Chapter Eighteen

In the Hyperion Hotel on Central Park West, Amery and Cathy were having sex.

That hadn't been the plan. Not at all. For a start, he was shattered from being up all night. He, Lee and Everard had only got back to the house at eleven this morning. And then he'd had to go straight back out. Today was the day he had decided to end things with Cathy. He had made up his mind on the drive home from the hospital. It couldn't go on. His family needed him. They'd had a few laughs, but now it was over. These things happened. What could you do?

He would meet her for lunch as planned, but he would tell her straight out that he wanted to end it. His life had become too complicated lately. On the train into town he had rehearsed what he would say. He would have to plan it out carefully, though. If he confessed that his wife had left him, she might start getting dangerous ideas. It was vital to keep it more general than that.

He needed some space. To be alone. To work on his marriage, for the sake of his children. Blah, blah, he knew the drill by now. He would make the enormous personal sacrifice of leaving her, all for the sake of his children and their happiness.

She should be with someone of her own age anyway. That was always a good tack to take. He was holding her back, narrowing her options; the world had so much to offer a young woman of her abilities.

He peered at his face in the mirror of the train's bathroom. 'I don't deserve you anyway,' he whispered, half lowering his eyes. 'Really, I don't,' he managed to gulp.

Back in his seat, he found himself thinking about the lyrics of an old song, as the towers of Manhattan came into view. It was just one of those things. Just one of those something flings. A flight to the moon. On something wings. What a pile of baloney that was. It was damn well *never* just one of those things. Maybe it was if you were Frank Sinatra, but it certainly wasn't if you were Doctor Milton Amery.

The train pulled into Grand Central. He was irritated to find that he couldn't get the lyrics out of his head. Round and round they buzzed, like a bee in a jam jar.

The city was quiet, empty and peaceful. He looked south along Park Avenue, so straight and long and gracious, the vanishing point down in the twenties. Was there a city anywhere as beautiful as this? Built from scratch by immigrants and refugees. He thought about a night when he and Ellen had visited the Empire State Building, though he couldn't remember when it was or what the circumstances had been. They had held hands and simply looked at the view. He'd found it so moving that for a while he couldn't speak. He'd had tears in his eyes coming down in the elevator.

For a moment he was tempted to change his mind about meeting Cathy, just turn left and keep on walking, all the way down to Battery Park. He saw himself jumping into the grimy water then, and starting to swim out towards the Verrazano Narrows. People would shout at him but he'd ignore them and continue. Out past Ellis Island and just keep going. He wondered how far he would get before he drowned. Maybe the sharks would get him instead.

She wasn't in the lobby when he arrived. He'd sat at a table and ordered a coffee, feeling hot and tired and irritated by the Muzak. He wondered how she would take his decision. Not well, he expected. But you never knew. Surely to God she would act like an adult. Perhaps that wouldn't be too much to ask.

She had turned up with the diamond choker still in its box, handed it back just as soon as they kissed.

'It's too much, Milton, I can't accept it.'

'But I want you to have it. Really I do.'

She shook her head and laughed. 'No, honestly, I couldn't.'

'But . . . for heaven's sake, why not?'

'What we have is very special, Milton. You don't need to buy me.'

'I'm going to leave it right here on the table.'

'Do that if you want. But I'm not taking it.'

There was a sharpness in her voice when she'd said that last sentence, a new tone he hadn't heard before. A woman in furs stared at them as she passed. He'd sighed and put the box in his inside pocket, feeling as though a bribe had just been refused.

Over lunch in the dining room the conversation was strained. The place was too formal; there were linen tablecloths and crystal glasses. The waiters moved around with a tactful unobtrusiveness that reminded Amery of stage hands changing scenery in the dark. It felt more like a place to begin just one of those things, not to end one.

She picked at her food, pushing it around with the fork. Then reached into her pocket and pulled out a small parcel.

'Hey, Santa came for you too,' she said.

It was a garish red and black silk tie, hand-painted with a motif of tiny butterflies.

'Isn't that marvellous?' he said, though he absolutely hated it. It looked to him like something Bruce Springsteen might wear around his head.

'Isn't it though?' she beamed. 'Soon as I saw it, I thought of you. Maybe I can get you to dress a little brighter in the New Year? Quit walking round like a Presbyterian minister. Or an FBI man.'

'Thank you,' he said. 'That's really very thoughtful.'

'I'm sorry if I was rude earlier,' she said.

'No, I'm the one who's sorry. It was wrong of me.'

'I don't like to be controlled, that's all.'

'I hadn't understood my gift as being controlling. If you felt it was, I apologise.'

She took his hand and squeezed it.

'You're adorable,' she said. 'I don't know what I ever did to deserve you.'

He felt a shrivelling sensation in his heart.

'You make me feel . . . so complete, Milton. I can't imagine ever being without you now.'

'That's really . . . terribly nice of you,' he managed to say.

'So how was your Christmas dinner, Milton?'

'It was fine.'

'You've been so busy at work lately. Must have been nice for you to spend some time at home.'

He wondered what was the correct response to that. 'Yes,' he tried. 'I suppose it was.'

She nodded. 'I guess you're uncomfortable talking with me about home. But that's OK. I understand.'

He said nothing, just took a sip of wine. But his mouth tasted sour, as though he hadn't brushed his teeth for a week. He was sorry he'd ordered the damn stuff now. Drinking at lunchtime always made him sleepy.

'How was your own day?' he ventured.

'It was nice. My brother and his girlfriend got engaged.'

'Oh, good.'

'I get to be a maid of honour,' she said. 'Flounce around in a big pink dress and get my ass pinched by somebody's pervy uncle.'

'Indeed.'

'Oh, yeah,' she said, remembering something. 'I brought these too.'

She reached into her pocket and placed a bundle of CDs on the table. Demented-looking youths leered from the covers, waving their fists and making offensive gestures. One image he found downright disturbing; a naked baby under water, paddling towards a dollar bill that was impaled on a fishing hook.

'We're having like a New Year clear-out sale in the store today. I thought your kids might like those.'

'That's kind of you. Thank you.'

'Say, maybe we could all get together some time? Me and Lee and Elizabeth?'

'Oh . . . well, yes. That might be nice.'

A waitress came and took the entrée plates away. This was the moment. It had to be now. He opened his mouth and took a deep breath.

'Left a little space for dessert?' he asked.

She smiled. 'I guess.'

'Would you like me to ask for the menu?'

'I was hoping we might order a treat from room service.'

He held his napkin to his lips. *Say it*, he thought. For God's sake, spit it out.

'OK,' he said. 'I'll go get a room.'

It was a single bed, four foot six wide, all they had available at such short notice. The bellboy had smirked – 'Have a good day now' – as he'd accepted the tip and closed the door.

Now here they were again, writhing on the bed, like two helpless and lost little animals. He hadn't even had the chance to get his trousers off. He looked down at her hard tanned hips, inhaled the limey smell of her hair. She kissed him deeply, sucking on the end of his tongue. She raised her legs and clutched his waist between her knees, pulling him closer, her calf winding around his lower back.

It excited him so much to observe her excitement. It was like being present at some remarkable natural phenomenon that ultimately had very little to do with you. Perhaps this was how the ancient druids had felt while sitting on a menhir and gazing up at an eclipse; involved and not involved, simultaneously. Shuddering and sighing, she dug her fingernails into his shoulders and gave a low laugh of throaty desire that almost made him climax.

As a young man interested in Russian history, he had found Bolshevik memoirs the most useful thing to focus on in these circumstances. There were few rushes of flaming ardour that could not be quelled by Trotsky's analysis of the regressive role of the lumpenproletariat. *It is the duty of every single organ of the party to penetrate the backward parts of the working class.* You didn't get sentences like that just anywhere.

Trotsky had served him exceedingly well. His early college relationships had been happy and fulfilling, he had found sex easy, it was something at which he excelled. Perhaps for that reason, he was the only young man in first-year medicine whose previous girlfriends all still spoke to him. They flashed through his consciousness now, a tangle of elastic and hastily loosened cheesecloth, adumbrated by the varnishy smell of the leatherette from the back seat of his first car. The girls he had known then were so uncomplicated. Nobody ever talked about sex. That was the great thing about the late sixties. Sex was just something you did if you could. You were tremendously grateful about it but you didn't analyse it too much; it was, in that sense, like being American. And if you had to fumble and fidget a bit before you got it right, why, that was all part of the fun of the thing. For God's sake, it was a bit of an adventure. It was more fun, more educational, more romantic.

When he'd met Ellen Donnelly, one sunny afternoon in third year, he had thought she was so beautiful that he couldn't stop looking at her. She had the loveliest face he had ever seen; an open, generous, gentle face without one single trace of guile. That night he had written in his journal that he had met the girl he was going to marry. She was dating idiotic Dick Spiggot at the time and it had taken quite some effort to woo her away. Spiggot was a moron, but what could you do? Sometimes – in fact, often – beautiful women seemed to like morons. When she'd laugh at one of his imbecilic jokes, at his asinine bray or his Donald Duck voice, Amery wanted to commit murder.

He arranged his timetable so he would bump into her outside lectures; he haunted the cafeteria when he knew she had a free period; skulked around the library late at night in the hope of finding her there alone.

She and Spiggot had been in a play at the time, some awful piece of tat by Eugene O'Neill. Amery attended every night for the remainder of the run, waiting until the lights were about to dim before slipping secretly into the back row. He would sit in the darkness transfixed by her movements, admiring her grace, the way she walked, the heartbreakingly inefficient way she held a cigarette. One night she had stumbled on her lines and corpsed with embarrassed laughter. A knot of helpless longing had formed in Amery's heart. When she came out at the end to acknowledge the applause, he wanted to stand up on his seat and bellow that he loved her. The next night he almost did. By the end of the run he was silently mouthing her dialogue along with her.

You can put that goddamn bottle down, mother. I've told you already, I'm leaving this town.

243

For three whole months they had just kissed and touched. But that was fine, he didn't want to rush things. Amery had a classmate who was Irish Catholic too; the boy had explained that they saw sex as evil. That, in the main, was what Catholics talked about in the confessional, the dark sinfulness of their physical urges. It made him weak with desire to think of her doing that. Imagine having sex with someone who was sure she was going to Hell for having it. Imagine the time she'd want to have before going. He began to have fantasies about being a priest.

They had gone dancing, to movies, to concerts in Central Park. He had introduced her to opera; she had brought him to see a strange rock group called the Velvet Underground. And then one night towards the end of that summer she had wondered aloud why he hadn't yet asked her to sleep with him. The first time they did, Trotsky let him down badly.

But there were other things you could think about to delay the inevitable. Random acts of complex multiplication had got him through their courtship. After they had married, there was the staggering cost of household insurance, the remembered image of a diaper on the kitchen floor, the mental planning-out of a demanding operation on someone's eyebags, and in later years – not that the need had arisen much in later years – the sheer physical appearance of President Gerald Ford. If ever a man could delay your orgasm, Ford could. The Republicans, it seemed, thought of everything.

And then, quite quickly, or so it seemed now, things had started to change between them. Before he had even truly begun to think of himself as a father, Elizabeth had started school and Lee was six months old. He had set up his own practice around then, and the following year Ellen had decided to apply for a teaching job. Without his noticing, their lives had somehow speeded up. It had worsened around the time her parents died, the time she had started to go to Ireland. By then Dan Quayle was beginning to gain national prominence, but his great usefulness was wasted, they hardly ever made love any more. They would tell each other they were simply too tired.

The counsellor woman he had seen with Ellen had said it

was wrong to think of sex as a task. And try as he might, Amery could not figure that out. All his adult life, he had assumed that was precisely what you were supposed to do. Given the facts of biology, not to mention the existence of feminism, wasn't that just being selfless?

Cathy moaned and pushed against him. He found himself mentally reciting the names of golf courses within a five-mile radius of his home. *Fenway, Saxon Woods, Quaker Ridge, Winged Foot.*

She began to gnaw on his chest now, her strong fingers rhythmically kneading his buttocks, her firm thighs writhing against his own.

Wykagyl . . . Bonnie Briar . . . Siwanoy . . . Leewood.

For some strange reason a joke came into his mind, that a taxi driver had told him once in Dublin. What was the definition of Irish foreplay? Brace yourself, Bridget, and start saying the rosary.

She began to lick and kiss his nipples. By way of response he gave a half-hearted, disconsolate thrust.

'Milton,' she sighed. 'Milton . . . Milton.'

He began picturing the train journey from home to work.

Scarsdale Station, he thought. *Crestwood, Tuckahoe, Bronxville, Fleetwood . . .*

'Yes,' she sighed. 'Oh God, yes.'

Mount Vernon West, Wakefield, Woodlawn . . .

'Oh, Jesus,' she groaned, squeezing his hips and pushing harder against him. 'I'm so close, Milton.'

Williams Bridge, Botanical Garden.

'Ahhh.'

Fordam . . . Tremont . . .

'Oh, God . . . I'm . . .'

Melrose.

'Yes!'

125th Street . . .

'Yess! . . . Oh God, yes. There. Harder.'

Grand . . . Central . . . Terminal . . . Station.

She screamed and grabbed him, shuddering wildly, sinking her teeth into his neck.

'Did you come?' he squeaked. He thought she probably had, but he desperately wanted to make her say something so she'd open her teeth and release his jugular.

'Don't stop, Milton . . . Please don't stop.'

'Cathy,' he said. 'I think we need to talk.'

'God, yes, yes . . . Talk dirty to me.'

'That isn't really what I meant.'

'Oh, yes,' she urged. 'Tell me what you're gonna do to me, Corporal.'

'I meant a talk about our relationship.'

She stopped moving. Opened her eyes.

'Now?'

'Well, yes . . . The fact is, I think it's time to end things between us.'

She grinned in disbelief. 'No way.'

'Yes. I'm sorry.'

She sat up on her elbows. 'Let me understand something. You're breaking up with me while you're *inside* me?'

'I realise the timing isn't the best.'

She plumped back down and put her hands to her face.

'The age of fucking chivalry,' she said.

He climbed delicately out of bed, pulled up his trousers, put on a robe.

'I understand that this may come as a shock to you. But I really feel it's time to let matters lie.'

She said nothing.

'I just feel I'm kind of holding you back. There's a great big world of experience out there, after all.'

She scoffed. 'Why don't you just tell me you don't deserve me? Isn't that the next line of the script here?'

He swallowed. 'There's no need to be insulting, Cathy.'

'I know there's no need to. It's just that it's fun.'

'I . . .'

'Do you think you could pass me my jeans before you get into your soliloquy?'

He picked them up and handed them to her. They were made of black leather and had a bondage strap attaching the knees. Eyebrows had been raised when they strolled across the lobby towards the elevators. He'd wondered if people thought he had procured some kind of S and M hooker. For one awful moment, he had thought the concierge might call the police.

She took a pack of cigarettes from the pocket and lit one up.

'Well . . . You're right, I know, Milton . . . I suppose I'm relieved.'

His heart gave a cautiously cheerful flutter. 'Why's that?'

'I guess I had some guilt. What we were doing never felt right.'

(Yesss. Thank you, God. Oh, Lord, thank you.)

He placed a reassuring hand on her shoulder. 'You haven't done much to justify guilt. If it's Ellen you're worried about, she certainly doesn't know.'

She looked up at him blankly.

'You really don't get it, do you?'

'Get what?'

She rolled her eyes. 'You think I owe your wife something, Milton? I'm not the one who fucking married her.'

'So . . . what do you feel guilty for?'

'Well, Jesus, what do you think? I've been seeing someone else. He'd be so upset if he knew what I'd been doing.'

Through the window, the sun was already setting over the skyscrapers. The sky was streaked with orange cloud. An aeroplane was slowly moving in from the west, a plume of purplish exhaust behind it.

'How long for?'

'Well . . . since before I met you.'

'I hadn't realised that.'

She sat up in bed and put on her bra, reaching her hands behind her back to clip it.

'Yeah. I have a boyfriend. We've been together three years.' She spoke matter-of-factly, as though answering a survey. 'He's a real good guy. You'd like him a lot.'

'So do you love him?'

She shrugged. 'I guess I wouldn't be marrying him if I didn't love him.'

'You're *marrying* him?'

247

'Well, yeah. Isn't that what you do when you love someone to death?'

'But . . . so why did we get involved, then?'

'Well, see, I didn't see it as involved exactly. I guess around the time Donny started asking me to get married I had some doubts. Because he's a great guy and the sex was mind-blowingly awesome, but, you know, the grass is always greener and all that. So I figured I'd sleep with someone else a few times and make a comparison. And then just . . . one thing led to another.'

'But it's been two years, Cathy. It's been more than that.'

'Time flies like an arrow,' she said. 'And fruit flies like a banana.'

'I see.' He sat on the edge of the bed. 'So may I ask how I compared?'

'Well, I don't want to hurt your feelings.'

'. . . I beg your pardon?'

'God, that came out wrong, sorry. I know you did your very best. Really, I couldn't fault you for enthusiasm.'

She put on her shirt and began to button it closed, whistling softly. When she had finished, she rolled up the sleeves and squinted around the room.

'Oh . . . Could you pass me my panties, Milton? I think they're on the floor there? By the trouser press?'

He picked them up and handed them to her.

She looked at them and grinned. 'I guess you tore 'em a little. With your teeth.'

She lay on her back and pulled them on, legs in the air, wriggling her butt. Her jeans she tugged on the same way, easing them up over her thighs and hips. Then she stepped out of the bed, tucking the hem of her shirt into the waistband, wrinkling her face with effort as she tried to pull up her zipper.

'What?' she said, working her waist button closed. 'You look a little . . . hurt or something. Like a cocker spaniel that didn't get a biscuit.'

'I don't know. I guess I sometimes thought that we might have had a future.'

She laughed out loud and pulled a face. 'Jesus, Milton. Are you totally nuts?'

'But I did think that. Is that so strange?'

'Let me understand this. You thought I'd want to get seriously involved with a married man who wants to screw me twice a week in some hotel room?'

'Well, I . . .'

'I think I deserve a little better than that. Don't you?'

She went into the bathroom and ran some water in the sink. He watched in the mirror as she washed her face and her long graceful neck. She pulled a comb from her hip pocket and began to tidy her hair.

'Oh, hey,' she said gently, coming back in. 'I can see you're upset. But we're adults. It happens. We had a few laughs and now it's over. And you should be with someone of your own age anyway.'

She took her jacket from the sofa and slipped it on, pulled a scarf from the pocket and wrapped it around her neck.

'*Vaya con Dios*. I gotta go sell records.'

'Look, Cathy. Please. I don't want things to end this way.'

'Well, neither do I, so . . .' She held out her hand and smiled brightly. 'Friends?'

'Well . . . I . . .' She took his hand and shook it a few times.

'Can I give you a little piece of advice, Milton? As a friend?'

'Why, yes. Of course.'

She picked up the Yellow Pages from the bedside locker and tossed it to him.

'Be all you can be, babe. Look under T. For therapists.'

WEDNESDAY,
28 DECEMBER 1994

Chapter Nineteen

He had agreed to meet her at half-eight for breakfast but when he woke up it was almost nine. Without shaving or showering he threw a handful of clothes into a shopping bag and left the house, taking time to lock the doors.

The morning was tartly cold; the air had a faint taste of peat. A muffling of snow dampened everything down. Three waxwings were pecking berries in the frozen hawthorn by the gate while the Bradleys' collie, De Valera, pawed sulkily at a marbled puddle. The bird tables, the cars in the driveways, the bins outside the bungalows were covered with crisp crystalline snow, the kind that melted fast in your palm when you tried to roll a snowball. In the distance a white sheet shrouded the Dublin Mountains. He made it into town in forty minutes, put the Mini on the double yellows outside Hannigan's Hotel.

She was in the lobby, at a table by herself, sipping tea and reading the *Irish Independent*. A bright smile illuminated her face when she saw him come in. She looked well rested, clear-eyed, contented.

'So, m'lady,' he said. 'Your chariot awaits. Sorry the driver couldn't wake himself up.'

'Want a cup of coffee before we go?'

'We better try and make a start. The roads aren't the Mae West today.'

'But I ordered you one. Look.'

She pulled a fluffy tea-cosy off a squat coffee pot and began to butter him a piece of toast.

'Sit down for five minutes, Martin. You look like the kind of man likes his coffee in the mornings.'

'I thought you'd be dying to get going.'

253

'I've waited forty-six years,' she shrugged. 'I think I can manage ten minutes more.'

He thought about the forthcoming journey as he chewed his toast. It felt exciting to be going away, escaping the city for the first time in months. How great it would be to leave the place behind. His clothes, his skin felt grubby with exhaust fumes, his heart dirtied by Dublin. He wondered if he would call to see Valerie's family. It had been so long now, they'd hardly recognise him. What would their attitude be now? What had Valerie told them about him lately?

She pulled a fold-up map from her pocket.

'So I worked out a route for us last night when I got back. Here.'

He glanced at the map and shook his head. 'We can't go that way, it would take too long.'

'But it's only a hundred and fifty miles.'

He laughed. 'A hundred and fifty Irish miles. On a hundred and fifty miles of Irish road. They've potholes up that end of the country like the Grand Canyon.'

'So what will it take? Four hours?'

'If we take the main road we'll be there in six. Maybe seven or eight if the weather's bad. Add in a bit of time for lunch, it'll be evening anyway by the time we hit Donegal.'

Her face took on a dark, disappointed look. She stared at the map hard, as though by staring she could alter its contours, and after a moment raised her free hand to smooth the hair from her forehead. The movement laid bare the silky, pale flesh of her inner wrist, and somehow gave her a helpless and frightened air, as though she had thought what he'd said unjust. His eyes fell on the shadowy outline of her collarbone. An ache of something that felt uneasily like longing filled him. She was so strong and so deeply wounded; fragility hung about her like a muted perfume, as it often did with people who seemed cheerful and brave when you met them first. He had a faint desire to stand up and embrace her, simply tell her he would do his best.

'Maybe this is stupid,' she sighed.

'Course it isn't. How do you mean?'

'It's just . . .' She looked away.

'I like being in your company, Ellen.'

'I know that,' she answered, quietly. 'You show me that.'

'Well then.'

She turned to him again. 'You're certain you want to do this, Martin? I understand completely if you want to change your mind.'

'Sure I'm sure. Why wouldn't I be?'

'It seems a bit crazy somehow. When we only met the other evening.'

'But I told you last night, I'm going anyway.'

'You didn't just say that?'

He laughed at her directness. 'No way. I've had it planned for months.'

She gave him an amused, disbelieving look. She had done something to her hair that made her appear younger. He wondered what exactly that might be.

'I swear to God,' he said. 'I had it planned before Christmas. That's why I took all this holiday now.'

'I'd insist on paying for half the gas.'

'I'd rather you didn't. But if you want to, that's fine.'

'It's not what I want. It's an absolute condition.'

'OK,' he shrugged.

'And I'd need to get some clothes first.'

'Some . . . ?'

'My clothes never turned up from the airport, you see. So I'm wearing all I possess right now. I don't want to meet my mother looking like a refugee.'

He wanted to tell her she looked beautiful then. But maybe that wasn't a good idea.

'Have you thought about it, Ellen? Exactly how you'll find her?'

Her eyes had a kind of unearthly clarity.

'I think her name is Margaret Derrington. Or Doherty.' She cut a piece of toast in half. 'And that she lives in Malin town. Or near it.'

'How d'you know that much?'

'We were briefly in touch by letter a few years back. Round 1986.'

'Oh.' He reached into his pocket. 'I forgot this, I'm sorry. I took it from your coat when I saw you in the hospital Christmas Day.'

She took the letter from him and looked at it closely, as though seeing it for the first time.

'I could barely read it, to be honest, Ellen. I just wanted to see if I could find who you were.'

'It's OK. I understand.'

'You have an address for her up there, do you?'

She shook her head. 'The condition of writing was that I had to do it through the local convent. Not try to find her directly.'

'Must have been hard to keep to that.'

'Impossible, actually. A few years ago we hired a private detective here in Dublin to see if he could find out a little more.'

'We?'

She blushed. 'I mean I. Sorry.' She folded her hands carefully. 'No, I did mean we. It was when my husband was still alive.'

'I see.'

'He went through the Donegal newspapers for the time I was born. Did a little cross-referencing in some files I'd found myself. She'd let one or two clues slip in her letters.' She smiled without looking at him. 'Maybe she wanted that. So Mr Freud would say. Like the criminal who wants to get caught.'

Aitken laughed. 'I haven't met too many of those.'

'You know what I mean though.'

'Yes, I do. It must have all been very stressful on you.'

She laughed. 'It wasn't so bad as a matter of fact. Turned out I was three months younger than I'd always thought.'

They finished their coffee and went outside.

Black-headed gulls were wheeling over the river. A group of boys went past with fishing rods and radios. He took her by the arm and led her to the Mini.

Inside the car felt cold as a fridge. She gave a small shiver and wrapped her arms around herself.

'Yowch,' she said. 'This Irish weather.'

'I'm afraid I'm not well up on where to buy women's clothes, Ellen.'

'I'm sure you must have gone with your wife.' Her playful tone made him smile. 'Or were you the typical Irish male in that regard?'

'I wasn't always invited,' he said.

'Do you know a charity store downtown? Like a secondhand place? I prefer to go to a place like that, if I can.'

'I think I know one. If I can remember where it is.'

He drove down the quays, turned over O'Connell Bridge making towards Stephen's Green. The streets were not as empty as he had imagined. The flower sellers were back in business at their stalls. Groups of tousled backpackers were strolling around taking photographs of each other. Three buskers pounded guitars by the Molly Malone statue. The city had already begun to shake itself out of the sleep of Christmas.

He parked in a multi-storey on Drury Street, led the way to an Oxfam shop on George's Street, a small, bright, place that smelt of incense and damp newspaper. It managed to be neat and somehow inviting despite the piles of shabby cardboard boxes that were stacked high in the corners. Handbags and rucksacks hung from the ceiling. An ornately scripted sign saying *Photocopying available* was leaning against a display mirror that was badly cracked. While she idled through the rails and racks, selecting a few blouses, he wandered down the back and began to flick through the cartons of old records.

There were albums here he hadn't seen in years. Naked John and Yoko peering speculatively over their shoulders. A badly crumpled *Velvet Underground*, with graffiti eyes scrawled on the cartoon banana. The Beatles staring gloomily from the sleeve of *Let It Be*, the black print of the cardboard bleached by time to light grey. How sad it was that someone had had to sell their records. Worse, some junkie had probably filched them, sold the lot for a tenner or swapped them for a fix.

Ellen was holding a wine-coloured shirt on a hanger up to the light, as though she were trying to see through it. An older woman, in an impressive churchy hat, was talking to her in an animated way, pointing at the sleeves and caressing the fabric. He drifted down to the bookshelves and started

257

to browse, half thinking he might buy something to read in Inishowen.

There were trashy airport thrillers and battered teach-yourself manuals, a couple of pornographic paperbacks and glitzy-jacketed bodice-rippers, a pamphlet by John O'Mahony SJ on Our Blessed Mother, Light of the Faithful.

A children's book caught his eye and made him start. *The Boys' Treasury of Irish Ghost Stories*. Its cellophane dust cover had been ripped in a horizontal zigzag and poorly repaired with Sellotape. A wrinkle ran down the cracked spine.

His stomach pulsed.

It couldn't be.

Not after six years, it couldn't be.

He took it down and half opened it at the flyleaf.

> *Robert Aitken is my name*
> *Ireland is my nation*
> *Glasthule is my dwelling place*
> *And heaven my destination.*

Tears pricked his eyes but he blinked them away.

He allowed the fragile book to fall open in his hands. *Dean Swift And The Haunting Of Marsh's Library*. He raised it to his face. The faded paper had a greenish, mouldy smell. His son's messy handwriting blurred before him again, its childishly flourishing curlicues and ornate capitals, the minuscule smiley faces in the dots over the i's. Valerie had bought it for him when he had the flu one time and had to miss the summer soccer tournament. The poor kid had been broken-hearted; he'd been training for months. Tumbling around the house all that sweltering June, in the Packie Bonner goal-keeping gloves he'd got the previous Christmas.

'Martin?'

When he turned, she was holding a dress up to herself. It was in a yellow and gold floral print pattern, old-fashioned and primly neat with a round lacy collar.

'What do you think?'

He swallowed back his tears again. 'Yeah. Nice.'

In fact he didn't like it at all. Not that it mattered, but he thought it was something a grandmother would wear. A grandmother probably had, before it ended up here.

'You think it's me?'

'I wouldn't know about that.'

She tutted, rolled her eyes to the ceiling, exchanged a meaningful glance with a nearby assistant.

'Surely you have an opinion you could give me?'

'I think it's very nice,' he said.

She put her hand on her hip and regarded him with mock irritation.

'I think it's lovely. Honest to God.'

'Femme fatale?'

'Sure.' He laughed. 'Oxfam *fatale*.'

She went through a dark doorway hung with strips of multi-coloured plastic and into the changing area at the back. He paid for the book and slipped it into his pocket, feeling an awkward light-headed unease now, as though the assistant might somehow know where it had come from and admonish him for ever having allowed it to be sold.

A middle-aged man sidled into the shop wearing baggy moleskin trousers, battered sneakers, a rumpled duffel coat. It was Jimmy Plunkett, a professional shoplifter and cheat. Back in 1970 he'd been Aitken's first arrest. Once or twice a year ever since they had celebrated their special relationship by repeating the event.

He watched for a while as Plunkett fingered through the rails. Poor old Jimmy. The state of him now. Such a handsome kid he was back then. But ten or twelve years ago he'd gone on to heroin, spiked himself up one Easter Monday night with what turned out to be rat poison. The seizure had almost burst his heart, had given him a stroke that left his mouth twisted halfway round his cheek. If you glanced at him quickly from the side-on position he had the look of a living Picasso. Not that it was anything much to laugh about. Though Jimmy himself often did.

He thought he'd better speak to him before he stole something.

'What's the crack, Jimmy, you bowsie?'

Plunkett whipped around, looking florid with guilt. He replaced a khaki shirt on a hanger and ran his fingers through his greasy yellow hair. His mangled face exploded into a smile.

'Jayzus Christ,' he piped, in his wheezy, feeble voice. 'Would you fuck off, you fat fuckeryeh.'

'Happy Christmas to you too, James.'

He shuffled over and shook Aitken's hand. 'What you doin in a gaff like this? They mustn't be payin yeh down at the piggery.'

'They'd want to be deckin me out in diamonds to make it worth dealin with gaugers like you.'

'Yeah, yeah. Yeh love me really. It's the likes of me keeps youse shites employed.'

'Yeah. Thanks a mill, Jimmy, for all you've done for me.'

Aitken glanced over his shoulder. Nobody was looking.

'Anything on you today, Jim?'

'Well . . . a little bitta percy, just . . . Don't tell me you're gonna do me?'

'Course I'm not . . . Let me have a ten off you?'

Plunkett sniffed, looked around carefully, reached into his pocket; handed over a small twist of tinfoil. Aitken slipped him a ten-pound note. Plunkett nodded and gave a soft cough.

'Yeah. So listen, Martin . . . I've somethin to tell yeh.'

'What's that?'

He beamed with pride. 'I'm off the gear.'

'No way. Are you?'

'Straight up, man. Serio. Off it three months next Tuesday. I'm on the phiseptone.' He gave a sudden shudder. 'Natalie says there's methadone in me madness.'

'Fair balls to you, Jimmy. That's fantastic news.'

'The phi makes it a bit easier. Takes the longin off a bit.'

'That's not easy and never was. You must be thrilled skinny with yourself.'

'I'm made up,' he agreed, 'if I can only stick it now.'

Plunkett went silent, his eyes flitting around the shop. Aitken found himself wondering what it was he wanted to steal.

'So what else has you busy this weather, Jimmy?'

He shrugged. 'Was knockin round the buildings for a while but it didn't work out. I'm back to bein an artist now.'

'An artist?'

'Yeah. Drawin the fuckin dole.'

He laughed loud at himself, his mouth opened wide, a hell's gate of raw gums and twisted black bicuspids.

'Better than puttin up in the Joy though, James.'

'Prolly be back there soon enough. Just a bit of a Christmas cease-fire, you know? Makes yeh feel bad to be robbin at Christmas.' He snuffled. 'Like little robbin fuckin redbreast.'

'You want to stop actin the maggot and stay well clear of that place, Jimmy. Specially now you're after kickin the old scag.'

Plunkett gave him a look like they both knew all about it. 'No bleedin choice, man. Be back to work now soon enough. In the New Year like. The baby needs clothes. And another one on the way.'

'Natalie's expecting again, is she?'

He gave a rueful sigh. 'Honest to the livin Christ, Martin, if I do as much as look at that mott she gets herself up the pole.' His pale sick eyes gave a sudden roll. 'True's fuck. She must have ovaries the size of bowlin balls.'

'Did you never hear tell of precautions in your life?'

'Sure she swore to Christ she was on the Benny Hill when I met her. But what can yeh do, man? I love the mare.'

'Tell her I was askin for her. She's a lovely girl.'

'She is, yeah. Be lost without her, Martin.'

'I haven't a breeze how an awful-lookin ibex like yourself ever got her.'

Jimmy grinned. 'I dunno either, sheriff. Must be me body she's after. Course some motts prefer the older man. Yeh know yerself.'

Rain splattered against the window. Ellen had emerged and was rummaging through a plywood tea chest of old shoes now, with three bright blouses draped over her arm.

'And how's the crack with yourself, Mr Aitken? Anythin strange or startlin this weather?'

'Not a thing, Jimmy. Just mopin along.'

'Yeah. You're lookin well. They give yeh your auld gun back yet, no?'

'Don't you think I woulda shot you by now if they had?'

Plunkett guffawed appreciatively. 'Very good, very good.' He licked his lips, which was difficult enough, and glanced over his shoulder. 'I can get yeh one if you want, Martin. Now there's a fella up my way . . .'

'Fuck off, Jimmy.'

'But . . .'

'You want me to have to lift you?'

Plunkett's face took on a sly look. 'Don't be getting arsey with me now, hairoil. You might need one soon enough. What I'm after hearin lately.'

'What's that?'

'It's all over the shop yeh lifted the Mouse Doogan, Friday. He's not what yeh might call happy about it.'

'Well, my heart pumps piss for him.'

Plunkett didn't laugh. 'Take the shite out of your lugs and listen up, sweat. That cunt Doogan is a shaggin psycho. He's twisted, man, him and all belongin to him. You wouldn't want to piss on his chips again, I'm tellin yeh. Cos that one's a bleedin space cadet.'

'I know what he is, OK?'

'Oh, y'do? Y'know there's talk he's after puttin out a contract on yeh?'

He could see that Plunkett wasn't joking. He lit a cigarette and forced a laugh. 'Course I do, Jimmy. What? You think I don't hear things these days?'

'Well, just, I'd be shockin careful, if I was you. Take it handy, keep the head down. Because that's one Comanche would slit your throat soon as pick his shaggin nose.'

In the corner of his eye, he saw Ellen approach him. He reached into his wallet and took out a fifty-pound note, which he pressed into Plunkett's fingers.

'What's that supposed to be?'

'It's a holy picture, Jimmy. What the fuck do you think?'

'But . . . Christ, Martin. I couldn't take that off yeh.'

'Take the bloody thing before I burst you. For the baby.'

He looked at the note. 'I dunno what to say, man.'

'Well, just shove it in your britches and say shag all, then. And I catch you robbin I'll reef the arm off you, Jimmy, and beat you to death with the wet end. I swear.'

'I better not let yeh catch me in that case.' He winked.

Plunkett was into his happy villain act now, a routine at which he wasn't as good as he thought any more. He was too sick, too frightened. Aitken had seen it too many times. It depressed him to see it being dusted off again. He'd always known Jimmy had more going on than that, more brains and resilience than any glib suburbanite; he couldn't have survived this long if he hadn't. Born somewhere else he'd have ended up in a boardroom, or ripping it up on the golf course with the boys. It was bad luck and geography that had put him in the way of the law, and to say it was much else was the filthiest lie of the lot. These days all he had left was to play the character, the lovable wise-cracking Dubbalin blackguard. And Aitken liked to play the cop. Neither of them would ever change now.

'You hear anything else about that mad prick Doogan, you gimme a bell and let me know, all right?'

'Sound,' said Plunkett. 'But keep it quiet, for Jayzus' sake. And he found out I told yeh, he'd plaster a jacks door with me.'

Ellen was standing behind them now. She hadn't made a good job of putting her coat back on, so the corner of her collar was tucked inside. She looked at Aitken quizzically. 'Ellen,' he said, 'this is . . .'

'Morning, Missus Aitken,' Plunkett grinned, saluting briefly. 'Lovely to meet at last.'

'Oh.'

'I'm a professional associate of the inspector here. The inspector's always talkin about you.'

'Oh, he is?'

'He is, he is, on me word of honour. Never done talkin about you, so he isn't. I love that woman like there's no tomorrow, Jimmy, I love her the way I love me own life. Sure he's famous for talkin about yeh, so he is.'

She turned to Aitken and smiled. 'That's so nice of you, honey.'

'My pleasure,' he replied.

'A wife likes to hear these things.'

He reached out to fix her collar. 'And a husband likes to say them, dear.'

'Look at the pair of yez,' Plunkett beamed, raising his hands in benediction. 'Still love's old sweet song after all these years. You're a marvellous example to us all, so yez are. Now I remember the mother once sayin to me . . .'

'Hey . . . Jimmy?'

'Yes, Mr Aitken?'

'Look after yourself, all right? Get somethin to eat.'

'Oh . . . OK. Keep it country.'

He left the shop, walking backwards, almost as though he intended to bow.

Chapter Twenty

They weren't prepared for the wind, which rushed up against them like a great flat wave, making his trouser legs flap as they walked back towards the car park. The ice and snow had begun to thaw; a gurgle of slushy water ran in the gutters, trickled and dripped from the awnings and rooftops. She kept stopping and dawdling by the shop windows, asking what he thought of these shoes and those sweaters.

'Really, Ellen, we should think about hitting the road. It's nearly twelve o'clock already.'

'I need to get just a few more things.'

'Like?'

'Like the kind of intimate items you wouldn't want to buy second-hand.'

'Oh.'

'Indeed. Oh. You know a department store around here?'

They went into a chainstore in the Stephen's Green mall, a vast, painfully bright place where the excessive heat gave the air a rubbery smell. While she bought underwear, tights and socks, he went to the cashpoint and tried to get two hundred pounds. The screen told him it would only allow him fifty.

He thought about what Plunkett had told him. Should he be worried? Was he being stalked even now? Was the guy he'd seen yesterday in the strange sunglasses something to do with it? EXCEEDED LIMIT, the screen insisted. Suddenly he had a sensation that someone was watching him again. He turned and let his eyes scan the shop. Women with prams and trolleys. Men with shopping baskets. Shrieking children racing the aisles. From above his head came a clicking, buzzing sound as a closed-circuit camera swivelled to focus on him.

Maybe, after all, there was nothing to worry about. Dublin

was the world capital of hearsay evidence; along with lamenting the traffic and the price of houses, rumour-mongering was the citizens' favourite pastime. Surely to Christ even a madman like Doogan wouldn't order you killed just for arresting him.

Back in the car she handed him a plastic bag. 'That's for you.'

When he opened it he found a thick blue sweater.

'What's this?'

'Just a gift.'

'There was no need, Ellen. Really.'

She shrugged. 'It's Christmas though.'

'Well . . . thanks. That's lovely.'

'Aren't you going to put it on?'

He took it out of its packet and pulled it over his head.

'It's nice on you,' she said. 'It brings out the colour of your eyes.'

He laughed. 'They didn't have it in red, no?'

'I guess not. But I'll keep looking.'

He drove out of the car park and up through town. The moon was already visible in the northern sky. Up through Dorset Street and out towards the suburbs.

YOU ARE NOW LEAVING DUBLIN CITY

They turned onto the N3 for Donegal.

*   *   *

It was something Amery had always liked to do when he had a little time, particularly during the holidays when the city was quiet: take an early train into town by himself and potter around his office for a while.

This morning when he arrived, a globe-shaped object swathed in bubble wrap was sitting in the corridor outside the surgery door, along with a note from the janitor to say it had been delivered last thing Christmas Eve. Assuming it was a gift from a colleague or a grateful patient, he picked it up and brought it inside.

The room was warm and smelt of stale coffee. He tuned his receptionist's radio to a light classical channel, picked up the

266

pile of mail from the welcome mat, raised the windows to let in some air.

He took the object and rested it on his knees. It felt satisfyingly heavy, a good solid handful. He snipped the tape with the point of a letter opener and carefully peeled back the layers of wrapping.

It was the new cross-section model he'd ordered, of a portion of the human skin. Its constituent parts were marked and labelled. Epidermis and basal layer, sweat gland and dermis, hair follicle and sebaceous gland.

He set it with care on his secretary's desk and spent some time simply admiring it. It was as absolutely beautiful as any Renaissance work of art. In fact it was more beautiful, because its purpose was definable and important. He said the word 'sebaceous' aloud. It thrilled him to say it, as it always had.

He loved the vocabulary that attended his profession. Tretinoin. Dermabrasion. Microsuction. Tyrosinase. To Amery, those words had an almost alchemical ring. They were redolent of wizardry, magic, sacrament. Subconjunctival blepharoplasty! Corrugator resection! Hydroquinone! His patients loved to hear those words too. They didn't want to know about facial scrapes and nose jobs. They wanted to hear *the correct language*. Everywhere you went now, language was debased. For God's sake, they wanted some beauty in their lives. Who would be merciless enough to deny them that?

It was all to do with turning back time. If not actually stopping the great celestial clock, then at least managing to slow it down a little – or, preferably, a lot. That was the great preoccupation of his profession. But then half of modern American medicine was almost religiously fixated on that, if people were only honest about it. Not that there was anything wrong with that either. Who was to say we should all accept decrepitude, crawl towards the grave without even a fight? Old Father Time had the cards marked, but you could reach under the table for an extra ace occasionally.

Some of his classmates who had gone into more conventional specialisms saw Amery's own as faintly ridiculous, regarded his patients as pathetic and vain. Even Ellen, he felt sure, had never been truly comfortable with the decision he had made shortly after qualifying to abandon his plans of becoming a geriatrician and opt instead for cosmetic medicine. Your husband being a plastic surgeon didn't play so good with the Save the Whale brigade, he imagined. It didn't give you the punch of being married to a heart man – or preferably a truck driver who'd had his balls blown off in Vietnam and who now did a little Native American-style pottery. Well, that was fine, it didn't bother him one jot. In time, he knew, they would all come to see he was right. For those old Manhattan ladies, those wrinkled womanly men – those beautiful girls who were already almost perfect but who said simply *no*, almost isn't enough – they weren't pitiful to him, they were heroes. They embodied the spirit that had made the country great. No wonder plastic surgery had been pioneered in America. Pioneer, for once, was the appropriate word. That's what they were, these frail stubborn New Yorkers he treated, with their puffy eyebags and pouchy buttocks, their wrinkles and frown lines and moles and carbuncles: brave frontiersmen, gallant pilgrims, setting out across the vast desert of ageing, the prairie of entropy, the wasteland of wasted time, to subdue and tame and fence off and make boundaries.

Yippie aye goddamn yay!

Only death itself couldn't be cheated. At least not for the moment, though in the future who could tell? He had several patients already who intended to be cryogenically frozen when their time came. And the research being done on human cloning would lead in the end to permanent rejuvenation. Nobody had published much on it yet, but that was where the science was leading; surely anyone with even a non-Ivy League brain could see it. Theoretically at least, people could stay forever young. Just like Bob Dylan said. That would be America's greatest bequest to the world – the gift of eternal youth lusted after by the sages of old.

He thought of something he'd heard in Ireland once; a time Ellen had dragged him along with her to mass. *The Word was made flesh and dwelt among us*. It was such an astonishingly beautiful image he had almost wept. The flesh was sacred;

it was miraculous and sanctified. Afterwards, when he'd told Ellen how he felt, she hadn't seemed to understand. In fact she'd looked at him as though he were nuts.

What had happened between himself and Ellen? He pictured them playing golf at Headford, the breeze blowing her hair and ruddying her face. Taking off her shoe in the hotel room and gently massaging her swollen foot. Sipping hot whiskies by the turf fire in the lobby. That trip was the year Lee turned five or six. They'd been happy then, or so it had honestly seemed. And now they weren't. But the line between those two fixed points had meandered so imperceptibly that he wouldn't have been able to trace it, never mind point to its beginning. Were they actually different people then? Over a period of two years, your skin was shed and completely replaced. Was it insane to think that had something to do with it? Was it your flesh that contained your soul?

Or had they ever been truly happy? Wasn't it rather the case that like two coterminous countries they were inextricably close, interdependent in all sorts of ways – but not actually one. Never truly unified. That had never happened and it wouldn't now. What they had come to love most was the border between them.

Cathy had left him, as he had wanted her to do for a long time, almost since the first occasion they had slept together. The way she had done it had hurt a little, but still, he could take it, he was glad it was over. It was all for the best. Cathy had been unique; there was no doubt about it. But someone else would come along soon. And she'd be unique too. Life would go on.

Men sometimes used the language of hunting to talk about courtship, but Amery felt that wasn't right. For him, it was demonstrably more like sports fishing. Dangle your bait. Sit back in your boat. Wait for the bite. Then reel in like crazy, as though your very salvation depended on this one act of mastery. Make sure your pals all got to know about it. Then almost immediately throw the catch back in.

He knew it wasn't modern to see it like that, but, nevertheless, that was the way it was. He had some mysterious thing that women wanted, he always had; there was nothing he could do

269

about it. Often, he thought, it might be that he came across as damaged. Perhaps it was just that they wanted to fix him up.

The buzzer sounded. That was odd, he wasn't expecting anyone. He went to the security screen and flicked it on. Outside was a strikingly attractive Asian woman in her late twenties. She turned and peered directly into the lens, as though she knew someone was looking at her. She had almond eyes, porcelain skin; a silver cross glittered on the soft part of her neck. A rush of expectancy crackled through him. 'What did I tell you,' he said aloud. 'Get your rod out, Milton old boy.'

He picked up the phone and with studied nonchalance said hello. Thrilled, he watched as she turned her fabulous face towards the lens again.

'May I schedule an appointment to meet with Doctor Amery?'

'This is he.'

'Oh.' She sounded surprised and happy. 'This is Doctor Amery himself?'

'This is Professor Amery, yes.'

Bait that hook, Milton. Cast it in deep.

'Wow. OK. Might I come in for a moment? I wasn't expecting to find you here in person.'

'Actually, surgery isn't open today. I was just attending to some administrative matters.'

'I know I don't have an appointment,' she said. 'But I promise I won't take more than a few moments of your time.'

'Well . . . I don't know. I *am* terribly busy.'

Play that fishy, Milton; string out your lure.

'Please,' she said. 'Won't you see if you can squeeze me in?'

'Oh, come on up then,' he said, with a vulnerable little chuckle. 'Come up and see me, make me smile.'

Squeeze her in. He'd do that all right. He grinned at himself in the mirror on his assistant's desk. Pinched the pallor out of his cheeks. Took out a throat spray and shot a squirt into his mouth. Let's face it, some men had it, others didn't. But he did. Big time. With extra mayo. A few moments later he heard her shoes click along the corridor. Sweet God, she was wearing stilettos. How much better could it possibly get?

A soft knock sounded on the door. He did a silent count to ten before opening it.

She was unbuckling the belt of her stylish leather raincoat, revealing a tight black blouse, short black skirt and red stockings.

'Come in, come in.'

Entering cautiously, she peered around as though in a church. She had a small linen knapsack on her back.

'Wow,' she said. 'So this is where it all happens?'

She was looking at the ceiling now, which he found a little off-putting. He wondered if he should mention that he didn't actually slice people open right here in the lobby. But then maybe that would give the wrong impression.

'You know my work?' he asked.

She gazed at him as though the answer was obvious. 'Oh yes, of course. Doesn't everyone?'

He led her from the reception room into his own office, a large, white-carpeted L-shaped room with a sofa and two armchairs as well as a desk. A bay window looked over the nearby roofs and, in the distance, the green oasis of the park. She gave a small gasp when she saw the view. He noticed that the cleaner had tilted the photograph he kept on his desk of Ellen and the children, in such a way that it couldn't be seen. Silently he cursed her. How stupid she was.

Some men of his acquaintance who ran around with girls made a point of pretending they were single. They would remove their wedding rings, hide pictures of the missus, speak always in the first person singular. But throughout his own two decades of extramarital angling, Amery had found it was actually best to have a photograph of your legal dependants prominently displayed every place you could reasonably display one. Your office, your wallet, on the dashboard of your Lexus. If he could have put a *baby seat* in the damn car, he would have; certainly, he'd kept Lee's there until the boy was practically pubescent. These displays of familial piety had the considerable double advantage of making you look like a down-home, sensitive, caring guy while simultaneously stating that you had serious obligations of a personal nature. You put those two factors together, multiply one by the other, divide by the square root of his dashing good looks, and the equation could only come out one way: a roll in the hay might well be on the cards, but don't go asking for anything else.

Over by the sofa, the beautiful woman was admiring his certificates, with her back to him now, standing on tiptoe to read them. Every time she stretched to see closer, the hem of her skirt rode up a couple of inches more. God in heaven. Sometimes life was good. He wanted to fall to his knees and gnaw her thighs. That supple waist! That shiny hair! Something about her made him want to sing.

She turned and regarded him with admiration.

'Smart guy,' she said.

'Oh well.' He shrugged. 'We do our best.'

'You must have every qualification there is.'

'I like to keep abreast, yes.'

She smiled. 'I bet you do.'

'But I find that side of medicine a little unchallenging. There's so much more to patient care than passing examinations.'

'Right,' she agreed. 'The personal touch.'

'I certainly hope I can offer that,' he agreed.

Deciding against the desk, he sat in the armchair, indicating that she should take the couch. She sat down slowly – Lord, so very slowly – smoothing her small shapely hands over her knees.

'So, tell me, my dear. What can we do for you?'

'Gosh, it's a little embarrassing. I don't know exactly how to begin.'

'Well then . . . just relax.' He picked up the remote control and switched on the music, a ridiculously evocative Chopin nocturne. Another flick of his finger made the curtains slide closed, the antique wall lamps he had bought in Verona now bathing the room in a dim lilac glow.

'Now.' He leaned forward and knotted his brows. 'Why don't you tell me exactly what's on your mind.'

She appeared nervous as she met his eyes. 'I really didn't expect to see you personally. I only intended to make an appointment.'

'There's no need to be embarrassed, Miss.' He smiled under-standingly. 'It is Miss, is it?'

'Miss Fong, yes.'

'So what can we do for you today, Miss Fong?'

She made as if to speak but then changed her mind and bowed her head. God, she was gorgeous. All that wonderful shyness. Already he was imagining how she'd look while having an orgasm.

'This is kind of hard for me,' she said.

There was nothing else for it now, he thought. It was time to get out his big harpoon.

'Tell you what,' he said softly. 'Let me guess.'

She looked up, surprised. 'You want to guess?'

'May I?'

'You really . . . think you can?'

'Some say it's a knack. I prefer to call it . . . my gift.'

She smiled pleasantly. 'Sure. OK.'

'Would you mind standing up for a moment?'

She did as he asked, tucking the hem of her blouse into the waist of her skirt, a gesture that made him swallow hard and think of Trotsky's exegesis of post-Marxian macroeconomics.

'Might I ask your first name? Mine is Milton.'

'Gloria,' she said.

'My, how lovely. Were your parents Latinists?'

'No,' she said. 'Van Morrison fans.'

'Ah, I see.' He laughed gently, yet masterfully. 'Best to keep these things on a friendly basis, don't you think?'

'I guess so, yes.'

'So. You'll be Gloria and I'll be . . . ?'

'Milton,' she smiled.

'Right. Exactly. Now, that's not so bad, is it?'

'No,' she agreed.

'Milton doesn't bite, now does he?'

'No,' she grinned. 'Not unless he's asked to.'

'Would you turn around for me please, Gloria?'

He watched, dry-mouthed, as she slowly rotated before him, arms outstretched like the ballerina on top of a jewellery box. He wanted to stand and yodel her name. A faint aroma of vanilla and musk flowed from her, which sent a flickering blaze through his nerve endings. It was absolutely obvious why she needed his professional help, but apart from that one all-too-apparent blemish, good God, she was astounding, so lithe and taut, so elegant yet so fantastically earthy. She turned through the final degrees of the circle and came to rest facing him again, arms folded demurely beneath her breasts. He summoned up his best sympathetic expression.

'Well . . . it's clear why you've come. Isn't it, dear?'

'It is?'

'I know it's hard for us to face up to it honestly, Gloria. But every precious diamond has its tiny flaw. And believe me, we can do a lot with buttocks like that.'

'We can?'

'Absolutely, absolutely. They really don't have to sag in that fashion. They've just lost their shape a little, is all, that's a natural thing over time. We'll have you back in your tightest jeans in two shakes of a lamb's tail.'

She nodded.

'Professor Amery . . .'

He raised an admonishing finger. 'Ah-ah. Milton, please.'

'Milton . . .'

'The thing, Gloria, about a woman's body . . . it needs to be treated with skill and tenderness. Like a fine musical instrument, really. A Stradivarius. Or a Bechstein, if you will.'

'I think there's been a little misunderstanding, Milton.'

He looked at her. 'There has?'

'I represent the firm of Galsworthy, Bligh, Brinksman, Hamburger.'

'And what might they do?'

'They might be attorneys.'

He swallowed. 'They might?'

'They might, yes.' She handed him a business card.

'Well . . . that's excellent. You're a talented young lady, Gloria, as well as a beautiful one. Now . . .'

She reached into her knapsack, took out a foolscap envelope which was rolled into a tube shape and secured with a rubber band. She placed it gently on the coffee table.

'What's that, Gloria?'

'That's a divorce claim and court summons, Milton.'

He chuckled.

'Your wife, our client, is suing you for four and a half million dollars.'

'What?'

'Four and one half million dollars, the holiday home in Saranac Lake, New York, half your stocks and bonds, a number of specified art works and one of the cars. Please consider yourself officially served as of now.'

She grabbed her bag and went to leave.

'Now, wait a second. Please . . . Don't . . . there's been some mistake here.'

'You're Doctor Milton Longfellow Amery, aren't you?'

'No.'

She squinted at him.

'Well, all right, yes, but . . .'

'And you're married to Ellen Donnelly Amery?'

'Yes, of course. But . . .'

'I guess you won't be for too much longer.'

'But . . . Do you know where my wife is right now?'

'I have no comment to make on that matter.'

'Please tell me.'

'I'm not at liberty to discuss anything, I'm afraid. My instructions are to serve you with these papers and then leave the premises.'

'Please. For God's sake. This will ruin me.'

'Professor Amery, would you kindly let go of my arm, sir?'

'Come on, you're an oriental. Surely to God you understand the importance of not losing face.'

She emitted a sound that was a little like a titter.

'Please, Miss Fong. Tell me. What am I supposed to do?'

'Why don't you fucking guess,' she smiled, 'Milton.'

And left the office, closing the door behind her.

Chapter Twenty-One

Just outside Dublin the road was closed and a half-hour tailback had already formed. There had been an accident a mile up ahead, a policewoman told them, a three-car pile-up that had left a man unconscious and two more with broken limbs. There were severe delays on the diversionary road through the forest but it was fairly clear of snow at least.

'It's the black ice you want to watch for,' she said. 'Keep strict to the speed limit and use the low gears.'

The road to which she pointed turned out to be little more than a boreen, with a badly broken surface and large potholes roughly filled with gravel. As she had predicted, there was almost no settled snow, because the branches of the overhanging conifers were so thick that even the daylight had difficulty peering through.

The road was choked with cars from the motorway, so that it was impossible to drive at more than a crawl. In the car ahead of them, three bored children were kneeling in the back, waving and pulling faces. Ellen laughed and waved in return. One of the trio, a grim-faced little tyke with spiky hair, stuck out his tongue and rolled his eyes. When Ellen repeated the gesture, he raised two fingers back at her, cackling with laughter, until one of his sisters cuffed him on the side of the head.

'That taught him, huh?' Ellen said.

'Good foot in the arse is what that chap needs.'

'You never did anything like that yourself, right?'

'Certainly not. Little altarboy.'

'Oh yeah. I bet.'

'I was. Swear to God.' He made the sign of the cross and intoned solemnly, '*Introibo ad altare Dei.*'

'Daily communicant, were you?'

'As a kid, yes. Believe it or not.'

'And as a grown-up?'

'I certainly went to mass a lot more when they started givin out the wine.' The car chugged maliciously. 'Free booze, you know? Can't be bad.'

They drove on in silence. In a clearing on the right a large oak had fallen, smashing through the roof of a metal shed. Men were working with chainsaws and axes, sawing off branches and loading them into a truck.

Before long the trees became even thicker and it felt as though they were driving through a tunnel. Here and there police were on duty, their luminous jackets bright yellow and orange. They directed the traffic with purpose and concentration as though there was some other way for it to go. A gust of wind sent a hail of pine cones splattering down on the roof of the Mini. The little boy in front raised his head again, smirking, bulging his cheeks, shoving his fingertips up his nose. A cop on a motorbike zoomed past with his lights flashing and his siren on.

'Did you ever do that?' she asked.

'What?'

'Ride a big bike? In your job?'

He laughed. 'I can't really see myself on one of those. Some old jalopy was the most I ever had.'

'Do you actually like the work?'

'It has its moments.'

'Tell me about some of the moments it has.'

He thought about her question as he drove along. A trip he had made maybe fifteen years ago came into his mind, on the night boat to England, accompanying a republican prisoner who was being extradited to face a bombing charge. They had talked about football, their children, music, the two of them sitting in the Pullman lounge, handcuffed together and eating chicken-in-a-basket. When the lights of Liverpool came into view the man had asked Aitken to buy him one last pint. Where he was going now, he joked, they wouldn't be likely to have Guinness on draught. He was resigned to his fate, he expected a life sentence. Aitken had felt strongly that his prisoner was innocent, but he'd had no choice except to deliver

277

him up. The officers from the anti-terrorist squad who'd been waiting at dawn on the embarkation dock grabbed the man by the hair as they dragged him into the squad car. Aitken had intervened, insisting he be treated fairly.

Afterwards he had walked around the centre of Liverpool, killing a few hours until it was time to get the boat home. It was close to Valerie's birthday. When the shops opened he had bought her a gift, then got a few small things for the kids. But all the way back on the restless, churning sea he hadn't been able to stop thinking of the prisoner. How could it be right to hand people over, when you knew for a fact they'd been beaten in custody, when they wouldn't get a fair trial? It had haunted him for months afterwards. He couldn't look at his own children without thinking of the man's two sons and three daughters. But later new intelligence had come to light. The prisoner was guilty, there was absolutely no doubt. This soft-spoken man who liked the Who and the Small Faces had taken an early morning plane from Dublin six months previously, placed a Semtex bomb in a litter bin in a London street, set the timer and cycled away. It was a miracle that only one person had been killed, a Pakistani shopkeeper on his way to work. It had taken him almost three weeks to die.

He glanced across and noticed Ellen was asleep, her left cheekbone leaning against the glass, her hands tucked between her crossed knees. He turned the heat up a little. She gave a troubled murmur and wrapped her arm around her neck.

Up ahead, he could see the glow of streetlights. The tunnel of trees came to an end and opened out on to a slightly larger road. There were no signposts in any direction. He pulled out and turned right, what he thought felt northwards again, towards Donegal.

He had only been driving for two hours, but already the city was far behind them. The land looked frozen, lunar, dead. Grey snow lay on the hedgerows and ditches, on the corrugated iron barns and cement milking parlours. It dusted the piles of plastic fertiliser sacks; it filled the iron bathtubs, surreal in the fields. Here and there men were working – repairing fence-posts, shovelling sleet out of gateways.

Off to his right a three-quarter moon was rising, pale and watery against the flat grey sky. To the west, over the mountains, the sun was sinking quickly. Before long it was so dark that he had to switch on his lights. Frustrated now, he felt himself tighten. It had been one of those days that had never got going. The possibility began to arise that they wouldn't make it to Inishowen tonight.

Being in the car was making him tired. His lower back was aching, his wounded leg was stiff and sore. He leaned beneath his seat to push it further backwards, only to find the control lever was stuck. Dusk was coming down faster now. He began to have the feeling he was lost. Perhaps he had taken a wrong turning. A few miles back the road had forked, then forked again five hundred yards later. Some minutes afterwards, as if to confirm his fear, he passed a twisted dead elm he knew he'd seen half an hour earlier. It was standing in the middle of a field, lonely as a lighthouse. Cursing softly, he pulled in to the edge, stopped the car; gingerly opened the glove box to look for a map. Ellen gave a soft restless snore. The glove box was full of rubbish: cassettes, old papers, empty cigarette boxes. But no map. He could have sworn he had one but it wasn't in there now.

He looked under his seat and in the driver's door pocket. An owl hooted close by. He looked at Ellen, asleep beside him. Where was her own map, he wondered? Had she even brought it with her? Had she left it at the hotel? Well, he couldn't just reach over and start searching through her pockets. And anyway, he didn't know where he was. What good was a map with no point of reference to help you read it? The fields around were flat and featureless; there was nothing obvious from which to take a bearing.

He pulled out and began to drive slowly through the dusk, trying to pick out some kind of landmark. He passed an abandoned pub with sheets of mossy corrugated iron in the windows and the words BRITS OUT spray-painted across the door. An old-fashioned telephone box, green as an apple. A humpback stone bridge over a gurgling stream. A statue of the Virgin Mary in a grotto close by on the bank. Ten minutes later

279

he came to a crossroads, took the left turn for no other reason than instinct. He found himself back on the track through the forest, only this time there was no traffic at all.

A wash of panic flowed through him like a drug. Where had all the cars gone? Was this the right direction? Where were the cops who had been on duty earlier? He stopped again and rolled down his window. The air was cold as iced water. Somewhere far away a dog was yelping. The wind made a rustling in the wet leaves and ferns.

In his rearview mirror he saw a single headlight. At first he thought it must be a motorbike. Maybe it was the cop they had seen earlier. But then he saw that it wasn't a bike, but a large car with one headlamp broken. It seemed to be approaching quite fast, a substantial black shape maybe a quarter-mile behind them. He watched it sink from view into a dip in the road. Relieved, he took out a cigarette and lit it. He would stop the driver and ask where he was. A fat, brown rabbit hopped out into the road in front of him, stopped and nuzzled at something on the ground. A twig cracked. It sat bolt upright on its hunkers, still as stone, breath steaming from its mouth.

He looked in his mirror again. The car appeared behind him on the brow of a hill. He flicked on his emergency flashers and waited. But the car stopped.

Its one light dipped and then went dead.

He stepped out of the Mini. There was no light at all now, apart from the clicking red glow of his emergency flashers, spreading blinks of colour across the rain-soaked road and the leaves.

He thought he could hear the car's engine still running.

He waved and beckoned. The car remained still. He waved again. Its engine cut out. It was so dark down the road that he could barely see the car now, let alone make out how many people were in it. Was it possible that they hadn't seen him? What the hell were they doing?

He waved both his arms now. 'Hello?' he called, louder than he intended. The lonesome bray of a donkey answered him back. Somewhere nearby, birds flapped out of trees.

He took a couple of cautious steps forward. The car started up and began to reverse away.

'Hey?' he shouted. 'Come back a second!'

He began to run hard along the track, his bad leg throbbing with pain. Gasps of breath came like rips inside his chest. By the time he got to the brow of the hill, the car was already five hundred yards away, doing a rapid and untidy three-point turn, its engine whining ferociously as though the driver were missing the gears.

'Come back,' he roared. 'I need help.'

He watched it speed off – swerving, righting – until its tail lights had disappeared from view.

'Bastards!' he yelled. 'Youse fucking bastards!'

His voice came back, a dull echo from the trees. Something in the ditch made a low, scuttling sound. A cow bawled from a field behind him.

Glumly he turned and started to trudge back the way he had come, soaked with perspiration, panting hard. How in the name of God could people do something like that? Leave you stranded in the armpit of nowhere. That would never happen in Dublin. A couple of drunken country bumpkins, he reckoned, beered up to their ugly country eyeballs. Off to find a sheep to molest. Dress it up in frillies and have a threesome. Bastards. That was all. Good old rural down-home bastards, whose parents were first cousins and shit-kickers with it. If he ever caught up with them, he'd . . .

He stopped in his tracks. There to his left was a tiny road, with a signpost for Tara nailed to a black tree trunk.

OK. Fine. So they'd showed him the way. But they hadn't meant to do it. They were still bastards.

'You're still bastards!' he yelled down the road.

The cow uttered a gloomy low.

When he got back to the Mini, Ellen was still asleep. He started up, turned, crossed the bridge; took the tiny road towards Tara.

Night had fallen completely now. As if brought on by the darkness, hunger started to gnaw at him. He realised he'd had nothing to eat all day except for the toast which she'd offered

281

him at breakfast. How pleasant that was, to sit by a fire having toast with her. How easy she was to be around. She gave a start and an anxious moan, but he felt he shouldn't wake her up. She twitched, muttered suddenly in her sleep, half-formed words he could barely make out.

Elizabeth . . . Elizabeth.

He wondered who that was.

When he looked at the clock it was almost half-five. He noticed her stir and begin to wake. Her hair was tousled and her moist eyes looked fearful. The strut of the window had left an indentation in her cheek.

'How was the Land of Nod?' he asked.

She peered at him hard, as though she didn't know who he was.

'Are you OK? You've just been asleep for a while.'

She yawned blearily, wrist to her mouth.

'God, how rude of me, Martin. I'm really sorry.'

'You're grand, don't worry.'

She lowered the sun visor and groaned at her reflection, licking her fingertips and smoothing her eyebrows.

'I look like the wreck of the *Edmund Fitzgerald.*'

'You don't,' he said. 'You just look tired.'

A thin spiralling worm of pain unwound slowly down his back.

'I'm so thirsty,' she said. 'Do we have any water?'

'We'll stop soon and get a cup of tea.'

She nodded. 'Be great. Are we nearly there?'

He laughed. 'Afraid not. We had a few problems while you were away with the fairies.'

'Problems?'

'Muggins here got lost and couldn't find the map.'

'It's here,' she said, taking it out of her pocket.

'Well . . . I don't really need it now.'

'So where are we?'

'We're near Tara.'

He glanced at the gauge and noticed that he was low on petrol. A flash of sheet lightning lit up the distant sky and mountains. Suddenly they were driving through a heavy shower of sleet. He jammed up the heater and switched on the wipers. They made a soft thrumm-thrumm as they glided back and forth, a sound he found oddly comforting. She tried to stretch now, and bumped her hands against the roof.

'Sleep a bit more if you like.'

'No, I'm fine.'

'We've a long old drive ahead of us still.'

The windscreen began to mist up. She reached out and cleaned a patch for him with her sleeve, then lazily traced her fingertips through the steam on her own side. 'I don't know what came over me. To sleep like that.'

'Really, you should have another little snooze. It'll be midnight now by the time we get to Donegal.'

She carved a spiral in the steam with her fingertip, leaning her head against the side window again. But she couldn't seem to get comfortable this time. She switched on the radio and turned up the volume. A man was reading the news in Irish. His voice was mellifluous, very clear and pure.

They listened for a few minutes, driving steadily on.

'Do you understand?' she asked him then.

He shook his head. 'I get the odd word.'

'Isn't it compulsory here in the schools?'

'It is, yeah. That's why nobody speaks it.'

She gave him a disapproving look.

'Well, come on.' He laughed. 'What's the point of a language that nobody speaks? I was never able to get the head round that.'

'It's a cultural thing,' she said.

He chuckled. 'Oh janey, is it?'

'Well, of course. It's part of being Irish.'

'My mate Ranj doesn't speak a word of it. But he's an Irish citizen. With an Irish wife and kids.'

'People do speak it. Down in the Gaeltacht.'

It amused him that she was getting so shirty. Only an American could inform you with such certainty that you weren't quite Irish enough to meet some objective standard.

'I know that,' he said. 'I do actually live here.'

'What's that supposed to mean? I don't live here so I can't have a point of view?'

He laughed again, though her abruptness was unnerving him. 'Of course you can. I didn't say that.'

'I don't live in South Africa either, but I have a point of view about apartheid.'

'We're a long way from apartheid here, Ellen.'

She scoffed. 'That's a matter of opinion, I guess.'

Chapter Twenty-Two

A stór mo chroi, in the strangers' land
There is plenty of weeping and wailing.
Where gems adorn the great and grand,
There are faces with hunger paling.

Half an hour later she still seemed to be sulking. The news programme was over, and a soft-voiced man was keening a lament. The Mini hit a pothole and made them both jump, but she folded her arms and stared determinedly away from him, showing no other reaction, remaining silent. The road swooped into a steep incline. The needle on the petrol gauge tilted down below the bottom horizontal of the E.

'Listen, I love the Gaeltacht,' he said. 'I used to go every summer with my kids.'

She said nothing.

'Look, Ellen, I didn't know you felt so strongly about it.'

Still she ignored him.

'To tell you the truth,' he said, 'I don't lose an awful lot of sleep over it myself.'

'Well, you damn well should,' she said huffily.

He felt a surge of irritation now. Bloody Americans. Honest to God, if there was one thing they loved it was telling you what to do. That was the national sport in America, ordering other people how to live. The liberals seemed as bad as the Bible-belters.

A stór mo chroi, in the evening mist
When the night is softly falling.
Turn away from the throng and list
And it's then you'll hear me calling.

The air in the car felt brittle. He wondered was there some way to move the conversation onwards. She reached out quickly and changed the station. Then took a cigarette from a pack and lit it, without offering him one.

A good-time blues number came on the radio and she turned it up.

'I like this one,' she said.

'You do?'

'Is it Jimmy Reed or Muddy?'

'Did anyone ever tell you, you're a fairly unusual nun?'

But she wasn't listening to him now. She had started to sing along, in a mock gravelly voice.

> Baby, baby, don't you treat me so mean.
> Asked you for water,
> But you gave me gasoline.

She turned and poked him gently in the side. 'Aren't you going to sing along?'

'I prefer songs about the potato famine.'

She laughed tenderly and slapped his arm.

'Come-all-yehs about being oppressed by the British,' he continued. '"Wrap the Green Flag Round Me, Boys". All that crack.'

She folded her arms and regarded him closely. 'You, my dear, are a very stubborn man. Anyone ever tell you that?'

'Now that you mention it, I don't think so.'

They rounded a corner. Her smile froze.

Two hundred yards ahead, a roadblock had been set up. Four glossy police cars were parked on the grass verge, blue lights flashing and back doors open. An army truck and a jeep had been backed into a creamery gateway. Soldiers were fanning out into the fields on both sides of the road while police scurried about with crime scene tape and lengths of scaffolding. A surly-faced corporal broke out of a group and approached, tilting his torso so his strapped machine gun swung into his hands.

Aitken rolled down his window quickly. He heard the crackle

of police radios, the excited shouts of men from over the hedges. A chopping mechanical sound filled the air. It took him a moment to identify it as a helicopter.

'Who are you?' the corporal said. He was a short, bunchy-necked, palely grim guy with depressed cheekbones and beady, sunken eyes.

'My name's Martin Aitken, I'm an inspector in the Guards.'

'From?'

'From Pearse Street station in Dublin.'

He pulled his identity badge from his pocket and flashed it. The soldier looked at it and shrugged.

'This road is closed. I'll have to ask you to turn around.'

'But I'm a cop.'

'Doesn't make any difference, you're not on my list.'

'But . . .'

'Nothing I can do for you tonight. We've a major security situation here. Doesn't matter if you're Christ Almighty. All right?'

The helicopter hovered into view from behind a wooded hill, its beam of sharp clean light sweeping slowly over the nearby fields.

'Can I speak to the officer in charge?'

'He's busy.'

'What happened here?'

'I'm not allowed to say.'

Aitken switched off the engine and went to step out. The soldier put his hand quickly on the door.

'I told you once, pal. Now I'll tell you the last time. The road is closed. Turn her round and get moving.'

'But this is bloody ridiculous . . . Look . . . I'm almost out of juice here. Can you not let me go on just a half-mile? I've to get to Donegal tonight.'

The corporal shook his head. 'You won't be going this route.'

'So what are we supposed to do?'

'That's up to you,' he said, raising his voice to compete with the approaching helicopter. 'I know there's a B-and-B about a mile back that way. You could do worse than put up there till morning.'

'But we can't do that. We're late already.'

'Look, if you want the gospel truth, boss, I don't give a flying fiddler's shite what you do. Just turn her round and get out of here. This minute.'

The helicopter was only two hundred yards away now, hovering low over the road, completely still. Its beam was moving along the hedges, tracking methodically in a long smooth sweep.

He heard the rising wail of a siren from the road behind him. An ambulance appeared from around the corner and sped past them, halting at the line of police cars. Two paramedics jumped out with a stretcher and an equipment box. A policeman beckoned them urgently into the field.

'What do you think?' Aitken said to Ellen.

'Suppose we'll have to do as he says.'

He turned the car, the corporal impatiently directing, and began to drive back down the narrow road.

The B-and-B that the corporal had mentioned was small and shabby with an overgrown garden. It had a sign in a window advertising rooms for rent, with the slogan PASSED FOR FOOD HYGIENE daubed on in red paint.

'Doesn't exactly look palatial, does it?'

She laughed. 'Really. Maybe we could do a little better than that.'

He drove on, into Tara town and down the tiny main street. There was a small hotel on the edge of the square. He swung into the car park at the back of the building.

Inside the lobby, people seemed to be going to some kind of function. Laughing men were wandering about in suits; women wore neat dresses and large flowery hats. The muffled sound of a country and western band could be heard, plunking bass, wailing pedal-steel guitar; it loudened and sharpened as the ballroom doors opened. A bride appeared in a flouncy cream dress, supping a pint of Guinness and smoking a cigarette, a bouquet of weary lilies clamped under her arm, a sulky-looking flower girl yawning at her side. Ellen went to use the bathroom. As Aitken joined the queue at the counter, he noticed the bride follow her in.

The desk clerk said there was nothing they could do. The hotel was completely full tonight.

'Surely you've something?' Aitken said. 'We're not fussy.'

'I appreciate that,' the clerk said, crossly, frowning as he searched through the registration ledger. 'But we're jammed to the rafters tonight.'

'Anything,' said Aitken. 'Anything at all.'

The man blew softly through his lips, his finger moving down the pages. 'If people only took the time and trouble to book, we'd be able to help them. But as it is, we're stuffed.' A young, heavily pregnant woman in a damask pinafore dress came out from an office behind the counter with a couple of files.

'Marian?' sighed the clerk. 'Is there anything we can do for this man here? He's stuck for a bed and I don't see a thing.'

'He didn't book?'

'No, he didn't.'

The woman shook her head decisively.

'We can't work miracles in that case,' she said, turning and going back into the office.

'Please,' said Aitken. 'We're very tired, we've been on the road since early, I'm nearly out of petrol.'

'Yes,' the clerk said. 'But you should have booked.'

By now Ellen had emerged from the bathroom. She came over wearily and stood by Aitken. Her face had a bleached-out, haggard look.

'They've nothing for us here,' Aitken said.

Ellen laughed. 'That must be a mistake.'

'I'm afraid not, Missus,' the clerk grinned. 'I've had a good look. We don't make mistakes like that around here.'

'Oh, is that right?'

'Yes, it is.'

'Now you listen to me, sir,' she said. 'My name is Sister Ellen Donnelly, do you understand? And I've come all the way from New York for my niece's wedding.'

The man's mouth opened. Aitken gaped at Ellen.

'All the way from America this morning. Do you know how long a journey that is? And I know for a fact there was a reservation for myself and my brother here. Because I called from my convent only last week. For Wednesday night, the 28th of December. Please check again.'

The clerk blushed. 'I'm sorry, Sister,' he stammered. 'It's just I don't have any record of that.'

'You must,' Ellen said firmly. 'Will you take another look for me please? It's hardly my fault if your records are poorly kept.'

He opened his book again, looking desperate. Small beads of sweat were forming on his forehead. Ellen refused to meet Aitken's glance, just tapped her fingernails on the surface of the counter, humming lightly along with the country music. The clerk glanced up from the book in an apologetic way. She shot him a look. He went back to it again.

The bride appeared from the ladies' room.

'Sarah, honey?' Ellen called.

She came over, smiling, still with her pint of Guinness, which she plonked down on top of the cigarette machine.

'Auntie Ellen,' she said, warmly. 'Is everything all right?'

'Oh yes, hon, just a minor problem. This nice man here says he can't see our booking.'

'Peter Foley,' said the bride, admonishingly. 'Auntie Ellen's after coming all the way from New York. You realise that?'

'Well, yes, love, I do. I don't know what's after happening, but . . .'

'She had to get special permission and all.'

The man looked fearful. 'Special permission?'

'That's right. From a bishop.'

'Well . . . why would . . .'

'For God's sake, the poor woman's in a silent order. She's hardly said a word in twenty-five years. And now you're going to ruin her trip to Ireland for my wedding? You have your shite, Peter Foley.'

'Excuse me a minute,' the clerk said hoarsely. He left them and scurried into the office.

Aitken looked at the bride and Ellen. Suddenly they both burst into laughter.

'Don't,' giggled the bride. 'Stop or they'll see us.'

'Do you mind,' said Aitken, 'if I ask what the fuck is going on?'

'Language, Martin, please.'

'Well, what though?'

She picked a postcard from the counter and looked at it closely. 'I just explained to Sarah about our little problem. She was kind enough to agree to help us out.'

'She . . . ? But how did you know they wouldn't have rooms?'

'For heaven's sakes, Martin, it's absolutely obvious.'

'Well . . . why?'

She shot him a look of mock confusion. 'Because there's a wedding on.'

She turned to the bride and they laughed again. 'Honestly, Sarah,' Ellen said. 'I sometimes truly think he lives in a world of his own.'

Through the venetian blinds they could see the man talking to the young woman. She stood up slowly behind her desk and gave an anxious glance out towards the lobby. Ellen waved. The clerk waved meekly back. The young woman turned and barked something at him. He shrank into his suit.

The woman came out, pursued by the clerk. She rushed to the counter and held her hand out to Ellen.

'Sister, I'm Marian Hamilton, the assistant manager here. I'm terribly sorry to hear you've been inconvenienced like this.'

'That's quite all right, dear. Please don't fret.'

'Peter here's going to take care of it for you. Aren't you, Peter?'

'Well, I'm certainly . . .'

'Aren't you, Peter?'

He nodded grimly and took out his book again. The manager asked if they'd had a nice trip.

'Oh, the flight was a little bumpy,' said Ellen. 'And the food wasn't very good. But apart from that it was pleasant enough.'

'Well, you're very welcome indeed to Tara,' said the manager. 'If you'll excuse me now I have work to do. But if there's anything more I can help you with, please let me know.'

She shot the clerk a glare of consummate disdain. He licked his lips nervously and performed a small bow. She clicked her tongue and returned to the office. He began to search through the book again, mumbling to himself; and then, after a few moments, gaped up at them hopefully. 'We've one small room there with twin single beds. It's out of action at the minute because we're redecorating. We could let you have that.'

Ellen calmly shook her head. 'That won't be acceptable, Peter. Father Martin will need a room of his own.'

The clerk looked at Aitken. 'Father Martin.'

Aitken managed a modest shrug.

'I swear to God Almighty the one room is all we have, Father. Please take it. Or Her Nibs'll crucify me upside down.'

'Oh, well in that case . . .' Aitken looked at Ellen pleadingly and she nodded.

'Right so,' said the bride, 'I'll see you later.'

'Yes, honey,' said Ellen. 'Thank you for that.'

The bride walked off in the direction of the bar. The clerk looked at Ellen and produced the register, his eyes gleaming with pride as though it was the Book of Kells.

'You're very welcome here, Sister. I'm sorry now if any offence was given.'

'That's quite all right, Peter,' she beamed. 'These little things happen. Father Martin, would you take care of the paperwork please? I'm going to get us a table for dinner.'

'But . . . dinner's actually finished, Sister.'

'Well then, Peter,' she said. 'All the more reason we better hurry up. I'll see you in the dining room in ten minutes, Martin. And don't be late. You heard what Peter said.'

She crossed the lobby towards the dining room. Aitken began to fill in the forms. The clerk watched her walk away, like a cowboy in a movie admiring the town's golden-hearted floozie.

'She's really in a silent order, is she?'

'She is,' said Aitken.

The clerk eyed the manager with cautious contempt through her window. 'I wish some other people were too,' he said.

'Indeed.'

'Did you come from north of the town, Father?'

'Yes.' He wondered now if he should address him as 'My child'.

'So . . . Did you see it?'

'What?'

The man was speaking with exaggerated calm but his eyes couldn't conceal his excitement. 'There was a shootout between the army and five IRA men.'

'Fuckin serious?' said Aitken.

The clerk looked a bit shocked.

'I mean, I'm sorry. Good Lord. I thought they were on cease-fire.'

The man peered at him. 'One tried to get away, so he did. They cornered him and pumped him with bullets.' He paused and licked his lips. 'Pumped him, they did. Shocking, Father. *Pumped* him. He died like a dog. With his guts hanging out of him like . . . sausages.'

'God bless now,' said Aitken, backing away nervously.

'Yes, Father. Thank you, Father.'

Men in morning suits were sitting on the stairway, sipping morosely at pints of Guinness. A queue of women had formed outside a bathroom on the landing. They fell silent as he walked past, down a corridor lined with photographs of pub fronts and Georgian doors in Dublin.

The bedroom was tiny and shockingly cold, with two narrow single beds, an old-fashioned aluminium washbowl and a metal jug on a narrow wooden table. A mahogany dressing-screen stood by the leaded window with a couple of paint-stained overalls slung over it. Here and there were tins of emulsion, with stiff brushes lying on top. In the bathroom the toilet had a strip of plastic across it, reading SANITISED FOR YOUR PROTECTION. A saucer balanced on the rim of the bath had several cigarette butts and an apple core in it.

After he had used the toilet, he went back inside and sat on one of the beds. The room smelt oppressive, of dusty air and acrid paint. He opened the window as far as he could. Snow was falling steadily on the street like blobs of cotton wool. He rolled a joint, called home and checked his messages.

'Hopalong, it's Ranj. Listen, that Yankee mott checked out while I was off, I thought you should know. And I just wondered if you fancied a game of pool or something. Gimme a buzz, OK?'

293

'Martin, it's Noreen Tynan here. Would you ever give me a ring about last evening? Hughie's been in shocking humour ever since.'

'Aitken, this is Assistant Commissioner Mellowes speaking. Please telephone my secretary and make an urgent appointment. You and I need to have a talk.'

The tape spooled forward again. 'Dad, it's me, Julie. You there?' His daughter's voice sounded curious and excited. 'You there, Dad? Come on, pick up. London calling.'

He could hear traffic moving in the background. Then Valerie's voice saying something he couldn't make out, but which made Julie laugh in a mischievous way. He had a sudden mental picture of the Charing Cross Road, the theatre fronts and Chinese restaurants and little secondhand bookshops. Valerie and the girls clustered together in a phone box.

'Well, Dad, we're in London, me and Ma and Claire. And we just rang you up to say how's it going.'

Leave a number, he thought. *Leave some number where I can get you.*

'You're not there, Dad, are you?' The surging sound of an articulated lorry cut across her voice. A groan of gears and a wheeze of compressed air. 'Well, look . . . we love you, Dad. OK? Bye.' She gave another gleeful chuckle. 'Oh, and Ma says don't do anything we wouldn't do.'

Two quick bleeps and the line went dead. Showband music was coming in through the window.

> *Her eyes they shone like diamonds,*
> *I thought her the queen of the land,*
> *With her hair hung over her shoulders,*
> *Tied up with a black velvet band.*

Chapter Twenty-Three

Amery had to admit it. He was lost in Yonkers.

For most of his adult life he had lived only fifteen miles away, in Scarsdale, yet he had never once driven these streets before. He wished he had thought to bring a map. Almost two o'clock and he'd had no success. An hour had passed in aimless searching and still he hadn't found the home of Howard Ackley, Ellen's co-volunteer at the charity bookstore.

He doubled back by the entrance to the raceway and drove on, his lack of planning infuriating him now. Come on, Milton, suck gut and pull through. Suddenly he saw the sign for Benson Avenue. He jammed on his brakes; the car behind started honking. He turned right into a messy street where the buildings had a hotch-potch look, as though each had been thrown up without regard to any other.

He parked by a copy shop, got out and started walking. This section of street was full of small redbrick houses, with stone steps and neat windowboxes. A little black girl in a front garden was whacking a tetherball. She stared at him hard as he passed by.

He came to number 27A. A rusted yellow Oldsmobile sat up on four concrete blocks, with a sticker on the rear window saying MCGOVERN FOR PRESIDENT. He went up to the door and looked for a bell or a knocker. Finding neither, he rapped three times with his knuckles.

The door was opened with startling speed by a sleepy-looking middle-aged man who was wrapped in a bath towel. He had a crinkled chicken-skin neck, saggy breasts, wild tufts of fleecy chest-hair.

'Yeah?' he grunted.

'I'm looking for Howard,' Amery said.

'You got a warrant?'

'I'm sorry?'

'You're a cop, right?'

'Pardon me?'

'We know our rights. Show your warrant or take a hike.'

The door slammed. He knocked again. The same man opened it, with sunglasses on now.

'I think there must be some mistake. I'm not a police officer.'

'You sure?'

'Of course I'm sure.' The man raised his sunglasses and blinked in the light. 'Look, I promise you, I'm not,' Amery repeated.

'OK.' The man nodded. 'You look like a cop, is all.'

'Is it possible to see Howard? I mean Mr Ackley.'

'What about?'

'It's a personal matter.'

'Why didden ya say. Guess you better come in.'

The door led straight into a sitting room that had dark wooden floorboards and rough pine furniture. Indian rugs and framed posters of cowboys decorated the walls; there were earthenware pots and bits of crockery on the shelves, a hessian hammock was slung between two stone pillars. It looked like the kind of place in which a gaucho with obsessive-compulsive tidying disorder might live. A seventies-style lava lamp glowed on top of the TV, but the lava was lying in a lump at the bottom, like a small dead alien in a specimen jar. A Keith Haring poster of two babies disco-dancing hung over a fireplace that contained a potted cactus.

'Howard's in the shower,' the man said. 'Park it there, officer. Take the weight off your sling-backs.'

Amery sat on the sofa.

The man adjusted his towel. Hopped up to perch on the breakfast bar. 'Howard tends to take a lot of showers,' he said.

'I see.'

'Howard's real clean.'

'I'm . . . sorry?'

'Are you an ex-boyfriend of Howard's or somethin?'

'No, I'm not.'

'So what you do, then? If you ain't a cop.'

'I'm a cosmetic surgeon. I practise in Manhattan.'
The man's eyes brightened.
'For real?'
'Yes. Why?'
'Man, I got this boil on my thigh that you would not believe. Can't hardly move most of the time.'
'Oh.'
'It's right here,' he said, parting his legs and pointing more at his crotch than his thigh. 'It hurts so bad I can't sleep at night.'
'Well, you probably need to get that attended to professionally.'
'Tell me sum I don't know. Can't afford that.'
'I really would advise it. A thing like that can turn nasty.'
The man nodded absently, then glared at Amery. 'You couldn't take a quick look at it, could you? I mean now you're here?'
'It isn't really my area of specialty.'
'You're a surgeon, right?'
'I'm more in the overall cosmetic area.'
The man scoffed. 'I got a boil the size of Texas two inches from my pecker. If that ain't the overall cosmetic area, tell me what is.'
'Really. I'd like to see Mr Ackley if that's at all possible.'
The man scowled violently, hopped down from the bar, went to the door and opened it.
'Hey, Rosie,' he called. 'Some cop who says he's a plastic surgeon here to see you.'
He left then, slamming the door behind him so hard that a framed photograph fell off the wall. Amery went to pick it up. It showed a workman balancing on one leg halfway up the Eiffel Tower. He dusted it off and set it on a table. A moment later, a piercing scream came from the back of the building. Another shriek sounded, but this one like a strangled yodel. Amery was paralysed with tension.

Had he even got the right house? If so, was that raving madman Ackley's lover? For God's sake, how could Ellen be friends with people like this?

He flicked through a current affairs magazine on the coffee

297

table. A third scream came – this one as bloodcurdling as the howl of a wolf, followed by a wild whoop like an Indian war cry. Amery's scalp prickled with fear. A ginger cat with one ear appeared and regarded him suspiciously. The sound of raucous male laughter came from a back room.

The door opened and Ackley strode in. He was tanned and well proportioned, in his late thirties, wearing cut-off denim shorts and a Hawaiian-style shirt that was sky blue and covered with parrots. His feet were bare and pointed outwards as he stood. He was red in the face and moist-eyed, as though he had only just stopped laughing.

'Hi there.' He beamed. 'Can I help you?'

'Yes.' Amery got up. 'That is, I hope so. Actually we've met before.'

Ackley pursed his lips for a moment.

'Nicaragua Solidarity Campaign?' he asked uncertainly.

'No.'

'Queer Nation?'

'No, no. We were introduced at a poetry reading some time ago. I'm Ellen's husband?'

'Ellen.'

'Ellen Amery. Or Donnelly. You help out with her at the charity store in Scarsdale?'

Ackley clicked his fingers. 'Oh, my gosh, yes, of course. At the rainforest evening. How are you? . . . Maldwyn, isn't it?'

'Milton.'

They shook hands.

'Milton. Right. I'm so sorry. We were in bed when you called. We kinda sleep late around here in the holidays.'

Amery laughed a little too wildly. 'That's OK. I sleep late myself sometimes.'

Ackley looked confused. 'Pardon me?'

'Is everything all right?' Amery asked. 'I heard some disturbing . . . sounds from in back.'

'Oh that. We were just horsing around. Little wake-up ritual we have.'

He opened his mouth and ululated so piercingly that the cat crashed off the breakfast bar and scurried behind the couch.

'How . . . fascinating,' Amery said.

'Right. You want to sit down or something, Maldwyn?'

Amery sat back down hard on the sofa. It was so deep that his feet almost left the floorboards. Ackley pulled out a folding wooden chair and sat on that.

Some time passed while they looked around.

'You have a beautiful home,' Amery said.

'Oh, thank you.' Ackley glanced down at his feet. He seemed surprised to find them there. 'Yes. It needs a lot of attention, a funky old place like this. But I figure that adobe wall-finish really works. Do you?'

'Well.' Amery looked at the walls uncertainly. 'It does seem to work, yes.'

'Good.' Ackley grinned. 'Excellent. I'm glad you think so. Geraldo, my partner, he's not so sure. Geraldo gets these real fixed views and stuff so I have to stick to my guns about design matters.'

Another terrible shriek came from the back of the house.

'You're in design yourself, are you?' said Amery.

'No, no.' He laughed as though the suggestion was preposterous. 'I sell real estate. Here in Yonkers.'

'Oh. I see. I wasn't aware of that.'

Some more time passed while they looked at the walls. Amery tried to think of something intelligent to say about them. But basically they were flat brown-coloured walls.

'So, Maldwyn.' Ackley clapped his hands. 'It's good to see you again.'

'Thank you.'

'I dunno. You've lost a little weight or something. Here. Round the face. I think that's maybe why I didn't recognise you at first.'

'I wasn't aware of that. But perhaps.'

'Ellen's back from London, is she?'

Suddenly the other man came back in. He was wearing tweed golf slacks now, carpet slippers that seemed several sizes too large and a pink and white striped T-shirt that said CAMP AS CHRISTMAS.

'Hey,' said Ackley.

'Is for horses,' said the man.

'You guys met already, right?' Ackley asked.

'Not officially,' Amery said. 'I guess you must be Geraldo?'

The two men looked at each other. Ackley laughed.

'Maldwyn,' he said. 'This is my dad, Cleveland Ackley.'

'Your father?'

'Pop, this is Maldwyn. Ellen's husband.'

'Whose?'

'You know Ellen, Pop. From the bookstore? The nice lady with the smile? Who buys you cake?'

'Who?'

'The lady you spoke to about the war. You showed her your photos of Normandy?'

The older man thought for a moment, looking utterly mystified. 'She never told me she was married to a cop. Ain't that a kick in the head.'

He sat on the arm of the sofa and picked up the cat, laying it on his thigh and stroking its back. 'How's my baby today?' he said to it. 'You're a good girl, huh?'

'Dad's staying with Geraldo and me over the holiday, Maldwyn.'

'Oh, that's nice. For a vacation?'

'Nope,' barked the man. 'I'm on the run from the cops.'

'Hey now, Pop,' said Ackley gently.

'Why are people here?' said his father, and stared at his hands. He laughed, suddenly, in a gulping, half-choked way, then began to shake his head as though he were afraid.

Ackley got up and went to him. He took his right hand and rubbed it softly. 'Hey, why don't you take your bath now, Dad. I ran it nice and hot. Just the way you like it.'

Cleveland Ackley looked like a frightened child. 'Will you stop by the bathroom and dry me later?'

'Course I will, Pop. And then we'll get dressed. And we'll go get a cup of coffee somewhere. Would you like that?'

The old man put the cat on the floor and nodded gravely. 'We have to go pick up your mom first, Howard,' he said.

Then he gazed around the room as though it seemed unfamiliar to him; he cocked his head and stared, as if strange music was coming from the furthest corner. He jumped up and took

300

an uneasy step towards the fireplace. Stood like that for several moments before turning slowly to look back at his son. Tears were trickling down his creased face. He raised his thumb and wiped them away.

'She's dead, isn't she?'

'Hey, Pop. Come on now.'

His lower lip curled, trembling lightly. 'Your mother . . . She isn't really here now, right, son?'

Ackley got up again and took him in his arms. 'It's OK, Cleveland. Just relax.'

The man was sobbing gently, his frail shoulders shaking. 'I'm so sorry, son . . . I thought I heard her.'

Ackley stroked his father's back. 'Don't worry, Pop. Everything's fine.'

'I'm sorry if I embarrassed you in front of your friend . . . I'm . . . just so . . .'

'You didn't embarrass anyone, Pop. Did he, Maldwyn?'

Amery got up and went to Ackley's father. 'It's been a real pleasure meeting you, Cleveland. I hope we can do that again some time soon.'

The man nodded. 'Thank you.' He shook Amery's outstretched hand.

Amery took out his wallet and gave him a business card. 'Say, I'd like you to call my secretary next week. Come into the city and see me about that little matter of your leg.'

The old man looked at the card. 'Thank you again. But I couldn't afford that.'

'I'd consider it an honour to help you, sir. Maybe we could get a bite of lunch together afterwards?'

The man dried his eyes on the hem of his shirt. 'That's very kind. You're a friend of my son?'

'He's a good friend of my wife, yes. Of our family.'

'He's a fine boy, isn't he?'

'Yes, he is, sir. A fine boy.'

The man nodded thoughtfully and shuffled out of the room, closing the door softly behind him. Amery could see Ackley looking at him. He sat back down; wished Ackley would stop.

'Thank you,' said Ackley. 'I don't know what to say.'

'No, no. My pleasure.'

'Ellen always says you're very generous. I'm touched. Thank you again.'

'You cope with him very well. Alzheimer's, is it?'

Ackley nodded and lit a cigarette. 'He's only out of the hospital for Christmas. He spends most holidays with me and Geraldo.' He looked across at Milton. 'And Ellen, of course. He loves Ellen.'

'It was actually Ellen I was wanting to talk to you about.'

'Oh, yes. I'm sorry. She called me from London the other morning. I hadn't seen her at the store for a while.'

'From London . . . I see. May I ask how you found her?'

'OK, I guess. Maybe a little preoccupied. We didn't talk for long. She got cut off and didn't call back.'

'I see. Thank you.'

Ackley looked at him. 'This isn't exactly any of my business here. But are you guys OK, Doctor Amery?'

'Actually, to be honest, we're having some problems.'

'We did sometimes wonder. Geraldo and me.'

'I think she's left me, Howard, is the truth of the thing.'

'Oh, you know what Ellen's like. She takes these notions. She's too independent.' He pulled a face. 'Matter of fact, she's a royal pain sometimes.'

His father called from the back of the house.

'I guess I better let you go,' Ackley said. 'Unless you'd care to join us for coffee?'

'Thank you,' said Amery. 'Thank you. I'd like that.'

Chapter Twenty-Four

In the small, neat dining room that looked over the main street, a pine-log fire was burning in a black iron grate. A portrait of a smiling Saint Patrick hung over it, with strings of red tinsel around the frame. The waitress had shown her to a table for two in the bay window, near a display case full of ornamental dolls in flamenco costumes. A leering redheaded leprechaun at the back of the cabinet caught her eye. He was brandishing a crooked blackthorn shillelagh, and had a greeting embroidered on his emerald jacket. IF YOU'RE IRISH, COME INTO THE PARLOUR.

A smell of roasted meat and rosemary hung over the room. The leaden windows were blanched with steam. From the kitchen she could hear a tenor voice singing a love aria, but in an exaggeratedly maudlin bleat that sent it up.

> *O soave fanciulla!*
> *Di mite circonfuso alba lunar!*

She had the vague feeling she had been here in this hotel before, but couldn't remember exactly when. Was it with the Westchester Women's Cultural League, 1986? The Boston Irish Sons of the Shamrock, back in the summer of '89? There had been so many little places just like this over the years since she'd been working with the group. So many chicken and mashed potato dinners, with people she hardly knew.

> *In te ravviso il sogno*
> *Ch'io vorrei sempre sognari!*

A thin young man peeked in through the dining-room door.

She thought it was odd that he was wearing sunglasses. Unusual things they were too, with small round lenses and thick white frames. He had a long neck and a dirty leather jacket. He peered quickly around the room and then almost as abruptly went away. How peculiar, she thought.

Dammi il braccio, o mia piccina . . .

A few moments later the man appeared again, but this time he entered and came straight to her table.

'I'm terrible sorry,' he said, in a broad Dublin accent, 'I wonder could I trouble you for a light there, Missus?'

She reached into her pocket and pulled out a book of matches. He touched her hand as he bent towards the flame and sucked. The flame went out and she handed him the matches. He struck one himself and lit his cigarette.

'Thankin you,' he grinned. As though he didn't mean it.

He leaned back his head and blew a smoke ring. 'Would you believe they ran outta matches behind the bar. Been gaspin for a smoke the last half-hour.'

'Glad to help,' she said.

He looked closely at the book of matches. 'Hannigan's Hotel,' he said. 'Isn't that in Dublin?'

'Yes. On the quays.'

He nodded. 'Thought it was. Nice place?'

'Yes, fine.'

'Sound, sound. Where you from yourself anyways?'

'New York,' she replied, wishing he would leave her, or wishing Aitken would hurry up. What the hell was keeping him so long upstairs?

'Ah,' he sighed. 'New York. Lovely. That's a place I always wanted to go.'

'It's a great city. I hope you do.'

'Well, you're very welcome to Ireland,' he said.

She had the idea he was waiting for an invitation to sit down. Was it possible that he was trying to hit on her?

'Myself and my husband come here a lot. We've had many memorable trips to Ireland.'

304

He grinned. 'I hope this one turns out as memorable.'

'I hope so too.'

'Trust me, love, I've a feelin it will. Be lucky now, all right?' He winked, turned and went away.

She picked up the menu and began to read it. But although she had hardly eaten all day, she didn't feel hungry. Her attention was drawn once again to the doorway. The bride and groom were standing by a fountain, arms around each other, posing for photographs.

She saw the young man sidle across the lobby towards the main door. A moment later he went past the window, jogging heavily along with his arms crossed in the rain and the collar of his leather jacket pulled up around his cheeks. The poor fellow looked soaked to the skin, as though every single muscle was trying to draw itself inwards. But still he was wearing his funny sunglasses. She watched him as he opened a saloon car and climbed quickly in, shaking his long wet hair, running his fingers through his fringe. He pulled out a mobile phone, tapped at it and spoke into it, took off his sunglasses and wiped them on his shirt. He seemed to be speaking intensely, angrily. Then all of a sudden he was shouting. She watched, intrigued. He was definitely yelling – now waving his free hand in the air, now stabbing at the dashboard with an extended finger. He tossed the phone over his shoulder on to the back seat. She saw him punch the steering wheel hard. A moment later he started the car, pulled out from the kerb so quickly that he caused a wizened old man on an antique-looking ladies' bicycle to swerve and almost topple. The car sped off down the street, the furious old man shaking his fist after it.

When Aitken came in he looked tense and weary. But he appeared a little younger too; she thought he might perhaps have shaved. He had on the same jacket and pants as earlier, but he'd replaced his shirt and sweater with a loose black polo neck that gave him, she thought, the look of a playwright.

'Very dapper,' she said.

'Oh, I know. God's bloody gift.'

He sat down and methodically unfolded his napkin, gazing

around the warm room as though he found something about it amusing. 'Sorry I was a while,' he said.

'Did you take a shower?'

'No, I was hearing confessions.'

A droll grin lit up his face. He snuffled with laughter, closed his eyes with mock piety and made a theatrical sign of the cross. She had a sudden urge to reach out and hold his hand.

'I hope the bride's mother doesn't die in the night, Ellen. I'll have to give her the last bloody rites.'

'I'm sure you'd do it beautifully,' she replied.

'Make a change from reading people their rights, I suppose. Though maybe it's not so different in the end.'

She wondered what exactly that was supposed to mean. A waiter with a pockmarked face emerged from the kitchen and took their order. She asked for grilled lamb chops and a glass of red wine. Aitken opted for steak and a Coca-Cola.

'I think you make an impressive priest, Martin. All your parishioners would fall in love with you.'

'Stop that now,' he replied, blushing. 'It's a bit late for God and me at this stage.'

The waiter came back with their drinks and a plate of cold meats that he said the chef thought they might like to share. Aitken took a bread roll and broke it in half. He seemed a little distracted now, as he absent-mindedly pulled the soft white dough from the crust, crumbling it softly between his fingers. She found herself trying to picture him with a gun in his hand, standing over the body of the man he had killed. How could that have happened? It was unimaginable.

'Well,' he said, 'we didn't have the day we thought we'd have.'

'Really,' she agreed.

'But the road to Hell is paved with good intentions.'

She laughed. 'Let's hope it isn't the road to Hell.'

He chinked her glass. 'Amen to that.'

He began to help them both to some meat, but it was a little greasy, so the slices stuck together and he had to separate them with the tip of his knife.

'I don't know if I like the look of that,' she said.

'You should try and eat. We don't want you getting sick.'

She allowed him to put more slices on her plate. It was such a simple and small thing to do, but she couldn't remember the last time anyone had done it.

'Now,' he said. 'We'll keep you right. That's the stuff to send the troops, eh?'

When he'd finished serving them, he paused and bowed his head. He seemed to be looking at the cutlery.

'Are you waiting for something, Martin?'

'Well, y'know.'

'I'm sorry?'

'I just thought you might like to say grace.'

'Oh.' She coloured. 'That's all right.'

'Don't they say it at the convent?'

'Well . . . Yes.'

He shrugged. 'You must be used to it, so.'

'Well . . . of course.'

'Sure blaze away, then. On the count of three.'

He looked so hopeful and childishly expectant, as though some kind of performance was about to begin. She bowed her head and joined her hands, frowning as she realised with a panic-inducing start that she couldn't remember the words of the grace before meals.

'Bless us, oh Lord,' he prompted.

'Bless us, oh Lord . . .'

'And these thy gifts . . .'

'Bless us, oh Lord . . . for this food and this companionship. For the unexpected kindness we find in people. Amen.'

He nodded back at her, looking faintly discomfited.

'Will that do?' she asked.

'Gameball, yeah. Very nice.'

They began to eat. For a while they said nothing.

His hand was only two inches from her own. She wondered what would happen if she allowed herself to touch it. Or simply brushed against his fingertips.

Instead she raised her glass and smiled. 'Here's to the elusive Inishowen.'

'I'll drink to that.' He raised his glass. 'Cheers, my dears.' He

307

took a sip, put down the glass; took another forkful of food. 'He's buried there, by the way. My son, I mean.'

'Where?'

'Inishowen.'

He continued eating, sawing at the ham, his eyes fixed hard on his plate. Although he had tried to say it casually, it was clear it was something he had wanted to say.

'Martin . . . you didn't tell me that.'

He shrugged. 'You didn't ask.' He ate some more. 'My ex-wife's people are from up that way.'

'My God . . . Are you absolutely sure you're OK about going?'

'Yeah. I thought it was about time I did.'

When the main course came, he ate hungrily. They finished the meal in complete silence. When the waiter asked if they wanted dessert or coffee, they both said no, they'd had enough.

'Will we head on up to the room so, Ellen?'

'I wouldn't mind a whiskey. Unless you're tired?'

'No, we've all night to sleep. It's only ten.'

The bar had closed early and a noisy crowd had spilled out into the lobby. Ellen slipped outside for a breath of fresh air.

Suddenly people clapped. A man strummed a guitar. The bridegroom stood up in the middle of the throng. Someone threw him a flower and he laughed. A hush fell then, and a chorus of shhhhhs, as he began to sing in a strong pure voice:

> *Twas early, early*
> *All in the spring,*
> *When the young birds did whistle and sweetly sing.*
> *Changing their notes*
> *From tree to tree,*
> *And the song they sang was Old Ireland Free.*

Aitken went to the counter, where the clerk was sleepily reading a newspaper.

'Ah,' said the clerk. 'Was dinner all right, Father?'

'It was heavenly,' said Aitken. 'But we'd like a nightcap now.'

'The bar's just after closing, Father. We've only an early licence here. I can get you a mineral or a glass of good Meath water.'

'We'd prefer a triple whiskey, if that was possible.'

'A triple whiskey,' the clerk said, flatly.

'Black Bush if you have it. Or Paddy.'

The clerk glanced guiltily over his shoulder before speaking. 'Father, I can't, really. We've had bother with the police all over the Christmas. If they pay us a visit I'd get into trouble.'

'Oh, it's not for me. Is that what you thought?'

The clerk laughed apprehensively. 'God, of course not, Father. For one of the wedding party, was it?'

'Well, no. It's for Sister.'

His face was expressionless. 'For Sister.'

'Yes.' Aitken leaned forward. 'Breaking no confidences or anything like that, but Sister has . . . a little problem that way.'

'I understand,' whispered the clerk. 'A lot of them do.'

Aitken whispered back. 'Between you and me and the wall, the bitch would suck it out of a dishcloth if she was let.'

'Go on.'

'If that one doesn't get her little drop going to bed, I couldn't be responsible for what might happen. There've been incidents before, I may tell you candidly.'

'Incidents.'

'Yes, Peter. Embarrassing incidents.'

'Of what nature, Father?'

'Well, let me put it this way. Come here to me.'

The man leaned in so close that Aitken could smell his aftershave.

'She flew over from America with Aer Lingus this morning, Peter. And they'd nothing stronger than beer on the plane.'

'*Yes?*'

'Well, she won't be flying back with them. If you get my drift. Not after the incident she caused over Canada.'

'Holy God, Father.' He clicked his tongue. 'It's a curse, isn't it? Boys, oh boys.'

'It is, Peter. A terrible curse.'

'I suppose I could let you have a little something for upstairs. But not a word to anyone else, Father. Or your woman inside'll brain me with a shovel.'

'Good man, good man,' hissed Aitken confidentially. 'A triple please, and a nice cup of tea.'

> *And as I was climbing the scaffold high*
> *My own dear father was standing nigh;*
> *But my own dear father did me deny.*
> *And the name he gave me*
> *Was the Croppy Boy.*

Chapter Twenty-Five

He opened the door and stood back, allowing her to enter. The room was dank, the windows greasy. A battered two-bar electric heater was sitting on the floor. The dressing screen he had noticed earlier had been opened fully and placed between the beds.

'Hey,' said Aitken. 'That's good, isn't it?'

'It certainly is, Father,' she replied.

'We don't want any occasions of sin,' he said.

Both the heater's bars were bravely glowing but failing to make any impact on the cold. Their breath came in globes of steam. Frost had begun to form on the windows; outside the wind's steady roars were levelling out all other sounds of the night. She looked around the miserable room.

'It's not great, I know, Ellen.'

'It's fine, Martin. Really.'

He lay down on the bed nearest to the door and took a sip of his tea. She went around the screen and sat on the other one. It felt too soft and springy and had a dip in the middle, as though someone had only just stepped out of it. She unlaced her shoes, took them off, put them on the floor, lay back herself.

'You OK?' he called, from beyond the screen.

'Just having lustful thoughts.'

'Very glad to hear it,' he laughed.

'If it wasn't for that screen, who knows what might happen.'

He said nothing to that. A draught fluttered the curtains. She heard the rasp of a match being struck. A moment later, smoke began to rise above his side of the screen.

'*Habemus papam*,' she called.

'Yeah. True enough.'

Outside in the street a truck trundled past, making the windows rattle.

'How's your whiskey anyway, Ellen?'

'It's excellent, thanks.'

'My tea is good too.'

'You wouldn't have a cigarette to spare, would you, Martin?'

'I wouldn't, sorry.'

'Damn, I'd really love one now.'

'Will I go down and see if I can get some more?'

'Maybe you'd just let me have a drag of yours?'

'Yeah . . . I'm not so sure you'd like mine, actually.'

'Hey, I'm not that fussy, am I? I smoke any brand.'

She heard the springs creak as he sighed heavily and stood up. He appeared around the screen with a very large joint.

'This brand comes from Morocco,' he grinned.

She began to laugh. He laughed back. Their laughter died at about the same time.

'Should I put it out?'

'It doesn't really bother me. Funny, I thought I recognised the smell.'

'You partake yourself?'

'Not for years.'

He held it towards her.

'No, thanks.' She laughed again, more softly. 'To tell you the truth, it always gave me a headache.'

He crushed it out on the lid of a paint can, kept crushing long after it was extinguished.

'So,' he said. 'What happens now?'

'You tell me.'

He came towards her and sat on the bed. His fingers moved gently towards her hair. She tilted her head and kissed the palm of his hand, then the inside of his wrist, the ball of his thumb. He allowed his fingers to lengthen slowly until they were cupping the side of her face.

Before she really knew what she was doing she was kissing him, a mellow kiss on the corner of his mouth. He kissed her back, took her hand in his. Branches tapped on the black

312

window. His arm moved around the small of her back. He seemed to be trembling as the kiss became more passionate. She slid her tongue between his lips and felt him pull away.

'I suppose this isn't such a great idea,' he said.

'No,' she replied, brushing her fingertips across his cheek.

'Maybe I should go.' He kissed her forehead. 'Sleep somewhere else.'

'Like where?' She kissed his chin.

'I don't know.' He chuckled. 'The car.'

'You can't sleep in the car, for God's sake.'

'It wouldn't be the first time.'

'If you wanted to stay here, Martin, that'd be all right.'

'If I wanted to stay here?'

'I mean stay the night. With me.'

'Let me get this straight. If I wanted to stay the night here. In this room?'

'In this bed.'

He laughed. 'You're a nun.'

'Yes.'

'You want me to spend the night with you, and you're a nun?'

'I mean just to sleep with me. I feel very close to you.'

'Whoa, whoa. Hey, listen, I know people say the Catholic Church is changing a lot these days, but Jayzus, Ellen, this is . . .'

His voice trailed off. She didn't return his laugh. He gaped around the room, scratching his head. 'Just to sleep together?' he said.

'I'm not the kind of nun who has sex on the first date.'

'Oh, you're not, huh? Just my luck.'

'Won't you take off your clothes, Martin, and come to bed.'

He snuffled with laughter. 'Would you stop that.'

'Please. As a favour.'

'Will you quit your messing for Jesus' sake.'

'Martin, I'm forty-six years old.'

'I prefer the older woman,' he smirked.

'Do you want me to kill you right now, Aitken?'

'Depends,' he said, 'how you were going to do it.'

313

'I am forty-six, you impertinent brat. I might never see another naked man as long as I live. I'll probably never be kissed again my whole life. There's nobody in the whole world wants to kiss me. And that's fine. I've no complaints. But just this one last time I'd like to see a naked man. Please.'

'No way.'

'Why not?'

'Are you daring me or something?' He pointed at her and grinned. 'Because you needn't think I won't.'

'So do.'

'I will, Ellen. I'm telling you.'

'Go on then.'

She watched him calmly while he sighed and stood up. His eyes were bright with glee as he took off his jacket and then his shoes. Next came his socks, slowly. 'You're serious about this, are you?' She nodded. He took off his sweater, revealing a T-shirt vest beneath. 'There, is that enough?' She shook her head and lay down on her side.

'Merciful hour of the livin Christ. If the Christian Brothers could see me now.'

'I'll send them a photo, Martin, don't worry.'

He opened his trousers and let them fall to the floor. 'This isn't a joke?' She shook her head again and told him no. His smile seemed to dissolve slowly, as though the light that gave it life was evaporating. He pulled off his vest, peeled his shorts down over his thighs and feet. He stood before her naked, his long arms hanging awkwardly. He said nothing. She could hear his breathing. He looked at the carpet, his head bowed low, as he moved his hand to cover his genitals. On his left shoulder was a faded pink tattoo of a heart with the letter 'V' inside it. Thin grey hair covered his chest, ran from his navel to his pubic bone. He had a thick purple scar across his right thigh, an incrustation of dead skin, dark cross-stitches zigzagging through it. His toenails were too long, his legs pale and wiry. Although he was stocky and had a small pot-belly, he was nevertheless a little trimmer than he appeared with his clothes on. Goose pimples began to form on his arms. He gave a small shudder and patted his stomach a few times. When he spoke all trace of merriment had gone from his voice.

'The Chippendales can sleep safe in their beds, huh?'

'You're beautiful,' she said.

'I'm sorry you couldn't have found a better specimen.' He tried to laugh. 'For the last naked man you're ever going to see.'

'You look gorgeous, Martin. Do you think you could undress me now?'

His hands were trembling as he helped her off with her sweater. She stood up and removed her slacks. She stepped out of her underpants and unhooked her bra, covering her breasts with her forearms. Naked they slid together under the quilt. She turned away from him; he eased his arm around her from behind. She switched off the lamp on the bedside table. The wind made a disconsolate complaining sound. Out on the road another truck roared past. She felt his small thick penis begin to harden against the back of her thigh.

'Martin,' she said.

'I'm embarrassed,' he murmured. 'I'm aroused by you.'

'That's all right,' she said.

'I don't see how that's one bit all right. I'm being sexually aroused by a nun here. I'm gonna be in therapy the rest of my bleedin life.'

'You're going to have an issue around being sexually aroused by nuns.'

'You're dead bloody right, I am, Sister. And that's one of the more expensive issues too, let me tell you.'

She switched the lamp on again and turned to look at him. 'You make me laugh so much, Martin.'

He touched her face, kissed the curve of her collarbone as though his lips were measuring it. 'You're lovely,' he said. 'I love being with you.'

'Can I tell you something?'

'What?'

'These days I probably need a laugh.'

He kissed her breast. 'Why's that?'

Her fingertips touched his mouth. 'It doesn't matter. But

something difficult has happened in my life. Something painful I don't want to talk about. But you make me laugh. You're a lovely, tender man. I'd run away with you given half a chance.'

'If you could, right?'

'Yes. If I could.'

'Well . . . Why couldn't you, so?'

'Because there wouldn't be any future to it, Martin. And that's the truth.'

It was when she put her arms around him again that he began to weep. She was glad that he did, because from the moment she had met him, back in Hannigan's Quayside Hotel, he had looked like a man whose hurt had become too much for him, a man who badly needed to cry. He raised his palms to his face, quietly shook with tears. For a long time hardly any sound came from him, just the frailest of tremulous sighs. Sometimes he shivered as he wept into his hands. Once, twice, he allowed himself to sob. She held his head gently, like a piece of brittle sculpture.

'I know,' she whispered. 'It's all right. I know.'

She moved her arms around his quivering shoulders, lowered her mouth to his hair.

THURSDAY, 29 DECEMBER 1994

Chapter Twenty-Six

The whine of a vacuum cleaner outside in the corridor woke her just after half-past eight. A fat blackbird was hopping up and down on the windowsill, pecking at bits of the loose plaster. The sheets were wrapped hard around her naked thighs. The central heating must have come on earlier; the room was airless, stultifyingly hot. Her mouth felt as though she had swallowed a handful of ashes. When she sat up to take a drink of water she saw the note on the pillow.

Gone to see about petrol. Will put 'do not disturb' sign on the door.
Yours sincerely, Martin

She took a long cool shower and then sat naked on the bed. It was so small and uncomfortable, this narrow little bed. She wondered how they had managed to sleep at all. It wasn't like the king-sized bed in Hannigan's Hotel. She could see them together, wrapped in each other's arms in a large cosy bed. How pleasant that would be right now. Simply to lie together and talk. How powerful and vivid that picture was. Could you remember something that had never happened?

Dressing, she noticed the glass of whiskey still sitting on the windowsill, almost as full as when he'd handed it to her last night. Its warm sour smell was colouring the air. She fetched it, thinking she'd bring it downstairs.

The clerk was standing like a sentry by the door to the dining room. It was as though he had been expecting her. Behind him yellow light shone, bathing him in a shimmering lacquer, such as a knight-angel might have in an icon. When she went to enter he stepped into her path. Regarded her seriously. Tapped on his watch.

'Now, you're after leaving it fierce late again there, Sister.'

'I know,' she agreed, 'I slept in.'

'Breakfast's over at nine on the button. That's the rule. We're short staffed.'

'I know. But maybe . . .'

He held up his hand. 'The rules is the rules. I didn't make them. Between ourselves, I was never asked me *opinion* on them. But there they are all the same.'

'But do you think – do you think – that you might be able to make an exception just this once?'

He gave an almost operatic display of disapproval.

'Please,' she said. 'I know I'm in the wrong.'

'Well.' He shook his head. 'I don't know.'

It would never cease to amaze her how men loved being apologised to by women.

'I'm so very sorry,' she said. 'Really, I am. Do you think you can find it in your heart to forgive me?'

'Well, then . . . I suppose anyone can make a mistake, Sister. We won't let you starve. But just this once, mind.'

Now he seemed to notice the glass of whiskey. He peered at it for a while, and then he peered at Ellen, with a concerned and sympathetic expression. What a kindly-looking man he was. The kind of man you could trust with anything.

'Would you not prefer a nice cup of tea, Sister?'

'Yes,' she smiled. 'Tea would be lovely.'

Understandingly, he took the glass and glanced around, as if looking for somewhere to put it. Finally he sloshed the contents into a pot plant and slipped the glass into his jacket pocket.

'Now,' he said. 'We'll get you sorted out.'

He stepped out of the doorway and beckoned her in with a graceful wave of his white cloth. The small room seemed to sing with clean light. A pretty young woman was just finishing vacuuming. She half turned and waved at Ellen and the clerk. The clerk sat Ellen down at the table in the window, placed a serviette across her knees and went into the kitchen.

It was the middle of the night in New York now. She

wondered if Milton would be awake. She pictured him in their bed, propped up on three pillows the way he liked, reading a book, maybe studying the notes for that lecture he was going to give at the Institute soon. How shocked he would be if he knew what had happened. How hurt, too. Or would he even care?

She thought about how he would get up in a few hours. He would shave and shower, floss his teeth, put on his fresh clothes. She thought about the musky scent of his cologne. She imagined him leaving the house and driving to the station. Maybe Elizabeth would do that for him from now on. Or maybe he would drive himself, or walk. He would want to go into the surgery today; that was a thing he liked to do in the holidays, just potter around his office and water the plants. He would stop at the news-stand outside Scarsdale station to buy the *New York Times* and a packet of mints. He wouldn't read more than the front-page headlines, but he'd bought it every day for twenty years. He was such a creature of habit. It was one of the things that annoyed her about him, but also – simultaneously – one of the things she loved most. He was such a solid man in so many ways. What a wonderful husband he would have been, for a woman he truly loved and didn't merely need. She tried hard to imagine how he would even begin to cope when he finally accepted what was happening. They would have to talk about it soon, the inescapable fact of what her illness meant, the absurdity and yet the truth of it. The end of their shared life would have to be faced. The thought stirred tears but she blinked them away. The clerk brought her a bowl of cornflakes and a cup of greasy-looking tea.

'That's absolutely all I can do for you,' he said. 'If it was known I done even that much I'd be horse-whipped from here to Dublin.'

'Thank you, that's lovely. I'm so sorry to trouble you.'

Five minutes later he brought a rack of hot, soggy toast, a basket of bread rolls, a little silver dish of marmalade.

'Thank you,' she said. 'You're very kind.'

'Indeed and I'm not.'

'You are. You're a godsend.'

He pantomimed a scoff. 'I've been called a few choice things around this place but that's a new one.'

He ran his finger around the collar of his shirt, peered back down at her.

'Just don't be leaving it so late next time, love.'

'No,' she said. 'I promise I won't.'

Outside in the street, people were shopping. A greengrocer was placing fat pears in his window, polishing them on his apron as though they were jewels, then setting them out reverently in neat pyramids. An old man in faded clothes was laughing with a priest. She saw the bride and groom clamber into a Volkswagen, turn to each other and kiss, before driving away. She lit her last cigarette and watched the smoke rise through the air, knowing, in her heart, that she would never see her home again. But that was all right now. She had found what she needed. The courage to say goodbye.

*

The morning sky was flat and watery grey. A pale crescent moon could be seen over the mountains, half obscured by fingers of streaky cloud. Fresh snow lay on the banks and ditches, it covered the fields in a glassy crust; the slow-moving cold front coming in from the north had frozen the dead leaves to stiffened wafers.

Shivering, Aitken inched along the road, cigarette in his mouth and a petrol can under his arm. He had failed to start the Mini, and the garage in the town was closed, so he had asked directions from a passing postman and set out to hike the two miles that led to the nearest Texaco.

The snow muffled the sound of his footsteps. The tip of his nose was painfully throbbing. His ears were smarting, pulsing with cold. After a while his whole face felt raw. His throat was sore from smoking and his shoes were letting in water. His limp was bad and his eyes felt itchy.

But things were even worse than that.

He had gone to bed with a nun. There was no getting around it. Not a lot had happened then, but still, he had taken his clothes off and got into bed with a naked nun. That was a fact. You couldn't change it. A nun had seen him with no clothes on. A mickey-dodger had seen his mickey. Well, he figured, stranger things had happened. But just at the moment he couldn't think of one. This was new. This was unique. Nun-bedding was now something he could put on his CV.

In the distance he saw a farmer approaching, with a crook in his hand and a sheepdog bouncing along at his feet.

His head was reeling as he trudged the road. The black trees looked weary, bent low with ice and snow. The fields were the colour of day-old mashed potato. It was a long time since he'd been to bed with anyone, let alone a person who had taken vows of celibacy. Had he been that stoned? Was he going a bit kinky? Was the fact that she was a nun part of it all? Back in his past, in the mists of his childhood, was there some erotic nun he had secretly desired? He certainly didn't think so. But who could say for certain?

Had she done this kind of thing before? Was she some sort of unusual nun that got a kick out of naked frolicking? Jumping Jesus, what would people say? If Valerie or the girls ever found out? What about the Assistant Commissioner? What about Hughie? You couldn't really say it was normal. PERVY POLICEMAN BONKS TWISTED SISTER.

He found himself thinking about some of the nuns he had known. There was Sister Immaculata who had taught him in junior school. She'd written on his report card once that frying insects with a magnifying glass was the only scientific activity for which he showed anything like aptitude. What would Sister Immaculata say if she ever heard? Not, of course, that she would. There probably wasn't a newsletter for nuns to brag about their sexual conquests. Although in America anything was possible.

'Grand morning, now,' the farmer said, passing him by with a nod.

'I went to bed with a nun last night,' Aitken said. In his mind.

Onwards he hiked until he came to a crossroads that looked familiar. In a nearby field stood a circle of feeble-looking shorthorn cows. Fretfully bleating sheep were spilling through a gap in the hedgerow. Was this where he and Ellen had been turned back last night? He thought it was, but he couldn't

323

be sure. He took the right turn and almost immediately saw a collection of police cars two hundred yards ahead.

As he approached, some of the sheep went trotting before him. A prison van had been driven into a ditch and was surrounded by barriers of fluorescent orange tape. Nearby a canvas shelter had been erected on scaffolding, and two armed soldiers were standing guard. Press photographers had gathered in the road, and a television crew was setting up a camera on top of a bank. A man who looked like a local sergeant was standing in the creamery gateway, legs slightly apart, hands behind his back, talking solemnly into a reporter's microphone. Uniformed policemen were sitting in a Garda truck, sipping from polystyrene cups. Over the blackthorn hedge to Aitken's right a couple of photographers were taking pictures of something on the ground.

'Well well. The dead arose and appeared to many.'

When he turned he saw a man grinning at him from the back seat of an unmarked Special Branch car.

'Johnny Duignan. Jesus Christ.'

Detective Superintendent Duignan stepped out of the Granada and offered his hand. He was an athletic-looking man, with a nonchalant, casual style, glittering hazel eyes set deep in a tanned face. He wore a bright red scarf wrapped around his throat. His deerstalker hat had its earflaps down.

'Jesus wept, Martin. What are you doing in this godforsaken kip?'

'Passing through and I ran out of juice. Taking a trip up north just.'

'You'll have your work cut out so. The roads are arse-ways altogether with the snow.'

'That right?'

'Four hours it took us to get up from Dublin. The N3's closed all the way up to Virginia. Where are you bound for?'

'Donegal.'

'I hope to Christ nobody's waiting on you.'

'It's that bad, is it?'

'Well, you could swing over towards Trim and on up by Cavan. Just don't be doing an Eddie Jordan on it. There was four people killed on the roads last night.'

'Christ. Was there?' He looked around. 'What happened here anyway, John?'

'Lad up on a rape, Martin. Bust out of the wagon and stabbed a guard in the head with a chisel.'

'Jesus.'

'Aye. Nasty it was.'

'Did he kill him?'

'Well, he's alive just about, but he's in intensive care down in Beaumont. Not too much hope. Poor bastard's got a lump out of his head you wouldn't fit in a hat.'

'Did you get him?'

He scowled. 'Not yet. Fucked off at speed. Look.'

Duignan pointed over the hedge, to where a ragged trail of footprints led across the white, hilly field, eventually disappearing into a copse of evergreens. On a high bank nearby stood an ancient ring fort of broken black stones. A trio of men with yelping Alsatians appeared from over the brow of the hill, the dogs sniffing the slush, straining hard on their leashes. A line of police came into view behind them, inching along slowly and scrutinising the ground.

'If we had the likes of yourself still with us in the Branch, Martin, the little gurrier'd be in a cell by now.'

'I don't know about that,' Aitken said.

'It's true and you do know it. But he'll not get too far in this weather, the same bad little hoor's melt. We've a second chopper on the way up from Dublin too.'

'Someone told me in the town it was a Provo thing.'

'Ach.' Duignan tutted. 'Wish it was, nearly. A Provo's a Provo. But this gauger here is a fuckin headcase.'

'So the cease-fire's holding up all right, is it?'

'Maybe it is, maybe it isn't. Things seem quiet, right enough. But you know what they're like, Martin. Our friends the peacemakers.'

'Yeah.'

'I know, I know. Anyways, how've you been keeping yourself, Martin?'

'Sound enough, Johnny. How's life with you?'

'Not a bother. Suckin diesel, as usual.'

'Maureen well?'

'Oh, the best, yeah. Still there anyway. Must be doin somethin right, says you. Though what it is I don't know.'

'And the kids?'

'Shane's the size of a carthorse now. Manners of one too. He'd shite trottin if he was let. But you know what these youngfellas are like, Martin. God help us all who have teenage sons, isn't that it?'

A long awkward pause settled on them now. The clumsiness of the remark seemed to bounce off the wet road like a ball.

'Yeah,' said Aitken finally. 'Boys'll be boys, right enough.'

Duignan nodded. 'Sure we were the same ourselves, I suppose.'

'And worse.'

'And worse right enough. And worse.' A soft laugh of reminiscence crinkled up his face. 'Martin, do you mind that time you, me and Billy French went on the skite up to Dublin from Tipp? When we were in training? And chatted up the three from Liverpool in Toner's?'

'Good crack, wasn't it?'

'Man alive, don't be talkin. I sometimes think that was the happiest weekend of me life.'

'It was some weekend right enough. That must be twenty-five years back now.'

'Going back down to Templemore on the train on the Sunday night. Billy asleep on the seat, do you remember? With the lipstick all over him. And you and me playing poker for bottle-tops. With the countryside rolling past. Not a care in the world between the three of us. And God, I remember thinking, we should enjoy this now. We'll be out on the beat in three months' time. And it won't always be like this.'

Aitken laughed. 'It wasn't either.'

'No, it wasn't. They did for poor old Billy in the end, the same peacemakers.' He shook his head. 'It gives me the gawks when I see them on the television. Ireland this and Ireland that. When they'd put a bullet in the head of a man like Billy.'

'I know,' Aitken said. 'It was terrible what happened.'

326

Duignan nodded. 'I was sorry to hear about your own news, Martin.'

'What news was that?'

'Ah, you know. About the job.'

'What about it?'

Duignan looked at him. 'Christ,' he said, quietly. 'You didn't know.'

'What?'

He peered around, face reddening with mortification.

'Sorry, Martin. I've a mouth on me like the Liffey.'

'What, Johnny? Did you hear something?'

'Not at all, it's nothing definite, Martin. Tell us anyway, how's the girls? Julie must be out of college now?'

'Tell me what you heard, Johnny.'

Duignan sighed and looked at his hands. 'Well, you didn't get it from me . . . But I heard they were letting you go, Martin. In the New Year.'

'What?'

'Look, it's only what I heard. It's probably just talk. You know the way people yak.'

'Jesus.'

'Look . . . someone I know was chewin it with Mellowes and your name came up. I knew you weren't exactly top of his Christmas card list. But apparently he wants you out.'

'Little sleeveen bollocks has me in his sights right enough.'

'I heard something about a motor going missing too. Was that right?'

'Yeah . . . That was right.'

'You're better off out of this crack anyway, Martin. It gets into your bones after a while.'

A woman officer in a bulletproof jacket beckoned to him.

'I better head, Martin. It was great seeing you. We should get together for a proper natter in the New Year.'

They shook hands.

'And listen, Martin, be sure and take turns with the driving today, all right? That snow sends up a terrible glare so it does.'

Aitken laughed. 'How do you know I've someone to take turns with?'

'Well, I just assumed. When I saw yourself and the youngfella.'

'What youngfella?'

'Well . . . The one walking with you. Who is he anyway?'

The wind gusted. Snow fell from an ash tree.

'How do you mean?'

Duignan looked nonplussed. 'Well, the young lad.'

'What young lad, John?'

'Well . . . the one I saw you with. Twenty or so. In the leather jacket. He was danderin along behind you when I noticed you coming. Down beyond there. At the crossroads. When you came around the corner.'

'There was nobody with me.'

Duignan shrugged. 'Well, he was right behind you ten minutes ago. Just at your shoulder. Like a couple of feet behind, just. He was so close I thought he must be with you. Just laggin back a bit or something.'

Aitken turned and looked around. The road was completely empty, except for a horned black ram that was bawling at the sky.

'So where did he go?'

'Jaze, I don't know, Martin. I looked away for a second. And when I looked again he wasn't there. I thought he must have nipped into the bushes for a riddle or something.'

'There was an auldfella I passed along the way. A farmer? Maybe he turned back?'

Duignan shook his head. 'This lad was in his twenties. In a leather jacket.'

'You're absolutely sure?'

'Yeah, course. A leather jacket and funny-looking sunglasses.'

'Boss,' the woman officer called again. 'You're needed over here.'

'I must have seen a ghost, Martin,' Duignan said.

Chapter Twenty-Seven

When he got back she was sitting at the window table in the breakfast room, wearing the flowery dress she'd bought in Dublin. Although she smiled when he came in, she looked tired this morning and even more pale than usual, with soft grey shadows around her eyes.

'Tea?' she said, making to pour him a cup.

He crossed and sat down opposite her. When she stretched to pour the milk in his tea, he got a fresh citrusy aroma of soap. The room looked oddly smaller in the daylight than it had the night before. Some of the tables had chairs on top of them. A couple of towers of dirty beer glasses had been stacked on a trolley by the kitchen door.

'Did you sleep all right?' he asked.

'Yes. I drifted off after a while.'

'That's good.'

'Yes.'

He sipped his tea. It was stewed and bitter.

'Did you, Martin?'

'Yes, I did.'

She produced a new pack of cigarettes, placed them on his side plate.

'What's that?'

'I asked the clerk to get some more. I smoked half of yours, after all.'

He opened the packet and offered her one. She shook her head. He lit one for himself.

'I went out to get some petrol. Sorry I took a while.'

'You found a gas station that was open?'

'Just outside the town.'

'OK.'

He looked around the table for an ashtray. There wasn't one, so he used his saucer. She kept staring around the room, towards the fireplace and the other tables, as though she was undecided or confused about something. She took a soggy piece of toast from the rack and cut it in half, then into quarters.

'If there's anything we need to talk about, Ellen . . .'

'No,' she said. 'Nothing at all.'

He reached across the table and took her hand. Her fingers immediately twined tightly around his. She looked like she was trying to think of something to say, but all she did was nod a few times, her fingertips massaging the backs of his knuckles, slowly folding them into a fist.

They left Tara, heading briefly south-west from the town, along a winding minor road that was slick with ice. Soon they came to a roadblock but were waved straight through by two weary-looking gardaí in sou'westers and waterproof leggings. A short time later, passing through Dunsany, they saw a squat red tractor trying to haul a Mercedes out of a ditch.

They came to a junction, turned on to a slightly better road and began to head northwards again. From time to time, off to their right, they saw the police helicopter moving through the sky. For a while it almost seemed that it was following them, tracking their progress as they crawled through four miles of roadworks. Then it was gone, except for a distant chucka-chucka that Aitken heard when he rolled down the window to flick out a cigarette. And then suddenly, as they crossed the Boyne near Trim, it loomed out of a distant cloud like a vicious black insect.

Snow began to fall, a gentle powder at first, but then faster and thicker in splats that stuck to the windscreen. Before long a wind came blustering up, shaking the trees on the road between Athboy and Crossakeel, sending three farmhands in a distant white field into a scurry for the ruined castle by the river. For the rest of the morning the snow came down in swirling sheets, through a shrieking wind that rocked the car from side to side on the longer stretches of open road. Passing a meadow on the approach to Oldcastle, the snow turned to

330

noisy hail, hammering down on the roof of the Mini, pelting the windows, clacking against the windscreen. He turned the heat up to maximum and put the wipers on full blast.

As he drove, he found himself pondering what Duignan had said about his job. They wanted him out. That was clear now. He wondered what would happen if he went to Mellowes and asked for another chance. How much he'd like that, the arrogant, craw-thumping pox-bottle. He could see his ugly farmboy's face, trying to rearrange itself into a merciful yet stern look. He'd get up and pace his oak-lined office, hands behind his back, talking to the ceiling, give the usual pompous moralising lecture before handing Aitken his walking papers anyway. Even if he didn't, the thought was sickening. Imagine having to ask that inbred moron for a favour. He knew in his heart it would never happen. He could go and shite, him and his files.

A flat pale-yellow cloud squatted over Lough Sheelin, the water was grey as the blade of an old knife. By the time they came through Ballyjamesduff, the countryside had begun to change subtly, the land more hilly, the houses more assuredly solid and prosperous. He turned back onto the main road again, where a roadblock across the opposite lanes had built up a four-mile tailback. They drove on past a gritting truck, from which drenched men were shovelling heaps of sand and salt. Soon they were moving through the drumlin-speckled landscape of Ulster.

Methodist and Presbyterian chapels appeared along the wayside, simple and stark, black as bibles, one outside New Inn flying the Saint George's Cross of England. Near Lavey, Sinn Fein posters were attached to the lampposts, fluttering in the wind like sodden green flags.

By lunchtime they had made it to Cavan, a town Aitken had never liked, where a fantastically crenellated Catholic church loomed over the streets like an emperor's palace.

He pulled into the forecourt of a bright new filling station that had a giant inflatable tiger's head roped to the roof. Ellen looked queasy, suddenly exhausted.

'What's the matter, Martin?'

'I think we're overheating a bit. I want to check the oil and water.'

She said she'd go and freshen up.

The taps in the public bathroom were of the type you had to press continuously to make the water flow. She wondered what kind of sadist had invented those. The plug was missing, so she improvised one with a lump of toilet paper, filling the sink and rinsing her hands and wrists. Bending then, she scooped the water over her face, massaging her temples, her brow and neck.

A sudden flare of pain rippled through her abdomen.

She stood bolt upright, transfixed with fear. No, she thought. Please not again. It was as though some living thing was inside her – she thought of a scorpion or a black-headed snake. Please, she thought. *Not now.* She pictured the creature coiling speculatively around her vertebrae, slithering its way between her ribs; silently begged for it to be appeased. Another burst of flaming pain bit into her, that doubled her up and made her clutch her stomach as though she could squeeze the burning away. The room seemed to swim. She gave a small stagger. She managed to make it into one of the stalls, lowered the lid of the toilet and sat down.

Her limbs felt loose as lengths of twine. The serpent unfurled, spreading fire through her torso. She gripped her knees and closed her eyes, tried to go into the centre of the pain. She imagined herself moving down a long fiery corridor, heard herself groan, in the back of her throat. Dry-mouthed, she gaped around at the graffiti-splattered walls, the childish obscenities and declarations of love. Gasping, she tried to read the words, find something – anything – on which to concentrate. Cock. Fuck. Ireland. Jesus. Her vision was blurry, moist, shimmering. Finally the pain melted away, as though oozing back into the marrow of her bones.

Drunk with shock she left the bathroom. The sun appeared from behind a fish-shaped brown cloud, spreading a hopeful glow over the forecourt. Over by the pumps, the Mini's bonnet was open, but she couldn't see where Aitken was. Black spots flickered before her eyes. She took several deep breaths and went into the shop.

332

It was the kind of bright, functional place that sold basic groceries. There were racks of chocolate bars, fridges of milk and Coke, wooden crates of footballs in red plastic nets. A radio was playing a folk station loudly. Three surly teenagers in matching tracksuits were idling by a Slush-Puppie machine, munching hot dogs, eyeing anyone who came in.

Outside on the forecourt she saw him now, bent over the open bonnet of the car and wearily shaking his head. He seemed to be talking to the engine, which made her laugh, though the pain inside her was still threatening. A youth in a dirty white overall stood up from behind the Mini's far side. He and Aitken began to roar with laughter. Aitken grabbed a spanner from him and shook it mockingly at the car. There he was, just outside. Perhaps everything would be all right now.

She went around the aisles, got some packets of biscuits, a couple of apples, a large bottle of mineral water.

The bored-looking girl behind the counter was reading a teenage magazine. She had a ragged punky look, dyed yellow hair, skull-shaped studs in both nostrils. She ran the fifty-pound note Ellen offered through an infrared machine before accepting it.

'I'm sorry I don't have anything smaller,' Ellen said.

The girl nodded. 'American, are you?'

'That's right.'

'Here on holiday?'

'Just passing through.'

'I wish I was,' the girl said glumly.

A fresh hand of pain gripped her spine now; she could feel its icy, clutching fingers.

'Are you all right there, Missus?' the girl asked.

'I'm fine, yes.'

'You're wild pale. About the face.'

'I just . . . You wouldn't have aspirin? Something like that?'

'No, sorry, we don't keep it. But there's a chemist up the town. Are you not feeling well?'

'I just have this toothache. It seems to have flared up badly today.'

The girl gave her a sympathetic look. She glanced over Ellen's shoulder, then leaned a little closer and spoke confidentially.

'I've some Ponstan myself in my jacket, if you'll hold on a wee minute. They're for period pain and things like that there, but maybe they'd do you?'

'That would be really kind of you. Thanks.'

The girl slipped into a back room and came back a few moments later with a mug of water and six white tablets.

'Oh, gosh. Thank you so much.'

'Here. Take two now and save the others. Drink this down. Are you sure you're all right?'

'Yes, I'll be fine now. Honestly.'

'Do you want to sit down in the back a wee while?'

'No, no. How much do I owe you for those?'

'Oh, not at all. Nothing.'

'You really are an angel.'

'Toothache can be awful. It's the worst pain there is nearly. I hope those bring it down a bit for you.'

A sudden thought drifted up.

'You wouldn't have a public telephone, would you?'

'Aye. Just over there by the door.'

She walked to the phone and looked at it for a moment. When she glanced at her watch it was just after one. That meant it was eight o'clock in New York. The coins in the palm of her hand felt hot.

Out on the forecourt Aitken was cleaning the windscreen.

Before she really knew what she was doing she had put in some change, dialled a long-distance number. She waited for the circuits to click into place, the thumping of her heart a ragged counterpoint to the thudding of the ceilidh music on the radio.

The phone rang four times. The sleepy voice of her son came on the line.

'Hello?'

In that instant she could almost see him, with his hair tousled up like an old bird's nest and his face milk white, as it always was in the mornings. She found herself wondering which phone he had picked up.

'Hello?' he said again, his voice echoing slightly. The line made a crackling, underwater sound.

She had a strong impulse to hang up straight away. What was it she wanted to say, after all? She should have thought about this, planned it out.

'Who is it?' he tried again. 'Is somebody there?'

Now she thought she could hear the dishwasher churning in the kitchen. She pictured him standing just inside the back door. For some reason she imagined him barefoot. What had got him up so early? He was rarely out of bed before eleven during the holidays.

'Mom? . . . Is that you?'

'Lee,' she blurted. 'It's me, honey.'

For a moment he said nothing. Then gave a quiet laugh.

'Mom. Jesus. Where the rusty fuck are you?'

'Don't swear, Lee. Is your father there?'

'He thinks you been kidnapped or something. Where are you?'

'Well, I haven't. Is he there?'

'He's out at work.'

'At work?'

'Yeah. So where are you, Mom?'

The line began to bleep. She fed the phone more change. She glanced through the window and across the forecourt. Aitken slammed down the bonnet, went to a spool of paper that was mounted on a pillar, ripped off a length and wiped his hands. He looked over, met her eyes and waved.

'I'm . . . it doesn't matter where I am.'

'Are you with the sex-aid guy?'

'The who?'

'That Florida guy with the weird name.'

'If you mean Dick Spiggot, no, I'm not.'

'OK.' He snuffled. 'Dick Spiggot. That really kills me.'

'My God, is that what your father thinks?'

'I never really know what he thinks, I guess.'

Aitken began to amble towards her, still rubbing his wet hands. A jeep pulled in and cut him off from her view. When it had passed he was looking straight at her. He did an exaggeratedly casual shrug, like a mafioso in a *Godfather* movie.

'So where are you, Mom? Are you OK?'

335

'I'm perfectly safe and well, honey. But I have to go now.'

Aitken tapped on his watch, jerking his thumb in the direction of the road. She gestured back at him that she wouldn't be long.

'I can't hear you so good, Mom. Is there a radio playing or something?'

She turned and put her hand over the phone. The girl was talking to the other teenagers, one of whom was fingering an invisible guitar and swinging his shoulders in time with the rhythm. 'I'm sorry,' Ellen called. 'Would you mind turning that down a moment?'

The girl put her hand to her mouth and ran in behind the counter, where she switched the ceilidh music off. She gave Ellen an apologetic look and mimed the word 'sorry'.

'Hello? Mom?'

'Yes, I'm here.'

'Where?'

'I can't say, Lee.'

The time delay was cutting them into each other now, making them pause too long between their sentences, giving the conversation an artificial feel.

'Are you coming home, Mom?'

'I have to go, Lee.'

'Why d'you run away like that?'

'There was something I had to take care of.'

'It isn't because of me?'

'Oh, Lee. Of course it isn't.'

Aitken put his hands on his hips. He shot her an impatient glare.

'Is it something to do with your real mom?'

She could hear her son's breathing. He had a habit of holding the phone too close to his mouth. Milton was always telling him it was unhygienic. She could picture him so clearly, sitting on the kitchen table with his feet on a chair, the way he always did when he spoke on the telephone. She had told him not to do it a thousand times.

'Why would you say that, honey?'

'I think about that sometimes. How much you must want to find her.'

'What would make you think about that, Lee?'

He was silent for what seemed like a long time.

'Because I know I'd want to find you,' he said then.

What a shockingly beautiful boy he was. How like Milton. Not at all like her. A memory flashed through her mind. Lee running in a sports-day race at school, back when he'd been seven or maybe eight. His heartbreakingly eager face as he'd galloped past her and Milton and into the home straight towards the tape.

'Lee Amery,' she quietly said. 'I don't know what I ever did to deserve a son as wonderful as you.'

'Right,' he said. 'Me too.'

On the other side of the glass, Aitken was standing with his back to her now, idly flicking at a rack of newspapers that was sitting just outside the door. She watched him pick one out and scan the front page.

'Hey, Mom, I got a flight simulator from Grandma and Grandad for Christmas. It's awesome.'

The line began to beep again. She had no more change.

'I have to go, honey.'

'Yeah. We all miss you, Mom.'

'I miss you too.'

'But I don't want you to worry about anything, Mom, OK? We'll all be . . .'

The line clicked and went dead.

Chapter Twenty-Eight

Something about Aitken had changed. She couldn't quite name it, but she was sure it was true. It was nothing he said, but things had altered. It was as though the light in the car was different.

The snow stopped. Mist was forming over the ivory-coloured fields. The winding shore of Lough Oughter came into view on the left. A flock of wild swans had congregated near a small island that was overgrown with conifers and withered rhododendrons. They sped by the ruin of an ancient church, a closed-down dance hall, a piebald mare tethered in a field near a circle of travellers' caravans and rusty pick-up trucks.

'Everything OK today, Martin?'

He gave a peremptory nod, eyes fixed hard on the road. 'Sure.'

Coming into Butler's Bridge, they passed a billboard saying ULSTER IS BEAUTIFUL, through which had been splashed a rough black X. On the far side of the town stood a giant green signpost for DERRY, DONEGAL, INISHOWEN PENINSULA. The place names had thick black lines spray-painted through them; their Irish equivalents had been daubed on instead. *Doire. Tir Conail. Inis Eoghain.*

There had been something on his mind since they'd left Cavan. She wondered if her making the phone call had annoyed him. She'd thought he had been joking when he'd looked so exasperated. But maybe he wasn't. Men often weren't, especially when it came to timetables for journeys.

How many arguments had she had with Milton about getting ready to go out, off on vacation, or just up to Saranac Lake for a weekend? When they were first married she had found it amusing. In ways, she had even found it attractive that he'd get so moody and ridiculous occasionally. She'd tease him about it, flirtatiously call him masterful. But after a time she could see it really did upset him when she was late. Once, *en route* to a wedding, he had even sworn at her about it. That had shocked her to the core. It was the only time she had ever heard him curse.

Another billboard loomed up by the roadside, showing a glorious lakeside scene with a border of medieval-style Celtic spirals and zigzags. THE ULSTER LAKES was the slogan this time. The words ARE IRISH! had been painted in.

'Look.' She laughed. 'Guess someone's been busy around here with the spray-cans.'

He said nothing at all, just squinted hard at the road.

There was clearly something wrong. She wasn't imagining it. It simply wasn't like him to be so silent. But she'd only slowed them down by five minutes. Surely it couldn't just be that.

Perhaps it was what had happened between them last night. Maybe he was frightened or confused about it. You couldn't blame him if that was so. Maybe, after all, she was frightened herself.

She looked at his profile, so grim and concentrated. His mouth was closed so hard that his chin was jutting out.

'Is there something on your mind, Martin?'

He shook his head.

'Would you like me to drive for a little while?'

'No. I'm fine to drive.'

'I really don't mind. I quite like driving. We could stop and get you a paper or something.'

'I already got a paper back at the garage.'

His voice was sharp. His hands gripped the wheel.

'Oh,' she said. 'OK. If you're sure.'

'Yes. I got myself a paper while you were on the phone.'

Was that supposed to be significant? When she looked at him again, his expression hadn't changed. What on earth was he trying to say? She felt real unease gnaw at her now. It was so difficult when men talked like this, inviting you to try and decode just what they meant.

'When you were on the phone to the convent. As you said. Right?'

'Yes.'

He nodded again. 'So how were all the sisters? Doing OK?'

'Well . . . yes, they're fine.'

Signs appeared saying WELCOME TO BELTURBET TOWN, but the landscape around was still rural and empty. On the crest of a long hill up ahead to the left a line of windmills stood like strange gods. She looked down at the map on her knees. Belturbet was the last town in the South. After that they would cross the border into Northern Ireland, drive up through Derry, then back into the Republic.

There wasn't much traffic on the narrow road. They eased past a lumbering tractor that was leaking spumes of diesel – the driver doffing his hat in cheerful salute as they overtook – then a ramshackle old brown Morris Minor with a black plastic sack taped into one of its windows. Aitken switched the radio on. A classical piano piece was playing, gentle, sparse; somehow brittle.

'So tell me,' he said. 'How do the other nuns feel about you being here?'

In an instant now, she knew what the matter was. The moment had come, as she'd known it must.

They swept past a blue and grey single-storey modern hotel. A banner hung over the entrance to the lobby.

THE FANTASTIC FRANCIS HARDY
FAITH HEALER
FOR ONE NIGHT ONLY

'Martin . . .'

'They don't mind, no? You coming to Ireland? They must be fierce tolerant altogether.'

'Please, Martin . . .'

He braked so quickly that they both jerked forward. He pulled in messily to the hard shoulder. The engine made a troubled gurgling sound.

'We need to have a talk, Ellen. Right now.'

'Yes.'

He peered straight ahead as though watching something specific on the road. It began to feel to her as though the car's interior was getting smaller. He reached out and switched off the ignition. The Morris Minor caught up and chugged past. Someone had written WASH ME in the grime on the back. She noticed that the exhaust pipe was dangling low, it seemed to be attached with some kind of rope.

'I think you've got something to tell me, Ellen.'

Her face felt hot, moist with sweat. 'What's that?'

'For Christ's sake, stop it! Don't insult me. All right?'

She watched the Morris Minor disappear around a bend. It trailed a small cloud of black smoke in its wake.

He pulled a folded-up newspaper from the door pocket and began to read aloud.

'Police have issued a description of a missing person, Ellen May Donnelly, of Scarsdale, New York, who is thought to be in the United Kingdom . . .'

A chilly sensation moved across her chest. He ran a finger roughly down the page to crease it open, before continuing in a voice he was clearly having to restrain:

'Ms Donnelly, a teacher at Fox Meadow School in her home town, has not been seen since last Wednesday night when she attended a social function held by a wealthy friend in the Bahamas . . .'

'Martin . . .'

He continued, insistent, his voice riding over her:

'Officers at Scotland Yard believe Ms Donnelly may have travelled from Nassau airport to London over the following night of the 22nd December, arriving at Heathrow early morning on the 23rd. She is in need of regular treatment

341

for a serious medical condition. It is possible that she may
have suffered blackouts, faints or memory loss. She is aged
47, and is five foot seven, of medium build, with greying
hair and green eyes. Witnesses are asked to contact their
nearest police station as soon as possible. A substantial
reward has been offered for information.'

He lowered the paper but still did not look at her. Two boys
and a woman were walking along the road towards them, with
a mangy three-legged dog dolefully trotting ahead, snuffling in
the ditches and chasing its tail.

'Forty-seven,' she said. 'What a cheek.'

He tossed the newspaper into her lap.

'There you go. Congratulations.'

At the bottom of the article was a smudged black and white
print of the photograph taken of herself and Milton at the Rotary
Club dinner back in September. Milton had been cropped out of
the picture, but you could still see his right arm on her waist. Her
eyes looked vague; a little frightened. Her mouth was open, as
though she'd been laughing at something. She thought she looked
disturbed and ugly. MISSING MUM, said the caption underneath.

She folded up the paper and put it in the glove box. Wiped
the misting windscreen with the back of her hand.

He opened his window and looked out for a while. The boys
were climbing a five-bar gate, pulling the yelping dog through by
the soft part of its neck. The woman was beautiful, in her early
thirties, wearing tight blue faded jeans and an oilskin jacket. She
was carrying a kite, Ellen noticed, as she climbed the stile at the
side of the gate.

'So what's the story, Ellen? Or don't I get told that?'

For some reason, Milton came into her mind now, an incident
from their honeymoon, in Positano. He had gone swimming one
afternoon after a heavy lunch of lobster ravioli and had gotten
into difficulties. She remembered glancing out at the sea from
her sun-bed, the horror of seeing him sink into the waves. It
was low season; the beach was almost deserted. As though in a
dream, she had begun to run through the water to try to reach
him, but the harder she had run, the stronger the waves seemed,

342

knocking her backwards and off balance. She remembered him appearing on the surface again, calling out in abject childlike terror, her sheer helplessness to do anything to save him. And in that moment she had thought he would die.

Even as she had plunged on towards him, her mouth and nostrils filling with salt water, her eyes stinging, she was imagining the unbearable pointlessness of her life without him. A huge wave slammed head-on into her, bowling her into an underwater somersault. By the time she had staggered to her feet, she couldn't even see him any more. Then after a moment she had seen his hands break the surface and she'd thrown herself into the swell again. In the event he had been saved by a German tourist who spoke no English and was vacationing alone. A powerful swimmer, he had pounded out through the current and managed to grab him, hauling him in towards the beach by the hair, lifting up his limp body when they got to the shallows, striding out of the water like a godly apparition. He'd laid Milton down on the sand and given him the kiss of life, repeatedly grunting the word 'nein' as he pumped on his sternum, as though he could save him by sheer will alone.

They had felt they should invite the man to dinner every night from then on. There the story of the rescue would be retold in mime, a pepperpot or sauce bottle representing Milton, a knife or fork standing in for fearless Hansi, the Kaiser of the breaststroke, as Milton had insisted on calling him. How very odd to think of that now. Where was Hansi when you needed him most?

'You're married,' said Aitken, 'aren't you, Ellen?'

'You can leave me here,' she said.

He scoffed. 'What are you talking about?'

'You can leave me here, Martin. Or maybe you'd be good enough to drive me back to Cavan.'

'So what's this so-called medical condition you have, then?'

Hansi was such a handsome man. Such a beautiful body, like an ancient Greek statue. All the girls on the beach would look at him when he went by. She wondered if he had ever met anyone afterwards. It was such a shame he'd had to holiday all by himself. He was so gentle and considerate she felt sure

343

he was gay. She pictured them now, Hansi and his partner, cooking Wiener schnitzel and watering their plants.

'Not in the mood for answering, no?'

'I'm dying, Martin,' she said.

The wind threw a handful of dust against the windscreen. Over the field on the right, two larks were whirling in a slow, graceful, figure-of-eight pattern. The younger of the two boys they had seen before was wearing yellow oilskins now and flying the kite.

'I'm dying.' She listened to the sound of the words. She had never said them out loud before. How strange they sounded. How ridiculous, really. Those were words other people said.

'I have cancer of the pancreas. It's beyond treatment. They've given me less than a year to live.'

The child began to move slowly across the field, tottering on the rutted frozen earth, tugging lightly on the cord while his brother watched him and shouted encouragement.

'So how am I to know that isn't another lie?'

She felt the tears begin to spill over her eyelids. He went to touch her but she pushed him back.

The boy with the kite was running clumsily, yowling with glee, being chased by the woman and the yapping, half-lame dog.

She stepped out of the car, slammed the door so hard that a cloudburst of birds came flapping out of the hedgerow. She began to walk quickly away.

'Running again?' Aitken yelled. 'Well, you just keep on running, Ellen. Don't let me stop you. *All right?*'

*

Ten minutes later he saw her on the opposite side of the road, striding determinedly towards the town, past a cluster of bungalows advertising bed and breakfast. Up ahead he could see the outskirts of Belturbet, the steeple of the church and a couple of shops.

He eased forward, pulled alongside her and rolled down the window. Her face was pink and swollen from crying.

'Get in,' he said.

She ignored him and kept walking, head high, swinging her arms. Grit flew in through the window, moistening his eyes. The wind threw a dead oak leaf against the windscreen. A priest came around the corner on a sputtering moped. He stared so hard as he rode slowly past that he almost went into a ditch.

'For God's sake get in,' Aitken said. 'You're being ridiculous.'

'I'm going to Inishowen if I have to walk all the way.'

'Well, that's quite a walk.'

'Please leave me alone. Or I'll call the police.'

'There's an answer to that, Ellen.'

She whipped around to face him. 'Martin Aitken, what the hell do you want from me? *What?*'

He shrugged. 'I want you to come to Inishowen.'

She shook her head bitterly and walked on again.

'Please.'

Suddenly she turned off the road, through a gate that was open to her right and into a long boggy field spread with tea-coloured snow. He pulled in to the verge and jumped out, quickening his stride to catch her up. He grabbed her by the elbow but she pulled away.

'Look, I'm sorry I said that . . . about you lying.'

'You think I'm lying?' She swung round and slapped him hard across the mouth. 'You think I'm lying, you bastard?' She gave a wrenching, agonised sob that twisted her face. 'Like people lie when they're going to die? Tell me I'm lying again. Go on. You son of a bitch.'

'Please.'

She pushed him away. He grabbed her by the wrists.

'Go on, Inspector. That's right. Do it.'

'Stop it. Please.'

'Come on, big man. You want to, don't you? Go ahead, knock a confession out of me.'

'Please, Ellen. Stop it now.'

She threw back her head, closed her streaming eyes and began to speak in a bitter, anguished monotone, as though she had once written down what she was saying before learning to say it off by heart.

'My name is Ellen May Roisín Donnelly, Inspector. I'm married to Doctor Milton Amery, a very nice, very damaged,

345

very silent man. A plastic surgeon who has sex in hotel rooms three times a week with a woman the age of our own daughter, a girl really, I taught her, who works in a punk rock record store on Bleecker Street and Broadway. Sometimes they have sex in his car too, Inspector. And actually I wouldn't even mind any more, Inspector, only that sometimes I can actually see her footprints on the glove compartment door, Inspector, because he can't even be bothered to clean them off when he's finished *fucking* her.'

'Ellen, please. Get back in the car.'

'So *I* do that. I clean off her footprints.' She pushed him away, now quivering with tears. 'And I'm dying, Inspector. OK? Do you understand? I am dying. My children don't know that in less than a year I'll be dead. Because I can't bring myself to tell them. That I'm dying right now from the inside out. That I smell of death. That my sweat stinks of death. That I'm afraid to kiss my children goodnight in case they get the smell of my insides rotting from my breath.'

She turned away, weeping, hands to her face.

'Ellen . . . I'm so sorry.'

They stood still for a moment, saying nothing. Her sobs came in painful breathy gulps. Up ahead, on the brow of the hill, a mangy black goat trotted into view. It stopped, frozen, watching them. Aitken felt the crystallised sludge soak through his shoes. Without turning to look at him, she raised her head. 'Did you ever hear of loneliness? Did you?'

He moved forward now and took her in his arms. The wind rushed up from the roadway and hit his back. Snow lay around like lumps of broken glass.

'I'm going to take care of you, love,' he said.

He held her tightly and felt her tremble.

'You'll never be lonely again. I swear.'

Chapter Twenty-Nine

Though the Manhattan office of Galsworthy, Bligh, Brinksman, Hamburger was closed for the Christmas and New Year holiday, Amery was trying to track down the partners.

This had proved extremely difficult. Bligh had gone bear shooting; Hamburger was attempting the land speed record; Brinksman was out of town for the weekend, having been booked to guest-present *Larry King Live*.

Finally he managed to get through to Julian Galsworthy at home – or, at least, at one of his several homes, a ski lodge in a frighteningly expensive part of Vermont.

Ellen's lawyer sounded pleasant and businesslike, but really, he said, this was now a matter for the courts.

'But she doesn't truly want to divorce me,' said Amery. 'We've just been experiencing some minor problems recently.'

Galsworthy sighed. 'That's not my information.'

'Well, what is?'

'Doctor Amery, look. Divorce work is expensive and time-consuming. We don't take it on unless the client truly wants that. I've been through all the options with Mrs Amery and I'm sorry to have to tell you, but she definitely wants a divorce.'

'But she doesn't . . . She couldn't.'

'Unfortunately, Doctor Amery, she does and she could. And as for the financial aspects, well, as the wife of a very wealthy man she's entitled to an adequate settlement.'

'An adequate settlement? Four and a half million dollars?'

'That's what we would consider adequate, yes. Now, if you'll excuse me, Doctor Amery, I'm spending time with my children today.'

'Say if I said I was open to negotiation?'

The lawyer made a strange burbling noise. 'I don't really know that Mrs Amery would be. But I suspect not, to be frank with you.'

'What the hell does she need four and a half million dollars for?'

'I didn't ask her that, to be honest. I wouldn't really see it as my area of specialty.'

'My wife is dying, for God's sakes.'

The lawyer chuckled. 'We're all doing that, Doctor Amery.'

'*She's* doing it in six months' time!'

'Well, her future plans are no concern of ours.'

'Her . . . what?'

'And no concern of yours either. At least not as soon as the order goes through.'

'I'll fight this, Galsworthy. I will, you know.'

'Yes. The last witness we placed under subpoena said you probably would.'

'What witness?'

'Your girlfriend of some two years? Miss Catherine Kenneally, I believe, from recollection?'

'Who?'

'Tell you what, Doctor Amery. Let me just slip out the old file here.'

Jesus Christ, Ellen knew about Cathy. Worse, she had a lawyer who brought his files on *vacation.*

'Ah, yes. Here we are. Catherine Jane Kenneally.'

'I have absolutely no idea who you're talking about.'

'Hmm. You do know she was a minor when you first had relations, do you?'

'We were just friends, for God's sakes. That's a dirty lie.'

A low, soft snigger came down the line. 'We've located a number of previous friends too.'

'Now look . . .'

'Would you like them in alphabetical order or simply at random?'

'Now listen . . .'

'Miss Michelle Nicolson, Mrs Reba Drabble, Mademoiselle Claudia Frenet, Miss Ruth Freud and her twin sister, Ethel.

Mrs Marion Astor, Professor Miriam Truffaut . . . Would you like me to go on, Doctor Amery?'

'No. No. I get the point.'

'Assistant Commissioner of Police, Jane Hemingway. Miss Taylor, Miss Farrelly, Miss Lewinsky, Miss Norman, Miss Blumenstein, Miss Gomez, Rabbi Sarah Duglacz, Miss Cabot, Fräulein Hoffman, Miss Spanker and Miss Brahms.'

'I've never met anyone called Spanker in my life.'

'Oh yes. This is good. A person named Spiggot.'

'Spiggot?'

'Yes. A Miss Muriel Spiggot of Indianapolis, Indiana. I believe she's the younger sister of a university friend of yours and Mrs Amery's?'

'Muriel says she and I had an affair?' He cackled. 'Have you seen her? I wouldn't touch her with *yours*, Galsworthy.'

'Oh no, no, sir, she didn't say that.'

'Thank the Lord for that much, at least.'

'No. She says you and her brother Dick were well-known homosexual lovers. Whilst at college.'

'She *what*?'

'Actually I'd heard that said myself. You know, around town.'

'What?'

'Look, I really have to go, Doctor Amery. Duty calls, as they say in the movies.'

'For God's sake, man. You must have some advice.'

'I'd advise you to hire a *really* first-class attorney, Doctor Amery. Believe you me, you're certainly going to need one.'

*   *   *

Once, back in the eighties – she couldn't remember when, and it didn't matter now – a stupid story had gotten into the local newspaper about how, according to some medieval astronomer, the world was going to end on the following Saturday night. She had ridiculed it, of course, to allay the children's fears. As for Milton, he'd banned that newspaper from the house and written o the editor to call him a moron.

Around two that Sunday morning she had happened to wake. It had been raining hard and the bedroom curtains were open.

Milton had been beside her, turned away, his joined hands pillowing the side of his head, his troubled breath rising and uneasily falling. He'd had a bad cold, the room smelt of eucalyptus rub. The white lace curtains were moving in the breeze. And suddenly the sky had gone dark. A bolt of jagged lightning had flashed; so long that it seemed to shred the space in the windowframe in two from top to bottom. The crack of thunder seemed to shake the house. A jangle of car alarms began. A gush of rain. Awesome darkness. Well, it was ridiculous. All that had happened was that a cloud had passed in front of the moon and the storm must have blown out the power for the street lamps. But in that darkness, for one fraction of a second, she had imagined that the world was truly about to end, that the earth was on the verge of being plunged back into preternatural, biblical chaos. And in that moment, Ellen Donnelly thought, she had received some revelation of what it would be to die.

She was going to die.

She was going to die.

What would it feel like? Would it hurt? Be pleasant? Would it be a little like falling asleep? But then, when you thought about it, what was falling asleep really *like*?

Her neighbours, Sarah Peterson and Hope Collins, would wash her body and dress her in grave-clothes. Then Sarah's husband Murray and their son Peagram would put her in a pine box and screw down the lid. Charlie Tomalin would drive her to the town crematorium in the fin-tailed Chevrolet hearse she'd seen him polish a thousand times on her way to do the Saturday supermarket trip. What a nice man Charlie was. Always ready with a joke, or a friendly wave. His son Charlie Junior had been killed in Vietnam. Charlie'd had bad times then; his wife had taken to drinking. Shortly afterwards she had developed Parkinson's and had to be put into a home. It had broken Charlie's heart to be without her, for months he hadn't been able to work at all. When the bank had tried to confiscate his business, Milton had helped him out financially without letting Ellen know. She had only found out when Charlie had told her. It was so typical of Milton. He was such a generous person.

When she'd tried to tell him she was proud of him for doing it, he had shrugged and blushed and gone back to his supper. 'You don't stand by and let a man's dignity be taken away.'

At the chapel of rest all the neighbours would be waiting. Some of her students might be there too. The town choir would sing 'Abide with Me' – that was what they always sang at funerals. Mitchum Doyle and Tommy Harris would place her casket on the rolling rubber track that was for all the world like a scaled-down baggage carousel. And then they would burn her.

What a strange thought. Her kindly neighbours – men who had sat opposite her at parent-teacher meetings, whose neat lawns Lee had mown as a Boy Scout, whose chatty wives she would see at the slimming class – would burn her body until it was gone.

And what would happen then? Would she stop existing?

Her mind recalled some lines from a childhood hymn. *Will there be any stars in my crown, Sweet Lord?* Sunlight streaming through stained-glass windows. Handsome Father Dumoulin holding up the chalice. 'We, girls, are an Easter people. None of us in this room is ever going to die.'

She pictured her family standing in the garden, Lee and Elizabeth in sweaters and raincoats, Milton in a suit, arms behind his back, rolling gently on the balls of his feet, the way he always did when something was tearing him up so badly he couldn't even speak. She even knew the suit he would wear, the dark grey stripe they had bought on that vacation in Paris, the one he always took on conference trips because it didn't crease easily or show the dirt. Reverend Hubbard would officiate at the service. He had married her and Milton one cold spring day under cherry trees, had baptised Lee and Elizabeth, taken them for Sunday school. She had taught his daughter to read and overcome a stammer. One day she had helped drag his wailing seven-year-old son out of the duck pond in the park, had dried him with a bath towel she'd happened to buy just five minutes earlier. Now he would say the prayers over her ashes. The children and Milton would scatter what was left of her over those rose bushes she had planted down near the tennis court. They'd go into the house and sit around. And their lives would simply continue without her.

She wondered if she would be able to see them still? Elizabeth and Lee? She felt a stab of grief at her heart.

Would she see Milton still? See him reading his notes on the train into work, his tender fingers on a patient's upturned face, see him walking the beautiful streets of Manhattan arm in arm with his latest girlfriend?

All these thoughts went through her mind as she sat alone in the waiting room of Cavan hospital.

Aitken had turned the car around and driven straight back to the town. She had told him she was all right, she wasn't in pain, but he had insisted. She needed a doctor.

Seated around were various festive season casualties. A plump, prematurely balding young man in a tartan shirt, his right hand wrapped in a bloodied linen tea towel. An eager little boy in knee-length football shorts, with one of those light-shade bandages around his neck. A slim teenage girl in a ballerina's tutu, her pale, oval face distended in pain, her graceful arms clutching her stomach as she rocked slowly back and forth, her mother's arm around her shoulder.

She caught the girl's glance and smiled sympathetically. The girl rolled her eyes and managed a brave little grin.

'Hang on in there,' Ellen said.

Aitken came in with two plastic cups of tea.

'They'll be a while yet,' he said. 'The doctors are up to their oxters.'

'Thanks.'

'Are you OK? You look very pale.'

'I do feel a little weak today. It tends to come and go.'

'Have some tea. Put lead in your pencil, eh?'

She took a sip that made her shudder. 'It's just a bit of wooziness. Really I'm fine.'

'Listen, I think we should head on back down to Dublin. Go out to Ranj in Dun Laoghaire, get you looked at properly. These are only culchie mullaghs up this neck of the woods.'

She shook her head. 'No, I'm fine.'

'Aren't you in pain?'

352

She shook her head again. 'You get used to it mostly. I had some drugs in my bag to help take care of the worst of it. The one that was stolen.'

A sudden pinch of agony deep in her chest made her wince.

'Jesus Christ. Hang on, I'll go get someone right now.'

'No,' she said, swallowing hard and bowing her head.

'If you're in pain, I . . .'

'Just stay with me, Martin . . . Just do that.'

The pain seemed to wrap itself around her heart, sharpening from an ache to a bright clean burn. She felt his hand on the back of her neck. The pain flowered up and quickly died away.

He took a sip of tea and grimaced.

'I'd say they waved a teabag over that two whole times. Would you?'

She laughed.

'They've a certain reputation up here in Cavan,' he said. 'They'd peel an orange without takin it out of their pockets.'

Her eyes fell on the mural that stretched the length of the waiting-room wall, with panels of children's Christmas drawings. A sad-looking camel with three big humps. A cartoon Joseph with a square smiling head, a matchstick Mary on a sky blue donkey, pursued by soldiers in helicopters and tanks. Three streaks of jagged brown crayon representing the manger, with wise men dressed in soccer outfits; leering shepherds watching cotton-wool sheep.

> *Wot are we going to call our baby, Mary?*
> *Well, Joseph, I was going to call him Mikey but instead we're calling him Jesus Christ!*
> *Hurray! Hurray! Happy bertie Jesus!*

He put his arm around her and clutched her elbow. Kissed her hair. Sipped his tea.

★   ★   ★

'Dad,' said Lee. 'I have something to tell you.'

When he looked up from the desk, his son was in the doorway. He saw that his plaster cast had been painted black and red with a circled capital 'A' adorning the shin. His hair had been slicked back hard across his scalp. He was wearing a padded skateboard glove on his right hand. He looked different since the accident, more grown-up somehow. It seemed ridiculous to think so, yet Amery couldn't help it.

'I had another call from Mom this morning.'

'You did?'

Lee nodded.

'Where was she?'

'I think she's in Ireland. Not in England.'

'Why's that?'

He limped into the study on his single crutch, wincing, holding on to the backs of the chairs.

'There was crappy Irish music playing on a radio in the background. I think she's gone to Ireland to find her mom.'

'Why do you think she'd be doing that all of a sudden?'

He sat down carefully on the edge of the desk. Balanced the crutch across his thighs. 'I don't know, Dad. You tell me.'

Amery looked at his son's face. Sometimes he reminded him so much of himself at that age. But mostly he seemed the incarnation of Ellen. He had her way of moving, of not speaking a thing straight out; the same perpetual almost comic half-frown that made him look suspicious and somehow too alert.

'Is there something wrong with Mom, Dad?'

'How do you mean?'

'Is Mom – you know – is she sick or something?'

Amery laughed. 'Of course she's not.'

'Are you scared to tell us, Dad?'

'My God, no. Where do you get these ideas, Lee?'

His son picked up a snowstorm paperweight and shook it gently. He stared hard at it, refusing to meet Amery's eyes. 'Because the first time she called – last week? – I asked her if we could all go to EuroDisney next year.'

'What did she say?'

'I just got the feeling we wouldn't be going.'

He slid down into a chair and regarded Amery closely.

'Maybe you should call the cops in Ireland, Dad.'

'I'll do that tomorrow. First thing.'

354

'Maybe you should call 'em right now, Dad.'

'It's night in Ireland now. I'll call them tomorrow.'

'OK.' Lee nodded. 'Whatever, Milton. Just don't say I didn't tell you this time.'

Chapter Thirty

'How far is Inishowen now?' she asked.

'We'll cross the border in five minutes, head on up through Enniskillen, Omagh, then Derry. Once you're out of Derry that's where Inishowen begins.' He looked at his watch. 'We'll be there in an hour and a half. Say by nine at the latest.'

'OK,' she said. 'Let's keep going.'

'There's a hotel I know in Red Castle, kind of a family place. They do mighty breakfasts. I thought we might put up there for the night.'

'Sounds good,' she replied.

They drove quickly through Belturbet, which had an eerie closed-down look. Before long, signs began to appear along the edge of the road saying BUREAU DE CHANGE 100 YARDS, STERLING NOTES ACCEPTED HERE, GOODS AT NORTHERN IRELAND PRICES. A wooden cut-out of a submachine gun had been fixed to the highest point of a lamppost and painted with the words BRITS GO HOME.

'I meant to ask you,' Aitken said. 'Have you ever been to the North before? With your group?'

'Belfast once, just after the hunger strikes. I was involved in fundraising back home for the prisoners' families.'

'Oh.' He laughed. 'Fair enough.'

'Is that funny to you?'

'No, no.'

'So why are you laughing? What's so amusing?'

'Now don't be jumpin on my back,' he said, gently. 'I just didn't know you were involved in that.'

'I felt very strongly about it. A lot of us did.'

'It was a mad auld time right enough.'

356

'It was a disgrace,' she said firmly. 'What was allowed to happen. I'm only sorry I didn't do more.'

A large green sign loomed up before them.

BORDER CHECKPOINT APPROACHING
SLOW DOWN AND DIM YOUR LIGHTS

'Here we go,' he grinned. 'The occupied territories.'

She smiled back wryly. '*Adios, Irlanda Libre.*'

The approach road was studded with fluorescent yellow speed bumps. A line of high metal walls began, which funnelled the cars into one long lane, at the end of which was a dark green, spotlit corrugated iron structure with a barrier post at which armed guards were on duty.

A short line of traffic had built up at the checkpoint. They eased past the raised barrier and into a wider fenced-off area that looked like a small car park. Around the barbed-wire perimeter were concrete posts with security cameras and more spotlights that spilled narrow pools of barium whiteness down into the darkness. On the right, soldiers and RUC officers were searching the back of an articulated truck, while the driver stood watching, smoking a cigarette. A sergeant with a clipboard seemed to be asking him questions. The driver kept taking off his cap and scratching his head, then madly gesticulating as he tried to explain something. Three men in luminous yellow uniforms with HM CUSTOMS stamped on the back appeared in the rear of the truck now, waving flashlights. They clambered out, hunkered down and beamed their torches around the wheels and axles. Two more men emerged from the truck, hefting wooden crates that looked extremely heavy.

A soldier stepped forward and held up his hand. His face was streaked with lines of black camouflage, the brim of his helmet down low over his eyes. A short-barrelled machine gun sat cradled in his arms. Aitken stopped and rolled down the window.

'Evening, sir,' the soldier said.

'Good evening yourself. How are you doing?'

The soldier looked taken aback to be asked. He gazed at

357

Aitken for a moment or two as though it might be some kind of trick question.

'Bit cooled,' he said then. He had a broad, North of England accent.

'You'd need your long johns on you in this weather, right enough.'

The soldier pursed his lips and nodded. 'Aye, true. Where you off to, sir?'

'We're headed up to Donegal for a few days.'

'Which part?'

'Inishowen.'

'I see. Would you have a bit of identification for us, please?'

Aitken pulled out his wallet and showed his badge. The soldier took it and looked at it closely, checking it against Aitken's face.

'Policeman, are you, sir?'

'I'm an inspector in the Gardaí, yes. Down south.'

A light rain began to fall as the soldier examined the badge. He shivered a little, closing the buttons at his throat. The radio on his shoulder bleeped.

'You from Newcastle yourself?' Aitken asked.

'Aye.'

'Howay the lads, eh?'

'Yes, sir. Exactly.'

'A Geordie, eh? Like Jackie Charlton. He's from up around there, isn't he?'

'Aye, from near enough,' the soldier grinned. 'Only he's Irish as well now, eh?'

'He is indeed,' Aitken said. 'He's practically running the country, in fact.'

The soldier chuckled and adjusted his chinstrap. 'This photo here?' He tapped it with his gloved fingertip. 'That's a photo of yourself, is it, sir?'

'That's me, yes.'

'Durnt look like you.'

'It was taken a few years ago.'

The soldier looked at it again. Held it up to the light.

'There's none of us getting any younger,' Aitken said.

358

'Stay there in the car,' the soldier said. 'We'll just take a moment.'

'OK.'

'You understand I'm asking you to stay there for me? Yourself and your wife both. Close the windows. And don't attempt to go moving the car, all right?'

'Yes, I understand. Is there something the matter?'

The soldier shook his head. 'Shunt think so. Just roll up your window for me. I'll be back in a mo.'

Aitken eased the window up. The soldier took a few steps away and said something sharp to a colleague who was standing in the shadows by the door of an office. Now three more soldiers slid slowly like ghosts out of the darkness. One of them, a well-built black man, took up a position in front of the car, facing it. The other two stood on either side, the man by the driver's door so close that Aitken could see a tattoo across the backs of his knuckles.

'What's going on?' Ellen said.

'Relax,' he told her. 'It's nothing at all.'

'I don't like this.'

'We'll be through in two shakes. Just take it easy.'

Up ahead of them a sleek fox scuttled across the tarmac, its bushy tail held high, a bird limp in its jaws. It padded under an armoured car, emerged a moment later and squeezed through the boundary wire.

'You know they can hear what we're saying, Martin?'

'Who can?'

'The Brits. They have microphones that can spy on a conversation, even inside a car.'

Aitken laughed. 'They don't, Ellen. For God's sake.'

'They do, I'm telling you. That's a well-known fact.'

'Hey, muggins,' Aitken called lightly towards a passing corporal who was leading an Alsatian on a leash. 'Who cuts your hair, you ugly-lookin ibex?'

The man kept going, the dog trotting lightly behind him. He stopped, then, suddenly, seemed to notice something. He turned and made a gesture to the black soldier in front of the car.

The black man began waving his hand at Aitken.

'What?' said Aitken.

He was pointing at something now.

'What is it?' Aitken called.

The man was jabbing his finger hard.

'I don't understand.'

'Your lights,' shouted the soldier. 'Kill your lights.'

Aitken went to do as he was told. His hand slipped and knocked the headlight lever. Whiteness blazed across the tarmac. The three soldiers immediately aimed their rifles. The corporal's hand went for his pistol.

'Kill them!' snapped the black soldier, lunging forward with his gun pointed at the windscreen. 'Kill them, I said!'

'OK,' yelled Aitken.

The soldier was bawling. 'Now, I said! *Right* now! Kill them!'

Darkness fell again over the roadway.

'OK,' Aitken called. 'They're off. They're off.'

The corporal barked something at the black soldier, who nodded apologetically and stood to attention. The corporal bent and removed the dog's lead. It lowered its nose and nuzzled at the ground, took a few cautions steps in the direction of the Mini. Stopped. A manhole cover took its attention; it gave a few speculative sniffs. It cocked its head, did a little sneeze, licked its mouth, trotted around slowly to Ellen's side. The tip of its tail swung past the passenger window. It gave a small, sharp yelp. Its claws could be heard scratching on the door.

'Martin,' Ellen said.

Suddenly it bounced up on its front legs with its face to her window, its long drooling tongue hanging over its teeth.

'Jesus Christ,' Ellen said.

'Just relax.' He grabbed her hand.

'I'm scared, Martin.'

'Don't be scared. Take it easy.'

The dog jumped down and trotted back to the corporal. He said something and it sank to a sullen sit. Across the way the soldier who had questioned them was talking to the RUC sergeant. The lorry driver kept trying to interrupt them; he seemed impatient and angry, but the sergeant was ignoring him. He took the garda badge and looked at it for a time, then stared over hard at the Mini.

He drew his raincoat tightly around him, crossed the tarmac, gesturing with his finger for Aitken to roll the window down.

He was a plump, stocky barrel of a man with neatly trimmed sandy sideburns, a beefy face and long loose arms. He looked like he once might have been a boxer. He saluted quickly and handed the badge in through the window.

'Mizzly auld night now, Inspector,' he said.

'It is,' agreed Aitken.

'Aye, surely. You're away up to Donegal, is it?'

'That's right.'

The sergeant bent down. His breath smelt of peppermint. Behind him, the rain dropped like oval beads through the spotlight beam.

'Well, the roads are wild bad now. You'll not want to swing off at Lifford, they've flooding there on the bridge, over on the Republic side. You can take it handy up thon way, through Omagh and on.'

'You mean Derry way?'

'Aye, by Londonderry. You'd be wiser.'

'Sound, I'll do that, thanks. I was going to do that anyway.'

The sergeant hunkered lower and peered across at Ellen. Rain streamed down the glossy peak of his cap. 'What about you, Missus?'

Ellen turned to him. 'What about me?'

His face was expressionless. 'Well . . . may I see some identification, please?'

She turned away and faced forward again, folding her arms in a decisive way. 'I have none.'

'No driver's licence? Credit card?'

'Nothing like that.'

'But . . . you must have something I could look at, surely?'

'I don't.'

'She had her bag stolen down in Dublin recently,' Aitken explained. 'All her papers and things were in it.'

361

The sergeant tutted sympathetically. 'Ach, no. That's a blumming nuisance.'

'But I can vouch for her,' Aitken said.

'Aye, of course.' He took out a small notebook and pulled a pen from his pocket, bending to speak across to Ellen again.

'Did you know,' he beamed, 'that the man who designed the White House had Ulster blood?'

She said nothing.

'Well . . . Might I ask your name then, Missus?'

'Ellen Donnelly. And it's Ms. To you.'

He shrugged and nodded; scribbled something in the note-book.

'And where in America would you be from exactly?'

'I'm from Scarsdale, New York. If that's any of your business.'

The sergeant squinted quizzically, as though he was amused. Then he sighed and pinched his bulbous red nose. 'With respect now, there's no need for that class of talk at all, so there isn't. I and my men don't want to detain you any longer than necessary. We've families to go home to at this time of the year. I've a job to do here, that's all. For everyone's good. I'm sure your husband here understands, in his own line of work.'

'He's not my husband.'

'Oh . . . I see.'

'Since when does every woman in the world have to have a husband?'

The sergeant peered at Aitken closely. His hooded eyes looked weary and sad. 'I'm sorry, I'm confused, sir. You told thon soldier this person was your wife.'

'I didn't actually. He just assumed she was.'

The sergeant stood and went to the soldier. They exchanged a few words and then both came back to the Mini. The sergeant appeared a little anxious now.

'Might I ask you to both step out for a moment please?'

'Is there a problem?' Aitken said.

'Not at all. Just we'll have to take a wee bit of your time if you don't mind. I'd like to have a quick look in the car there.'

Ellen whipped around towards him again, her eyes narrowed

362

to slits of anger. 'Where the hell do you get off harassing us like this?'

He did a mock double-take of disbelief.

'What gives you the right? That uniform, is it?'

'Ellen, please,' Aitken sighed.

The sergeant's smile faded. 'Get out of that car. Now.'

'Why don't you come here and just get me out of it?'

'Ellen, for Jesus' sake. Do as he says.'

She turned forward again. The soldiers around the car had raised their weapons. The man on the right had a small spotlight attached to the barrel of his rifle, and this was shining straight into her eyes. She raised her hand and covered her face. The rain started to surge down harder. A dull boom of thunder sounded in the distance. The sergeant opened the driver's door and beckoned to Aitken to climb out, gesturing to him to open his jacket. Two women RUC officers in bulletproof vests and leather gloves came to the passenger door and quickly opened it.

The sergeant began to pat Aitken's pockets. 'Step out of the car slowly on your own side, Miss, with your hands in the air.'

'This is all a misunderstanding, Sergeant,' Aitken said. 'Now come on, let's just . . .'

'In the air. Right now. Both of you, please.'

She stepped out, painfully, and raised her arms. The women officers began to search her, checking her coat, her armpits, her torso. One of them squatted down and began feeling her thighs, the backs of her knees, around her buttocks.

'Could you spread your legs please, Miss?' she said.

Ellen stepped back. 'Get the hell off me. Right now.'

'I have the legal power to do this, Miss. We can do it here or beyond at the station.'

'Oh, I see. I suppose you'll strip-search me there, will you?'

'Only if we have to. That's up to you.'

'How dare you?' Ellen seethed. 'How dare you threaten me like that? Who the hell do you think you are?'

The woman turned to the officer. 'Sergeant?'

'Look, my friend isn't well,' Aitken said. 'She's really not.'

363

The man looked at him. 'I'd say there's a deal of truth in that, right enough.'

'She has a severe medical condition. She's in a lot of discomfort. We've just spent five hours in Cavan hospital where she had to have a very painful injection.'

The wind made a sighing, lonesome sound. The sergeant stared at Ellen for a time without saying anything.

'Leave her be,' he said then. The women released her and stood still. He nodded at them to leave.

'What's your name?' Ellen asked angrily.

'Ruttledge,' the man replied. 'Sergeant Mervyn Albert Ruttledge. My number is G7 9267A. Anything else you'd like to know?'

'You'll be sorry for that little display, Sergeant Ruttledge.' She pronounced his rank as though it amused her. 'You'll be damn sorry about this. I am a very good friend of the American ambassador. Your superiors will be hearing about this matter first thing in the morning.'

'Yes, madam,' the sergeant said softly, without looking at her. He was beaming his torch around the interior of the Mini now, letting it slide over the back seat and the rear window shelf. He climbed into the driver's seat then, lowered the sun visors, checked the door pockets, under the floor mats.

In the glove compartment he found her bundle of letters. He took them out and held them up.

'What are these, madam?'

'They're personal papers.'

'I thought all your personal papers were stolen in Dublin.'

'Give those back.'

He began leafing through them, examining them closely by the light of his torch.

'I said give those to me, Mister. Right now.'

He ignored her and continued reading, wiping his nose from time to time with the back of his glove. When he had finished he held them out towards her and she snapped them from him.

'Give you some thrill, does it? Invading people's privacy like that?'

'Ellen, for God's sake,' Aitken said.

364

The sergeant sighed deeply and climbed out of the car. His eyes seemed to be scanning the hills.

'Tell me, madam,' he said, without looking at her. 'What precisely have I done to offend you here tonight?'

She said nothing.

'It might interest you to know,' he continued, 'that we have reports of subversive activity in this area. That a woman was attacked near here last month. That a very dangerous rapist escaped from prison only down the road in the Republic last night.'

'Oh, I see. And I look like him, do I?'

'I am making the point. I have a job to do.'

'So go ahead. Go do it. Don't you have some kids to harass or something?'

He looked at her now. 'Don't you think I have children myself, Mrs Donnelly?'

'They must be real proud of their father.'

'Ellen, that's enough,' Aitken said.

'I hope they're proud, yes,' the man said. 'I hope they might have some reason to be.'

'Oh yes. Very proud.'

'But the way I see it myself, Missus, respect tends to be earned so it does. Like trust.'

'Oh, I'm sure they're proud, yes. Wearing that uniform and harassing innocent people. For the so-called crime of being Irish.'

The sergeant laughed. 'I'm Irish myself, Missus. Unlike some of us here.'

'And as for your wife, she must be really proud too.'

The sergeant's smile slowly died. He looked at Ellen and nodded a few times. 'Well, I believe I won't dignify that remark, if you don't mind. I'll bid you goodnight at that point.' He turned to Aitken and saluted again. 'Goodnight to you too, sir. I'm sorry if we upset your companion. No offence was meant. We were only doing our job.'

'Goodnight,' Aitken said.

The sergeant held out his hand. Aitken shook it.

'I'll wish you welcome and a safe journey,' the sergeant said.

365

Ellen got back into the Mini and slammed the door. The sergeant turned and walked slowly down the road. He paused, looked away over the field, as though something unusual was happening in it. A constable approached and offered him a cigarette. He took it, bent to light it, then walked on a few yards into a small metal hut, closing the door gently behind him. After a few moments the constable went and knocked on the door. Some words were exchanged. Then the man closed the door and came back up the road to the checkpoint.

'You can go on now, sir,' he said to Aitken.

'Is he all right?'

'Aye. I think it was the comment about his wife did it, sir.'

'What about it?'

'Well . . . three years ago, his wife was in a bomb, sir. She's been in a wheelchair ever since.'

'Jesus Christ . . . Can I have another word with him?'

'I think you should go now, sir. You're holding up the cars behind.'

He got back in, pulled slowly away from the checkpoint, the Mini bouncing lightly as it rolled over the speed bumps. He could see the sergeant through the window of the shed, standing still, smoking, with his back to the glass.

Chapter Thirty-One

'Well, that was great,' he said. 'Well done.'

They were driving along a straight new road, its smooth surface gleaming in the rain.

'Don't start, Martin.'

He scoffed. 'I amn't the one who started anything.'

'I'm allowed to have my feelings about it.'

'Nobody said you weren't.'

'Don't you have any feelings about it yourself?'

'No, I fuckin don't, if you must know, Ellen!'

The vehemence of his own voice surprised him.

'I can't afford the luxury of havin feelings about it.'

He wasn't sure what that meant, but he thought it was probably true.

She grabbed a cigarette and lit it. 'I don't know how any intelligent person could not have feelings about it.'

'My feeling about it is that it's a pain in the hole. Who the fuck wants the place anyway? Cut it off and float it into the fuckin Atlantic for all I care.' He ran out of steam. Felt a headache begin to pulse. 'Jesus, beautiful. The fourth green field. And gobshites in America snivellin into their green beer about it.'

'What does that mean?'

'I live here, Ellen. That's what it means.'

'What is that supposed to *mean*, Martin? Some people's ancestors were forced to leave and that makes them less Irish than everyone else?'

'Save it, Ellen, will you, for Jesus' sake? Your ancestors.'

'Who should I save it for?'

'For the Scarsdale fuckin branch of the Troops Out movement. Bake an apple pie and buy an Armalite.'

She folded her arms and looked away out her window. He

drove on, feeling weary now. His headache sharpened suddenly, spilling pain across his scalp. Gleaming cats' eyes retreated into the middle distance. The dark expanse of Lough Erne appeared on the right, speckled with small islands that were overgrown with trees. Soon they were passing through Derrylin. On the far side of the town they saw an army patrol, two teenage Asian soldiers walking slowly backwards along the road, an armoured car trundling ahead of them with its spotlight on, sweeping the fields.

From then on the small towns seemed to spread into each other, each with an RUC station wrapped in sheets of armour plating, lookout towers bristling with cameras, thick nests of barbed wire and electric fencing. Some of the towns had kerb-stones daubed with red, white and blue paint, lampposts hung with Union Jacks and Ulster flags. Slogans flashed past on the gables of houses. NO SURRENDER TO THE IRA. ARMED RESIST-ANCE. UVF.

And then other villages had Irish tricolours flying; walls painted with murals of fists bursting chains apart; burning crowns, hooded figures brandishing pistols and machine guns. IRELAND UNITED IS IRELAND FREE. NO TO SECTARIAN ORANGE MARCHES. DISBAND THE RUC.

Mackan. Bellanaleck. Enniskillen. He drove through the town and towards the north.

The date of the Enniskillen bombing came into his mind. The 8th of November 1987. It was the day of Julie's thirteenth birthday. He recalled picking up the phone in the hallway, just as her fancy-dressed schoolfriends were trooping in for the party. Eleven people had been killed in the North. Warnings were coming in fast about retaliation. There were intelligence reports about car bombs being planned for the South. All police leave in Dublin was cancelled immediately.

That night Valerie and Julie had wept watching the news. Aitken had been close to tears himself. A middle-aged, soft-spoken man named Wilson had described how he had held his daughter Marie's hand; told her he loved her as she died in the rubble. It was one of only two times the troubles in the North had made Valerie cry. The other was back in the summer of '75, when three members of the Miami Showband – the band to whose music they had had their first dance, to whose innocently corny waltzes they had fallen in love – were murdered on a roadside by the UVF. Anthony Geraghty. Fran O'Toole. Brian McCoy. Three more names.

'So pointless.' That was all she could say through her tears. 'So pointless. So fucking pointless. When's it going to stop, Martin?'

Whitehill. Irvinestown. Tummery. Dromore. So completely Ulster, those place names, how rich they sounded when spoken by the locals, how foreign when uttered by anyone else. How many times had he driven this road with Valerie and the kids? It was a journey he could probably do in his sleep. Passing through Clanabogan he thought about Robbie. One summer afternoon, when he was five or six, they had stopped here for chips and lemonade while on their way up to see Valerie's family. The woman in the café had been friendly and charming. There were kittens in the yard outside; she'd brought the kids to see them. Robbie had seized on the name of the place, pronouncing it theatrically in the local accent, *Clawnaboogan*, as though delighted to discover he'd been able to do that. What a funny little kid he was sometimes. *Dadday, can we stawp at Clawnaboogan.*

He drove on. It was dark now. Along the open stretches of country road, nothing but blackness could be seen on either side; a blackness made only the more thick and mysterious by the blazing beams of the roadside lights.

On the main roundabout outside Omagh, an RUC patrol was on duty. A young woman constable in a flak-jacket peered quickly through the windscreen before waving them on.

Mountjoy. Newtownstewart. Sion Mills. Strabane. The pain behind his eyes was pulsing hard.

Ballymagorry. New Buildings. Then the stretch of straight road up to Waterside that somehow always seemed longer than its three or four miles. Still Ellen remained resolutely silent, immune in a haze of cigarette smoke.

At last Derry came looming into view, its streetlights twinkling on the hills and reflecting in the Foyle, its steeples breaking

369

into the skyline. He crossed the long bridge and entered the city, continued along parallel to the river, following the signs for Donegal and Inishowen.

This was a part of the town he had always liked, with warehouses, grain stores, cranes along the dockside. It was quiet now; there was nobody around. The cobbled streets were slick with rain. Suddenly he saw a new hotel on the left. He pulled into the car park and switched off the engine.

'I'm tired,' he said. 'I'd like to stay here.'

'I gathered that.'

When they climbed out of the car the cold air smelt of fish. Gulls were widly screaming, complaining. She walked away from him into the hotel.

He took out his bag and followed her in. The large bright lobby was decorated with potted plants; an ornamental fountain bubbled near the registration desk, an expensive-looking tapestry with a motif of Celtic crosses and round towers covered the walls. A Muzak version of 'Danny Boy' was playing. Waiters in bow ties moved between the tables. It looked like the kind of place businesspeople would use.

'How many rooms will I get?' he asked.

'As many as you want for all I care.'

He went up to the counter and checked them in.

'I got two,' he told her.

'Fine with me,' she answered, snapping a key from him and making to walk away.

'Ellen,' he said, and she stopped and turned.

'We'll need to make an early start in the morning.'

'I won't be here in the morning,' she said.

*　　*　　*

Elizabeth lunged and served straight into the net. She tried again and missed the court completely, the ball disappearing into the rose bushes by the garden wall.

'Cool,' chuckled Everard, who was kneeling by the net-post, the only ball-boy Amery had ever seen who was clad from head to toe in black leather.

Four and a half million dollars. He threw the ball high, slammed it over the net. Elizabeth neatly bopped it back. Four

370

and a half. It was so specific. *Pock* went the ball, bouncing off
his racket. It skidded off her baseline and into the rockery.
Four and a half million dollars. That was several thousand
blepharoplasties, endless hundreds of Botox injections, suffi-
cient cash to lift the face of the Eiger, enough liposuction for
a small country in South America. Everard slouched across the
court, scuffing his feet, rolling his shoulders.

Elizabeth pulled another ball from her skirt pocket and
chucked it disconsolately over to her father. They rallied it
back and forth a few times, waiting for Everard to reappear
from the foliage. She wouldn't play properly unless Everard
was watching. Completely illogical, but there you were. That
was the part of Elizabeth that would always be Ellen. The
boredom of waiting began to irritate him. The ball went over,
the ball came back. Amery began to imagine that they were
playing for the elements of Ellen's proposed settlement. He
dropped down a powerful and cunning lob. That saved the
house in Saranac Lake. Elizabeth gaped up at him, served
one back over lightly. He walloped it back, straight to her
feet. That was the Miró etching in the bag. She retrieved
it, picked it up, bounced it a few times. Then slammed it
over as hard as she could, grunting with effort as her racket
swooped to hit it. He clattered it back with the full force
of his smash; she only just managed to get out of the way.
That was the ownership of the Lexus taken care of, along
with Lee's custody and Great Uncle Byron's diamond pinky
ring.

He'd show Ellen. He really would. The damn cheek, when
you thought about it.

'Jesus, Dad,' Elizabeth said. 'What the hell's with you today?'

'I don't like losing any day. Now serve if you're serving.'

'It's only a game, Dad. Chill out, for Christ's sake.'

'It may be only a game to you. But if we're going to play, we
may as well do so to win.'

She gazed across at him curiously, wrinkling her nose. Everard
peeped up from the bushes, like some kind of semi-extinct jungle
creature.

'I can't find the ball,' he said.

Suddenly Lee appeared at his bedroom window, yelling out and wildly beckoning.

Elizabeth snickered. 'Saved by the bell.'

'What is it, Lee? What's the matter?'

'Quick, Dad, quick. The cops are on the line.'

Up in the hall, Lee looked excited as he handed over the phone to his father.

'Doctor Amery, this is Agent Polk here at the FBI. I have some information regarding your wife.'

'Yes?'

'We've had a call from the police in Ireland.'

'From Dublin?'

'No, from Belfast. It seems your wife crossed the border into Northern Ireland two hours ago. Her name came up on their computer as a reported missing person.'

Amery sat down. 'Was she OK?'

'I don't know, sir. She seemed to be.'

'Was she alone?'

'Well, that's the bizarre part, sir. She appeared to be travelling with an Irish police officer, a Martin Joseph Philip Aitken. Do you know an individual by that name?'

Everard and Elizabeth came into the hall. Lee made a face at them and turned away.

'I don't think so. But Ellen knows a lot of people in Ireland.'

From down the line Amery now thought he could hear the sound of fingers tapping on a keyboard.

'Are you writing down what I'm saying, Agent Polk?'

'Would she have any particular reason to be in Northern Ireland, sir?'

'I don't really know. She goes to Ireland often.'

'How often would that be?'

'I guess once a year. Why? There's nothing to be suspicious about here, is there?'

'Sir, there is one odd thing, yes.'

'What's that?'

'Well, five minutes after they passed through, another man arrived at the checkpoint. A younger man who gave his name as Doogan.'

372

'And?'

'He said he was travelling with your wife and her companion and had gotten a little delayed. Apparently they're having some bad weather over there in Ireland right now.'

'Well . . . what's odd about that?'

'It's just that neither of them mentioned him, sir. And his name didn't check out.'

'I'm sorry?'

'They ran a check on him, sir, at the border. Either he was using a false name or the car he was driving wasn't his.'

'Well . . . I assume they arrested him?'

Elizabeth approached, looking concerned.

'They only ran the check after he'd left the border area, sir. I believe they're looking for him right now.'

'This is all most bizarre.'

'There's nothing at all I need to know here, is there, sir?'

Amery laughed. 'How do you mean?'

'Would you describe your wife as a radical, Doctor Amery?'

'Well . . . she's interested in various issues, I suppose.'

There was another burst of frantic keyboard tapping.

'Excuse me, Agent Polk, I asked before if you were writing down what I was saying.'

'OK. Thank you for your help, Doctor Amery. We'll keep you apprised of further developments.'

'Now hold on a minute. If there's . . .'

'Thank you, sir. Happy holidays.'

* * *

In the city of Chicago
When the evening shadows fall,
There are people dreaming
Of the hills of Donegal.

It was half-past ten and the hotel bar was full. Aitken was sitting in a corner by himself, sipping sulkily at his third tonic water and listening to the three-piece traditional folk band belt it out from a stage down the far end.

His headache had eased but he still wasn't happy. Not for the first time in his adult life, he reflected that a night in an Irish pub

373

could be a disconcerting experience. People were drinking and milling around, chatting each other up, laughing and joking. A man was putting up decorations for a New Year's Eve party. A woman was selling raffle tickets for a hamper. And all the while the people did this, there was a band in the corner singing about death.

He felt it was odd. He often had. The songs the Irish sang at funerals could sometimes be quite cheerful, occasionally even raucous. But when the very same people were enjoying themselves in a pub the ballads in the background were of such lachrymose misery that they'd turn Barry Manilow into an existentialist.

> *At the Copa.*
> *Copa Cabana.*
> *The hottest spot north of Buncrana.*

They had started off with 'Danny Boy', a song about death, then progressed to 'Carrickfergus', a song about death, before neatly segueing into 'Boolavogue', a song about death. For light relief and a little textural variety they were finishing this part of their set with 'In the City of Chicago', a song about having to emigrate because of the great Irish potato famine, thereby successfully avoiding death, or at least successfully postponing it somewhat.

He wondered if he could write a traditional Irish song himself. A good old lament. Maybe a lullaby. He swigged down his tonic water and thought hard about it.

> *Toora loora loora;*
> *Toora loora lie;*
> *Toora loora loora;*
> *We're going to fucking die.*

His mobile rang in his jacket pocket. He had a strange impulse to put it in the fire.

'Martin, it's Ranji. Where are you?'

For some reason, he didn't want Singh to know.

'I'm at home, Ranj. Where are you?'

'Oh yeah? Can I call around?'

374

'I'm in bed. I've got the flu.'

'You're not at home, you mendacious Irish bollocks. I'm outside your tip of a house right now.'

'You're outside my house?'

'Yes, you lying get. I can tell it's yours by the smell. Now fess up, Hopalong. Where the hell are you?'

'Jesus, Ranj, I'm on holidays, OK? It's Christmas. What do you want?'

'Why don't you tell *me*, Martin?'

'I dunno. What? You've got a floater or something?'

'I'll float your aggravating mick arse, man, right up the Liffey when I see you. That woman you came in to see Christmas Day? The American? She's very seriously ill. You know that? And she ran away from home?'

'Yeah? So what? What are you telling me for?'

'I've had your charming constabulary colleagues down at the hospital tonight, asking about her, Martin. And asking about you.'

'What do you mean, asking about me?'

'Look, I was told you were seen in some hotel in Dublin with her. Hannigan's, is that right? Some dump on the quays.'

'I haven't a breeze what you're on about, Ranj.'

'Well, some flatfoot who went to close down the bar Stephen's Night says he saw you there giving her the eyeball, the two of you skulling down pints like it's going out of fashion.'

'Well . . . so what?'

'Look, Martin, personally I don't give a cricketer's fart. But the woman is dying. Did you know that?'

'Yeah,' he said. 'I knew that.'

'So did you know there's talk of her husband coming over from the States to get her? Apparently he's gonna be here next week with some head-the-ball from the FBI. They'd be here already if it wasn't for some plane strike.'

He looked up and saw her come into the lounge. She was wearing a black dress he didn't know she had.

'Sorry, Ranj,' he said. 'You're breakin up on me there.'

'Ring me straight back, Martin. OK? This is absolutely urgent. I'm in the car. You . . .'

He switched off the phone and put it in his pocket.

He saw her go up to the bar and order something. The band came back on and plugged in their guitars, banged their bodhráns, adjusted their beards. The barman handed her a glass of whiskey and a bottle of tonic water. She took them and came to Aitken, sitting down without a word.

'Well,' he said.

'Fine, thanks.'

'Great band, aren't they?'

'Marvellous,' she said.

'The future of rock and roll,' he said.

She lit a cigarette. Looked at the band.

'Don't you think you shouldn't be smoking so much, Ellen?'

'It hardly matters at this point, does it?'

He took one himself and lit it off hers.

> *The blessings of a poor old man*
> *Be with you night and day,*
> *The blessings of a lonely man*
> *Whose heart will soon be clay;*
> *It's all of heaven I'd ask of God*
> *Upon my dying day,*
> *I'd soar and soar, for ever more,*
> *Above you, Galway Bay.*

She stubbed her cigarette out in the ashtray.

'Will you come to bed with me, Martin?' she said.

*   *   *

When he came out of the bathroom he was still wearing his socks and a pair of underpants that were way too big. He looked a bit like an old-fashioned all-in wrestler. The skin on his chest was blotchy and red.

'Were you planning on keeping those on?' she asked.

'Well, yeah,' he said. 'I believe in protection.'

'I imagine you've found those very effective.'

He stripped off completely and lay down beside her. He smelt of apple shampoo and the hotel's cheap shower gel, beneath that a faint nutty aroma of sweat.

'There you are anyway,' he said.

'Here I am.'

He took her face gently and kissed her mouth. She kissed him back, moved her hands to his hips. His own hand came to rest on her stomach. They kissed again; he tasted of toothpaste. He rolled on to his belly and looked into her eyes.

'You're so lovely,' he told her. 'I could look at you all night.'

'Two kids later,' she laughed. 'I don't know about that.'

'You are, Ellen. Completely lovely.'

They kissed for a long time more then, holding each other, moving closer together so their bodies touched. Her hand moved to his right thigh, her fingertips touched the skein of his scar. His flesh felt rough there, a thin line of flint. He kissed her mouth, her eyebrows, her nose. They pulled back the sheet and rolled beneath it. His fingers touched her breasts, softly resting between them. His hand felt so light now, as though it was made of water. Their mouths kneaded against each other, their tongues and lips touching as she moved her hand to between his thighs.

'I guess someone's happy to see me,' she said.

He peeped downwards and scowled.

'Gas old things, aren't they? The hassle they cause.'

'You're beautiful there,' she said, touching him again.

He gave a small shudder of pleasure. 'Oh, I am indeed. I should be in a glass case in the National Museum.'

'How's that feel? Nice?'

'I could probably get to like it right enough.'

'I think I could too.' He shivered and sighed.

She pulled back the sheet and kissed his chest and ribs; lowered her mouth, kissed the insides of his thighs. He took her shoulders and drew her silently back to him.

'You don't like that?'

'It's just been a long time.'

'For me too.'

He held her close and looked at her. 'There wouldn't have ever been much in the way of gymnastics. Even at the best of times.'

377

'Oh, OK,' she said, folding her arms. 'I don't want you then. Off you go.'

'Ah, you do.' He nibbled her chin. 'I'll go downstairs now and borrow some Orangeman's uniform.'

She laughed. 'Oh, yes please.'

'I'd look well in the auld sash and the bowler though, wouldn't I? And me nip.'

'I think I'd prefer the Easter Rising.'

He howled with laughter and lay down on his back. She kissed his face gently and stroked his forehead. He kissed her neck for a long time, then took her hands in his own and kissed her breasts. He moved down slowly over her ribcage, her navel, her abdomen. As he went to move lower, she felt herself tense.

'Can we turn out the light, Martin?'

'What's the matter, pet?'

'I'm just a little self-conscious,' she said.

'There's no need to be.'

'I know. I am, though. It's just I'm so out of practice.'

He laughed. 'Me too. I need to do a bit of revision.'

'What you were doing was beautiful,' she said.

He reached out and flicked off the bedside lamp. She felt him wrap his arms around her, the softness of his lips on her collarbone, the touch of his hands, the press of her shoulder into his chest. Slowly his features began to form in the darkness. She could see his eyes shining, the curve of his mouth.

'You're so lovely to be with,' he whispered.

'So are you.'

As his mouth moved lower, she felt herself grow tense again and moved her hand between her legs. He began lightly kissing the backs of her fingers, licking in between them, softly biting on her knuckles. That made her laugh. He gave a low, self-mocking growl. She laughed again. He touched her wrists and kissed them. She moved her fingers into his thick hair.

She came quite quickly, crying out gently. He rested the side of his face on her abdomen, breathing softly, sometimes kissing her, reaching down to massage her toes and the ball of her foot. She could feel his heart pulsing against her thigh, the smell of his body sharper now, his open mouth warm on her skin.

'You know what just happened, Martin?'

'An asthma attack, was it?'

She flicked his shoulders with her fingertips.

'Sorry.'

'Come here.'

He moved up and lay alongside her, sliding his arm around her waist.

'You're so completely beautiful,' he said.

'You make me feel that way.' She kissed his cheek. 'I think I forgot that such pleasure existed.'

'Do you want to go to sleep now?'

'What do you think?'

He nodded. 'Are you sure?'

'Can't you feel that I am?' She took his hand. 'Touch me.'

He was trembling a little as he moved to lie above her. His skin wet, his hair smelling of soap. He held himself on his arms and moved slowly forward. She felt tears well up and touched his hot face.

'Hey,' she said. 'I guess we fit.'

He smiled, leaned his weight on his elbows, holding her face in his hands, kissing her mouth tenderly, as he began to move. She slid her right calf across the backs of his knees, her fingers pressing softly between his shoulders.

'I think I'm having a little well-known problem,' he said.

'It doesn't matter. It's lovely, Martin.'

'Bit of a let-down,' he laughed, quietly. 'You should have met me when I was nineteen.'

She reached up to touch his lips. Pushed his damp fringe out of his eyes. He opened his mouth and softly sucked her little finger. He slid his hand between their abdomens and down her body, his fingertips gently circling her mound as he nuzzled her ear.

'I'm going to come again,' she whispered.

'Do.'

She felt him harden a little as she climaxed. She reached her hands down his back, heard him gasp with pleasure, and then whimper softly, as his torso and legs began to quiver.

'Come inside me, Martin,' she murmured.

379

'I can't, love,' he whispered back. 'I'm sorry.'
She moved her hands around his shoulders.
'I'm so sorry, Ellen,' he said.
'Lie still,' she said. 'Just be still. My love.'

FRIDAY, 30 DECEMBER 1994

Chapter Thirty-Two

Just after quarter-past two in the morning, Amery thought he heard a speculative knock on his bedroom door. He turned in his sleep, told himself it was nothing – but there followed what sounded like a low snigger that someone was trying hard to quell. He sat up in bed, feeling woozy and strange. Though he hadn't been drinking, he felt a little drunk. A wheat-coloured quarter moon was shining through a gap in the curtains. The house seemed quiet, very still. He looked around at the dark shapes in the room, wondered if he had been dreaming after all.

The knock came again. And then once more.

'Hello?' he called. 'Who is that?'

The door creaked slowly open to a shaft of yellow light. For a moment he was certain it was some crazed intruder or burgling psychopath. Perhaps a patient whose procedure had gone wrong. 'I said, who is it? Show your face.'

If he shouted loud enough, he told himself, he might manage to wake Lee or Elizabeth.

'Hello?' he shrieked. 'I've called the cops.'

A black shadow crept along the landing wall.

Amery's heart turned a slow sickening somersault.

There was a figure out there, in looming silhouette, with what looked like a long-handled shovel in its grip.

'I warn you,' he yelped. 'I have a gun.'

There was no response. He gaped towards the windows. They were closed and locked, the storm shutters half down.

'I was in the Marine Corps, I tell you. I've been trained to kill with my bare hands.'

The clock ticked. An owl hooted. Lee shuffled into his father's bedroom, leaning on the shovel as though it was his crutch.

He was followed by Elizabeth. Who was wielding a chainsaw.

They stood still as statues, just looking at him. They were both in pyjamas and crumpled dressing gowns. Their faces wore serious, stressed expressions. Lee slowly raised the shovel. He stood there measuring its weight in both hands.

'Jesus,' laughed Amery.

But they didn't laugh back.

They stared right at him, almost sculpturally inscrutable.

'Hey,' he croaked, his voice throaty with sleep. 'What the heck's going on here, guys?'

Neither said anything. Elizabeth switched on one of the wall-lamps. She came further into the room, went to the window, carefully placed the chainsaw on the Shaker table. Lee remained where he was, standing upright in the path to the doorway, shouldering the shovel like a sentry on parade.

Eyeing her father closely now, Elizabeth took a pack of cigarettes from the pocket of her robe.

'You mind if I smoke, Pops?'

'No, no.' He heard himself titter nervously. 'Please go ahead.'

Could he somehow make a bolt for the door? Get past Lee and down the stairs? What the hell were they going to do to him? She lit a cigarette and took a long, deep drag. Billowed a globe of smoke in his direction.

'So, Dad,' she said. 'Me and Lee have made a difficult decision.'

'Oh?'

She nodded. Pushed her hair behind her ears. 'I'm gonna tell you the truth here, Dad. I'm not too sure you're going to exactly like it.'

Lee gave a grunting malicious snigger.

'He probably won't like it one little bit.'

'It might even hurt a little,' Elizabeth said.

'But it has to be done,' Lee snapped.

'Oh yeah,' she agreed. 'It absolutely has to be done.'

Lee shot her a challenging look. 'You're not gonna back out now, are you?'

'I'm in for the whole nine yards,' she said calmly. 'You just do your part and don't worry about me.'

384

'Now, guys,' tried Amery, 'I think we're all a little tired here. And upset.'

'No, Dad, I'm not tired,' Elizabeth said, fixing her eyes on his. 'I never felt so awake in all my life.'

His stomach churned. 'We couldn't talk things over in the morning?'

She shook her head. 'It's too late for talking, Popsicle. I'm sorry. Really.'

'The decision is made,' Lee said, quietly. 'I think you better prepare yourself, Dad.'

Elizabeth took another long drag of her cigarette. Lee turned and gently closed the door.

Good God. So it had finally come to this. He wondered if begging for mercy could possibly change things. Or perhaps he could offer them the keys of the safe. There must be almost forty thousand in there. He glanced at the chainsaw, then at the shovel. His legs felt weak as he imagined what was to come, just exactly what damage those could do. For Christ's sake. A chainsaw and a shovel. Even those evil Menendez brothers had had the decency to use shotguns on their parents.

Honest to God, you give in to your wife, send your children to liberal schools. Look at how things come out in the end.

'You must have known this was coming for a while,' Elizabeth said.

'I . . . I didn't really think things were as serious as this.'

She laughed, lightly. 'Come on, Popsicle. You knew very well. You were just in denial.'

'Yeah,' said Lee. 'Major denial.'

'If I've been in denial,' Amery said, 'I'm truly sorry. But we can make it OK.'

'You want us to spell it out for you?' she asked impatiently. 'Or should we just go ahead and get right down to it?'

'No, no . . . Spell it out . . . Take your time.'

She looked at Lee. He shrugged his assent.

'Well, the thing of it is, Dad,' Elizabeth said, 'we're gonna have to go to Ireland and get Mom ourselves.'

385

The clock on the locker said 02:18. He told himself that when it got to 02:19 his heart might well start beating again.

'I'm sorry?' he said.

'We got it all planned,' Lee explained. 'We've been talking it over since Christmas Eve.'

'Oh. I see. How wonderful. It hasn't occurred to you that we don't know exactly where she is? On an island of four and a half million people?'

'Come on, Dad,' sighed Elizabeth. 'We all know where she is.'

He croaked with mocking bitter laughter. 'Oh, is that right? Perhaps someone would be good enough to impart that particular nugget of information to me.'

'Stop stalling, Popsicle. She's the only place in Ireland she's never been before.'

'Where's that?'

'Don't you really see?' she said pleadingly. 'She's gone to Inishowen. Where her real mom was from. Why do you think she never went there before?'

He found that he couldn't meet her eyes. 'What about the baggage handlers being on strike? There are no flights. You must know that.'

'We've got all that figured out, Dad. We know exactly what we're gonna do.'

'Oh yes? And what is this touchingly communal first-person-plural entity known as "we" "gonna" do? Damn well *surf* there?'

She nodded to Lee. He put down the shovel, went and opened the door, stuck his head out into the corridor. 'OK,' he called. 'You can come in now.'

In sauntered Dick Spiggot, grinning like the presenter of a 1950s game-show. He had on light blue golf slacks, two-tone spats and a canary yellow sports jacket with his intertwined initials emblazoned on the breast pocket. He was also, unfortunately, carrying a cane.

'Well, hey there, Milton old sportaroonie.'

'Dick? . . . My Lord . . . what are you doing here?'

He came further in and looked around, laughing as though

386

the room amused him. 'Well now, I just happened to be in the neighbourhood and I couldn't wait to see your miserable old twisted face again.' He toddled over to the bed and gave Amery a playfully manful punch on the shoulder.

'Dick . . . I . . .'

Spiggot grabbed him by the cheek and made his flesh flap. 'What the hell do you think, good buddy? I'm here to pay you a visit, of course.'

His pinching fingers released Amery's face and began to poke him hard in the ribs.

'Look at you, you handsome bastard. Slim as a goddamn . . . Mormon or something.'

Amery sat up. His head was reeling. He found himself drawing the quilt up to his neck. 'I'm going to level with you at this point, Dick. The thing is, we've had a little . . . situation in the family here.'

'Yeah, I know. Ellen's gone AWOL to find her mother. The kids told me.'

'They told you?'

'Hell, yes. And I rode to the rescue just as soon as I could.'

Amery turned to Lee and Elizabeth. 'You called him? In the Bahamas?'

'Well, yeah. This afternoon.'

'And I came right away. Just landed not half an hour ago.'

'Look . . . it's the middle of the damn night here, Dick.'

'I know, yeah.'

'But . . . but . . . the baggage handlers. The strike. How'd you get here?'

'Oh, I don't really bother with public transport, Milton.' He put on a camp expression and clamped his hand to his hip. 'I mean, that's just *so* yesterday's pizza.'

Lee and Elizabeth snickered.

'You're not telling me you hired a plane?'

He reached into his sports jacket pocket and brought out a set of keys.

'I brought my own.'

'You brought your own plane?'

'Well.' He shrugged modestly. 'One of them, yeah.'

'How cool is that, Dad,' Lee said.

Spiggot took a hold of the quilt and tugged it hard. 'Uppenzy duppenzy, Milton old sport. Hands off cocks, hands on socks.'

Amery yanked the cover back over himself. 'Now just hold on a damn second, Dick. You think you can just waltz in here and take everything over? Like some damn cocktail party? Is that it?'

Spiggot was still smiling, but in a different way. When he spoke again his voice had an edge. 'Tell me what you think yourself, Milton. That I'm going to leave a woman I've known thirty years to run around scared without a friend in the world?'

Amery said nothing.

'I don't think so, Milton. That isn't going to happen. And if I was sick and far from home she'd do the same for me.'

'Please, Dick . . . The children don't know.'

'We do know, Dad,' Elizabeth said.

He looked at his daughter's beautiful face.

'We do know,' she said again. 'And you know we know, Dad. We're not stupid.'

Spiggot walked away slowly into the bay window. He sat down on the edge of the table, looking through the gap in the curtains as though something was moving outside on the lawn. For a long time nobody said anything.

Lee came over and sat on the bed.

'Hey, don't cry, Dad,' he whispered, taking his father's hand. 'Everything's gonna be OK now, I promise.'

Sobs began to rack Amery's body. He screwed his eyes shut and tried to stop. Lee reached an arm around his shoulders. 'We're here for you, Dad. Everything's all right.'

'Hey,' Spiggot sighed then, making to rise. 'Maybe I should leave you guys alone to talk a while.'

'No.' Elizabeth shook her head, wiping away her tears with her thumbs. 'There'll be time enough for talking when we bring Mom home.'

Amery looked up at her. 'How come you never said anything about it, baby?'

'I guess we thought you didn't want that, Dad.'

388

'Come on, sport,' said Spiggot quietly. 'Let's go, OK?'

'I can't, Dick.'

'Course you can.'

'I just . . .' He shook his head helplessly. 'I can't do it.'

'Come on, buddy. It'll be a blast. A brand-new three-passenger Learjet Challenger 604? Parked yonder at Westchester Airport with a full tank of gas and a new set of tyres. With the Rolling Stones on the tape deck and the Rolling Rock in the icebox. And me and Elizabeth are gonna cross the Atlantic in that thing right now. If anyone wants to hitch a ride.'

He turned to Elizabeth and beamed. 'Isn't that right?'

'It does seem to be,' Elizabeth said.

'Hey,' said Lee. 'That's not fair. Why can't I come?'

'Because you can't,' said Elizabeth.

'But that sucks the big one and blows *bubbles*,' Lee whined.

Spiggot regarded him with a curious expression. He was clearly not a man accustomed to teenagers.

'You like planes, Jerry Lee?'

'Yeah.'

'Ever been in a Lear before?'

Lee scoffed. 'Right. As if.'

'Then you can tag along too, I guess. Go get your coat and a change of undies. And bring that snow-shovel I told you to get, kiddo. There's enough snow out there to freeze a witch's tit.'

Lee grabbed the shovel and actually scampered through the door. Amery couldn't remember the last time he had seen his son move so fast.

Now Spiggot was gazing across the room at something. 'Is that . . . ?' He pointed. 'Is that . . . a chainsaw?'

'Oh that,' said Elizabeth. 'It said on the radio there were trees down on the airport road. We thought we should bring it just in case.'

Spiggot picked it up. He raised it to the light and examined it approvingly, as though it was some kind of rare fossil from the Pleistocene era. 'Well now, Elizabeth,' he beamed, tugging lightly on the starter cord so that the motor gave a series of

389

sputtering coughs. 'We got you, me and little junior on board. Only one member of the family left. Be a shame to leave him out of the trip, wouldn't it?'

'Sure would,' Elizabeth grinned.

The door opened and Everard clanked in, clad in what appeared to be full battledress, complete with rising sun bandanna around his forehead and bandoleer over his shoulder.

'Hey,' said Spiggot. 'Here he is now.'

Everard thrust out his right gauntlet.

'Nice meeting you, sir. That is, Mr Spiggot.'

'Call me Uncle Dick, son,' Spiggot said, pumping him by the hand so vigorously and lengthily that Everard's clothes and piercings made an especially celebratory jangle. 'Now come on, Milton, hit the floor.'

'I thought there was only room for three passengers.'

'We'll strap your body to one wing and your ego to the other. Now.' He tapped his watch. 'It's 2.30 here. So it's 7.30 a.m. in Europe. We take off from County Airfield in an hour, we get over there four tomorrow afternoon. Local time.'

'I'm not going,' Amery said.

Spiggot turned, grinning, and revved the chainsaw viciously. 'Get out of that bed and be a man to your wife, or so help me, I'll make you into an English work of art.'

*   *   *

Just after 7.30 Ellen awoke with a start. For a moment she didn't know exactly where she was. What a remarkable dream she'd been having. She rolled around and looked at Aitken. He was sprawled face down on the flattened pillow with his mouth wide open and his tongue sticking out.

She went to the minibar and got an orange juice. She felt so uneasy, full of anxiety. She found it difficult to get back to sleep.

*   *   *

The Learjet sat gleaming proudly on the tarmac, a vision of chrome and polished steel. A leggy reclining Vargas girl in a scarlet négligé was painted down the side, with the words SPIGGOT SEVEN ONE running across the label of the champagne

390

bottle in her hand. A stairway led to an open doorway just to the right of her scarlet stilettos.

'Awesome,' said Lee. 'This is the latest model, right, Uncle Dick?'

'Sure is, Jerry Lee. It's got transonic wing design, damage-tolerant airframe.'

'Triple-redundant hydraulic systems?'

'What else, kid? This baby is the deal. They don't call me King Lear for nothing.'

The interior of the passenger cabin was decorated in dark leather and mahogany, like a compressed version of an Edwardian English gentleman's club, only with two TV screens set into a wall. Everard and Elizabeth sat down and strapped in. Spiggot pulled the door closed behind them and turned the airlock.

He led Amery and Lee to the cockpit, flicked a few switches and tapped on a microphone. A screeching sound boomed from the speakers.

'Gentlemen, this is Spiggot Seven One. Requesting clearance for immediate eastward takeoff.'

A sleepy voice came back. 'Hey, good morning there, Spiggot Seven One. Please identify your co-pilot.'

Spiggot nudged Amery. 'That's you, Sport. Your name is Ward Stradlater.'

'What?'

'There wouldn't have been room for everyone if I'd brought the real co-pilot.'

'This is co-pilot Ward Stradlater here.' Spiggot was expansively miming him the words. 'We're . . . ah . . . here. That is, we're . . .'

Spiggot rolled his eyes and grabbed the microphone.

'We're having a highly technological problem, gentlemen, known as the co-pilot being a stuttering asshole.'

As they taxied out from the terminal building, Spiggot produced a bottle of Jack Daniels, uncorking it with his teeth and spitting the stopper across the cockpit in a violently contemptuous manner. The wind blew so hard that an airsock stood out parallel to the ground. Spiggot turned the plane around. The spotlights flickered on down each side of the runway. He hit the throttle and eased the joystick forward. The plane began to race along the tarmac, bobbing and shuddering as it picked up speed.

'Oh, man,' said Lee. 'This is too cool.'

'Dick?' said Amery.

The front wheels lifted.

'Dick? *For God's sake!*'

'What's the matter?'

'I've just thought of something. We've forgotten our passports.'

'Too late now, pal, sorry.'

The plane shook a little as it left the ground. The sound of Everard and Elizabeth clapping and wolf-whistling came from the cabin.

Spiggot took a long slug of the whiskey, emitted a porcine snort of satisfaction, threw back his head and started to sing 'I Just Dropped In To See What Condition My Condition Was In'. Amery's stomach began to turn inside out. With a series of hoots, barks and piercing rebel yells from the pilot, the Lear rose up over Westchester County, levelling out at ten thousand feet.

'Thank you, Jesus,' said Spiggot, wiping his brow. 'Now comes the tricky part, I guess.'

He grabbed the microphone and spat into it a few times. 'Ladies and gentlemen, good morning and welcome. We'll be commencing our in-flight service shortly. In the meantime, sit back, hang loose and take the weight off your brains.'

He switched off the microphone and pointed to a drawer.

'Hey, Lee? Get me the charts, kid.'

Lee rummaged for a moment and handed him a map.

'Hmmm. OK. You said Holland, right, Milton?'

'I'm sorry?' Amery was already feeling weak with nausea.

'Ellen's in Holland? Yes?'

'She's in *Ireland*, you fool.'

'No way. Is she?'

'Yes!'

Chuckling, Spiggot pointed and winked, pinching his nose as he tittered. 'So easy, Milton. So fuckin easy.'

The plane banked gently and gave a small shudder. Spiggot began to examine the map.

'You've plotted a course, have you, Dick? Is that the correct terminology?'

'Well, yeah, Milton, I guess so. Like we're here and Ireland's over there. So I thought I'd just pedal her over that direction.'

'That's it? You don't use computers?'

'For Christ's sake, Milton, you fly to Canada and turn right. Fucking geese manage it every year.'

'You do actually have a pilot's licence, do you, Dick?'

'Oh sure, sure,' he nodded. 'You want a beer, Milton?'

'Well done. That's an achievement to be mighty proud of.'

'Hmm?'

'That's a difficult thing to get, I'm sure. A pilot's licence.'

Spiggot chuckled. 'Not in Zambia.'

'I beg your pardon?'

He snapped the cap off a beer bottle with his teeth, gagging as he almost swallowed it. 'Fifty dollars in downtown Lusaka. They give 'em out free when you go to a whorehouse.'

'You told me you had a United States pilot's licence.'

'I don't think I used those words exactly.'

'For God's sake, Dick. You absolutely did.'

'Don't be such a damn stickler, Milton. We're up here, aren't we? What more do you want?'

'I want you to be qualified to fly this thing.'

Spiggot laughed softly. 'You sad sap. Of course I have a licence.'

'Oh . . . OK, Dick. Just wanted to be certain.'

'You're an embarrassment sometimes, Milton. You really are. If I didn't love you as much as I do, I think I'd want to beat you senseless with a monkey wrench.'

Chapter Thirty-Three

When the phone rang it was almost 12.30. The girl at the reception desk said they needed the room back. Checkout time had come and gone.

The bed was empty. He wondered where she was. He couldn't believe he had slept for so long. A few moments later she came in from the corridor, wrapped in a scarf and his own overcoat, her face a glowing pink. She had cardboard cups of milky coffee and a couple of bread rolls in a paper bag.

'Where'd you get to?' he asked her.

'Just for a walk,' she smiled, and kissed him. He went to kiss her back and draw her into bed, but she laughed and pushed him back down.

'Come on, Inspector,' she said, tapping on her watch. 'The bad guys are getting away out there.'

They drove out of Derry and northward again. Soon, without realising, they had crossed into the Republic – the only sign they had done so a bright green post-box outside a pub, and, a little further on, an electronic billboard with rotating vertical slats.

INISHOWEN
FOR THE TIME OF YOUR LIFE

The poster showed two flame-haired children climbing a heathery hillock, while a clutter of sheep and black-faced rams stared blankly at the viewer. The slats turned. Another picture formed. A scarlet can of Coca-Cola with cartoon bubbles.

They could see the creamy peak of Slieve Snaght on their left, the grey-blue slash of Lough Foyle to their right, as they took the eastern coast road that led up the peninsula. Within five minutes the landscape had already begun to change – slowly enough at first; there were still redbrick blocks of retirement apartments, modern shops and petrol stations on a roadway that also had thatched cottages. But then the spaces between the buildings began to grow longer, the mounds of outcropping granite in the backfields more rough and large. The cottages seemed poorer; some were falling down. A few Aitken knew from the old days had been demolished and replaced with bungalows. Small ragged fields appeared now, patches of dark bog and rush-infested swampland, rhomboid swathes of black scrub walled off with rough stones on the steep sides of the hills. As you moved further north the land was so marshy or rocky that he'd often wondered why anyone would bother fencing it in. But then, as Aitken's father-in-law had told him once, the poorer the land, the better the wall. People with hardly anything in the world needed to protect what little they did have.

They stopped in Moville for a cup of coffee, listened to Roy Orbison on the pub jukebox. Afterwards they strolled up the main street past the Inishowen Co-op, past the grim-faced convent that looked like a Victorian mental home, past an ugly stone-clad modern church with a turret on the roof. She bought a couple of disposable cameras in a newsagent's shop.

They went back to the car and started up again. He wondered if she wanted to go straight to Malin now. A possibility had woken him in the middle of the night that he hoped she had at least considered. What if her mother had died?

The sun came out and gleamed on the water. As he drove, he asked himself if he should mention what had occurred to him. Surely she must have faced that herself?

She looked across and smiled, rested her hand on his thigh. Maybe he'd ask her later, or at least try to hint at it.

A small fairground had been set up on the seafront at Greencastle, with bumper cars and a rifle range, ranks of slot machines, a ghost train painted with leering skeletons and phantoms. Off to the right fishing boats were chugging out to sea and a black speedboat was pulling a tiny water-skier.

They stopped briefly at Stroove – she wanted to take a picture of the black and white lighthouse – then drove on into a sudden shower of rain that died almost as quickly as it had started.

The road began to rise. As they climbed higher, the wind came swooping up from the lough, sending the mounds of dead leaves into a wild swirling dance.

'Hey,' she said suddenly, 'can you go back a little ways? Do we have time?'

He looked over his shoulder and reversed thirty yards. A signpost for Inishowen Head pointed up to the right.

'Let's go up there,' she said, excitedly.

'Sure,' he nodded, although in truth he didn't want to. This was a place he could do without revisiting.

The road was steep, still slippery with frost, heavily rutted. Stacks of wet black turf lay all around. In the fields on either side huddled sheep and sad-faced heifers. The car slithered sideways and scraped against a boulder. He jammed it into first, crawled on up towards the summit.

He parked in a lay-by and they got out.

The sea air was cold and damp up here, so tangy with salt it felt as though you could take crunchy bites out of it. Down below them, herring gulls turned, swooping at the water as though attacking the white-capped waves. He watched one pluck a fish from a churning pool and rise up fast, banking in the breeze.

One summer night twenty-five years ago he and Valerie had lain half naked in the heather and watched those weird lights across the bay in Derry. That was August 1969, the night before the Turas, the annual pilgrimage to the holy well down near the beach. He was eighteen, she nineteen; they hadn't even known each other a month. They had found what was happening over the water exciting and strange, watched on for an hour as though it had nothing to do with them, silently passing each other cigarettes. In Belfast that night Bombay Street was burning. But he and Valerie didn't know it at the time, just as they didn't know she was already pregnant, that everything in their lives was about to change.

It occurred to him now that the whole course of his life had already been plotted by then, that he could trace the most important things that had since happened right back to the night they had seen those glittering lights and thought them the ghosts of the famine dead. It almost made him laugh out loud to think about it now. It was so random it was terrifying.

When he turned, she had drifted a little away from him, halfway down the winding gravel path that led to the strip of beach below. She was bending her knees a little, taking photographs of the sea. Somehow it moved him to see her concentration.

He found himself wondering whom the photographs were for. Her children maybe? Perhaps her husband? What would happen when this journey was over? Would she simply say goodbye and go back to her life? If he told the truth – if he even knew it now – was that in fact what he wanted her to do?

Though it pained him to do it, he imagined her husband, a successful plastic surgeon in uptown New York. He pictured a man who was elegantly dressed, with manicured fingernails, salt-and-pepper hair. A man who had his suits made to measure, even though he was slim enough to buy them off the peg. A man who would have no problem tying a tie.

He wondered was he handsome. He must be, Aitken supposed, if half of what she had said about his womanising was true.

It rolled up in his mind like a slow, grey wave that he had fallen in love with a woman who was dying. He allowed the thought to come and then to flow away. There was nothing else to do with it.

It came again. This woman is dying. He groped for a way to make sense of the fact, find some kind of framework in which to locate it.

Suddenly she slipped, half lost her footing; her right hand shot out to steady herself on the back of a bench.

'Hey, Missus,' he called out, 'be careful down there.'

She came back up, wincing, limping against the steep gradient. He held out his hand to help her. When she took it, he tugged a little too hard and she ended up pressed against his chest. She slid her arms around his waist and kissed him briefly. Her narrow eyebrows were flecked with sea spray. Her lips looked dry and slightly cracked at the corners. Her irises were a darker shade of green than usual.

'Are you all right? Did you hurt yourself?'

'No.'

'Will we head on, so?'

'It's beautiful, isn't it, Martin?'

'Yeah. It's grand.'

She turned to look at the sea again. He stood behind her, his arms wrapped around her body, resting his chin on the top of her head. Down to the right they could see the big wheel at the Greencastle funfair, turning slowly, its coloured lights flashing. Sparks were flying from the metal ceiling of the dodgem track. She took his hands and moved them inside her coat. They stood like that for a long time.

'Tell me a story or something,' she said.

He laughed. 'I don't know any stories. Only dirty ones.'

'You must know one. Or make one up.'

The wind brought a broken burst of carnival music up from the fairground. A brown trawler slid into view, chugging steadily through the waves towards the open sea. From the stern a small tricolour was flying. Two men in orange oilskins could be seen on the deck.

'There's a story they tell about this place,' he said.

'So tell me that one.'

'Well, way back when, in the days of yore. When men were men and sheep were nervous. Poor old Saint Somebody – Saint Columba, I think – he was fecked out of Ireland. For robbing some book, I believe it was.'

She chuckled. 'He couldn't have robbed it, not if he was a saint.'

'All the robbers are saints here in Ireland. I meet some very pious types in my line of work.'

She gave his hand an affectionate squeeze. 'You're making this story up, I think.'

'No, no. It's the gospel truth.'

'Go on then,' she said. 'It better be good.'

'Well, your man, Saint Something, gets chucked out on his arse into banishment, you see. And the story goes, he was sailing along down below there – just where that trawler is now – and didn't he get this longing to see Derry, where he had a church,

398

one last time. So he stopped his boat and climbed up here. And he blessed a holy well or something, on his way up. There's supposed to be a cross in the stone to this day where he carved it with his finger. And then up he came here, and he had a look over beyond to Derry. And he burst into tears, the poor old codger.'

She laughed. 'Why'd he do that?'

'I suppose he knew he'd never see it again.'

There was a long silence, broken only by the shrill cry of the gulls. What he had said hung in the air. A cow peered through a nearby hedge, blinking and chewing. It uttered a low gloomy bellow. Another gust of churning music drifted up on the breeze. He cursed himself for not thinking before he'd spoken.

'And that's the whole story, is it?' she said.

'I can't remember the end,' he told her. 'That's just the beginning. If you think about it properly.'

She nodded. 'So where'd he go then?'

'Off to Iona, I think it was. One of them faraway places anyway.'

'And where'd he end up at the end of his travels?'

'Ended up running a pub in Chicago. Married a nurse from Tipperary. Called Bridget. Had seventeen big red-faced sons all sweating Irish stew into their armpits.'

'And built the railroad to California,' she said. 'You forgot that part.'

'He did, yeah. With his bare hands and a box of matchsticks.'

'And then he ran for President, right?'

'He did, of course. And discovered Jimi Hendrix.'

'What a talented little saint he was.'

The sun appeared from behind a cloud, spreading a sudden glow of gold over the water. She shaded her eyes with her outstretched fingers. A cormorant skimmed the trawler's white wake. Slowly the light faded again.

'My mother – my real mother – she mentioned this place in one of her letters. She said it was the most beautiful view in Ireland.'

'It's a nice old view, right enough.'

'Will we go on?' she said. 'I've seen it now.'

They got back in the car and started up again, eased back down on to the main road. A farmer appeared from a gate, driving cows. When he saw the Mini coming he raised his stick and softly tapped on a heifer's behind, chivvying her through a gap in a broken dry-stone wall. One by one the others followed, swinging their tails, nibbling at each other's ears. The man tipped his hat as they passed him by. He was wearing plastic fertiliser bags over his feet.

The road rose up in a gentle slope but almost immediately curled around in a hairpin, back towards Greencastle and Moville, so that suddenly the sea was on their left. It looked greyer and colder from up here on the cliffs. Had the road changed in six years? Or was his recollection somehow letting him down? He stopped, took out the map, tried to get a fix on where they were.

'Is it painful for you to be here?' she asked him suddenly.

'No,' he said. 'It isn't that.'

'Your wife was from here?'

He nodded. 'From Carndonagh. Over the other side.'

'You must have a lot of memories of the place.'

'Not really,' he said. 'I've a terrible memory.'

'You don't like to talk about her, do you?'

He laughed. 'About as much as you like to talk about your husband.'

He pulled out again, drove straight on. A digger sat in a bog, its claw in the air, near a broken, blackened cottage with a scrawny thatch that was fluttering with snowdrops.

'I'm divorcing him,' she said. 'He'll have been served the papers by now.'

'Do you think he'll come to Ireland to try and find you?'

'I wouldn't think so. He never has before.'

'You've done this before, then? Disappeared?'

'I'm not exactly proud of it, but yes. It's a selfish thing to do, I guess.'

'I don't think there's anyone who's never fantasised about it. Just vamoosing somewhere. Starting again.'

He came to a crossroads and slowed to a stop.

'What's the matter?' she asked.

He lit a cigarette.

'We can get to Malin this way,' he said. 'You know. The town where your mother lives.'

'I know,' she said. 'I saw a signpost earlier. Way back at Quigley's Point.'

'So did I. But I thought you might need a bit more time.'

Splats of rain smacked against the windscreen. She rolled down her window and put out her fingers.

'Do you think what I'm doing is unfair, Martin? When she's asked me not to do it?'

'I suppose it depends on what you're going to do exactly.'

She wiped her forehead with her pale wet hand.

'Have you changed your mind about it, Ellen?'

She said nothing. Just looked out at the road.

'Don't be thinking you have to go and find her, just because we're here. All right? If you've changed your mind, that's fine.'

Still she was silent.

'Or there's tomorrow, if you want. Do you need more time to think it over?'

Please, he thought. *At least say there's tomorrow.*

She moved her hand across to take his. He raised it to his mouth and kissed it.

'Do you think about her much, Ellen?'

She nodded. 'When I was young that used to happen a lot. At odd times. Like once when I was a student, I was in this stupid play in college. Some nights I'd look out from behind the curtains and imagine she was there. I'd get this weird feeling. That someone who loved me was out there in the darkness watching me. And I remember thinking about her on my wedding day. And when the children were born. Maybe especially then.'

'Anyone could understand that,' he said.

She laughed. 'Not anyone.'

'Most people, then.'

'I'd imagine that one day I might *see* her just once. I don't know. Maybe go to the town she lived in, see her in the distance. In a store or something. Having her hair done. Shopping for groceries. Maybe watch her going past in a car. To see her just once and then let go. That I wouldn't have to go blowing into her life like some . . .' Her fingers seemed to search for the word.

'Hurricane,' he said.

'Yes, exactly. Like some hurricane. But then, in time, even that feeling passed. There were whole years I hardly thought about her at all, to be honest. Things were suddenly so busy. With the children, or school. With the group. I don't know. There was always something else. A counsellor I was seeing for a while with my husband told me I made myself busy as a way of not dealing with it.'

Aitken laughed. 'They have gas theories, those lads.'

'But that wasn't right. I just *was* busy. But I think when I got my news. About what was going to happen to me.' She looked suddenly down at her hands and when she spoke again, it was with care and precision. 'I think that when I got my news – my diagnosis – I just thought, I can't allow myself to die without knowing where I'm from. That doing that just wouldn't be possible somehow . . . Because that would mean I'd never really lived.'

She gave a thoughtful nod of agreement, as if someone else had been speaking.

'Yes,' she said. 'I think that's it. Do you know what I mean?'

'I think so, yeah.'

'But isn't there something else we should do first, Martin?'

'What's that?'

'Isn't there an appointment of your own you need to keep?'

In a way, he was hoping she would have forgotten. Now he was here, something in him didn't want to go. He saw it as foolish, sentimental – even maudlin. Was he suddenly a man who pottered around graveyards, mouthing useless prayers he didn't believe?

'Would you like to go pay your respects by yourself, Martin? You could drop me off somewhere. Meet me later?'

He thought about it.

'I'd understand completely, Martin.'

'I'd like if you came with me. If that'd be all right.'

'Of course it would. If you're sure I'm not invading something.'

'We'd have to drive through Malin to get there, Ellen.'

She kissed his hand and smiled bravely. 'It's time,' she said. 'I'm ready now.'

He started up, turned right and took the road west.

The teak-coloured hills sloped away up to the left. He thought of their names as he drove along, a teasing game he and Valerie used to play in their courtship, a kiss for every name he could remember. Crockbrack, Crockavishane, Crocknanoneen, Crockatlishna, Sheshkinbane, Shones Hill, Crockrawer, Crockroosky. There wasn't a mile of one of them he and Valerie hadn't walked. Sometimes he would dream about them still.

He thought about Valerie and the girls being in London. Wondered what they were doing just at that moment. How funny, he thought, if they were to ring him right now. What would he say? And what would they answer?

And what would the girls make of Ellen? Was she the kind of woman they'd get along with? Was it foolish even to think in those terms, to start into imagining what could never be?

The drive seemed to pass quickly. When she saw the sign announcing the town's name she gave a playfully anxious groan. He put his hand on the back of her neck. They crossed the Ballyboe River and drove into Malin.

It was an odd-shaped, elongated town, off-centre somehow, but with a certain grace. It had changed a little in the six years since his last visit, the day of the funeral. There was a modern health clinic, a new burger bar on the main street; there was a tourist office with bright colourful posters outside. And the place had a clean, youthful look. There were banners over the streets saying HAPPY NEW YEAR and WELCOME 1995. Malin was a town he had always associated with old people, but the people in the streets today were almost all young. He drove past the church where he had been married, past the stern-faced national school that faced out on the sea, took the road that hugged the bay.

A left turn just north of the town led them to the church at Lag.

'Well, then,' he told her. 'This is it.'

From out on the road, the small grey-slated church looked

neat, as though it had been freshly whitewashed. But closer up the wash was flaking badly. The arched windows had been fitted with chicken wire; the lintel over the main door was cracked and bowed, the decayed guttering along the eaves had leaked rusty orange drips down the tops of the gables. It was a strangely childish building, he had always thought, a bit like an illustration in a book of fairytales. It was more of a T-shape than a true cruciform; where the altar would have been in a conventional church was a little room at the back with a chimney-stack on top. The oaken doors were bolted and padlocked. A Celtic cross on the apex of one of the side walls was broken in half. There was a stale smell of urine near the main doorway; cider bottles and lager cans were strewn on the ground.

It looked like a place that had been abandoned for years, though a sign in the window announced Sunday mass tomorrow, with special prayers for a peaceful New Year in Northern Ireland.

A gust of biting wind brought a redolence of sea and bogland. Next to the church, in a mean field of rushes and alder scrub, sodden sheep were sadly bawling at each other. As Ellen and Aitken climbed the rough steps that led to the graveyard, a scrawny grey donkey trotted out from a thicket and poked his neck hopefully over the wall.

Someone had cut the grass in the graveyard recently. It was short and tidy, neat as a golf green. In the far corner was a pile of mouldy compost, tied down under a length of black plastic sacking that was weighted at the edges with bits of brick. A rusting scythe lay against a fence. A few beech trees stood around in gnarled knots.

He stopped dead. Peered up at the sky.

'Hey,' she said, linking his arm. 'You can do this.'

He half turned and looked over his shoulder. A dirty saloon car with Dublin plates came into view, travelling quickly from the direction of Malin. It slowed a little when it came to the church, then suddenly sped up, heading north.

'Is something wrong, Martin?'

'I don't know.' He laughed. 'Did you ever get the feeling you were being followed?'

She shrugged. 'Not really.'

They walked on, down rows of granite stones and alabaster crosses with oversized wooden rosary beads laid out on the gravel, others with heart-shaped marble plaques displaying black and white photographs of those who had died. Gortnamullin, Crega, Slievebawn, Drumavohy. Some of the places whose names were carved into the stones barely existed any more.

Keenagh, Urbalreagh. The scut of a rabbit scurrying into a clump of whins. Coshquin. Francistown, Glengad Mountain. They walked the winding path and came to his grave.

Robert Rory Aitken
1979–1988
Beloved son of Martin and Valerie (née Houghton)
Suffer The Little Children To Come Unto Me

The simple headstone was cracked and faded, pale yellow lichen filling the indentations of the letters. Between the marble beams that defined the grave's shape the once white pebbles looked dirty and slimy, sprouting here and there with swaying nettles and tufts of snipe-grass. A metal urn intended for flowers was toppled and snapped off from its base, jagged holes rusted into its sides. Pieces of a broken lager bottle were lying near the stone.

His first conscious sensation was a feeling of shame. He found himself wishing Ellen wasn't there. He clenched his fingers into small tight fists, so hard that his nails dug into his palms. He didn't want her to see him cry.

She slipped her hand into his pocket, wrapped it around his wrist.

'Poor kid,' he said. 'To die on the side of the road like that.'

'I know,' she murmured.

'Bad enough for it to happen at all. But to think of a child dying alone.'

'Should I leave you be for a minute?'

'Thanks.'

She walked off down the path. He leaned in and began to scrape the moss out of the carved letters. It was grown so

405

thick it was hard to get at, but he worked with his fingertips for ten minutes, then with a piece of broken twig, until Robbie's name had blackened and deepened. He stood the urn against the stone, collected up the bits of broken bottle and threw them into a hedge. He had a powerful urge to speak aloud to his son, but for some reason found that he couldn't do that.

When he looked down the pathway her back was turned. He reached into his pocket and took out the book. *The Boys' Treasury of Irish Ghost Stories.* A breeze blustered up; rain began to spit. Kneeling now, his fingers raked a small hollow in the gravel. He put in the book and covered it over.

A few minutes later, she came back up the path with a small bunch of snowdrops and wild ferns. She handed him the flowers. He put them in the urn. She knelt down herself and arranged them more neatly.

'Listen,' he said, 'thanks for coming with me.'

'There's something I want to say to you, Martin.'

'What?'

'It sounds stupid.'

'Well . . . what is it?'

'It was what you said earlier. About him being so alone.'

'What about it?'

Tears filled her eyes. 'I'll take good care of him for you, Martin,' she said.

He moved forward and took her in his arms. 'Don't be talking like that,' he whispered. Her hands came up and touched his shoulders. They stood very still for a few minutes more.

It was just as they turned around to leave that he saw a glint of light from high up on Soldiers Hill.

'Hey?' he shouted. 'Who's up there?'

The despondent call of sheep was the only reply.

A man stepped out of a copse of whins with a pair of binoculars around his neck. He looked down at them, waved and walked away.

Chapter Thirty-Four

In the tiny bathroom at the back of the plane, Amery had just finished being violently sick. Air travel had never agreed with him. But this was something new and disturbing. He peered at his miserable face in the mirror. He looked like downtown Jersey City on legs.

When he got back from the bathroom, Lee was perched on Spiggot's lap, happily operating some kind of control that made a plastic panel on the nearest console flash on and off. Spiggot beckoned him in and pointed up ahead.

Through the front window, away in the distance, a filigree-thin strip of dark green had appeared. Far below them they could see a fishing boat.

'Land ho,' Spiggot said. 'ETA one hour or so.'

A crackling voice suddenly burst from the speaker. 'Four One Eight. This is air traffic control in Donegal, Ireland. Identify yourself, please.'

'Top o' the mornin, little Irish buddies,' called Spiggot cheerfully. 'And how do the leprechauns be doin, begorrah?'

'Four One Eight. You have entered Irish air space. Please identify yourself immediately and give your course.'

'Ten Four.' Spiggot shot Amery a wink. 'This is United States Air Force Two, carrying President and Mrs Clinton. Who am I speaking with, sir?'

'Jesus Christ, Dick,' Amery sighed. Lee gave a soft bark of delight.

The radio went silent for what seemed like a long time.

'Say again, Four One Eight.'

Spiggot nodded and did a thumbs-up at Lee. 'Ten Four, this is Flight Captain John Hancock on USAF Two. I have the President and the First Lady on board.'

407

'You have entered Irish air space without clearance, Four One Eight.'

'Oh yeah? You gonna shoot us down, cowboy?'

'Repeat. You have no clearance for approach. Take evasive course immediately.'

'That's a negatory, flight control. Intend to land at Donegal airport as ordered.'

'That won't be possible, Four One Eight. Repeat, you must evade without delay.'

Spiggot went quiet and took a long swig of beer. Then a light of pure evil clicked on in his eyes. He picked up the microphone and cleared his throat.

'Your superior around just now, Donegal?'

'Affirmative, Four One Eight. He's here beside me.'

'Do me a favour and put him on, sir. The President would like to speak with him personally.'

Chuckling gleefully, Spiggot lit a cigar. Closed his eyes and counted to five.

'Good mawnin,' he said, then, in a hoarse, wheezing voice. 'This is Praysdent Clinton speaking. Say, Chelsea, baby, put yo seatbailt awn.'

'Yes, Daddy,' Lee piped. Spiggot collapsed in a fit of giggles.

'Is everything all right?' the radio asked.

Spiggot managed to stop cackling. He coughed seriously into the microphone. 'Who is this ah am addressing now, please?'

A nervous voice came back. 'This is Supervisor Michael Lyons here in Donegal. It's a great honour to speak to you, sir.'

Spiggot nodded modestly. 'Ah know it, Mike.'

'You're on . . . a private visit, is it, Mister President?'

'This heah's a prahvat veezut, yessuh. T'express ma sawlidariddy with thuh Arish people at this momentus tam in they trubbled histree. Y'heah?'

'Sir, I'm terribly sorry. But I have to get some official clearance for this.'

'But ah feel yo pain,' said Spiggot tearfully.

'Well, I know you do, sir. And we're awfully grateful. But you see . . .'

'Hillary feels it too. Matter of fact, she feels it even more than me. Ain't that right, darlin?'

'Sho nuff, baby,' Lee squeaked.

Spiggot guffawed so explosively that a ball of snot rocketed from his nostrils and stuck to the windscreen. Lee stuffed his hand into his mouth and crawled from the seat, sinking to his knees in a fit of helpless laughter.

'Sir, I don't mean any offence, but this is really most irregular.'

Spiggot rose to his feet and puffed out his chest. 'Well, ah mo tell yew what, Mike. We're gonna land this baby in one hour. So get those pussyass leprechauns off the runway. And lock up yo daughters! *Caws Billy's back in town!!*'

'Sir . . .'

'God bless America! Over and out!'

Spiggot barely managed to switch off the radio, quacking with duck-like squawks of painful mirth. He and Lee were hooting with laughter, tears rolling down their purple faces. He pulled a handkerchief from his blazer pocket and dabbed at his cheeks, smacking his thigh hard with his other hand. Suddenly he stopped and glared at Amery.

'Step out back with me, Milton. I want to show you something.'

He leapt up and made for the cockpit door.

'But . . . What about the engine, Dick?'

Spiggot sighed. 'It's on autopilot, sap-head. It has been since we took off. Now come on.'

'We can't leave Lee up here by himself.'

'We'll just be a second. It's absolutely fine.'

Amery laughed. 'Dick, I'm not leaving Lee in charge alone. What if there's some kind of emergency?'

'Jesus Christ, Milton, we'll be ten feet away. Why can't you trust the kid for once in your life?'

Amery looked at Lee. He was wearing Spiggot's headphones. They were too large; they made him look like Mickey Mouse.

'Can I, Dad? Please?'

'Jeez, Lee . . . I don't know.'

'Please, Dad?'

'Well . . . Don't touch anything.'

'Wow, *cool*.'

'Just sit there. OK? Don't move. And don't touch anything.'

'I won't. I swear.' He held up his hands. 'I'll sit like this until you guys get back.'

They left the cockpit and entered the cabin.

On a couch-style seat down at the back, Everard and Elizabeth were asleep in each other's arms. She had her hand inside his tunic, Amery noticed, and was resting the side of her face on his chest.

Spiggot was on his knees, rummaging in a locker. 'Hey, I brought this with me. I thought you might like it.'

He produced a thick, worn-looking scrapbook with a skull and crossbones decal on the cover and a sticker saying GRATEFUL DEAD. Inside the book were old posters and cuttings, leaflets and photographs from their student days. A flyer for a production of *Macbeth* showed Ellen in Elizabethan costume. Another – this one for a comedy revue – had her standing to attention in a 1940s US army uniform beside a pretty girl whose name neither of them could remember. A third showed Ellen and Amery at a Hallowe'en party, dressed as ghosts. Ellen was smiling straight into the lens, toasting the photographer with a raised glass of wine.

'Man, she was something. Wasn't she, Milton?'

'She was,' said Amery. 'She really was.'

Spiggot flicked through a few more pages. There was a picture of him and Ellen in Central Park, blowing kisses at the camera. Another of himself, Amery and Mike Brockleton, arms around each other, in graduation gowns. One of an anti-Vietnam demonstration Ellen had helped to organise in college. She and a black boy were in the foreground with bullhorns, while an almost unrecognisably scrawny Spiggot handed out leaflets to passers-by.

'Hey, you remember this one, Milton?'

The photograph was blurred and badly off-centre. It showed Ellen outside a bar on Houston Street linking arms with a mop-haired and solemn Bob Dylan.

'My Lord,' Amery laughed, 'I haven't seen that in years.'

'You remember that day?'

'Of course I do, yes.'

They'd been walking along Houston, he and Ellen, accompanied by Spiggot and a group of student friends, when Dylan had been spotted talking to a girl through the window of a diner on the corner of West Broadway. They'd all been scared to approach him but Ellen had insisted. She'd crossed the street and introduced herself, chatted to Dylan and the girl for a few minutes, then beckoned the friends over to meet him. He'd been far more amiable than any of them would have imagined, signing autographs, cracking cryptic jokes. Afterwards they had all been so happy and excited. Amery's heart had felt like it would burst with pride. To think he had a girlfriend who could do something like that.

Spiggot flicked on through the last few pages. A flyer for a sit-in. A pressed dried flower. A large Polaroid of his sister, Muriel, doing a grimace of almost preternatural hideousness.

'Poor old Moosefeatures Muriel.' Spiggot chuckled. 'Beautiful person. But a face like a bag of fucking spanners.' He turned to Amery and made a gagging gesture. Then he gave the photo an affectionate kiss, closed the book and put it back in the locker.

'By the way, Dick,' Amery said. 'There was something I was meaning to ask you. About Muriel?'

'Oh yeah?'

'You wouldn't have ever told her that you and I . . . that you and I were homosexual lovers in college. Would you?'

Spiggot gaped at him. *'What?'*

'Only someone told me recently you'd said that. Naturally I didn't believe it. I mean, even you wouldn't say something as ludicrous as that. Right?'

Spiggot began to look embarrassed and hot. He glanced around the cabin and then at his watch.

'You . . . you didn't say that, did you, Dick?'

'I don't think I put it like that exactly.'

Amery heard himself chortle. 'How do you mean? Not like that exactly.'

'Well, it might have been, you know . . . wishful thinking. I sometimes do that. When I've had a few Tequila Sunrises.'

Amery looked at him. 'You're not . . . gay, are you, Dick?'

Spiggot appeared to be thinking about it hard, as though it was somehow a difficult question.

411

'I mean, you've been married four times. Right, Dick?'

'Well, five, really. If you count Consuela.'

'So you're clearly not gay, then.'

Spiggot nodded glumly but he didn't look convinced.

'*Dick?*'

'Well, no, I wouldn't actually choose to define myself as gay.' He nodded again. 'Gay is not the word I'd use. If I had to tick a box like in a survey or something.'

'Don't play linguistic games with me, Dick.'

Spiggot gave a sudden lascivious grin. 'You sure?'

'Take that animalistic look off your face. I am asking you candidly. Are you a homosexual?'

He shrugged. 'I guess I tend to cover the old waterfront. As it were.'

'What's that supposed to mean? You're not . . . bisexual or something?'

'Jesus. All these restrictive categories, Milton.' He poked him. 'You're a regular label queen, aren't you?'

'So you're bi, then. Is what you're saying.'

'No, I'm tri.'

'Tri? What in hell is that?'

'I'm trisexual,' he beamed. 'I'll try anything once.'

The plane bumped over a small wave of turbulence. Spiggot stood up and cracked his knuckles.

'Jesus Christ.' Amery sighed. 'I always thought you had designs on Ellen.'

'Nope. It was always you, buddy.'

'Me?'

'Well, you looked so restrained and neat back in those days.' He chuckled. 'You had that Ralph Lauren preppy thing going. I guess I wanted to mess you up a little. Drool all over your polo shirt. Unravel your cummerbund.'

'What are you talking about? I was never a preppy.'

'Oh, you were and you know it. Docksider Doris.'

Spiggot turned to glance through the cabin window. 'We better get back up front. Come on.' He turned to Amery with a mischievous glint. 'Unless you'd rather stay here and join the mile-high club?'

'Thank you, no.'

'I hear they're accepting members at the moment.'

'I'll thank you not to mention the word "member" in my presence again. Now. Please. After you.'

Amery got up. Spiggot stopped dead.

'Shit,' he said.

'What's wrong?'

'Shit. Look. The cockpit door's closed.'

'Is that a problem?'

'Well, in a way, yeah.'

'Why?'

'It's an experimental security door I had fitted. Cast iron. To stop the pilot being attacked by some lunatic.'

'To stop? . . . Why in God's name did you do that?'

Spiggot laughed hollowly. 'You've obviously never flown with Consuela.'

'So . . .'

'So it can't be opened from this side.'

'But the pilot can open it himself, right?'

'It's coded not to be openable for an hour.'

'Jesus Christ Almighty, Dick. That's a child up there. In a fucking plaster cast!'

'Stop freaking out, Milton, let me think.'

He rushed to a window. Amery followed.

'Fuck. *Fuck!* That's Ireland up ahead.'

Land was indeed coming into view, a vista of mountains hazy in the fog. Spiggot was sweating. Chewing on his knuckles.

'Wait a second,' Amery said. 'I've got it. We just won't land until after that.'

'What?'

'We'll just keep flying until the hour is up.'

'Well, that's the unfortunate thing of it, Milton.' He looked at his watch. 'We're going to run out of fuel in like twenty-five minutes.'

Amery rushed to the door and began to pound on it.

'Son?' he yelled. 'Open up. Can you hear me?'

There was a muffled banging from inside the cockpit.

'It won't open,' Lee called.

413

'Hang on, son. Take it easy, OK?'

'OK. Dad? What's going on out there?'

'Lee,' yelled Spiggot. 'Now just relax. You see the small red dial just in front of the joystick?'

'Yeah.'

'What's it say, kiddo?'

'It says fourteen hundred, Uncle Dick. No. Wait a second. Twelve hundred and fifty.'

'Jesus.'

'What? *What?*'

'Strike twenty-five minutes, Milton. It's actually nineteen.'

Everard woke up to find Doctor Milton Amery attacking the cockpit door with a chainsaw and Spiggot wildly flailing at it with a shovel.

'What's the matter?' Elizabeth murmured, stirring.

'This does not look like a completely cool situation,' he observed.

'Everard,' Amery yelled. 'Quick. We need to break down this door.'

'Too late, Milton,' Spiggot panted. '*We're losing altitude.* I think one of the engines must have just cut.'

'Jesus. *Lee?* Are you there, Lee?'

'Hey, Chelsea,' roared Spiggot. 'You're gonna have to land the plane by yourself. You think you can do that, baby mine?'

'Yes, Daddy,' Lee called back. 'Just as soon as I finish my manicure.'

When Amery turned, Spiggot was doubled over, his head rocking up and down with helpless laughter.

'Dick?'

He staggered forward, speechless with mirth, pressed the combination lock and the door swung open. Lee was slumped in the pilot's seat, holding his sides, making strangled noises of abandoned glee. He held out his hand. Spiggot high-fived him.

'Lee?' said Amery.

'Guess we gotcha, Dad.'

Spiggot picked up the radio handset.

'Donegal?' he said. 'Miss Clinton's coming in.'

Chapter Thirty-Five

She was still at the pool table when he came back into the bar, leaning on her cue and staring hard out the window. Her cigarette was propped vertically on the rim of the table, burned almost down to the filter, trailing smoke into the air.

'Hey there, fast Eddie,' he said.

She tried to smile but her face was gaunt with anxiety now. As soon as they'd driven back into Malin, she'd gone silent. He'd only suggested coffee or a drink to give her a chance to calm down. In truth he was anxious to press on now. It was almost four o'clock. Another day was dying.

'You want to play another frame?'

She laughed. 'I told you before, I always lose.'

'We could play a last one anyway? If you're not ready to go yet.'

She touched the baize with her fingertips, clacked two of the striped balls together. 'One more coffee instead, maybe? Let me get my head together.'

'Sure.'

He went to the bar and ordered coffees. The barwoman nodded and disappeared into a cubby-hole.

He noticed the local phone book on the counter, picked it up, brought it back to the table. She was sitting beside the jukebox now, lighting a fresh cigarette from the end of the burnt-down one. She had just opened her third pack of the day.

'I got this,' he said, showing her the phone book.

She looked at it blankly, as though she didn't know what he meant.

'Well . . . what was the name the detective gave you that time?'

'Derrington or Doherty. I think he said Railway Road.'

'Why don't we start by looking her up? See if we could maybe give her a call.'

She appeared to think about his suggestion for a while before finally agreeing. He sat down. The waitress brought two mugs of coffee and a plate of biscuits. He looked through the book but there wasn't a Derrington listed.

'Not there?' she said.

'Must be ex-directory. But that's all right. We could go down to the police station and ask there. They'd have an electoral register in the office. They might even know her by name in a place this size.'

She said nothing. He looked at his watch.

'Look . . . Will we get somewhere to stay and do this tomorrow?'

'No,' she murmured. 'Let's do it today.'

'It's just that it's getting on a bit, Ellen.'

'Yes. You're right.'

'Will we head so?' he asked her gently. She nodded, stood up suddenly, took a last gulp of coffee.

She took his arm as they left the pub.

Outside the light was turning to gold. Men were hanging New Year's bunting between the windows over the shops. One was contentedly singing to himself as he stretched to tie a knot in the flags:

There's brandy in Boston at ten cents a quart, boys;
The ale in New Brunswick is a penny a glass.
And there's wine in that sweet town they call Montreal, boys;
At inn after inn we will drink as we pass.

'We'll go in the car, OK?'

'Thanks. I'll be fine now, Martin. Honestly.'

'I know you will.'

He gave her a small kiss. She touched his face. They linked arms again and walked on towards the Mini.

He stopped dead.

His heart whirled.

Robbie was standing on the opposite corner.

A young woman went by on a motorbike. The man at the foot of the ladder called out 'Ho!' to the one who was singing. The sun spread a wash of burnished light over the flagstones.

And we'll call for a bumper of ale, wine and brandy
For to drink in remembrance of those far away.
Our hearts will be warm at the thoughts of old Ireland,
When we're in the green fields of Amerikay.

He stood very still in the shadow of a building, wearing a Manchester United shirt, knee-length shorts, black and white trainers, soccer boots. His head was raised, thrust far back, as though he was watching the men put up the banners. He had a dirty white football at his feet. Ice-cream from the cone in his right hand was melting over his slender wrist.

He turned slowly and noticed Aitken. Met his gaze, steady, unflinching. The dying sun spilled a soft golden light around him. He raised his fingers to shield his eyes – then seemed to gulp with mocking laughter and turned away again.

Heart thudding, Aitken took a step towards him.

'Martin Aitken? That isn't you?'

When he glanced towards the voice, he saw a plump, middle-aged, open-faced woman with light grey hair tied in a bun. She had just emerged from a supermarket and was carrying a bag of groceries.

'Well, the Lord save us,' she said in amazement. 'Would you look at the cut of you.'

She came towards him cautiously and held out her hand. Blood was pumping hard through his arms.

'Do you not remember me?' she smiled. 'I'm Karen Connors. Houghton that was.'

She turned towards the boy and called out sharply to him. Then smiled again at Aitken and shook her head in amazement.

'It's Valerie's cousin. Karen Houghton. Do you not mind me now, Martin? When we danced at your wedding?'

The boy trudged gloomily over to her with his hands deep in his pockets. He allowed her to lick her fingertips and rub a smudge of ice cream off his cheek.

417

'God, the state of you, pet,' she laughed. 'Martin, this is Feargal, my youngest. Say hello to the man here, Feargal.'

The boy nodded vaguely but he didn't say hello. He wiped his nose on the backs of his knuckles, then rubbed his hand down the side of his shorts.

'Karen,' Aitken finally managed to say. 'I thought you were in Australia.'

'Well, New Zealand it was, that's right. But we're back this four year now.'

Still half numb with shock, he tried to collect himself. 'It must be nearly fifteen since I saw you last.'

'God, it must, it must. But you've not changed much, Martin. I knew your face the minute I seen you.'

He couldn't take his eyes away from the boy. The same long eyelashes, the same pale skin, so thin and white it seemed almost transparent, blue veins lightly pulsing in his temples. He was peering up at Aitken now, swallowing hard sometimes as though he was afraid. Even the way he stood was the same, awkwardly, holding his weight on his heels.

'Cold enough the day,' Karen said to Ellen.

'It is,' said Ellen. 'But it's not as bad as yesterday.'

'I'm sorry, Karen,' Aitken said, 'this is Ellen Donnelly.'

The two women shook hands warmly.

'Nice to meet you,' Ellen said.

'And you,' said Karen, with a pleasant smile, though he could see her silently weighing Ellen up.

She moved her bag of groceries to her other arm. 'God, Martin Aitken, this is a turn-up. How's life been treating you all this time?'

'Grand, Karen. And you?'

'Ups and downs, the same as ever. I'm divorced now myself. You probably heard that.'

'I had, yes. I'm sorry, Karen.'

'Oh, well, there it is. So I'm on the lookout for a toy boy these days. A handsome fella who'll dress me in diamonds. With a huge big farm and a bad heart condition.' She looked down at her son, who was hugging her leg. 'Isn't that right, pet?'

'No,' he said crossly.

She ruffled his shirt collar. He scoffed, shrugged her off; shoved his thumb into his mouth.

'You know your cousins Julie and Claire, pet? From Dublin?'

He nodded and scowled.

'Well, this nice man here is their daddy, pet. He's a big boss man in the police down in Dublin.'

The boy's face was bright red now. He wasn't enjoying being on show. His mother smoothed down his unruly hair. He stepped quickly behind the skirt of her dress.

'We're a wee bit shy sometimes,' his mother explained. 'But we had Valerie up with us for a fortnight in the summer with the girls, Martin. And the wee lassie too. She's a right wee dote, isn't she?'

'She is,' he said. 'We're all very fond of her.'

'Feargal here fair fell for her, so he did.'

'I did not, Mammy,' the boy snapped.

She looked down at him and pulled a serious face. 'I think I know a little man who'd like to go in beyond and look at the computer games.'

He nodded solemnly.

'Go on over, so. But just for a minute, mind. And don't be giving any cheek to the man or he'll skelp the backside off you, so he will.'

He crossed the street with a doleful trudge and went into a shop that had PCs in the window. She laughed to herself as she watched him go.

'They're all wild keen for the games these days. And the price of them too. They'd have you in the poorhouse before they'd be finished.'

'He's very like Robbie,' Aitken said.

'Aye,' she agreed. 'Valerie says that.'

'It gave me a bit of a start when I saw him before. I really . . .' His voice trailed off into silence.

She bowed her head for a moment before looking at him again. 'We were sorry we couldn't make it home for the funeral, Martin. It was a stage when things were bad between Sean and me.'

'Well,' he said, 'I know what that's like.'

The sun went back in. They seemed to be stuck now. There were too many ways for the conversation to go and none of them seemed comfortable or completely appropriate. She looked up at him and put on a smile.

'What has you up this end of the country so, Martin?'

'Oh . . . We're just paying a little visit.'

'Aye. Well, you didn't bring any good weather from Dublin. It's been awful now all over the Christmas. And they say it'll freeze over again tonight.'

'Actually, Karen, now you're here, you might be able to help us with something?'

'Aye, surely.'

'The thing is, we need some directions. We're looking for a Railway Road here in the town?'

She curled her lip and looked confused. 'Lord, I'd be happy to help, Martin, the dear knows. But there's no Railway Road here in Malin. I'm in the post office now so I'd know if there was.'

'That's the address we have. Railway Road.'

She shook her head. 'But there's no railway here, Martin, as you know. So how would there be a Railway Road?'

'Are you sure?'

'Certain sure, Martin. There's no road by that name in the town, nor never was that I know of. Who is it you're after?'

He glanced at Ellen. She looked sick and pale.

'We're doing this bit of local history research, Karen, and looking for a person called Derrington.'

'Or Doherty,' Ellen said. 'She'd be a lady in her late sixties maybe.'

'Well, Dohertys are here by the thousand, love. Throw a stone over a ditch in Inishowen you'd hit a Doherty. But as for Derringtons.' She pulled a face and shook her head. 'Lord, I'm not being terrible helpful today, but I don't remember any Derringtons, love. Not here in Malin nor any place around. Are you sure you have the right town, you are?'

'We're sure,' Ellen said. 'The sister in charge of the convent wrote me about it.'

'Sister Mary Rose?'

'You know her?'

420

Karen laughed. 'Lord, do I what? Everyone knows poor Sister Mary, she's an institution in these parts, God love her. Though she's not been well at all this last few years. Very old for her age, they say.'

'How do you know her, Karen?' Aitken asked.

'She taught me English in senior school, Martin. I'm sure she'd've taught Valerie too. A right angry speywife she was sometimes. A proper bee. But she got the results all the same.'

She looked down the street as though she was thinking. 'Derrington, Derrington. I don't know. Unless you go direct and ask Sister Rose about it?'

'At the convent?'

She shook her head. 'The convent's been closed down and sold for apartments this last five years, Martin. She's down below in the old people's home.'

He turned to Ellen. 'Will we do that, so?'

'It might be worth your while,' Karen said. 'Though I'd have to warn ye, they say she's gone a bit soft upstairs this last few years.'

The door of the computer shop opened and a laughing old man appeared. 'Missus, for God's sake, come over here. This chap of yours is causing ructions.'

She clicked her tongue. 'Scuse me, Martin.' She put down her bag of groceries and jogged across the street, disappearing into the shop.

Ellen's eyes were wide and frightened.

'What's the matter?'

She said nothing.

He took her hand. 'We'll find her, don't worry. It's just some mistake.'

'No,' she said. 'It isn't that.'

'So what is it?'

'You know what you said before? About being followed?'

'Yeah?'

'Don't look, Martin. But there's a guy down the end of the street in a leather jacket. I saw him in the hotel back in Tara.'

'Is he wearing sunglasses?'

She looked surprised. 'With white rims, yes. Why?'

'Jesus.'

'He's watching us. Definitely.'

Across the street, Karen and Feargal came out of the shop.

'What's going on, Martin?'

'Go find the old folks' home. I'll catch you up.'

'No way. I'm not leaving you.'

He grabbed her wrist. 'Listen. Just do what I tell you, all right? Everything'll be fine.'

'What's happening, though?'

'Nothing.'

'Are you in some kind of trouble?'

He laughed. 'Course not.'

Karen and the boy came back across the street. Feargal had a plastic bag under his arm.

'We're going down that way,' Karen smiled. 'Near the old folks' place. We'd be happy to show you the way if you like.'

'Go,' Aitken said. 'I'll be there in twenty minutes.'

'No, Martin,' Ellen said.

'Go. Now. Is that all right with you, Karen?'

She shrugged. 'Well, of course. If you're sure. You're going to follow us on, are you, Martin?'

'Yes. There's just a message I have to do first.'

He watched Ellen leave with Karen and the child, then went to the supermarket window and looked in. Out of the corner of his eye he thought he could see the man now. He had crossed to Aitken's side of the street and was hunkering down to look at a car. He shot a quick glance. It was definitely the same guy.

Aitken slipped quickly into the supermarket. A radio was playing the four o'clock news. An item about a peace march in Derry tomorrow. Behind the counter a girl was counting change. He went straight to her, pulled out his badge.

'I'm a cop, OK?' She looked at it and nodded. 'Now do something for me, love? All right?'

She looked excited. 'What?'

'Call the police and tell them to get here fast.'

'I . . .'

'Don't be frightened. Just do it right now. And don't say a

thing to anyone who comes in after me. Just call them fast, then do exactly as normal.'

He ran down an aisle, slid behind a pile of cans. Sweat was forming between his shoulders. He watched the girl pick up the phone and dial. A few moments later she hung up; glanced down towards him looking terrified. He gestured for her to look away.

The man in the leather jacket came in and went to the newspaper rack. He idled there for a while, flicking through some magazines. Picked up a few and went to the counter. Asked for a packet of cigarettes and a lighter.

The newsreader was talking about some local farmer who'd won a prize in the national lottery. Up at the counter the man suddenly laughed. He leaned in close to the girl and said something. She backed away. He laughed again.

The man turned, as though about to leave. But then he turned back grinning, towards the rear of the shop. He stuck the magazines into the pockets of his jacket. Slowly began to walk down one of the two aisles.

Aitken crept up the other one, in the direction of the door, peering cautiously through the shelves as he moved. The man leaned up, as if reaching for something. His jacket swayed open. A fat black pistol was tucked into his belt.

Suddenly another man appeared in the doorway. He was heavy and bald, wearing a black trench coat. He stepped in quickly, slamming the door behind him.

'What's going on?' the girl said.

'Shut it,' he snapped. 'Just keep still, you'll be grand.'

Aitken turned. Saw a doorway down the back. Ran for it.

He found himself in a long, narrow storeroom with no windows. The metal door in the far wall was locked and bolted. He hammered it a few times but it was solid as stone. Crouched behind a pile of boxes, his heart whomping against his ribs.

He heard the man's footsteps come slowly down the aisle. Pause for a moment – and then enter the room.

The radio began to play a country song. The lights went out. The girl screamed. The radio went dead. She screamed again, 'Let me *go*.'

423

There was silence now, except for the sound of the man's breathing and a soft pulsing buzz that was coming from a chest freezer. From the far side of the metal door a dog gave a melancholy bark.

'Come out,' the man said, quietly.

Aitken didn't move.

'I'm not gonna tell you again, sweat. Get out here now or I'll blow yeh apart where you are.'

Aitken stood up and stepped out.

The man grinned. He had the gun in his right hand. With his left he was casually eating an apple.

'Nice to meet you, Martin,' he said.

Aitken said nothing.

'Should auld acquaintance be forgot, eh? And never brought to mind.' He smirked. 'Gonna be a real happy New Year for you, Martin. I'm gonna see to that. Personally.'

'Who are you?'

He gestured with the gun. 'Get the paws up. Now.'

Aitken did as he was told. Down the aisle he could see the other man by the door. He, too, had produced a gun and was turning around the OPEN/CLOSED sign.

'All right in there, Michael?' he called from the doorway. He had a heavy Belfast accent.

'Never better,' the man yelled back. 'This won't take a minute. Is the car on its way?'

'Yeah.'

'What's wrong with the lights?'

'Powercut or somethin, Michael. They're off all down the street.'

'What's this about?' Aitken said.

'I think you know well what it's about, Martin.'

'I don't. I swear.'

'Oh, OK, you don't so.' He laughed gently and sat down on a crate, regarding him closely, crunching on the apple. 'Babe in the woods, isn't that right, Martin. Poor little Aitken. The innocent abroad.'

He reached into his pocket, took out a pair of handcuffs and tossed them across. They landed on a flour sack.

'Put those on, Martin.'

'Now look . . . we can talk this over.'

A glare of hatred narrowed the man's eyes. 'Get them on right now, yeh miserable prick, or I'll rip you a new arsehole for yerself.'

He put the cuffs on.

'Lock 'em. Unless you'd like them down yer gullet.'

He clicked them closed.

'Now,' said the man, 'this is nice, isn't it?'

'Just tell me what's going on, all right?'

The man stood up, walked across, jammed the mouth of the gun against Aitken's forehead.

'Does the name Doogan mean anything to eh, Martin?'

'No.'

He chuckled and gazed around the room. 'Oh, now, I think it does, Martin. Yeh shot Mickey dead back in '88. And arrested his brother just last week. For nothing.'

'Michael,' roared the man at the door.

'What?'

A police car braked hard outside the shop with its blue lights flashing.

'Company, Michael!'

He turned quickly. Whipped back to face Aitken.

'You little fuck,' Aitken said. 'You're finished now. And so is that bollocks, Doogan.'

For one long moment the man looked stupefied. Then he threw back his head and roared with laughter.

'You stupid, shite-for-brains thick, Martin.'

He grabbed Aitken by the hair, dragged him down the aisle and into the street. Threw him into the back of the squad car.

A small crowd had gathered outside the shop. The men on their ladders were looking thunderstruck.

'OK,' the gunman grinned at the driver. 'Let's go, Sergeant. Put your welly down.'

Chapter Thirty-Six

The grandfather clock struck half-past five. A whole hour of waiting and Aitken still hadn't arrived. She wondered what could have happened to him.

The visitors' lounge of the old people's home was a dark, old-fashioned, high-ceilinged chamber that smelt of mothballs and furniture polish. The power was still off. Candles had been lit. Gas lamps puttered softly on the walls, their low hiss seeming to whisper of melancholy. The room was so large that the glow of the fire failed to reach the furthest corners, where dressing screens, standard lamps, cupboards of bog oak and black mahogany watched from the shadows like ghostly servants.

In the bay window stood a brass telescope trained at the stars. The clock counted out a drowsy plack-plock. Night had fallen; the sky was black and grey. The moon hung over the peak of Slieve Snaght. Sometimes cars passed the wrought-iron gate at the end of the drive; she could see the headlight beams before seeing the cars. Once a motorbike sped towards Malin. But it wouldn't have surprised her to see a highwayman ride by. This house, this room, seemed unchanged for a century.

Leather-bound books filled an applewood case. She read on the spine of one thick volume *Dwellynges, Buildynges & Diverse General Landholdynges in Her Majesties Loyalle Plantations in Ulster*. Around the walls were faded Ordnance Survey maps, portraits of young men in First World War uniforms, oleographs of the Sacred Heart and Patrick Pearse. Overstuffed red leather armchairs were arranged in a square around a frayed rug on which stood a reading lectern with an ancient, opened bible. Above the fireplace hung a long discoloured tapestry of a three-masted schooner pulling out from a quayside.

A young orderly came in wearing a cardigan over his crumpled blue and white uniform. A gentle Donegal accent gave his voice a singsong quality.

'It's nearly the end of visiting time,' he said, with an apologetic look, as though it was he who was disappointed.

'I don't know where my friend can be,' Ellen replied.

'I'm sorry, Miss, it's just that I can't really wait any more myself. But you can come back tomorrow if that's easier for you.'

Ellen looked across at the clock.

'No,' she said. 'I'd like to see her now, if that's all right.'

'The power's not back yet and our generator's gone. You'll have to mind how you go, all right?'

'Yes,' said Ellen. 'I'll follow you.'

The orderly lit a candle and led her out of the room, across a cold, stone-flagged hallway, up a long flight of bare wooden stairs. The house was in darkness, redolent of damp and mould, full of sudden turnings and steep stairways. Ellen found herself thinking of poor Miss Havisham, crazed by love and stalking her mansion. How fearfully her students would laugh when she read those passages to them. Along the landings were framed coats of arms, mounted stags' heads, crossed swords and pikestaffs. As they passed one door, they heard a woman singing a lullaby; passing another she thought she could hear a man reciting a prayer. Apart from that, you would have thought the house was empty, though the orderly assured her it was almost completely full.

At a solid oak door the orderly paused and gently knocked. By the candlelight Ellen could see an antique map on the nearby wall. *Le Royaume d'Irlande, divisé en ses quatre provinces, et subdivisé en Comtés: 1778.* When no answer came, the orderly knocked again. Still there was no reply, but he turned the handle anyway.

'Ten minutes,' he whispered. 'No more, please.'

He pushed the door open and they went inside.

The old woman in the bed looked more dead than alive. White candles had been lit on a table by her feet. The skin on her face and the backs of her hands looked like crinkled parchment. A fire was burning feebly in a black metal grate. The draught from the window made the shadows dance.

The orderly approached the bed and touched her wrist.

427

'Now, precious,' he said, 'here's the lady come to see you. Sit you up there like a good girl.'

The old nun gave a small cough but said nothing. Rain began to pitter against the window, trickling its shadowed image down the dirty floral wallpaper.

'Are you awake, love? Here's this lady from America.'

A strange, sickly-sweet aroma drifted through the hot room; the dying lilies in the jug on the washstand, Ellen thought. Beneath that a sour bodily smell.

The fire gave a sudden crack that made Ellen turn to look. There were clusters of ivy leaves pinned around the mantel.

The old woman wheezed, her frail breath catching scratchily as though her throat were full of phlegm. She coughed and spat into a metal bowl by her pillow. Spluttered again, her torso shaking. Gave a groan of enervation and misery.

The orderly wiped her mouth with a clump of toilet paper, then took a blanket from a dresser and spread it over the coverlet. The nun gave a low gurgle of discomfort as he tucked the blanket around her feet. Then she coughed again and lightly sighed.

Ellen moved closer. The old woman gaped up, her eyes bloodshot, her creased skin too loose for her cheeks. She had a thin strip of hair across her upper lip. Her face, like a map, was etched with lines.

'I'll let you be,' the orderly said. 'This lady just wants to ask you something.'

He glanced at Ellen, tapped his watch with a smile. He stoked up the fire and left the room.

A long moment passed. The fire fizzed and sparked as though the coal was wet. A leafy twig flared up, spilling evanescent light from the grate.

'My name is Ellen Donnelly, Sister. I think you know me as Ellen Amery.'

The old woman was deathly still for a time. Then she shook her head in weary reluctance, her strained breath coming in short, croaking rasps. From somewhere in the building the sound of muffled piano music could be heard.

'So you've come,' she said at last, in a tremulous whisper.

She eased herself slowly up on the pillow, her crumpled features distended with effort and pain. 'Come closer, child.' She swallowed hard. 'Let me see your face.'

Ellen sat on the edge of the bed. The nun squinted at her, trembling slightly.

'Aye,' she said softly. 'You have her looks.'

'Did you know her well?'

'Well enough.'

'What was her name?'

'It was Margaret Doherty.' She wiped her mouth with the back of her shaking bony hand. 'A bright wee girl. From up near Balleelaghan.'

'And my father?'

She nodded several times. 'Stephen, he was called. Stevie Derrington.'

'Can you tell me a little about how they met?'

The nun tried to sit up further, but gave a grunt of pain that twisted her face into a mask of agony. Ellen leaned over and propped the pillows behind her. The woman eased down grievously into them, folded her thin arms across her chest. Her fragile wrists looked brittle as twigs. She seemed to be waiting for her breathing to settle, until finally, calmed, she began to speak again.

'She lived out by the mountain, near the good Protestant land.'

'Yes.'

'And living out there would mean she would pass the Derringtons' orchard . . . on her way to school each day . . . Out by Carrowmore way. Near Faragan Hill . . . The son of the family came to work there . . . An innocent face on him . . . like a shiny new apple.'

'Tell me more about him.'

'The bonniest boy you'd meet . . . in a year's travel.' She gave a frail laugh of reminiscence.

'Go on.'

'One day as she passed the orchard . . . he threw her an apple.' She coughed again, hard, and drew the sheet up her body.

'And she fell in love with this boy? From the orchard?'

429

Her milky, bloodied eyes suddenly filled with moisture. 'Certain sure. She fell in love.' She sighed and sniffed. 'And that pained her, this bright wee girl . . . for she knew a bonny boy like that'd not want a plain wee thing like her . . .'

The old woman's face took on an abstracted look, but when she spoke again her voice came stronger.

'Until a certain day in school the old nun summoned her to the office. She'd lost some auld copybook and hadn't it been handed in. And in that book she had written him a wee love letter never meant for the sending. And their two names together inside a heart.' She chuckled grimly and closed her eyes. 'Ach, she went mad entirely, the same poor old nun. Home the girl was sent and no mercy shown . . . All the way to Balleelaghan in tears . . . and when she came in, her mother was at her baking. She was feared she'd be angry as the crotchety old sister, but no.'

'She wasn't?'

Again the woman waited for her breathing to subside. 'She said those feelings were what made the birds sing.' She moved her hand across her breast. 'That Stevie Derrington seemed a tender boy. That she should get to know him and ask him questions . . . for a young man loved to be asked questions about himself.'

Ellen laughed. But the nun's face darkened.

'But when her father came in from the fields, he saw it different.'

'Why was that?'

'The boy was a Protestant.' She coughed. 'Aye. A planter. His ancestors had done some great wrong to the girl's, had put them off their land in the penal times. When the girl cheeked her father back on the matter . . . he gave her such a beating as she'd never had before. Until she ran from the house . . . She ran to the boy.'

She raised the coverlet and dried her mouth with it.

'Well, at sunset that evening he was still at his work. And he must have heard the creak of the orchard gate closing. Because he turned about and gazed across at her.'

'May I ask how you know this?' Ellen said.

The old woman stilled. Her weary eyes widened, as though suddenly seeing a ghostly vision in the room. 'He turned around, aye. And the birds stopped their twittering.'

430

'How do you know, Sister?'

'A halo of golden sunlight all around him.' She raised her quivering hands. 'Like that . . . And he touched her lips with his fingers and smiled.'

'She told you all this?'

'And vowed he had loved her since first he ever saw her. Could get no rest for thinking of her . . . And she told him then . . . that she loved him too.'

She made a little plucking motion on the front of her night-dress. Then twitched, as though she had just woken from a dream. 'And he started to cry, as he touched her . . . told her he had never believed such love was possible in this midden of a world . . . Margaret Doherty. Over again. As though her name was a prayer. And then she cried too. She cried for the love of him.'

The old nun reached up and wiped her eyes. Her lips stiffened as she began to weep. Ellen reached out slowly and took her by the hand.

'They had happy times?'

'Aye. Blessed times. Until one night love made them lose their reason.'

'She must have been so frightened.'

She nodded. 'So terrified then she thought she would die . . . The boy said they would marry, he'd brave it out and tell his father. But he was never able . . . In the end, she had to tell her mother, for the time was coming when she could no more hide what happened.

'Her own father was told she might have TB. For that was raging in the country then. And if he had known the truth he would have put her out to walk the roads. She was sent away to a kindly relative. An aunt who lived near Sligo town. Having agreed with her mother that she'd give up the child . . . to an orphanage before returning home. And never breathe word more about it.'

'So she did?'

The old woman shook her head. 'It fair drove her astray to imagine leaving the wean . . . She wrote to her mother, who said she must. But she came back to Donegal, bringing the wean . . . only thinking that if she brought the wee angel with her,

431

her mother would soften and take it into the house. And that somehow, in time, her father might understand.'

'So what happened?'

'She had written she would meet her mother in Buncrana . . . She was waiting close by when the Sligo bus came in. But when she saw the wean along, her mother fair lost her reason . . . And things were about to get worse for them both.'

'How was that?'

'It being Christmas Eve market day, the town was full of farmers. As they stood in disagreement, the girl and her mother . . . her father came strolling the square and saw them. He looked at the wean. Then he looked at the girl . . . And in that instant she could see that he had understood everything.'

The old woman gave a sob.

'Never one word did her father utter. But took the child from her arms and walked out of the town.'

Ellen softly squeezed her hand. The nun's face began to crumple with pain.

'Wild late that night he came back alone to the house . . . a drenching of mud all over his clothes. The girl begged him to tell her where was her child. "We must never speak of it again," was all he said. "Never again. Do you hear? It never happened."'

She screwed her eyes closed and silently wept.

'It's all right,' Ellen murmured.

'Christ forgive me.'

The woman wept quietly for a short time more. She looked up at Ellen then, her face wet and twisted with grief.

'I never meant you harm,' she whispered. 'As God is my judge.'

'I know,' said Ellen. 'Please believe me.'

'Were you loved? By those you went to?'

'I was loved, yes.'

The woman nodded and reached out for a glass. Ellen took it and held it to her lips. She took a sip of water and lay back down.

'Mercy Christ,' she sighed. 'Have pity on me.'

'Maybe you should rest now.'

'In a while. Sit in closer . . . What joy to see you.'

She reached up and briefly touched Ellen's chin. For a minute or two no words passed between them. Then she closed her

432

eyes for such a long time that Ellen thought she must have fallen asleep.

The rain had started to come down harder, a sibilance that had grown to fill the room without her noticing it. She left the bedside and went to the window. Where was Aitken? What had happened? Stars were glittering in the distant sky. When she turned back the old woman had opened her eyes.

'Maybe I should go,' Ellen said.

'Please don't. Stay on a while.'

She came back over and sat on the bed.

'Is there anything else you want to tell me?'

'Just that . . . Christmas misery was all I had that year. I prayed and prayed, half astray with fear and shame. And then it occurred to me what must be done to atone.'

'What was that?'

'I wrote the boy a letter but got no reply. So on New Year's Day I walked the nine miles out to his people's house to see him. Such a picture of a house it was . . . With a great long driveway . . . Oaks and maples all around . . .'

A soft smile lit her eyes, but quickly faded.

'His father barred the door to me.' She shuddered at the memory. 'A good, decent man his father had been once. But hurt somehow. So his heart had hardened. Me and mine were never any good. Romish bitches and sons of bitches that he'd lief have hung from his own trees . . .' A sob convulsed her, which she tried to swallow back.

'And then . . . then walking down the driveway, I met his mother coming from the town. Who told me Stevie had run away off, on the boat to England . . . Having given no reason but that he was broken-hearted by my letter . . . had pleaded to be let go and join the British army. When I heard that, I thought I would die. How I cursed God for what I had written.'

'His mother asked permission to speak plain. Sat me down on a bench . . . and smiled kindly as she took my hands. She understood that I was a spiritual person. She was a spiritual person too, she said. And that would be something we'd have in common, despite all the ancient trouble . . . That there'd been too much talk of the past in this accursed country.

433

'But, she said, to be one of those poor old crusty dears up above in the convent? To be a nun? You don't want that, do you, Margaret? That the flyboys of the town laugh at as they go about? . . . And I said, yes, I do, Mrs Derrington.

'But God wouldn't want that for you, angel, she softly said. A bonny girl like you and her life stretched out before her like a ballgown on a bed . . . And I told her yes, I knew God did want that.

'But never to have a child of your own, love? Never to bring a brave new life into this beautiful world?' Tears were streaming down the old woman's face. 'And I said, yes, Mrs Derrington, never to bear a child of my own. But to be mother instead to many children . . . And without word more she stood and left in tears. And I walked home to Balleelaghan through the snow.'

'And when the boy came back from England?'

She made to speak, but tears overcame her. Instead, she simply shook her head.

'What about his family?'

'His people's house was burned in the Troubles . . . The land sold shortly after. And all his family moved away.'

'Where are they now?'

She shook her head again and shivered. 'Three hundred years they lived in this country . . . To have even their very name forgotten.'

'But you think of him still?'

The old woman nodded, eyes misting. She took another small sip of water. There was silence for a while in the small, stifling room.

'If only we'd gone away together,' she said.

The firelight moved; a coal jumped out and clattered against the scuttle, sending ghostly shadows leaping across the walls. A sodden blackbird landed on the windowsill and flapped its wings, before taking off again.

'Stay with me a wee while more,' she murmured. 'Stay close now while I rest me a little.'

By the time the orderly came back to the room, Margaret Doherty from Balleelaghan was asleep. The fire had burned down low in the grate.

434

Chapter Thirty-Seven

The Inish Times, **30** *December* 1994

A THOUGHT FOR THE DAY

Last week we enjoyed the welcome opportunity to view
the architect's plans to the barque of Saint Peter on the
road between Letterkenny and Derry in the beautiful little
hamlet of Newtowncunningham. We must say that this
boat-like modern church will be gracious and lovely in
every way . . .

Aitken's eye fell on the article, while his questioner paced the
interrogation room floor. He turned a page casually and began
reading the sports results. COCKHILL SET TO CAUSE A SUR-
PRISE NEXT SEASON? It was important not to show what you
were feeling. It was vital not to panic now. He flipped back to
the front of the paper.

STOP PRESS: PLANE CRAZY

Gardaí in Dungloe are investigating a bizarre incident in
which a private jet valued at five million dollars was landed
at Carraigfinn airport today by a thirteen-year-old boy
from New York masquerading as a member of President
Clinton's family. A number of foreign nationals are helping
the Gardaí with their inquiries. They had apparently tried
to enter the country without passports.

They had taken his watch away when they'd brought him in, but he thought it might be eight or half-past by now. He wondered where Ellen might be. Had something happened? Was she all right?

**Grain Farmers Urged To Attend Meeting
Buncrana Country Market And Fair
Moville Presbyterian Church Announces
New Year Service**

Detective Michael Duggan of the Special Branch turned to him and smirked.

'Havin a good read there, are yeh, Martin?'

Aitken shrugged and turned a page. Duggan snapped the newspaper from him, screwed it into a ball, tossed it into a corner. He took off his white-rimmed sunglasses and sat down at the table.

'There'll be plenty of time to catch up on your readin when yer in the Joy, believe you me.'

'I told you before, I don't know what you're on about.'

'I'd say there's a few heads in there'd love to meet yeh again, Martin. Renew a few old friendships. Y'know? Or maybe we'll lurry yeh down to Portlaoise. See if there's any room in the Provie wing.'

'I want a lawyer,' Aitken said.

Duggan laughed. 'And I want a Mercedes. But it doesn't look like I'm gonna get one, does it?'

From above them came the sound of heavy footsteps, boots clomping over a wooden floor.

'No,' sighed Duggan, 'I'll never get the Merc. But that's because I make do with me salary, Martin. That's cos I don't have me mitts in the till.'

'Neither do I,' Aitken said.

'Me hole you don't, Martin. Yeh fuckin liar.'

'Get me a lawyer. I'm saying nothing else.'

Duggan took an orange from his pocket and began to peel it carefully.

'You know they still talk about yeh, Martin, in the Branch? Bit of a legend in your own lunchtime. Famous man. A class act.'

Aitken said nothing.

'They say yeh weren't like some of the others. The wildmen, you know? The fuckin culchies. Beatin up Shinners in the backs of cars. Knockin confessions outta junkies and knackers. They say that crack wasn't your cup of tea.'

He bit at the peel of the orange and spat some out.

'Want a bit of this, Martin?'

'No.'

He gnawed again at the peel.

'Funny thing, Martin. An orange.'

'Is it?'

He nodded thoughtfully. 'I heard about this shockin practice used to go on back them times. Where they'd get a bag of oranges and clatter some Provo round the bollocks with them till he squealed. Tie his hands behind his back and beat him stupid. Hurts like Jayzus, a bag of oranges, but it doesn't leave a mark, apparently. But they say Saint Martin of Glasthule wasn't into that carry-on.'

Aitken laughed. 'Is this the best you can do, kid?'

'Oh, don't worry, Martin.' Duggan smiled. 'You're gonna see the best I can do real soon.'

He pulled out a tissue and wiped the juice from his hands. Then he sucked his fingers one by one. 'And I hear they used to say you'd a great memory, Martin. Back when you were a branchman. Not a ticket giver.'

'They used to say a lot of things.'

'Let me help yeh jog the old memory, Martin.'

'Go on, if you want.'

'October the 5th, 1988, there was a robbery done on a bank in Dalkey. Gang made a pig's mickey of it in the end. Remember that?'

'Course.'

'Mmm.' Duggan slurped on a piece of orange. 'That's the one where yeh gunned down Mickey Doogan.'

'That was all investigated before.'

'Put a bullet in his face. Didn't yeh, Martin? Stuck the Smith and Wesson in his kisser and let him have a taste.'

'He shot me first.'

Duggan grinned. 'Is that right now?'

437

'You want to see the hole in my leg?'

'I don't want to see any of your holes, Martin, thanks all the same.'

'I need to speak to Mellowes. Or someone from head office.'

Duggan chuckled. 'Yeh windy, yellow bastard. Who d'y'think put me tailin you only Mellowes?'

'Then I want to speak to someone else.'

'Gas thing about that bank job, Martin. Sixty grand of the take never turned up.'

'Don't you think I know that? I was on the bloody case. While you were still squeezin your acne spots.'

'So where is it, Martin?'

'Where's what?'

'Where's the dough that went for a walk?'

'How would I know where it is?'

Duggan sighed and shook his head. 'You're so full of shit it's comin out yer ears, man. Now tell me where it is, we can sort this all out.'

'I don't know. How *would* I know?'

Duggan broke the orange into segments and began to eat them one by one.

'You'd know,' he said. 'Because yeh took it, Martin.'

Aitken laughed and sat back in his chair.

'You filched it off Mickey when yeh thought no one was lookin. And hid it somewhere. Little pension, wasn't that the crack, Martin? Nice little nest egg for the old-age fund.'

'Would you fuck off, for Jesus' sake.'

Duggan clicked his tongue and shook his head sorrowfully. 'There's language to be usin. I'm fuckin shocked.'

'Look. There's some kind of misunderstanding going on here.'

'We've a witness who copped yeh nickin it, Martin.'

'You couldn't have. Because that didn't happen.'

'Mousey Doogan saw you himself. Picked it up and shoved it down yer kecks.'

Aitken laughed out loud. 'That lying prick? He'd swear a hole in an iron pot if he thought it'd get at me.'

'That's good, Martin. That's hilarious now. You callin some-

438

one else a liar.'

'Look . . . I don't know what you're talkin about, son.'

Duggan's eyes glimmered with merriment. He brought out a notebook and flicked it open. Began to read in a serious voice. 'Your Honour, he checks into a hotel makin out he's a priest. And the mott he's knockin around with is Mother Teresa.'

'That was a misunderstanding.'

'My Lord, he tells the doctor he's sick at home in the scratcher, when him and the nudie nun are trottin the bogs like Bonnie and Clyde.'

'How do you know what I said to Ranj?'

He grinned and ran his fingers through his long dirty hair. 'The walls have ears, Martin. Never talk on the phone. Surely you remember that from the old days, no?'

'Look . . . I'm involved in this personal situation, that's all.'

'It wouldn't be in a certain bone-yard around here, would it? The bread?'

Aitken said nothing.

'Only you seemed very interested when I saw you there this mornin. Down on the knees and havin a good rummage. Came out real nice in the photos I took.'

'That's my son's grave. All right?'

Duggan laughed. 'Oh, that's right. Yer son.'

'Leave him out of this, I'm warnin you.'

'Poor little kid. Never visited his grave before, did you, Martin?'

'I didn't have the chance.'

'Not once in six years. Funny that.'

'I don't see that it's any of your business.'

'You think he'd like to know his daddy's a fuckin robber? Better off dead really, isn't he, Martin?'

Aitken lunged across the table and grabbed him by the throat. Duggan punched him hard in the stomach, then shoved him against the wall, swinging a kick at his knee. He dragged him to his feet and threw him back in the chair.

'You're finished, Martin. You crooked fuck.'

He opened the door and called for an officer. A cadaverous

young garda came in looking worried.

'Take this miserable has-been and put him in the cells. Then go and get me a bag of oranges.'

*　　*　　*

The supermarket where she had left him was closed and shuttered; across from the pub, the Mini was gone.

Was it possible that he had simply left her here? Surely he hadn't? But what had happened? Who was the man who'd been following them earlier?

A strange feeling of being watched even now came over her. She buttoned up her coat and started to walk out of the town.

*　　*　　*

The sergeant dragged him down the corridor and threw him into a cell.

He clambered to his feet and grabbed at the bars.

'Call Detective Superintendent Johnny Duignan. He's attached to the Special Branch down in Dublin.'

'Now don't be making it worse for yourself,' the sergeant said.

'Just give him a call and tell him what's happened. Please.'

The sergeant rolled his eyes and walked away, his footsteps echoing down the steel corridor. Aitken kicked hard at the gate. He heard the metal door slam at the end of the passage.

'*Wait!*'

He turned.

Two middle-aged men were asleep on the bunk beds. The one on the top was handsome and slim, snoring loudly with his hands beneath his head. The other was wearing a yellow blazer with the initials DS embroidered on the breast pocket. He seemed to be talking softly in his sleep.

'*Milton . . . I love you . . . I love you, Milton.*'

Christ, thought Aitken, just my luck.

Stuck in the drunk-tank with a poetry fan.

He lay down on the floor and covered himself with a blanket. Sleep rolled up over him like a slow-moving fog.

*　　*　　*

A wild swoop of wind came and then another. The long low

440

bawling of frightened animals, the gush of rain on the bracken and the leaves. She pressed on along the muddy track, her body almost sideways to the wind as she walked, her feet faltering, tripping, staggering; now tottering childishly forward as the gust suddenly died. Where was the signpost? Had she somehow missed it?

Rain ran down her face, down the back of her neck. The wind roared up again, changing direction, pushing her backwards. Now she thought she could hear the sea from over the lumpy fields to her right. She climbed down into the ditch, pulled herself up the thorny bank; parted the barbed-wire fence and managed to squeeze through, snagging the hem of her skirt on the way. Briars and rocks lay all around, clumps of nettle and spiny rushes. Slithering through muck, her feet unsteady. She slipped then, a bang of stone on the base of her spine, her hands sinking into soft mud.

On again, fighting the gust, until up ahead she thought she saw the beam of Stroove lighthouse. Suddenly the ground became more solid. A narrow bog road, rutted, uneven, graven with long narrow potholes. Her soaked feet crunched through frozen puddles, past a ruined cottage of square black stones, through a deserted haggard with a broken pigsty guarded by the rusted heap of a plough. Through bracken and frondage then, alder scrub and whins, rough grasses, knotted ash and blackthorn. A quarter moon slid out of a rocklike cloud. Over a battered stile, on the brow of a hill a turf-stack dragon, through crumbling rabbit warrens and tussocked fields. Now a winding mucky track that was spongy as bog – and then into bog itself, her feet sinking and ankles soaked. A sucking squelch as her leg sank in to the knee. A field of thistles slowly rising towards a copse of sallies. She could hear the surge and dash of the sea now, pebbles lifted and smashed on the beach by the waves, the babble and shriek of gulls and cormorants. The ray of the lighthouse gliding across the clouds.

★   ★   ★

He shuddered awake in darkness, hands flailing at the air.

He could hear his own pulse, pumping steadily. He whispered her name but no answer came. His back was aching, his right leg completely numb. It took a few moments to realise he was still in the cell.

He sat up painfully, rubbed at his eyes. The cell was cold; it smelt of cement. UP THE PROVOS was scrawled on a wall. He saw that the other two men were gone. Though it felt like he had slept for only five minutes, the sky beyond the window was velvet black and there was no sound at all except for the storm.

Slowly he managed to get to his feet. A shiver ran through him and made him clutch his arms. He climbed onto the narrow wooden bench and craned his neck to see out the tiny strip of window. The glass was wet, cracked in a Z shape. Out in the corridor a fluorescent light flickered on. A few moments later, a weary-looking sergeant he hadn't seen before came up the passage with a mug of tea.

He opened the gate and stepped inside.

'You can go,' he said. 'Your car's out in the yard.'

'I can?'

'Some big noise called Duignan gave us a call. Assured us you'd present yourself down in Dublin tomorrow.'

'What time is it now?' He took the tea.

'It's just after four in the morning.'

'Jayzus Christ. Is it?'

The sergeant nodded and went to the bunks, where he folded the blankets and stacked them neatly.

'Did anyone come and ask for me?'

'A woman came, yes. An American lady. But it was to bail out her husband.'

'Her what?'

'The chap in the cell with you.'

'That was her *husband*?'

'One of them, aye. Her husband and a friend. They were fetched up here earlier from Dungloe.'

'But . . .'

'Lookit, I don't know the details. I wasn't on duty.'

Aitken sat down and put his head in his hands.

'Are you feeling all right?' the sergeant said.

'Did she ask for me at all?'

'She did, yes, apparently, but we couldn't let you go.'

'Why the fuck not?'

He shrugged. 'We hadn't heard from Duignan yet. We were under strict orders to keep you here.'

442

'Did she say she'd come back? Or where she's staying tonight?'

'She didn't say anything. Is something the matter?'

'Let me out. Quick.'

'Have you somewhere to sleep?'

'Come on. Let me out.'

The centre of the town was deserted and still. The gutters were gurgling and overflowing with rain. A litter-bin overturned with a clanging sound and spilled its rubbish into the wind. He hiked back up in the direction of the supermarket where she'd left him, but nobody was around, the place seemed dead. One of the streetlights was flickering, buzzing. He crossed the street, feeling stupid and confused. In the window of the electrical shop the television screens were showing the test-card; a computer was flashing a pattern of stars. He leaned his forehead against the glass. Behind him the streetlight flashed on and died again. A shadow moved in the back of the shop. He squinted and stared. Two red gleaming eyes peered back. He knocked on the window and called 'hello?' A black mongrel on a long length of chain trotted out from behind the counter and gave him a curious look. It licked its mouth in a slobbering yawn, then sat down on its haunches and slumped its chin to the floor. He turned and walked back down into the town.

The lights were off in all the houses; the shops and bars were shuttered up and locked. The only hotel he knew had a sign in the doorway saying it was closed until January. He wondered if there was another hotel in Malin, but he couldn't see one now and couldn't remember if there was.

He stopped and lit a cigarette, tried to think clearly. Was it possible that she had simply gone? Surely that couldn't have happened? She would at least have left a note. Or had her husband somehow forced her?

He heard a burst of wild laughter now, from the far end of the dark street. He walked down cautiously until he came to a bus shelter. A group of teenagers sat huddled inside, sharing bottles of cider and cans of Guinness.

They gaped up at him, grinning drunkenly.

443

'How's she cuttin?' one of them said. He had bright pink hair and a safety pin in his cheek.

'I'm looking for a woman.'

Another boy sniggered. 'Aren't we all, horse.' His friends jeered and began to jostle him. He pucked one on the arm and slurped at his beer.

'She's in her forties. Very pale in the face. With an American accent.'

'Yee haw,' the same boy snickered. 'Ride 'em, cowboy.'

'Fuck up, you,' a girl laughed back.

He thrust his neck towards her and leered. 'Here's me face if you want a lift home.'

'I'd want to be hard up,' she cooed, to a chorus of catcalls and chuckles.

The laughter slowly died and the kids went silent. They looked so young, no more than sixteen. The boy with the pink hair was blinking rapidly, rocking gently back and forth, sometimes giggling but for no clear reason. A girl in the corner seemed to be asleep, her close-cropped head leaning on an older boy's shoulder.

'So you can't help me?' Aitken said. 'She's forty-six. Wearing a raincoat.'

A boy who was sitting on the floor gaped up, eyes rolling. 'I shpoke . . .' – his tongue was numb with drink – 'I . . . shpoke to . . . a woman like that . . . two hours ago. But over –' he waved his arm – 'over there.'

'Where?'

He gestured again, but vaguely. 'Y'know . . . Down . . . near Shroove.'

'Are you sure?'

He nodded a few times, his head lolling badly, as though he had no muscles in his neck. 'Certain sure, aye. Ashked me the way up . . . towards the cliffs so she did.'

The boy with the pink hair slapped his arm a few times. 'Did you show her the way, you durty bastard? Hoh? Did ye give her the auld tour of the scenery? Hoh?'

'And I . . . thried to stop her goin up . . . I . . . Because . . . it's wild rough up there the night so tis.'

His head sank so low that his chin touched his chest. Aitken knelt and touched his arm.

'Near Stroove, you say? Near Inishowen Head?'

He gave a shudder and nodded. 'Swhat she said . . . the head is where I want . . . Inshone . . . An . . . I . . . Missus . . .' He closed his eyes and slumped sideways against the bus stop.

Aitken slowly stood.

Inishowen Head.

He began to walk.

Inishowen Head.

He quickened his pace, now light-headed with fear.

Inishowen Head. The place of goodbyes.

Chapter Thirty-Eight

The sea spread out below her like a black glossy sheet. Across the water in Derry the glinting lights, the dark ancient shapes of the hills and woods. Pinpricks of whiteness speckling the sky. Cameolopardalis. Cancer. The starry plough.

Her fingers traced the wet outline of the letters.

He turned away from Ireland, entered a pact,
He crossed the sea in ships, the sanctuary of the whales.

She leaned back against the plinth and pulled out a pack of cigarettes. There was only one left. That almost made her laugh.

*   *   *

The beam of his headlamps the tube of light he roared through.

*   *   *

She took out the last cigarette and carefully lit it. Her mouth and nose filled with smoke. She tossed the packet over the edge of the cliff.

The wind roared like a monster, caught the pack, threw it upwards. She fancied she could hear the beating of wings.

Chapter Thirty-Nine

S he was standing with her back to him, quite near to the edge, her shoulders low and her hands in her pockets. Spray flew up through the air before her, splooshing down on the pebbles and tufts of weed.

His breathing was heavy, his chest and throat aching. As though sensing his presence she turned to face him. Her clothes were ripped, her face streaked with mud. But her face had a tightened, composed look he hadn't seen before.

'Hi,' he said.

'Hi, yourself.'

'How's it going?'

'Never better, Martin.'

A battering of wind pushed him sideways. The ground was sedgy, soft as marshmallow. The odour of sea and wet eucalyptus hung in the air.

'You know your husband and family are here?'

'I know, yes.'

'Gas, eh?'

She wrapped her coat tight around herself. 'I went to the police station to ask if they'd seen you. It was quite a surprise. As you can imagine.'

'Did you talk to him?'

'Sure.' She nodded. 'That is, he talked to me.'

'So what did he say?'

She looked up at the sky, wrinkling her nose. Twigs and leaves danced through the air; a gannet gave a lonely squawk. She turned to face him, arms tightly folded. 'I don't suppose you could spare a smoke, Martin? I seem to be all out. As usual.'

He approached and gave her a cigarette. When he lit it, she wrapped her hands around his. But when he tried to take her in

447

his arms she stepped quickly away and back towards the edge. She held it like a dart, between her thumb and index finger, took a deep, hard drag.

'You really ought to jack that in, you know, Ellen.'

'This is my last one ever. I promise.'

'So what did he say? Your husband, I mean?'

'Oh, yes, let's see.' She tilted her head as though trying to remember some speech. 'He asked how could I leave a twenty-one-year marriage for a man I knew less than a week.' Another strong drag made her scowl and cough. 'But then you'd have to say that was a good question, I guess. To be absolutely fair, that is.'

'Well, it's always good to be absolutely fair.'

'It is, yeah. You get points for that.'

He took a small step towards her.

'We went to a hotel down in Carndonagh,' she said. 'It seemed very nice. There were log fires. I imagine you must have gone there with your wife.'

'Oh,' he said. 'Which one?'

'Which wife?'

'No, Groucho. Which hotel.'

She smiled guiltily. 'I'm afraid I didn't stay long enough to remember the name.'

She eased closer to the cliff-edge and looked straight out at the sea. A wave crashed on the stones below. He asked her what she was doing now.

'I think you know what I'm doing, Inspector.'

He went to grab her forearm. She backed away so quickly that she half stumbled, her feet only inches from the edge now.

'Just take it easy, Ellen . . . OK?'

'Don't try to stop me, Martin.'

'Ellen . . . Come home with me. Let me take care of you.'

She shook her head firmly and took another drag, a plume of smoke drifting up her nose. 'This is going to happen, Martin.'

'No.'

'It was always going to happen. Right from day one.'

'Come on now, Ellen, I don't believe that.'

'Well, you should, my dear. It's why I came in the first place.'

448

'You didn't come to Ireland to end things like this.'

'Why not?' She laughed, lightly. 'I'm already dead, after all.' She took a last pull on the sodden cigarette, holding it by the filter it had burnt so low. 'But that's probably all right, I guess. You hear about worse things than being dead.'

'You have children,' he said.

She nodded. 'Yes, I do. And this way they get to remember a mother. Not some wrinkled gasping witch in an oxygen tent. Because that's what would happen, Martin, in six months' time.'

'There's always hope.'

'Yes.' She smiled. 'That's what hurts the most.'

'I want to take care of you, Ellen.'

'Thank you. What a lovely man you are.'

'Oh, I know,' he said. 'Bleedin marvellous.'

'But you are. I hope you know that. Nobody's ever said that to me before.'

'So don't do this, then.'

She peered at him quizzically, as though she were amused. 'I really don't think you get this, Martin. I'm not afraid. Honestly I'm not.'

'I am, though. To be without you.'

'Oh, you won't ever be without me.'

'What's that supposed to mean?'

'You always had me. And I always had you.' She tied the coat-belt tight around her waist. 'I think we were together before I ever met you. Before I was ever born, I mean. It was only a homecoming. Or something like that.'

He laughed and ran his fingers through his drenched hair. 'Jesus, Missus, you're a howl sometimes. The fuckin terrible rubbish you come out with.'

She laughed back. 'I'm full of it, I know. But then again, I always have been.'

She bent and stepped quickly out of her shoes. When she rose again her face was dark with purposefulness.

'Don't come near me, Martin, I'm warning you.'

His mouth was dry. 'Relax now, Ellen. Take it easy, all right?'

449

'One more step and it'll be on your conscience. I mean it.'
He stopped and raised his hands in a silent plea.
'So.' She was shaking. 'Do me one favour, Martin?'
'Anything you want. But just don't do this.'
'You know when you're having a truly shitty day?'
'Yeah?'
'Well, just remember that once in your life – for one week anyway – you were loved the way you deserved to be.'
'Ellen . . .'
'Deal?'
'Ellen, don't be talking like this.'
'I hate goodbyes, Martin.'
'So don't say one.'
'OK, then.' She shrugged. 'See you round, I guess.'
She turned towards the sea and pulled her hands from her pockets. Quickly made the sign of the cross.
'Mom,' came a call.
Aitken whipped around.
A beautiful girl was standing on the path with a flashlight. A young man who seemed to be wearing a bandanna was at her side and happily waving.

SATURDAY, 31 JANUARY 1994

Chapter Forty

I t was eight o'clock on New Year's Eve and the Amery family with their friend Dick Spiggot were seated in the dining room of the Shelbourne Hotel.

Fat red candles were burning on the tables. Ivy and holly wreaths hung on the walls. Everard had been asked to wear a dinner jacket and tie, which had put him into a sulky mood. As an act of proletarian defiance he had stomped upstairs in his borrowed tuxedo and come back down in a nose ring the size of a saucer, having spiked up his hair using toothpaste as gel. His whole head was emitting a powerful odour of mint. The smell made Amery wish he had ordered the lamb.

He took a small forkful of salmon mayonnaise, a light sip of the chilled vintage Chablis. Near him a young woman in a long black dress was playing a traditional Irish melody on a harp. Sommeliers and bus boys in neat white jackets moved graciously about, surveyed by a head waiter. The elegant room hummed with polite chatter, the occasional laugh broken by the chink of glass on glass.

Ellen was sitting at the far end of the table, Lee and Elizabeth closest to her. There was a tall, ornate candelabra in the way so he couldn't see the whole of her face, but he knew she looked tired, she had all day. He himself had been saddled with Everard and Spiggot, neither of whom was exactly his ideal New Year's Eve companion; Everard glum when not being downright antsy, Spiggot half drunk on champagne cocktails.

But what could you do? You had to be grateful. At least they had found her, and in one piece too. The time for questions could come later. It would too, he'd see to that. He suspected she had some answering to do about a certain policeman she'd been gadding about with. Love of God, a damn *policeman*. What

453

would they say back at the country club? But what the hell. He could show a little nobility. If she came clean and pleaded for his forgiveness, why, he'd be more than happy to give it. What was a little trifling infidelity, after all, in such a long and successful marriage? It wouldn't be easy, but somehow he'd find it in his heart to be big. Cut the poor thing a little slack. She was only human, when you thought about it.

He sipped his wine and envisioned the touching scene. Marital harmony restored at last. He would take her weeping face in his strong hands, smile reassuringly; do his rough manly laugh. But not too rough, he'd be fragile too. He'd let her know this was a struggle for him; she had hurt him a lot, but he'd try to move on. She would sob and say she didn't deserve him. He would pat her on the back and say that wasn't literally true. She'd bury her forehead in his solid shoulder. Then he'd grasp her in his arms and bend her backwards and give her a kiss that would make her glad to be a woman. And who knew what might happen next? Because in some strange way that he didn't understand he found it quite arousing to imagine forgiving her. Why, he'd forgive the living daylights out of her if necessary. It was New Year's Eve. He'd forgive everyone.

The Shelbourne had been his own idea. It was a place he knew she had always liked, but they'd never actually stayed here before. He'd made a point of borrowing Spiggot's phone on the way down in the Lear from Donegal, had loudly booked five superior rooms. It might be a way of saying he wanted to make a fresh start. Granted, the arrangement would be shockingly expensive. But it wasn't every day your divorce was called off.

In the event, his decision had almost caused an argument. Elizabeth had asked him why they needed five rooms.

'The first is for your mother and me. That is to say, my beautiful wife and I' – he'd given Ellen an admiring glance but she hadn't looked back – 'the second is for Dick, our wonderful pilot. Then you, three, Lee four, Everard five. I make that five rooms unless my math is somewhat out.'

'But Everard and I are gonna be sharing.'

'I'm afraid that's where you're mistaken, Elizabeth. Everard and you are not "gonna" be sharing.'

454

'Is that right?'

'Yes, it is.'

'It isn't, Dad.'

'We'll see about that.'

Lee sniggered and nudged his sister. 'Looks like you're gonna be doing it up some alley. But I guess that's nothing new for you.'

She'd grabbed the soft part of his forearm and pinched him so hard that he'd shrieked.

'Jesus Christ . . . You retarded bitch.'

'Me retarded? You nasty little imbecile.'

'You slut-featured Nazi sadistic trash.'

'Burgerface.'

'Mattressback.'

'Just because you can't get a girlfriend, acne-boy.'

'Ha! You mean just because *you'd* screw a stiff breeze if you got the chance.'

In the taxi from Dublin airport, the feeling was tense. They were tired, as Amery had pointed out. They had all been through a difficult time.

At the hotel, things had got even worse. Spiggot had insisted that his room was too small and had demanded the largest suite they had, then caused a commotion by complaining that it too was totally inadequate. When the manager had come up to sort matters out, Spiggot had almost succeeded in getting barred. He had tucked a hundred-dollar bill into the manager's pocket and asked where a single guy with few sexual hang-ups might find himself a good time around here.

Back in their own room, Ellen hadn't said a word. She'd taken a long bath and got dressed in the bathroom, only emerging when it was time to go. She was wearing Amery's belated Christmas present to her: a pearl and diamond choker from Tiffany's that had cost fifteen thousand five hundred dollars. It was an absolutely perfect fit.

'You look beautiful tonight,' he'd told her, and she'd nodded.

'It's time to meet the others,' she said.

'I've made a decision I think you should know about, Ellen.'

455

'What's that?'

'I'm going back to college and do some retraining. In the New Year.'

'What kind?'

'I've been thinking about working with older patients. Alzheimer's, you know. Things like that. I just feel it's maybe time for a fresh start.'

'You used to want to do that when I met you first,' she said.

'I know. I should have, as you always said. I think it might have made me a happier person. And a better husband.'

'I always thought it was your gift, that's all.'

They'd all met down in the dining room at quarter to eight. There was salmon boiled and sole poached, scallops seared and beef marinaded. 'I'll have lobster to start,' Spiggot quipped to the waiter, 'bored to death by the *maître d'*.'

The appetisers came. Wine was poured. Ellen was still almost completely silent, pushing her food around with her cutlery. From time to time Lee would mumble something to her and she'd smile back at him or touch his face. Ten minutes had passed without any shared conversation. Everard looked completely exhausted, as though he might nod off into his vichyssoise.

Spiggot looked at Amery in a meaningful way, pleading with his eyes for him to get a conversation going. Amery shrugged back at him, feeling hot and desperate. All around them people were enjoying themselves. Here at his own table, it was like being at a wake.

'Well, I like this joint,' Spiggot suddenly said, gazing around at the chandeliers and velvet furnishings.

'I do too,' Amery said gratefully.

'Yeah. Real classy. Those high ceilings.'

'Ellen and I have always liked it.' He stretched so he could see her face. 'Haven't we, dear?'

'Pardon me?' she said, without looking at him.

'I was just saying to Dick. We've always liked the Shelbourne, haven't we?'

'Yes,' she said. 'We always have.'

She picked up a jug and poured herself a glass of water. But she didn't take a drink, just twisted the tumbler around in her fingers.

'That's . . . what I was saying,' Amery said.

'I think I might buy it,' Spiggot said. 'It kinda reminds me of home. In ways.'

'What makes you think they'd want to sell it, Uncle Dick?' Elizabeth asked.

Spiggot chuckled. 'Oh, they'd sell it, honey. They'd sell you anything in this country.' He forked a mound of lobster into his mouth. 'Matter of fact, if the price was right they'd sell you the damn *country*. And throw in the Isle of Man.'

An elderly lady at the next table looked at him. He chewed thoughtfully, now sucking on a claw. 'Course, Spiggot is a very Irish name,' he said.

'It is?'

'Sure it is. This guy in a tartan shop down the street was telling me earlier. Very knowledgeable heavy-duty tartan dude with a beard. Certificates and shit all over his walls. He's running me up a dress.'

'You mean a kilt?'

'Yeah. Like a skirt.' He beamed proudly. 'In the official Spiggot family tartan. Is that cool or is that cool?'

'That's so cool it's almost hot,' Lee said.

'You want one yourself, Jerry Lee?'

'Oh . . . no, thanks, Uncle Dick.'

'You sure? It's not a problem. I can go tell him now.'

'How would you go tell him? Isn't his store closed tonight?'

Spiggot shook his head. 'He's upstairs right now in that rat-box glorified roach-motel of a suite for midgets they sold me. Fiddling away on his sewing machine and shit. I can go call him up and tell him make an extra.'

'Honest, Uncle Dick. It's fine, really.'

Spiggot's attention now seemed to be taken by the harpist. She finished a tune with a flourish of arpeggios. Polite applause rippled around the room. Spiggot stuck his fingers into his mouth and released a shrill whistle of appreciation.

The harpist looked across in horror.

'Pluck it, baby,' he called encouragingly.

457

She gave him a nervous grin and began a new tune, a tender sentimental melody that made people go 'aah'.

'Strum that mother. *Strum* the bitch.'

A woman at the next table got up and left. Spiggot wiped his hands on the tablecloth. The head waiter came over looking concerned.

'Is everything . . . ?'

'Everything's bitchin,' Spiggot said.

'Might I ask sir to just . . . keep it down a little?'

Spiggot pushed a banknote into his hand. 'Don't worry bout it, Elvis. Just havin a good time, buddy.'

'Well . . . Yes, sir. Thank you, sir.'

'No,' beamed Spiggot cherubically. 'Thank *you*, sir.'

The waiter slid away and back to his station, where he went into anxious huddled conference with two colleagues.

A new waiter came and removed the starter plates. Silence descended once more over the table.

'You see that harp, Everard?' Spiggot said.

'Yes, sir.'

'I bet that would really hurt if somebody forced your head through it. Through the strings, I mean. Sideways.'

'Not if your head was flat, sir.'

'True.'

'Or very thin.'

'Conceded. But that's some serious tension she's got going on there.'

'Yes, sir. It certainly is.'

Spiggot nodded disconsolately. Time passed. A squad of waiters brought the main courses and set them out. The plates had old-fashioned covers over them and at the appointed moment the waiters whipped them off theatrically.

'Say,' Spiggot whooped. 'Look at that, Lee, my man. Sight for sore eyes, isn't it? Chow down!'

Lee looked at it, but he didn't seem impressed. Elizabeth sighed heavily and began to eat. Everard stared at his dish of boiled broccoli as though secretly he'd truncheon his grandmother for a steak.

Spiggot shook his napkin and tucked it into his collar. He

458

broke off a turkey wing and began to gnaw on it, emitting small but lustful gurgles of satisfaction.

A few moments passed while everyone ate. Lee turned and glared at Elizabeth. 'Did you fart?' he said.

She continued eating and refused to look at him.

'I said, did you fart?'

'Are you addressing me?'

'Well, somebody cut the cheese in here. Had to be you.'

'You probably just breathed out suddenly, you slime.'

'Jesus, that's good coming from . . .'

Ellen slammed down her cutlery.

'Stop it!' she snapped. 'Stop accusing each other. Do you hear me? I don't want to hear one word more of this . . . *crapology*!'

A waiter turned and looked at her. Lee bowed his head and went into a sulk.

Ellen looked like she was about to say something else. Instead she pushed away her plate and lit a cigarette. With a shaking hand she poured another glass of water, then sat back a little from the table and peered into the fireplace.

Lee began viciously plucking the petals off a carnation. Amery's clothes felt clammy and tight.

'So,' he said brightly. 'What time do we leave tomorrow, Dick?'

Spiggot looked relieved to be spoken to. 'Well, we get going at noon, we'll be home by 2.30 local time.' Amery nodded encouragingly. Spiggot drank more wine. 'I may then allow you to drag me to your local fleapit golf course, Doris. See if you're going round in less than a hundred these days.'

'That would be pleasant. Then fair wind back to Nassau?'

'Actually I thought I might hang out in Scarsdale a couple days. Been too long since I've seen you guys properly.'

'You'd be welcome to stay with us, Dick. Wouldn't he, dear?'

Ellen said nothing.

'Well,' said Amery, to the whole table. 'This is very agreeable, isn't it, everyone? Being all together as a family again.'

Various grunts and coughs came back. Elizabeth seemed to be looking at the floor.

459

'I think it's fair to say we've all been through a difficult time. And a challenging time. But all's well that ends well.' He picked up his glass. 'So perhaps this would be an opportune moment to propose a toast. To a fresh start and a happy New Year.'

He shunted sideways and smiled down towards his wife.

'And to forgiveness,' he said.

Ellen looked at him.

'To what?' she said.

'Well . . . to forgiveness, dear. We all make mistakes.'

She put her glass back on its coaster. Across the room an old man began to laugh. She crushed her cigarette out in the marble ashtray, picked up the pack and slipped it into her pocket. She folded her napkin and stood up slowly. Unclipped the diamond choker and put it on her side plate. Then came down the length of the table.

'Dick,' she said quietly, touching his arm. 'Is there another bedroom in your suite?'

He stared at his plate and said nothing.

'Is there, Dick?'

He sighed and nodded back. She squeezed his shoulder quickly and left the room.

Lee and Elizabeth watched her go. Everard raised his hands to his forehead. Spiggot was still staring at his plate.

'More wine, anyone?' Amery asked.

SUNDAY, 1 JANUARY 1995

A t quarter to three on New Year's morning Doctor Milton Amery was still awake.

His body clock was completely confused, he had more than a touch of indigestion, and the hotel room was far hotter than he liked. Even with all the windows wide open the room was sweltering, as though sucked clean of air. The sheets and pillowcases were moist with his sweat. The radiator was making a loud rhythmic click.

He could hear people singing in the street outside. They sounded happy and drunk. He wondered where they'd been.

He pictured Ellen, asleep down the corridor. How beautiful she looked when she was asleep. How gentle, somehow, how inspiring of reverence. When they'd first married, there were nights he'd lie awake for hours and just look at her. Once, he'd lain awake till dawn, simply watching the side of her face. At breakfast he'd been ashamed to tell her why he was so tired; embarrassed and frightened by the rawness of his love. Now, awake again, in a strange distant city he'd never liked, the thought suddenly flowered like a weed in his heart that he would never see her sleeping face again.

Was there any point in trying to persuade her one more time? What if he went down there right now? Knocked on the door and begged for a last chance. But what was left that hadn't been said?

A thirst salted up in the back of his throat. He got out of bed and padded across the carpet but there was no mineral water left in the minibar. He picked up the phone and dialled reception. It rang ten times but no answer came. Perhaps the staff had all gone home. He found himself picturing a weary Irish waiter, fast asleep in the arms of his loving waitress wife.

He pulled on his clothes, thinking he might go out for a walk.

Downstairs, the foyer was dark and deserted. Stacks of seats were piled up by the dining-room door. He went to the concierge's desk and rang the bell. Nobody came. He rang again.

He saw now through the windows of the revolving door that there were people standing outside on the street. He thought he could hear a familiar voice. He bent a little and peered out. Spiggot was among them, laughing excitedly with a middle-aged woman, braying inanely like a drunken mule. They threw their arms around each other and hugged. Well, it was either hugging or all-in wrestling. It was quite hard to tell.

It was only when he turned to go back upstairs that he saw Lee in the armchair across the lobby.

He was sitting side on, with his legs over the arm, sipping a can of Coke and stroking a cat.

'Hey,' said Amery.

'Ho,' said Lee.

'Kinda late to be up, isn't it?'

'Nope. It's early.'

'You have things on your mind, son?'

'I guess.'

'You mind if your dad sat with you a while?'

'Sure.'

Amery wasn't sure if that was a yes or a no, but he sat down anyway.

'So,' he said, 'I think I know what some of those things might be.'

'I doubt it.' Lee swigged some Coke. The cat rolled over and pawed at the air.

'You want to stay here in Ireland, right? With your mom?'

Lee gazed down at the cat and ruffled its ears. It opened its mouth and gave a soft *mraow* of pleasure.

'Yeah,' said Lee.

'I figured you probably did.'

'You want some Coke, Dad?' Amery accepted the can and took a swig. The liquid was warm and flat and felt sticky in his mouth.

'How would that work, son? Have you thought about that?'

'I'd stay here with Mom when you guys go home tomorrow.'

'I see. And what about school?'

He rolled his eyes. 'They do actually have schools in Ireland, Milton.'

464

'Well, yes. I suppose they do.'

'I'm sure they're just as mind-warping and fascistic as the schools in America.'

'Wouldn't you miss your friends back home?'

'Yeah, really. Crowd of pussies.'

'Indeed.' Amery took another swig of Coke. 'Though I'm not entirely certain that "crowd" is the correct collective noun for that particular feline item.'

'I'll look it up and let you know, Milton.'

'Isn't there anyone else you'd miss?'

Lee said nothing. He peered up at the ceiling. Outside on the street a bottle was smashed. A yelp of inebriated embarrassment echoed through the lobby.

'You know I don't want to let this happen, Lee?'

His son nodded.

'I really don't want you to do this, soldier.'

'I knew you wouldn't.'

'I don't think it's the right thing, is all.'

'What *I* think is someone has to stay here with Mom.'

'You know Elizabeth will be coming over regularly? And I will be too. When things settle down a little between us. We're going to see to it that Mom has the very best of care.'

'Someone has to be with her all the time now. It's not as if we're gonna have the chance for too much longer.'

The cat leapt down and slunk over to the grate, where it rubbed its back languidly on the coal bucket.

'Say,' said Amery, 'you want to go for a walk with your dad?'

Lee grimaced. 'Now?'

'Why not?'

'Not really, no. I'm a little tired.'

'You're a very honourable and remarkable boy, Lee.'

He scratched his neck. 'Whatever.'

'I think you must have got that from your mother.'

'I got it free in a pack of cornflakes.'

'You're so like her. You're a fine boy.'

Lee half turned and gave him a look. 'I'm not one tiny bit like her, Dad.'

'I love you very much. You know that, don't you?'

'Whatever. I'm gonna go to bed now. You coming up too?'

'I'm going to stay here a little while longer. See if there's any night staff still alive.'

His son slid out of the chair, stretched his arms and yawned. He picked up his crutch and put it over his shoulder.

'You're cool with this, Dad? My not going home?'

'I will be, yes.'

'OK. Thanks.'

Spiggot came tottering in with a bottle of Jack Daniels and a pint glass. He was wearing a floppy tartan fisherman's beret and a kilt that didn't quite reach his knees.

'Hey,' he said. 'Here's the party.'

'Night, Uncle Dickless,' Lee grinned.

'Night, Jerry Lee, old pal of mine.'

Lee shook his hand and limped away through the lobby. Spiggot came over and threw a log in the fire. Then he plopped down into an armchair with his thighs wide apart. He raised the bottle to his lips and took a long hard swig.

'So, Doris. I heard what you said to the little prince.'

'Many congratulations on your not being deaf.'

'Proud of you, buddy. That can't be easy.'

'I don't see that pride is an appropriate response.'

Spiggot shrugged. 'You love someone, you set them free.' He took another slug. 'As Sting so economically put it.'

'Spare me your dime-store banalities, would you, Dick? And close your legs for heaven's sake. You look like some particularly unappetising variety of low-rent . . . Caledonian . . . call-girl.'

'Oh. OK.' He opened them wider and arched his back so his chest protruded. When that got no reaction he crossed his legs demurely, tucking the hem of his kilt between his thighs.

A gust of wind came down the chimney and startled the cat. The coals glowed briefly and then darkened again.

Spiggot got up and went to the fire. He knelt down and poked at it half-heartedly until a couple of pale yellow flames began to flicker from a log. He hummed a snatch of a tune that Amery vaguely recognised, then eased to his feet and stood with his back to the glow.

466

He raised his kilt and gently wriggled his behind; continued to lilt, with his eyes half shut.

'Would you kindly stop doing that?' Amery said.

'What? I'm just toasting the old muffins.'

'Well, stop, for pity's sake. It's only six hours since I ate.'

Spiggot sighed and looked around as though bored. Took another long glug from the whiskey bottle.

'Say,' he said then. 'Can I kiss you, Doris?'

'No, you can't.'

'Oh, come on. One little smooch, for old times' sake.'

'No.'

'No tongues, I swear. And no hickies.'

'Jesus Christ. Have you lost your damn hearing as well as your mind?'

'Ah,' he beamed. 'Just my heart.'

'You don't have a heart,' Amery said. 'You have an answering machine where that particular organ should be.'

'Oh, doctor,' said Spiggot. 'Be rough with me.'

'Give me a drink and shut your mouth. And *stop looking at me like that, all right?*'

★　★　★

When Aitken and Hughie came out from the office and into the hall of Pearse Street police station, Doctor Ranjiv Singh was standing by the noticeboard, smoking a cigarette and looking at the WANTED posters.

'Yo, Hopalong,' said Singh. 'What's the crack?'

'Jayzus,' said Aitken. 'What are you doing here?'

'Christ, now there's a warm Irish welcome. Came by to see how you were, I suppose.'

'If I was any better I couldn't stick it, Ranj. Now get out of me way and bury me decent.'

'What's in them boxes? Your Christmas bonus?'

'Funny, Ranj. I just quit.'

The door behind them opened. The Assistant Commissioner poked his head through.

'And one last thing,' he barked. 'Before you go.'

'Suffering Christ. What do you want from me now, Mellowes?'

'That's *Assistant Commissioner* Mellowes to you.'

'Not any more, it isn't, pal. It's Shirley shaggin Temple if I want it to be.'

Hughie gave a burp of guilty laughter. The AC stepped towards him and shot him a look. Hughie seemed to wither a little, pulling his head inside his shirt like a turtle. Then the AC glared at Aitken and pursed his lips thoughtfully. He looked like he was about to plunge into the depths of an opinion, but was apprehensive about where exactly he might come up.

'Aitken. I have a question to ask you.'

'It's Martin actually. Or *Mister* Aitken to you.'

'Well . . . Martin, then. Did you remove those files from this office?'

'Why would I do that, Mr Mellowes?'

The AC's face took on an anxious expression. 'The fact is, I just had a look in your filing cabinet . . . Martin. And a number of papers on some very important and controversial cases are gone. Cases going back to the 1970s. The so-called Heavy Gang. Alleged brutality. The usual crack.'

'Oh. Those.'

'Now you know very well the ones I mean, Martin.'

'You never really told me why you needed them, sir.'

'I needed to study some detail, that's all.'

'Oh. Well, I'll see to it personally you can study them very soon, sir.'

'Thank you . . . Martin. That would be good of you.'

'Pleasure,' said Aitken. 'Now I have to go. You right, Ranj?'

The AC sighed regretfully and held out his hand. 'You'll be missed, Martin. I may tell you that candidly. I'm sorry now for the misunderstanding about the Doogan money. But forgive and forget, eh? Let bygones be bygones. As we all have to do these days, what? Cease-fire and all that.'

Aitken accepted his hand and shook it warmly.

'I think I can say . . . Martin . . . that although we had our run-ins over the years, it was a pleasure indeed to work with you always.'

'Yes, sir. Thank you, sir.'

'You had your little ways. And I had mine.'

468

'You certainly fucking did, sir, you terrible bollocks.'

'I'm sorry?'

'Just . . . your little ways, sir. I was agreeing with you.'

'Hmm. Yes.' The AC stared at Hughie, who was gnawing his lip.

'Don't you have something better to do than stand around here like some class of outmoded household ornament, Tynan?'

'Yes, sir. Sorry, sir.'

He shook hands with Aitken and disappeared through the doors. The AC seemed to notice Singh for the first time now.

'Excuse me,' he said. 'Are you delivering something?'

'Why?' said Singh. 'Are you?'

'He's a friend of mine,' Aitken said.

'Oh. Yes. Well, very good. As I was saying, Martin, I had my ways and you had yours. But then, every exceptionally talented policeman does.' He began to lead Aitken towards the door. 'And we didn't always see eye to eye, God knows. But I'd like to think we could share a joke about it now if we met, for example, at the golf club. Or at a charity social event of some kind, for cruelty to animals or battered Bosnians perhaps. Something of that nature.'

'Yes, sir. I'd like that too.'

'Of course you would, of course you would. And I wish you the very best of luck with your future.'

'You're not the worst, sir, I have to admit it. I wish you all the very best of luck with your own future too.'

'Good man, good man. God bless you indeed. And you'll drop those files in to me some time, will you?'

'Well, there's no need really, sir.' Aitken nodded. 'They'll be in the *Irish Times* tomorrow.'

The AC stopped walking. He turned to look at Aitken.

'They're running a front-page story, I believe, sir.'

The AC's face began to do something unusual. It was as though it was trying to turn itself inside out. Finally it settled in a fixed stony grin, like a gargoyle's.

He gave a hearty man-to-man chortle and slapped Aitken playfully on the shoulder.

'God now, Martin, you're a terrible chancer altogether. If I didn't know you better I'd nearly take you seriously.'

'Would you, sir? That's gas.'

The AC's eyes darkened. 'But of course you . . . you wouldn't.'

'Oh, I would.'

'But of course . . . you didn't?'

'I'm afraid I did, sir. Great old yarn they make too. I believe you feature pretty prominently yourself. Though I haven't had the chance to read them all just yet.'

'I . . .'

'*Irish Times*, sir. Tomorrow morning.'

'You . . .'

'Have a nice retirement yourself, won't you, sir. I'll love you and leave you now if I may.'

The AC pointed a trembling finger. 'I'll get you for this, Aitken. By Christ I will. By the time I'm finished, you'll be *swilling out public toilets*.'

'Fuck you too, sir. And the sheep you rode in on.'

The AC marched back through the swing doors and roared at someone.

'So, Hopalong,' said Singh. 'You're a free man.'

'Yeah.'

'So what are you gonna do for a living?'

'I'm thinkin of sellin my body, actually.'

'Great.' Singh pushed the door open for him. 'By the pound or the kilo?'

'You fancy a game of pool, Ranj?'

'Sure.'

He picked up his boxes and went out into the street. Put them into the boot of the Mini.

'Hey,' said Singh, nodding for him to look.

Ellen was standing on the corner near the cinema with a good-looking boy who had pale yellow hair. The boy had a plaster cast and was leaning on a crutch. Ellen raised her hand and cautiously waved.

'Fuck,' said Aitken.

'Happy New Year, Inspector.'

'Jayzus, Ellen. Same to you.'

470

'This is my son,' she said. 'Lee, this is Martin.'

He went over and shook hands with the boy, who stared up at him with a bored expression. He was a bright-faced kid, but he looked like he had seen plenty of trouble. There were grey rings around his pensive eyes, a certain coltish awkwardness in the way he stood.

'We figured we'd come by and say hello,' Ellen said. 'Me and my young man here are going to be finding some place to live. Near Saint Michael's Hospital. Doctor Singh's going to be looking after my pain control from now on.'

Aitken turned to Singh, who nodded.

'We've worked out a balance,' Ellen said. 'So I can keep on reading and getting around. For as long as possible. I think I'm going to find that important.'

'That's good news,' Aitken said.

'Yeah.' She smiled, though her face was wan. 'So if you ever want to come hang out, Doctor here knows where we'll be.'

Aitken looked at the boy. 'You like to play pool?'

'Some,' shrugged Lee, as though he couldn't care less.

'Any good?'

'So-so.'

He turned to Ellen. 'How about you?'

She pulled a scowl. 'I like to play but I always lose.'

'Let's play anyway . . . All right?'

'OK,' she agreed. 'Let's play anyway.'

'I know a place down on the quays,' said Singh.

'Best of five,' Aitken said. 'Loser buys the chips after.'

She and Singh led the way, the doctor linking her arm as they walked down towards the river. He seemed excited as he showed her the buildings, waving his arm in a gracious motion, pointing out features of special historical interest. She was clearly pretending not to know what they were. 'Oh,' she was saying. 'How terribly interesting. Look at that. My, how marvellous.'

After a moment it started to rain. He noticed the boy wasn't beside him now. He turned to see him staring in a travel agent's window.

'Hey,' he called. 'Come on there, Scout.'

The boy limped towards him and passed him by. He put his

good foot into a puddle and kicked at the muddy water. Then he limped on ahead with his right hand in his pocket, splashing the end of his crutch in the water as he went.

Aitken fell into step beside the boy and put his arm around his shoulder. The rain fell harder, colder; like an insult.

ACKNOWLEDGEMENTS

Grateful acknowledgement is made to my editor, Geoff Mulligan, and to Dermot Bolger, Isobel Dixon, Kevin Holohan, Beth Humphries, John McDermott, Peter McLaurin, David Milner, Eilean Ni Chuillcanain, the O'Connor family, Michael Casey, Jane Suiter, Colm Toibin, the Tyrone Guthrie Centre at Annaghmarkerrig, County Monaghan, Ireland, and to my agents, Carole Blake and Conrad Williams at Blake Friedmann Literary, TV and Film Agency, London. The dedication of this novel to my wife Anne-Marie is utterly inadequate thanks for her kindness, solidarity and patience.

Acknowledgement is made to the Garda press office in Dublin for general information on Irish police training, procedures and ranks. Any errors or distortions are my own. None of the characters in the novel is based in any way on an actual Garda, of any rank, whether serving or retired. *Inishowen* is a work of fiction. No similarity is intended with actual persons and none should be inferred. Specifically no suggestion is made that any actual Assistant Commissioner of the Garda or member of the Special Branch, whether serving or retired, is or was corrupt or unprofessional in any way.

Reproduction of lines from 'Advent' by Patrick Kavanagh is by permission of the Trustees of the estate of Katherine Kavanagh. Reproduction of lines from 'Burnt Norton' from *Four Quartets* by TS Eliot is by permission of Faber & Faber publishers. Reproduction of lyrics from 'Same Old Story' by Rory Gallagher (from *Taste*, Polydor Records, 583042) is by permission of BMG Music Publishing, Strange Music and the estate of Rory Gallagher.

Rory Gallagher's only recorded version of 'Out On The Western Plain' by Huddie Ledbetter appears on *Against The Grain* (Castle Communications CLACD233). Despite efforts, ownership of the lyrics as recorded could not be ascertained. (NB: The lyrics used in the Gallagher version bear no relation to that of the song by that title and author published by Tro-Essex Music Ltd and registered with the MCPS.) To avoid possible copyright infringement new lyrics were used in this novel.

Versions of some of the traditional songs quoted have been recorded on 'Rainy Sundays, Windy Dreams' by Andy Irvine (Wundertute Music 8884), 'The Best Of Dolores Keane' (Torc Music 206), 'No Stranger' by Sean Keane (Grapevine 250), Luke Kelly: The Collection (CH1041), 'Undocumented Dancing' by Pat Kilbride (Green Linnet 1120), 'After The Break' by Planxty (Tara 3001) and 'Irish Songs You Know By Heart' by The Erin's Isle Singers (Laserlight Celtic 21115).